SECRETS OF VAN BUREN UNIVERSITY

SUPERSTITION

JAMES BLAKEY

CITY OWL
PRESS

SUPERSTITION
The Secrets of Van Buren University, Book 1

CITY OWL PRESS
www.cityowlpress.com

Cover Design by MiblArt. All stock photos licensed appropriately.

Edited by Danielle DeVor.

For information on subsidiary rights, please contact the publisher at info@cityowlpress.com.

Print Edition ISBN: 978-1-64898-491-4

Digital Edition ISBN: 978-1-64898-492-1

Printed in the United States of America

To Dr. Churchill L. Blakey, M.D. (1938-2023)
I still miss you, Dad.

PRAISE FOR JAMES BLAKEY

"James Blakey's *Superstition* is a fast-paced mystery filled with twists and turns that kept me on my toes and guessing until the final reveal. Brimming with action and lead by dynamic characters, *Superstition* was a perfect balance of sharp-edged crime and lighthearted comedy; of bouncy cheerleaders, charming nerds, and rebellious journalists. Van Buren University has some serious secrets, and you'll finish this book thirsty for more." — *Meagan Jennett, Author of You Know Her*

"Blakey delivers a quirky 'whodunit' murder mystery with *Superstition*. A coming-of-age story, readers will be hunting for the truth right along with Jerry, a dedicated student reporter facing the social and academic challenges of navigating collegiate life, until the dramatic conclusion." — *H M DuVal, Author of the Dream Walker series*

"Is it appropriate to call a series of tragic deaths a fun read? Perhaps thrilling is a better description? Entertaining? An easy read? Blakey skillfully manages to make *Superstition* all of these. I felt like I was sitting at the same table with this cast of characters." — *William Zanotti, Author of The Link series*

"What the *Final Destination* films do for cheating death, Blakey's *Superstition* does for anyone cursed with bad luck, giving it a fun and deadly twist." — *Bill Blume, Author of West of Apocalypse*

"*Superstition* is a riveting, twisting puzzle that conjures up the question: what would you be willing to sacrifice in order to be successful - or lucky in love? Derringer Award-winning author James Blakey masterfully interweaves dark magic, *Superstition*, and cool, scrappy tech in this bewitching and highly addictive paranormal thriller." — *Lisa Nanni-Messegee, screenwriter of Holiday for Heroes, and author of the upcoming four book series, The Triumvirate*

"James Blakey's skills as a short story writer shine just as brightly on the larger stage of his debut novel. The tensions and turmoil of university life, expertly detailed, provide a rich landscape for this taut, twisty thriller." — *Art Taylor, Edgar Award-winning author of The Adventure of the Castle Thief and Other Expeditions and Indiscretions*

"James Blakey's *Superstition* is a fresh, funny novel brimming with magic and mystery. Lucky readers are in for a treat!" — *Adam Meyer, Author of The Last Domino*

"Great story with likable, believable characters and a fun, action packed plot." — *A.K. Lang, Author of The Gathering of the Three*

"Blakey's solid storytelling has tons of potential. An author to watch!" — *J.S. Furlong, Award-winning author of The Unimaginables series*

CAST OF CHARACTERS

Jerry Williams

Journalism Major
Van Buren University Sophomore
General Assignment Reporter for *The Chronicle*

Jerry's Friends

Mike Kwon

Jerry's Roommate
Electrical Engineering Major, Sophomore

Busby Tilden

Jerry's Girlfriend
Pre-Med, Sophomore

Miranda Sanchez

Busby's Roommate and Best Friend
English Major, Sophomore

Rick Tilden

Busby's Brother
Sports Management Major, Senior

Dmitri Popov

Miranda's Boyfriend
Philosophy Major, Junior

Vince Murphy

Rick's Best Friend
Physical Therapy Major, Senior

The Chronicle Staff

Vanessa Howley

Editor
Journalism Major, Junior

Noah Chen

Sports Reporter
Physics Major, Freshman

Fallon Ahern

Arts & Culture Critic
Gender Studies Major, Junior

Laurie Inverso

Campus Beat Reporter
English Major, Junior

Brandon Payer

General Assignment Reporter
Psychology Major, Senior

The Cheerleaders

Darla Jaggard

Assistant Captain
Chemical Engineering Major, Sophomore

Talia Decker

Point, Darla's Best Friend
Electrical Engineering Major, Sophomore

Veronica Decker

Tumbler, Talia's Twin Sister
Psychology Major, Sophomore

Cassie McGlaughlin

Flyer
Speech Pathology Major, Freshman

Marcus Reed

Base
Physical Therapy Major, Junior

Erica Nightlinger

Coach

Other Students

Lucy Davenport

Darla's Roommate
Wilderness Management Major, Junior

"Sam"

Mysterious publisher of *The Underground*

Vicky Tran

Fallon's Girlfriend
English Major, Senior

Beth Powers

President of the VBU Skeptics Club
Philosophy Major, Junior

Martha Gracehart

National Anthem Singer
Theater Arts Major, Senior

Brianna Sorenson

Rick's Friend
Elementary Education Major, Junior

Jackie DiBernardo

Brianna's Best Friend
Elementary Education Major, Sophomore

Priya Modi

Pre-Law, Freshman

Kate Fletcher

Undeclared Major, Freshman

Angela "Anj" Heatwole

Nursing Major, Freshman

Van Buren University Administration & Faculty

Dr. Janelle Thornton-Gaston, EdD	Chancellor
Chief George Characopus	Head of Campus Police
Dr. Mark Johnson, PhD	Adjunct Professor of Geology
Dr. Ellen Harding, PhD	Professor of Sociology
Don Gehring	Athletic Director
Rodney Case	Chief Information Officer
Maureen Stepanian	Legal Counsel
Julie Fredericton	Director of Media Relations
Skip Stetter	Athletic Trainer

Townies

Alan Berg	First Amendment & Civil Rights Lawyer
Allison Adams	Criminal Defense Attorney Married to Alan Berg
Mitchell Grant	Editor of *The Stuyvesant Whig*
Kirk Clayton	Stuyvesant County Sheriff's Deputy
Paul Wysocki	Retired *Stuyvesant Whig* reporter
Richard Mercer	Stuyvesant County Sheriff's Detective
Tom Rodgers & Milo	Resident of East Stuyvesant and his dog

"I know he's a good general, but is he lucky?"

— Attributed to Napoleon Bonaparte

PROLOGUE
SEPTEMBER

SATURDAY 1:13AM

Her headlamp illuminating the way, the college student trudged to the campfire circle and dumped another armful of sticks and leaves.

Satisfied with the pile, she rested on a boulder, her breath visible in the chilly air as she retrieved a bottle of water. To her right, an Adirondack 46er loomed. Above, a cloudless sky of stars twinkled, no city to drown their light.

Easier to try this at the nature preserve back on campus, but even at this late hour that risked awkward encounters with pot-smoking art majors or insomniac townies.

From her overstuffed green-and-gold backpack, she retrieved half a dozen copies of the college newspaper. She crumpled the pages, placing them strategically amongst the branches, then marinated the heap with charcoal lighter fluid.

She struck a match and tossed it. Orange flames erupted, blinding her for a second, enveloping her in a wave of heat. The hypnotizing fire reminded her of summer camping trips with her father. *Should have brought marshmallows.*

Her phone chimed. Five minutes until the new moon.

She pulled out the shrink-wrapped lamb chops, on sale for $9.99 per pound at Price Chopper. The student wouldn't, couldn't, sacrifice a living animal for the power she craved. Even the thought of touching raw meat filled her disgust. She slipped on a pair of latex gloves liberated from biology lab, then tossed the chops into the flames.

The scent of burning meat filled the air. She hoped to finish before any bears or wolves arrived.

She retrieved the blue textbook, turning to the marked page. Squinting at the diagram, then the sky, she oriented herself, zeroing in on Orion's Belt. A couple of moon widths to the east, she located Alpha Monocerotis.

Of course, that wasn't what the Picts called the star two millennia ago when they ruled what today is Scotland. No one knew their name for it. Almost all their knowledge had been lost. One scrap that survived: their high priestesses worshipped this star for luck.

No bars on her phone. Not a problem. The student pulled the folded printout from her pocket, silently rehearsing the spell. There wasn't a person alive who could reconstruct the enchantment the way the Picts originally spoke it. Her new friends on the dark web assured her that Modern English would work fine, as long as it rhymed.

The past few weeks, she experimented with charms and simple conjuring. Enough to prove to herself that magic was real, and she possessed the power to wield it.

The phone beeped. *Now.*

She stood before the fire, hand raised to the sky, pointing at the faint red star.

The paper rippled in the wind. She focused on the magic, emptying her mind of all other thoughts.

As she recited the words, all feeling receded, as if her consciousness left her physical form behind, merging with the fire, the star, the spell.

Goddesses of the Night, hear my plea
Bring Success and Prosperity
My offering to you, a favored sheep
A promise to you, I will always keep

To my endeavors great and small
I call upon you, one and all

With a whisper soft and a heart so true
I conjure Fortune to come anew

Bring me riches, bring me fame
And banish all my doubts and shame
I summon the forces of Star and Sky
To grant me Destiny that cannot die

By my will and desire so strong
This Magic now shall not go wrong
Bringing Luck to my life at last
So mote it be, this Spell is cast.

She became aware: clothes sticking to her sweat-drenched body, mouth dry, hair plastered to her head, heart pounding. She stumbled to the boulder, resting, regaining her strength.

An owl screeched in the darkness. Good sign? Owls were supposed to be magical. Or was that some Harry Potter nonsense?

The owl quieted. No crickets at this altitude. No sound but the wind and faint jet engines as red-and-green navigation lights hurried across the sky.

The student didn't look or feel different. No supernatural power coursing through her veins. No enhanced perceptions allowing her to observe a secret world. No ethereal light enveloping her.

How anticlimactic. What do you expect for $9.99 per pound?

No way to know if she cast the spell correctly.

No way to test if the magic was working.

No way to tell if this ceremony was a big waste of time.

Not waiting for any predators that caught the scent of the sacrifice, she doused the flames with three bottles of water, then buried the ashes with her collapsible shovel.

Only you can prevent forest fires.

She scoured the area, gathering any trash.

Leave no trace.

She slipped the pack on her back and began the four-mile hike to the trailhead. She stifled a yawn. At least it was downhill.

Thirty minutes on the trail and her mind was numb. Legs on auto. Step, step, step. Leaves crunching in her feet. Another three miles to go. All she wanted was to get back to her dorm, make a cup of hot cocoa, and crawl into bed.

Gack! A spider web across the trail on her face, in her mouth. She spit and raised a hand as the toe of her hiking boot caught a root. She pitched forward, losing her balance, falling toward the sharp rocks on this section of the trail. Arms flailing, she couldn't stop herself. In the darkness, her hand grabbed a branch, wrenching her shoulder, but arresting her fall.

The student righted herself, let out a deep breath, her palm scraped and scratched. Need to be careful. Could have broken a leg or worse. Been stranded with no way to call for help. And no one knew she was up here. Pretty lucky.

A smile spread across her face.

Pretty lucky.

"It works!" she shouted into the night.

CHAPTER 1
OCTOBER

Darla Jaggard's calves burned as she dashed up the concrete steps two at a time. The air was unusually warm for early autumn in upstate New York, and perspiration trickled down her back. Behind her, three trim figures in shiny green-and-gold warm-up suits, carrying matching gym bags, struggled to keep pace.

"Last one to the top is a rotten egg!" With a burst of speed, Darla, her honey-blonde hair secured with red ribbons, pulled away from the others. Two older brothers and a beauty queen mother made life a contest for as long as she could remember.

Descending students, coeds with a glare in their eyes, boys twisting their necks to watch, hustled to one side for fear of being run over.

Darla reached the top, tossed her bag, planted her feet, and launched into a backflip. Knees tucked tight to her body, she spun like a pinwheel and nailed a perfect landing. Flashing the smile of an Olympic champion gracing a box of breakfast cereal, she raised her arms in a *V* and announced, "I win." Her green eyes grew wide, and a frown replaced her smile. "You split the group!" She pointed an accusing finger at Cassie McGlaughlin.

Cassie, a dark-haired freshman and last of the four girls, slowed as she approached the top step and dropped her bag. "What are you talking about?" She leaned over, hands on knees, catching her breath.

"You ran up the other side." Darla pointed to the rusty metal railing dividing the steps. "The three of us were on this side."

Darla sneered and crossed her arms. The other two girls, Talia and Veronica, flanked Darla, striking identical poses hands on their hips, auburn hair pulled back, hazel eyes narrowed, and lips pressed into thin lines.

"And?" Cassie arched an eyebrow.

Darla let out an exaggerated sigh. "Everyone knows that's bad luck. Worse than taking a selfie with a black cat. Who knows what could happen? We might not get a bid for Dallas or lose a sponsor." Her eyes sparkled as she concocted the solution. "Unless you go back down and run up our side." She made a walking motion with her fingers.

Talia and Veronica nodded in simultaneous agreement, as if Darla's brain controlled both girls' actions.

Clouds darkened the sky, and a few scattered raindrops fell.

"Where do you come up with all these nutty ideas?" Cassie shook her head, "You're all delusional, and we're late. Coach isn't going to be happy." She picked up her gym bag. "If you think it's such a big deal, why don't you and the *Olsen twins* run back down and come up my side?" She stuck out her tongue, turned, and disappeared through the glass double doors of the gymnasium.

Darla's face reddened. "Sometimes she can be such a b—"

Inside the poorly lit gymnasium, a single faded banner hung from the rafters: Van Buren University Men's Basketball — 1947 Presidential Conference Champions. The ancient air-conditioning system rattled loudly as if to announce it wasn't dead, while circulating muggy air filled with the scent of bubble gum, cherry lip gloss, and sweat.

Marcus Reed, six-four with dark, curly hair, stood on the ratty black safety mat covering a third of the basketball court. He supported Cassie with a muscular arm and a sturdy hand. With a plastic smile, she leaned forward and raised her right leg, her body contorting into a capital *T*. She counted five, her body becoming more unsteady with each number. As she shakily returned to an upright position, Marcus's arm collapsed. Cassie tumbled through the air, but Marcus recovered, grunting as she landed in his arms.

Nearby, twenty-five other cheerleaders in T-shirts and shorts practiced tosses, leaps, and flips. A few girls stretched on the mat, gossiping or scrolling through phones. Heavy rain pounded the gymnasium roof. A couple guys placed buckets to catch the water dripping from the ceiling.

Coach Erica Nightlinger, her mousy brown hair pulled back in a perpetual ponytail, observed her squad. Perhaps half the boys were on performance enhancers, while a third of the girls could have eating disorders. She hadn't specifically encouraged her team to endanger their health through drugs and starvation, but she did turn a blind eye. According to the rumblings from the Athletic Department, this was her last year unless she brought home a championship. If she couldn't transform this third-rate cheer team into a contender, Nightlinger would be back to teaching dance in strip malls to uncoordinated tweens and their helicopter mothers.

"Okay, let's bring it in. Stragglers too!" She waved at the three late arrivals running penalty laps around the perimeter.

The team assembled on the mat in a semi-circle facing Nightlinger.

"It's less than a month until Nationals. We can't let up now. No matter how hard you're trying, no matter how sore, how tired, you can always give more. Here's proof." She held up her left hand to display a gold championship ring. "I wear this ring every day to remind myself of what I've accomplished. You can achieve this, too, if you make the commitment."

The truth was that Nightlinger bought the ring off eBay. The year that Lyndon Johnson State won the National Championship, she was on academic probation. Too many late nights at Smokey Joe's combined with eight a.m. Intro to Statistics.

She raised her hand over head. "Do you want this?"

"Yes!" the squad replied in chorus.

"Again, louder. Do you want this?"

"Yes!" The answer echoed throughout the gym.

"Better! And if necessary, I'll put myself in there. And you know I will."

That elicited a round of nervous laughter from the squad. Within a pound or two of her cheer weight, Nightlinger would insert herself into the practices when the squad floundered. In moments of desperation, she would concoct schemes where she assumed the identity of one of the girls, placing herself on the squad when they competed at Nationals.

"Circle up." The coach made a clockwise motion with her arm.

The squad formed a ring, their right hands touching in the center. "One, two, three! Statesmen!"

"Let's do this." Nightlinger pointed at her squad. "Arms straight and no boring faces."

The cheerleaders struck poses and displayed a series of winks, open mouths, and dropped jaws.

Nightlinger pressed play on the ancient boombox, and static crackled at maximum volume. Cheerleaders covered their ears. She fiddled with the device for a few moments before giving up. "Who's got a phone with the playlist that I can borrow?"

A brunette tossed her iPhone to the coach. Nightlinger hooked up the phone to the sound system and pressed play. High-energy techno-jazz boomed from the sound system, echoing throughout the gym.

Girls leapt, spun, and bounced into back flips. Marcus and another boy locked their wrists to form a basket. Cassie hopped into the basket, steadying herself on their shoulders. Two spotters placed their hands under the others. With a mighty effort, the four propelled her twenty feet into the air.

At the apex, Cassie split her legs, touching her toes. She descended toward waiting arms. A deafening roar of thunder filled the gymnasium, and the lights flickered. In the momentary darkness, her foot collided with someone's head, redirecting her fall. Marcus scrambled to catch her, but Cassie slammed to the floor, eating mat.

The rest of the team continued performing basket catches, rewinds, and liberties. The routine slowly came to a standstill as the squad realized something was amiss. Cassie lay motionless on the mat.

"Why is everybody stopping?" Nightlinger threw up her hands. "McGlaughlin, you go down like that in Dallas, you better not lie there. You get hurt, you roll off."

The squad made a half-hearted attempt to pick up the performance while Cassie remained unmoving. Nightlinger blew her whistle and killed the music. She walked over and knelt by Cassie, who had managed to sit up. The girl moved her jaw, wheezing, but no words were forthcoming.

Nightlinger placed a hand on the cheerleader's shoulder. "Take it easy. You got the wind knocked out of you." She shouted at her team, "Everyone, you have two minutes. Grab a drink!"

A variety of water bottles, electrolyte replacements, and energy drinks were retrieved from gym bags and guzzled.

Cassie gasped until her breathing returned to normal. A blank look crossed her face. "What happened, did I fall?"

Nightlinger looked around at the squad. "Anyone see? Did she hit her head?" The question was met by shrugs and stares. She pointed an accusing finger at Marcus. "You should have caught her. You're better than that."

Marcus shrugged. "But Coach, the lights went out."

"*But Coach, the lights went out,*" Nightlinger mocked. "We've been rehearsing this routine for weeks. You should be able to do it blindfolded." She dismissed Marcus with a wave of her hand. "Rokozny." The coach pointed at a strawberry-blonde stunter. "Go find a trainer."

The girl scampered off through a side entrance.

Ridiculous, thought Nightlinger. *The basketball team gets three trainers and God knows how many assistants, for half as many athletes, while I get less than nothing for the most dangerous sport on campus. Someday, we're going to get sued. And I'll be there to say 'I told you so.' If I'm not fired first.*

"I'll watch her, Coach." Marcus offered Cassie a hand and lifted her to her feet. "Lean on me." Even using Marcus for support, Cassie wobbled. "I have an idea." He reached behind her knees and hefted her up.

Secure in his arms, Cassie locked her hands around Marcus's neck, pulled their faces closer, and gazed into his sky-blue eyes. "My hero."

Nightlinger observed the goofy grins on both their faces. Last thing her team needed was romantic complications sparking jealousy among the rest of the squad, then the harsh feelings between Cassie and Marcus after the inevitable break-up. The coach would stop this budding flirtation before it destroyed her team. She followed Marcus across the court to the bleachers.

He gently placed Cassie in the first row, then sat next to her and held her hand. "Okay?"

"Yeah, I think so." Cassie squeezed his hand. Music again filled the gym, and the cheerleaders resumed their routine. "You should probably join the squad."

"Nah, I've got to keep an eye on our number one flyer."

"Uh, uh." Nightlinger pointed at Marcus. "You need to get in there. And no more mistakes."

"Okay." Marcus squeezed Cassie's hand once more, then jogged over to the other cheerleaders and resumed his place in the routine.

"You're going to be okay." Nightlinger sat next to Cassie. "Here comes help."

Skip Stetter, one of the basketball team trainers, jogged across the court. He wore a green VBU polo and khakis. In his right hand, he carried a med kit. He knelt next to Cassie and pulled a laminated 8.5" x 11" sheet from his bag.

"What happened, did I fall?" Cassie said again.

Skip searched for the concussion protocols on the sheet.

"Don't you know what to do?" Nightlinger stared at Skip.

Skip stared at the instructions. "This is very technical. I don't want to get it wrong."

"What happened, did I fall?"

"She keeps asking the same thing," Nightlinger slumped her shoulders. "She got the wind knocked out of her. No one's sure if she hit her head or what."

"Just let me do this." Skip grabbed Cassie's wrist, felt for a pulse, and checked his watch. "Fifty-two beats per minute. An athlete's heart." He released her wrist. "I'm going to ask you a few questions. Can you tell me your name?"

"Cassie." Her tone implied everyone should know it.

"Very good, Cassie. And do you know what day of the week it is?"

"It's Wednesday." She squinted at him. "Why?"

"These are the questions on the sheet. And where are you?"

She sighed. "Van Buren U. In the gym."

"Very good. Three for three."

"Is she going to be all right?" Nightlinger leaned forward trying to read the sheet in Skip's hands.

"Have to check a few more things." Skip reached into his bag for a penlight and aimed the beam into Cassie's brown eyes. Her pupils shrank to the size of pinheads. "Cassie, I want you to follow the light with your eyes while keeping your head still." He motioned the pen to the left, then back to the right.

Cassie's eyes didn't move. She stared straight ahead.

He leaned closer. "Cassie, can you hear me?"

"What happened, did I fall?"

Skip waved the pen in front of her face. "I want you to follow the light with your eyes."

"What light? Everything just went black." Her body shuddered. "I can't see!"

He clicked off the penlight. "Are you sure?"

"Yes, I'm sure! How could I not be?" she screamed, then broke into tears.

Nightlinger wrapped her arms around Cassie in a tight hug. "Everything's going to be okay," she whispered.

Skip pulled out his phone. "I better call 9-1-1."

CHAPTER 2

J
erry Williams, sophomore and general assignment reporter, stared at his article on the monitor, struggling to come up with the proper adverb. His phone buzzed.

> Busby: Where you at?

> Jerry: Newsroom

> Busby: Lunch at sc?

> Jerry: Sure. See you at 12

"Hey Jer, can you look at this story for me? I'm struggling to come up with a hook."

Jerry powered off his phone, shoved it in his pocket, and spun in his roller chair._Noah Chen, his bleached blond undercut styled into a towering quiff, sat at his desk behind a box of donuts. Powdered sugar clung to his lips and covered the shield of his blue Captain America T-shirt.

"Sure thing, Noah. What are you working on?" Jerry leaned back, lifted his feet, and propped them on the corner of Noah's desk.

"Thanks." The skinny freshman handed Jerry a sheet of paper and grabbed another donut. "I'm doing a story on the women's lacrosse team."

"You're in luck. I covered boy's lacrosse in high school." Jerry scanned the article. "Yeah, this is a pretty dry read. You need to drop the reader into the action or set the stakes." He lowered his voice, impersonating a radio announcer. "This Sunday, the Van Buren University Lady Statesmen lacrosse team faces a do-or-die confrontation when they battle their cross-state archrivals, the Grover Cl—"

"The two sports are entirely different," Fallon Ahern interrupted, her Boston accent slicing through the room. *The tah spahts ah uttely differan.* The tiny junior's eyes were almost obscured behind wire-rimmed glasses and dirty-blonde bangs. She wore an unbuttoned red-and-black checkered flannel shirt over a white tee and black jeans. There wasn't a subject that Fallon didn't have an opinion on, and she perpetually inserted herself into every possible conversation.

Fallon rose from her desk, snatching the paper from Jerry's hand. "The first thing you need to know about the men's game is the focus is on speed and power." *Powa.* She made a swooping motion with an imaginary lacrosse stick. "But women's is strategic." With her index finger, she tapped the side of her head. "It's all about finesse and control."

"Interesting." Noah scribbled a note.

"So it's like sex?" Jerry snickered.

Fallon groaned. Noah rolled his eyes.

"Hey, you wanted a hook." Jerry reached across Noah's desk and stole a jelly donut from the box.

"On second thought, I should figure it out myself." Noah grabbed the article from Fallon.

Jerry lifted his shoulders in indifference. "Suit yourself."

"Whatever." Fallon cocked her head, listening to a conversation between Laurie and Brandon about campus transportation, and headed toward them. "Actually, the reason the circulator bus is always late is because..."

"Uh, oh." Noah's eyes widened. "Vanessa's heading this way, and she doesn't look h—"

"Jerry, get your dirty high-top sneakers off that desk!" Vanessa Howley's Texas accent boomed throughout the office like a small-town sheriff lecturing an out-of-state speeder. "This is my newsroom, not your living room." *Notch yur livin ruum.*

Jerry swung his black Chuck Taylors to the floor. He adjusted his six-foot, two-inch frame in the too small chair, and his blue eyes met the gaze of the angry editor.

Unlike the rest of the staff of *The Chronicle*, Vanessa always dressed professionally: this morning a blue blazer over a white blouse paired with a tan skirt and sensible heels. A junior from the upper-class suburbs of Fort Worth, she was the first Black woman to lead the college paper in its one hundred-and-twenty-six-year history. Under her leadership, *The Chronicle* won a slew of honors, including an award for investigative reporting from the Upstate New York Press Association.

"Hey, Chief." Jerry flashed his best attempt at a disarming smile. "Are you done editing my story on the fast-running parking meters?"

"No, I have to let the university's lawyers look at it."

"Lawyers? What for? It's thoroughly researched. Did you talk to my source?"

Vanessa nodded. "I did. I'm not entirely convinced by her story. Plus, she isn't willing to go on the record."

"Of course she isn't. Her job is at risk."

Vanessa sighed. "We're talking parking meters, not Watergate."

Jerry set down his donut, pulled open a drawer, and retrieved his notes. "I've got aggrieved students with tickets, and a bunch of 'No comments' from the Parking Administration." He tapped his watch. "I timed some of the meters myself. They *do* run fast. This is an enormous scandal."

"The administration claims that there may be a bug affecting a few of the meters and they're looking into it."

"Which is noted in my story." Jerry held up his notes and research.

"But you wrote it in such a manner as to suggest that they are lying."

"Because they *are* lying, Vanessa. I don't understand why you have to run this by anyone!"

Chatter and typing stopped. All eyes locked on the confrontation.

Vanessa gave Jerry a hard stare. "You don't need to know because I'm the editor, and you're the reporter."

Jerry was wide-eyed and incredulous. "Do you know how much time I spent researching this? Pleading with my source in the Parking Department? You want the paper to win another award? This story is a lock."

"This isn't about awards; this is about responsible journalism." Vanessa crossed her arms. "I won't accuse the administration unless I have evidence to my satisfaction. If I want to land a job at the *New York Times* after I graduate, I can't afford any scandals."

"That's what this is all about? Playing it safe instead of breaking stories? Is the *Times* even going to be in business by the time you graduate?"

Throughout the newsroom, reporters audibly gasped at the remark.

Vanessa narrowed her eyes. "What is that supposed to mean?"

Jerry knew he had gone too far and softened his tone. "Sorry. So I'm clear, that was a comment on the *Times's* business prospects, not your academic progress."

"That's it." Vanessa drew a finger across her neck. "I'm killing your story."

How could she do this to him? Unable to control his temper, Jerry blurted out, "I bet *The Underground* would run it."

Vanessa laughed. "I thought you wanted to be a respected reporter. You want to work for that rag? Be my guest. It's little better than a collegiate *InfoWars*."

Jerry clenched his jaw. "No, I don't want to work for them. I enjoy working here. I want to uncover lies, expose corruption, tell stories that matter."

"Well, you're in luck. I have a new assignment for you." Vanessa held up the paper in her hand. "One of the cheerleaders injured herself at practice. Hit her head so hard she's in the hospital."

"Cheerleaders?" A pained look crossed Jerry's face. "You've got to be kidding. I can't think of anything that matters less."

"They're as much a part of the campus as you or me." Vanessa sat on the corner of Jerry's desk. "You've got talent, Jerry. But you're undisciplined. You want to be the ace reporter, you want to tell stories that matter? Here's your opportunity. Do a little digging. See if any other cheerleaders have been hurt. Check into the injury rate. I've heard it's worse than any other program on campus. This could be huge."

"Why don't you give the story to Noah?" Jerry glanced behind him. "He covers sports."

Noah dropped his donut and raised his hands in defense. "Hey, hey. Don't get me involved."

"Noah." Vanessa glared at him. "Stay out of this."

"But, I—"

"Out! I said." Vanessa pointed an accusing finger.

The sports reporter slumped in his chair and stared at his computer screen.

Vanessa returned her gaze to Jerry. She held up three fingers and counted. "One: Noah's going to be busy reporting on the groundbreaking for the new football stadium. Two: Cheerleading's not a sport. No reason to send a sports reporter to cover it. Three: I'm the editor. I give out the assignments."

"Four: This is lame. You kill a story I've spent weeks on and send me to cover Sis-Boom-Rah? C'mon, Vanessa."

She let out a weary breath. "I'm serious Jerry. You take this assignment, or you're done. I'm running a newspaper here, not herding armadillos." Above his head, she dangled the assignment sheet like tempting a kitten with a strand of yarn.

Jerry wondered how things had spiraled out of control so quickly. Okay, he didn't wonder. He shouldn't have argued with Vanessa in front of the entire newsroom. He needed to back down. No way he could explain to his dad that he was fired from the school newspaper. And his parking meter story might still have a chance. Vanessa's lawyers could give it their approval.

Vanessa won, and Jerry would suck it up. He lowered his chin to his chest and grabbed the sheet from her hand. "Fine, I'll do it."

Vanessa stood and looked around at the reporters staring at her and Jerry. "Get back to work. We have a newspaper to put out." She walked back to her office and slammed the door.

CHAPTER 3

W hile Professor Johnson droned on, Busby Tilden slipped her phone out of her purse and texted.

> Busby: Where you at?

> Jerry: Newsroom

> Busby: Lunch at sc?

> Jerry: Sure. See you at 12

Miranda Sanchez elbowed Busby in the ribs.

"What?" Busby looked up from her phone to see Professor Johnson in his tweed jacket, smirk on his face, arms crossed, tapping his foot impatiently, glaring at her.

"Please answer the question, Ms. Tilden."

The lecture hall was dead silent. All eyes on Busby.

"Interglacial," Miranda whispered without moving her lips.

Busby sat up straighter, mustering fake confidence. "Winter glaciers."

A smattering of laughter rippled from the class.

The fifty-something professor rolled his brown eyes and shook his head in disgust. "Ms. Tilden, I'm certain with whomever you are texting seems much more interesting than the epochs of Earth's history, but please try to restrain yourself in the future." He glanced around the lecture hall. "Can anyone who *was* paying attention answer my question?"

Hands from two dozen students shot up, while Busby slouched as low as possible in her seat. The class continued for another interminable fifteen minutes.

When the bell rang, Busby was the first to stand. She grabbed Miranda's hand. "C'mon, Sanchez, let's meet Williams for lunch."

Busby and Miranda climbed the steps of the Student Center to the second-floor cafeteria, arriving moments before the noon rush. Busby grabbed a tray, passing by the fried chicken and pizza slices. She breathed through her mouth, avoiding the smells. How could people eat that junk? She selected a garden salad and a banana. At the drink fountain, she filled a glass with unsweetened iced tea. Miranda grabbed half a tuna sub, strawberry yogurt, and a Diet Sprite.

The volume of the room rose as a crush of students pushed through the doors. The two roommates headed to their traditional table along the far wall of the cafeteria, where Busby's brother Rick was seated. He wore a green-and-gold varsity jacket. A plate of cheese nachos sat on the table before him.

Busby took the chair next to Rick, kissing him on the forehead. Miranda sat on the other side of Busby.

"Hey guys!" Mike Kwon, electrical engineering major, set down his tray of grilled cheese and tomato soup and grabbed the spot opposite Miranda. Mike wore a white polo shirt and thick-rimmed glasses. His dark hair an uncombed mess. "Where's Jerry?"

"I was going to ask you the same thing, Kwon." Busby scowled. "He said he'd meet us here at noon."

"I'm sure he'll turn up." Mike shrugged. "But get a load of this, I was talking with Coma Guy an—"

"Coma Guy?" Rick mumbled through a mouthful of chips.

"Yeah, tall dude with stringy blond hair. Looks like he's in a perpetual daze. I forget his real name. You must have seen him around campus. Anyway, he tipped me off to a brand new crypto coin. This is a chance to get in on the ground floor. It's going to make BitCoin look like Monopoly money."

Miranda tapped her phone. "I question the wisdom of taking advice from someone named 'Coma Guy,' financial or otherwise."

"He wasn't really in a coma. It's just that there are a couple of months where he can't remember what happened."

"That's much better." Busby peeled her banana.

Miranda spotted Jerry in his black-and-red striped rugby shirt meandering across the room. She raised both arms and waved widely.

Mike ignored Miranda's theatrics. "Anyway, Coma Guy tells me..."

Jerry balanced his tray of a bacon cheeseburger, curly fries, and a double chocolate shake while he scanned the student center cafeteria. He smiled when he spotted Miranda waving. As he negotiated his way through the chaotic lunchtime crowd toward his trio of friends, his smile disappeared. The trio was a foursome.

On the near side of the table sat his best friend and roommate, Mike Kwon, moving his hands animatedly.

"Hey guys." Jerry slapped Mike on the back and took the open seat next to him.

"Perfect timing." Miranda barely looked up from her phone that seemed permanently attached to her hand. Her jet-black hair was pulled back into a ponytail, and she wore a gray "Property of The Miami Dolphins" T-shirt. "You saved us from Mike's latest Coma Guy pitch."

"Hey, this is a chance to make some real money." Mike rubbed his fingers together.

Jerry leaned across the table to kiss Busby, her red hair down today, resting on the shoulders of denim jacket.

Instead of meeting the kiss, she raised her watch and pointed to the time. "Glad you could make it, Williams." A hint of annoyance in her east Tennessee accent.

Jerry leaned back and sat. "Yeah, sorry about that. I was—"

"Well, if it isn't Jimmy Olsen," Rick interrupted, his accent thicker, almost a twang. *Jemmy Olsun.*

Jerry silently counted five. As much as he adored Busby, he couldn't stand Rick. Loud. Obnoxious. And full of himself. Typical football player. "I think you mean Clark Kent. Jimmy Olsen's a photographer. I'm a reporter."

"You ain't no Superman, kid. You need one of those old-timey hats with a card that says 'Press' tucked in the band."

Kid? "Yeah, that's what I need."

"And one of those cameras with the oversized flash bulb." Rick pantomimed taking photographs. "Ker-chunk. Ker-chunk."

"Knock it off, Rick." Busby punched him in the shoulder.

Mike held up his hands. "Does *anyone* want to hear what Coma Guy had to say?" The table ignored him.

Miranda pointed with her phone at Jerry's tray. "I see you haven't changed your eating habits."

"Soggiest bacon and limpest fries in the New York State." Jerry lifted his drink and sucked on the straw. "But the shake makes it all worthwhile."

"That stuff will kill you dead, Williams." Busby jabbed at her salad and lifted a forkful of greens.

"Thank you, Dr. Tilden."

"I don't have to graduate from medical school to know that crap's not good for you. My arteries are hardening just by being in the same zip code."

"I'll take your advice under consideration." Baiting Busby, Jerry grabbed the ketchup, drenched his fries, and stuffed a half dozen into his mouth.

Busby let a deep exhale escape her lips. "Charming, Williams. It's your funeral."

Vince Murphy, his oversized neck straining the collar of his Van Buren U. sweatshirt, sat next to Rick and fist-bumped him. Vince leaned forward to peer at Miranda. "Hey, Miranda. How are you doing?"

"Fine." She didn't look up.

"I wanted to tell you I got an 'A' on that paper about Shaq that you wrote for me. I—"

"It's Eugene O'Neill, not Shaquille, and can we not talk about it in front of hundreds of witnesses?" Still staring at her phone, she swirled her free hand in a three-sixty, pointing at the other tables.

"Sure, sorry." Vince swallowed hard. "If you're not busy later, maybe we could h—"

Miranda finally turned to face him. "No, I already told you. I have a boyfriend."

Vince's face burned beet red. "Whatever." He reached across the table to snag a couple of fries off Jerry's tray and knocked over the saltshaker, white crystals spilling across the table.

"Great hands!" Jerry clapped. "I'm sure the team will have no trouble dominating Fillmore this weekend."

"Don't pay him any mind, Vince." Rick turned to Busby. "As much as I've enjoyed your company, sis, we have to go. Places to be. People to do." Rick stood and pointed at Jerry. "Bus my tray, Peter Parker." He made another picture-taking motion with his hands, and he and Vince left guffawing.

"Peter Parker's not a reporter. He's a photogr..." Jerry's voice trailed off. "Buzz, did you ever consider that your brother might be adopted?"

She sipped her iced tea and dismissed the idea with a wave of her hand. "You wouldn't say that if you met Daddy. Rick is just like him."

"Maybe you're the one who's adopted." Jerry chuckled.

"Nice one." Mike high-fived his roommate.

Busby scrunched up her face and fumed, unable to respond with a snappy comeback. She grabbed a fry off Jerry's tray and tossed it at him. It bounced off his forehead. He snatched it out of the air and jammed it in his mouth.

Jerry beamed with delight. "That's the best you got?"

"She's had a rough day." Miranda clucked her tongue. "Professor Johnson called on her while she was texting. Busby had no idea what the question was and totally whiffed in front of the entire class."

"Texting in class?" Mike made the shame-shame gesture with his fingers.

Busby glared at him. "Kwon, it's a stupid geology course, and I'm pre-med. Plus, it's pass-fail. When I save some patient's life by sticking a new heart inside of her, she isn't going to care if I don't know the difference between magma and lava."

"Magma is molten rocks beneath the earth. It's lava once it's on the surface." Miranda didn't look up from her phone.

Mike chuckled. "Someone's paying attention in class"."

Busby raised an eyebrow. "Sanchez, you want to talk about how Murphy has a crush on you? Because I think that's adorable."

Miranda frowned, tilted her head down, and continued tapping on her phone.

"Speaking of texting, this is a good time to segue into my latest invention." Mike reached into his backpack and pulled out a metallic copper box, the length and width of an iPad, but two inches thick. Switches, dials, and lights covered the top.

Jerry leaned closer. "What's that?"

"Cell phone jammer. Watch." Mike grabbed the black power cord originating from the box, plugging it into a wall outlet. He flicked a few switches, and three green lights blinked.

"Hey, I've got zero bars," Miranda whined.

"Brilliant, Kwon." Busby pointed at the copper box. "But you can buy jammers on the Internet for two hundred bucks."

Mike shook his head. "Not like this. I can jam selective frequencies: Bluetooth, Wi-Fi, cell phones, AM, FM, VHF, UHF, you name it. And it has directional capabilities. You can even create schedules. Imagine what the college would pay for one of these babies that can blanket a lecture hall. No more distracted students. No more cheating on exams."

Jerry peered at the jammer. "Do you have one that powerful?"

"Not yet. I need some start-up capital." He looked at his friends. "This is your chance to get in on the ground floor. A once-in-a-lifetime opportunity. This could be bigger than Google and Facebook combined."

"Aren't jammers illegal?" Miranda whispered.

"Asks the girl who's writing English papers for the football team. Sure, there are federal regulations against them, but so what? That's how big companies get so big. Break rules and move fast." Mike put his hand on Jerry's shoulder. "What do you say, roomie? Ready to invest?"

"Invest what? Hello? Starving journalism major." He removed Mike's hand from his shoulder.

"Busby?" Mike looked at her hopefully.

"Sorry, Kwon. All my spare cash is in a numbered account in the Caymans."

"Miranda?"

"Can't. As a condition of my parole, I am prohibited from investing in any illicit schemes."

"You're on parole?" Mike was wide-eyed. "What did you do?"

"Nothing, you idiot. That was a joke. I'm not putting my money into your stupid cell jammer."

"Fine, but after I go IPO," Mike pointed at the others one by one, "none of you are getting an invitation to cruise the Caribbean on my two-hundred-foot yacht."

Miranda waved her phone in Mike's face. "You want to shut that thing off? I need to text Dmitri."

Mike flicked off the jammer and slipped it back into his bag. Miranda tapped away on her phone.

"One o'clock chem lab. I have to get going." Busby stood. "Sanchez, you want to walk with me?"

"I'm headed to West Campus to see my guy."

"Okay." Busby picked up her tray. "You're coming by to change my oil this afternoon, right Williams?"

"Is that what you kids are calling it these days?" Mike snickered.

Miranda groaned and threw a balled-up napkin at Mike.

Jerry lips curled downward. "Buzz, I can't. Got an assignment. That's why I was late."

"You've been promising you'd do it for the last three weeks. *Buzz, don't pay to change your oil. Buzz, don't trust those clowns at Twenty-Minute Lube,*" she sneered.

Jerry's shoulders slumped. "Sorry, but I finally had it out with Vanessa, and now she's punishing me. Maybe I can do it tomorrow, but this afternoon, I have to interview a bunch of cheerleaders."

"Cheerleaders?" Mike's eyes widened. "That doesn't sound like much of a punishment to me."

Miranda looked up from her phone. "Shut up, Mike."

Mike ignored her. "Think about it, Jerry. Glossy hair. Lithe. Flexible. And they wear those tiny little skirts."

Jerry nodded. "You make a good point."

"Do you think it would be okay if I tagged along? Maybe you need someone to take photos?"

"Really, Mike." Miranda jabbed her finger at him. "Put a cork in it."

"I suppose I could use some help." Jerry leaned toward Mike. "What's it worth to you?"

"Oh, man. Don't make me beg. It's not—"

"Fine!" Busby slammed her tray on the table. Heads around the cafeteria turned at the sound. "Williams, you'd rather hang out with some bleached-blonde airheads whose greatest challenge is spelling out 'statesmen' than keep your promises to me? Go ahead, see if I care."

As Busby stormed off, Jerry glared at Mike. "Thanks for helping."

Mike grimaced. "You're blaming me?"

"I tried to warn you guys, but you wouldn't listen." Miranda held up her phone and snapped a photo of Jerry and Mike. "Let me caption this: Guys are morons."

Jerry sighed. "I should go after her and apologize."

"That's the *last* thing you should do." Miranda slipped her phone into her purse. "You need to give her space and time to cool off. And next time try not drooling over other girls."

"C'mon Miranda, that's not fair."

"My advice is only helpful if you take it." Miranda stood, grabbed her tray, and walked away.

CHAPTER 4

"Thanks for letting me come along, Jerry." A Canon EOS 70D camera dangled from the strap looped around Mike's neck. His backpack bulged with the rest of his photography equipment.

Jerry raised a finger. "Remember, I need you to take some decent photos. This story has to shine if I'm going to get out of Vanessa's doghouse."

They exited the quad and climbed the cracked concrete steps that led to the walk to the gymnasium.

"Of course. What else would I be doing?"

Jerry rolled his eyes. "Oh, I don't know. Maybe use this opportunity to hit on some cheerleaders and find a new girlfriend?"

"Bah! The idea never occurred to me." Mike's lips curled into a smile. "Besides, Amanda's coming back to me any day now."

"And you know this how?"

"I'm stalking her Instagram. It's obvious the poor girl can't live without me."

"I follow her too." Jerry tapped his phone. "And she sure looks pretty broken up here on the miniature golf course."

Mike grabbed the phone and glared at the photo of dark-haired Amanda. Some muscled blond dude with his arms around her waist helped her line up a putt through a clown's mouth. "Two can play this game. Wait till Amanda sees some photos of me and the cheerleaders. Especially in their uniforms."

"Sorry to disappoint, but we're going to a practice. They'll be in T-shirts and shorts."

"Nope." Mike's face lit up. "I contacted the coach. Asked her to have a few girls in uniform and full makeup for photos."

"You contacted the coach?" Jerry stopped and faced his roommate. "This is *my* story. You're not even on staff with *The Chronicle.*"

Mike faked taking a snapshot. "Does Vanessa need a photographer?"

Jerry started up the steps. "Don't get me started on her."

They reached the top, turned left, and headed toward the gym entrance. Along an intersecting sidewalk, a lone girl stood and offered them a friendly wave.

Jerry waved back. "Do you know her?"

"No, why?"

"Seems like she knows us."

The girl approached with a deliberate stride. She was short, maybe 5'1" or 5'2", with reddish-brown hair in a wedge cut under a navy-blue beret. She wore a black T-shirt with a photo of Edward Snowden captioned in Cyrillic, black jeans, and oversized hiking boots.

"Jerry Williams from *The Chronicle*, right?" She offered her hand.

"Yeah." Jerry cautiously accepted the hand and shook. This was the first time someone recognized him from the paper. "And you are?"

She ignored his question. "I really liked your piece on the no-show Board of Trustee members. Nice bit of investigative work."

"Thanks."

"But what's your name?" Mike stared at her.

She gave a half-smile. "You can call me Sam."

"Short for Samantha?"

"I don't know. I just made it up." Sam squinted at Mike. "You must be Noah Chen."

"No, I'm not Noah. Astonishingly, all Asians don't look alike." Mike folded his arms.

Sam looked contrite. "Honest mistake. I thought you were with *The Chronicle.*" She turned to Jerry. "Can we talk in private?"

"No need for the cloak-and-dagger routine." Mike hefted his camera bag onto his shoulder. "I've got better places to be." He stormed off toward the gymnasium.

Sam watched Mike disappear through the glass double doors. "Your friend needs to lighten up."

"His name is Mike."

"Mike? Wait, Mike Kwon? The guy with the cell jammer?"

Jerry glared at her. "How do you even know about that? Or who I am? Are you some kind of fangirl?"

"Fangirl? Like a groupie?" She laughed. "Far from it."

"So, what's your deal then?"

A few scattered raindrops fell.

"Let's sit down under that tree, okay? It's been a long day." Sam started for the bench, but Jerry remained where he was. She took a few steps, realized he wasn't following. "Trust me, this will be worth your while."

Jerry glanced at the gymnasium and checked his watch. "Okay, but this can't take too long." He took a seat on the bench. "I have a story to write on this che—"

"A story on the injured cheerleader, I know."

"You want to stop showing off how much you know and tell me what's going on, *Sam*?"

She blew out her breath. "I understand that it's rude to not reveal my name. But I'm not only protecting myself, but you too."

"Protecting me from what?"

Sam didn't answer; her gaze distracted by a squirrel dashing across the grass. She reached into her pocket, retrieved a peanut, and tossed it to the animal. He picked it up with his front paws and cracked the shell with his teeth.

Sam looked back at Jerry. "How's that parking meter story coming along?"

"Are you with the NSA?"

"Vanessa killed it, didn't she?"

Jerry spread his arms wide in exasperation. "Yes."

"What reason did she give?"

"She claimed the anonymous source is weak. Which is bull. Plus, something about lawyers. I stopped listening at that point."

"The real reason she's spiking it is because the chancellor's office came down on her hard."

"The chancellor? Why?"

"The administration is behind in fundraising, and they can't afford another scandal."

Jerry narrowed his eyes. "And how do you know all this?"

Her mouth twisted into an amused smile. "It's the twenty-first century. There are no more secrets."

The squirrel finished eating the peanut. He stood on his hind legs, six feet away, looking hopefully at Sam.

She threw another peanut. "Do you want to get your story out?"

"How? You just said the administration killed it. The town paper won't have any interest in it. Are you suggesting that I start a Substack? While I'm at it, I could include some photos of my cat."

"You don't have a cat."

Jerry stood. "This is way too creepy. You're way too creepy. I'm out of here."

"Wait." Sam grabbed his hand. "I'm sorry. And that's not something I say often. And even when I do, I usually don't mean it."

Jerry removed his hand from her grip. "You're not helping yourself."

"Come on, sit back down." She patted the bench. "I thought you'd figure it out on your own."

Jerry frowned and reluctantly sat. "Well, obviously I'm dense, so just tell me what's going on."

Sam looked around. No one nearby. She leaned close, with a conspiratorial glint in her eye, and whispered, "I'm with *The Underground*."

"*The Underground!*"

"Shush!" Sam put a finger to his lips. "Part of the secret of our success is our anonymity. Don't go shouting it all over campus."

"*The Underground?*" Jerry whispered.

"Are you just going to keep repeating that?"

"*The Underground.*" Jerry shook his head in disbelief.

Sam kicked him in the shin with the toe of her hiking boot.

"Ow! What was that for?"

"You were beginning to sound like you were stuck in an infinite loop.

Now that I've solved that problem, I am authorized to inform you that we're interested in having you write for us."

"Who's us?"

The Underground." She gave a sharp exhale of annoyance. "We just went over that."

"I meant specifically. Who runs *The Underground*?"

"Can't tell you."

"What's your name?"

Sam sighed again. "Can't tell you that either."

"What can you tell me?"

"We want you to join our team. There's some technical stuff about encryption that I'll have to school you on, but basically, we like your work and want you to report for us."

"I don't know." Jerry was still trying to process the offer. "I like the idea of writing for a publication that people hold in their hands. I have fond memories of my family swapping sections of the newspaper over breakfast."

"Print is dead. In a couple of years, *The Chronicle* will transition to a completely online publication. All papers will."

"I guess. But there's no byline, right? In all the stories on *The Underground* I've ever read, the reporters' names were aliases."

Sam reached up and rapped her knuckles on his head. "Hello, McFly? Anybody home? Anonymity is your friend."

"Don't do that!" Jerry smoothed his hair. "Yeah, but if I write for you guys, I'll never get any credit."

"You want to feel good about yourself? You want people to stare and point as you walk by and say that's Jerry Williams, the great reporter, or you do you want to write stories that matter?"

"Can't I do both?"

"On this campus? Apparently not." Sam gave a 'what can you do?' shrug. "It's your choice. Have your good work buried by the administration while your name is attached to puff pieces on cheerleaders, or get your story and make a difference, even if no one knows you broke it."

"And then there's the other thing?"

"What other thing?"

"You know. *The Underground*'s got a reputation for stories that might not be entirely accurate."

Sam crossed her arms. "Can you provide me with an example?"

"What about that one about the CIA contracting with Van Buren psychology profs to develop enhanced interrogation techniques?"

"What about it? That's a solid bit of reporting."

"But the university denied it."

"Of course they did."

"And so did the government."

"Are you really that naïve, Jerry? Maybe you aren't cut out to write for us."

"Can I at least think about it?"

"Sure, take your time. We're not going anywhere." Sam stood. The rain was falling harder now.

"Okay, how can I contact you?"

Sam smirked. "You're really not getting this whole anonymity thing, are you? We'll be in touch."

As Sam walked away, Jerry wondered if Vanessa was really killing his stories at the behest of the university administration. Sam's claim possessed the air of plausibility. But it was just that: a claim. Like any good reporter, he'd have to dig to learn it was the truth. He picked up his backpack and jogged toward the gym entrance, trying to dodge the raindrops.

CHAPTER 5

The truck straddled the painted white line, taking up two spaces in the Student Center parking lot, its menacing silver grill daring anyone to object. And what a magnificent truck it was: a gleaming black F-250 with a King Cab, tinted windows, skid plates, both the Off-Road and High-Capacity Towing packages, and an LED light bar. MSRP: $79,735. The truck and a no-show job were a gift to Rick from an alumnus and booster who owned the local Ford dealership.

The engine roared to life, its eight cylinders rattling like a machine gun. Tires squealed and students jumped out of the way as Rick turned left out of the lot and accelerated onto the street.

Vince flipped on the radio. A deafening blare of twangy pop country erupted from the truck's six speakers.

Rick pointed at the stereo. "You want to turn that thing down?"

Vince dulled the noise.

"So, what's the deal with you and that chick?"

Vince bit his lip. Rick was always on the lookout for some weakness to exploit or mock. "No deal. Miranda helps me with some papers for English."

"No deal? Is that why you were mooning over her back at lunch?" Rick grinned wickedly. "Pretty sure there's a little more than paper writing going on here."

"I wasn't mooning." Vince jabbed his finger at Rick. "And Miranda's nice."

"Nice?" Rick shook his head in disgust. "God Almighty. We're on the football team, and you want nice. We can have whoever we want, whatever we want, whenever we want. And you settle for nice."

"What's your point?"

"*What's your point?*" Rick mimicked Vince in a high-pitched voice. "Hi, I'm Vince. Will you go out with me?" He contorted his face into an over-exaggerated frown.

"That's not how I sound."

Rick opened the center console, retrieved a can of beer, popped the top, and took a swig. "No, dude, that's exactly how you sound. Quite frankly, it's embarrassing. I say this not only as a teammate, but as your friend."

Vince scowled. *Some friend.* "Do you know anything about Miranda's boyfriend? Maybe you could ask your sister to find out?"

"Jesus H. Christ! Will you listen to yourself? This is not high school." Steering with his knee, Rick pulled out his phone and texted, eyes flicking between the screen and the road. "Fortunately, I have the cure for what ails you."

"And what crazy idea is that?"

"I know a girl. She *is* crazy, plus a lot of other things. I'm delighted to say she's definitely not nice. And she's got a friend. For your sake, I hope she's also—"

Rick's phone chirped. He glanced at the text and smiled. "You're in luck. We're going to pick them up."

Without slowing, Rick spun the steering wheel. Tires screeched, and Vince's momentum slammed him into the door. As Rick executed the U-turn in the middle of traffic, cars in both directions blew their horns, and angry drivers cursed him.

A five-minute drive took them to South Campus. Under the leafy green trees lining Harrison Street outside Marcy Hall, Rick pulled into a handicapped spot and texted: HERE

Priya Modi guided her white Audi Q5 down the street, careful to stay below the speed limit and watchful of pedestrians. She turned right at the corner onto Harrison and frowned. A black truck occupied the handicapped spot outside her dorm. The truck was comically oversized; it looked like it could be responsible for climate change all by itself.

Priya let out a long, weary breath. The college really needed to add more handicapped spots. She contemplated the close to half mile walk from the parking garage back to her dorm and absentmindedly reached down and ran her hand across the ceramic prosthetic extending beneath her left knee.

As her car crept closer to the truck, she noticed the license plate was standard. She squinted but didn't see a placard hanging from the mirror, and the driver was still in the truck. Her resignation turned to anger. She pulled up to within ten feet and leaned on the horn.

The driver of the truck rolled down his window, stuck out his arm, and made a motion for Priya to pass by. She kept leaning on the horn. The driver hopped out of the truck, a beer can in his hand, and swaggered toward her car. Big guy with a neck like a tree trunk. Probably some kind of athlete, which would explain why he was acting like a jerk.

He stopped at the driver's door, trying to peer through the Audi's tinted glass. She rolled down her window.

The jerk spread his arms wide. "There's plenty of room. Go on by."

"You're in my parking spot." Priya pointed at the truck.

"*Your* spot?" He laughed. "I don't see your name on it."

"It's right here, you Neanderthal." She tapped the blue-and-white handicapped placard hanging from her rearview mirror.

"What's your handicap? You look okay to me."

Priya was stunned. She didn't have a response. She couldn't believe this colossal idiot was arguing over her rightful parking space.

The jerk jabbed his finger at her. "Did your foot-doctor daddy forge your application for handicapped access in between submitting phony claims to Medicare?"

Priya wouldn't dignify this cretin with an answer. She was glad she hadn't said anything before. She raised the window and leaned on the horn.

The skies darkened. A few raindrops splattered on the windshield.

He leaned against the Audi, crossed his arms, and shouted. "Keep at it! The more you honk, the longer I'm going to stay in that spot!"

"We'll see what the school police have to say about this." Priya tapped the phone mounted on her dashboard, snapped video of the truck, then angled the phone at Rick. She touched the controls on the steering wheel.

First, the Audi's speakers rang, then a female voice answered, "Van Buren University Campus Police."

"Hi, I'm at Marcy Hall, and there's a black truck parked illegally in the handicapped spot."

"Let me check if there's an officer in the area."

A blonde and a brunette exited the dorm and approached the truck. The blonde, wearing a white tee and jeans, waved at the jerk.

"You're in luck!" he shouted through the closed window. "We're out of here." He guzzled the rest of the beer, crushed the can, and dropped it on the hood of the Audi.

"Hold on, I think the truck is leaving." Priya leaned on the horn again.

With deliberate slowness, Rick walked back to the truck, gave the blonde a quick embrace, and climbed into the driver's seat. The girls slid in the back, the blonde behind Rick and the brunette behind Vince.

"Glad you could make it, ladies." Rick reached into the console for two more beers, passing them back. "Enjoy." He gunned the engine, a puff of black exhaust enveloping the Audi, screeched tires, and pulled into the street.

"Brianna," Rick addressed the blonde sitting behind him. "Introduce me to your friend."

"I'm Jackie." She wore a lavender sweatshirt with an embroidered unicorn and her hair in a high ponytail.

"Brianna, Jackie. In the passenger seat is Van Buren's starting tight end, Vince Murphy."

Vince turned in his seat. "Hi Brianna, Jackie. Nice to meet you."

Rick silently mouthed 'Nice to meet you' and cringed.

The rain fell harder.

"Where are we going?" Briana rested her head against the window.

"It's a beautiful thing." Rick shifted gears. "Wherever we are, that's where the party is."

Jackie leaned forward. "Can you be a little more specific?"

"Ah, an intellectual." Rick guffawed. "Brianna warned me you were smart like that."

"What did you get me into?" Jackie whispered to Brianna.

"Relax." She leaned close so the boys couldn't hear. "I can handle Rick."

Rick tapped the steering wheel. "We're going to Engine Eighty-Nine. It's a bar off Wolfe on the far side of town. Hot food. Cold drafts. Good tunes. And plenty of room to dance."

"I don't have ID." Jackie threw herself back in the seat.

"Doesn't matter. You're with us. The owner is a big football fan. Another perk of being on the team. No one will hassle us."

They were off campus now, on a two-lane road, passing farms, heading toward town. Thick clouds obscured the mountains. The sky was almost black. Sheets of rain pelted the windshield. Rick flipped the wipers to maximum speed. Visibility was close to zero.

"Maybe you should slow down." Jackie pulled the seatbelt shoulder strap across her body and buckled in.

Rick heard the click. "Scared? You have to push through. Fear is a barrier to success. Like weakness. Coach explained it to us."

"Sounds like warmed-over pop psychology to me," Jackie said.

Brianna glared at her. "What are you doing?"

Rick raised his voice. "Who invited you anyway?"

"Back off, Rick." Vince put a hand on his friend's shoulder. "The lady is entitled to her opinion."

"Yeah," Jackie crossed her arms. "I'm entitled to my opinion that you should really slow down."

"Brianna?" Rick made eye contact with her in the rearview mirror.

"Better safe than sorry. I vote we slow down."

Rick erupted in laughter. "Fortunately, this truck is not a democracy, and we're not ruled by timid girls." He stepped on the accelerator, and the truck lurched forward.

A bolt of lightning flashed to their right, striking an empty field. A cacophony of thunder engulfed them a moment later.

"Three thousand feet!" Jackie yelled.

"What?" Vince turned to look at her.

"That last bolt struck three thousand feet away."

"How can you tell?"

"I counted. Three seconds between the flash and the thunder. Sound travels at a little over a thousand feet per second in the air. That's about three thousand feet or three-fifths of a mile."

"Jackie, are you some kind of science nerd?" Rick growled.

"No, just curious about things."

Vince faced the backseat. "What's your major, Jackie?"

Rick moaned and grabbed another beer. "We can't get to the bar fast enough."

"Look out!" Brianna screamed.

A set of headlights on the wrong side of the road bore down on the truck.

Rick slammed on the brakes. Brianna reached for her seatbelt. Jackie shut her eyes. Vince braced himself against the dashboard. Rick spun the wheel hard to the right, sending the truck into a sideways skid. The oncoming tractor-trailer clipped the Ford, sending it careening off the road, where it slammed into a telephone pole, coming to rest on its side in a ditch.

As the eighteen-wheeler continued on its way, the wind and the roar of thunder drowned out the blaring of the Ford's horn.

CHAPTER 6

With one knee on the gymnasium floor, Mike cradled the camera. Through the viewfinder, he framed the twin cheerleaders, standing back-to-back in their green-and-gold uniforms. Eyes twinkled, and smiles dazzled while he snapped away.

Mike checked the results and shook his head. "Let's try that one again."

The girls relaxed for a moment, then resumed their poses as the camera clicked.

"Okay." Mike rose from his knee and pointed to the cheerleader on the left. "Talia, you face me directly. Veronica, stand at a ninety-degree angle, resting your right forearm on your sister's left shoulder."

Sitting on the bleachers, Darla shouted, "Remember to smolder, girls!"

The two arranged themselves as requested, adopted a vacant look in their eyes, and pursed their lips.

"You're on fire! My camera lens is melting."

"Van Buren student owes his roommate big time," Jerry said in his radio announcer's voice as he slapped a hand on Mike's back.

"This is great, Jerry! I got some group shots of the squad, and some action stuff too." Mike nodded at the blonde on the bleachers. "But Darla suggested that I do some posed shots of her and her friends."

"Excuse me." Darla hopped off the bleachers and stood in front of Jerry with her arms crossed. "Cheerleading practice is closed to outsiders. You'll have to leave."

"It's okay." Mike put a hand on his roommate' shoulder. "This is my friend, Jerry."

Darla arched an eyebrow. "You're friends with Michael?"

"Well, friendship is a tricky thing." Jerry removed Mike's hand. "I'm actually from the school newspaper. Unlike other people." He glared at his roommate. "I'm here to write a story about the cheerleader who was injured. I interviewed the coach, and she said I should talk with you, if you're Darla."

"Oh, you're the one doing the article. I'm Darla Jaggard, Assistant Cheerleading Captain. That's Jaggard with one *J* and two *Gs*." She grabbed Jerry by the hand, then looked at the twins. "You two keep working with Michael."

Darla dragged Jerry toward the bleachers. She was dressed in the same uniform as the other two cheerleaders: a sleeveless green top with Statesmen printed in gold script across the front, a green skirt trimmed with gold and ending significantly above her knees, tiny white socks, and green athletic shoes. Matching ribbons secured her honey-blonde hair.

Initially, Jerry thought the tiny sparkles on Darla's face were glistening sweat, but with a second glance, he determined it was glittery make-up. Her lips were painted sports-car red. And she smelled like someone set off a bomb in a candy shop: bubble gum, chocolate, and Peeps. The effect was like a punch in the gut, and he found it challenging to breathe.

They took seats in the first row, and Jerry forced himself to maintain eye contact, staring at irises the color of a putting green framed by impossibly long lashes.

"This is so exciting!" Darla tapped away on her phone. "We're going to be in the school newspaper."

"I'm not sure *exciting* is the word I would choose to describe what happened to your teammate."

"Oh right." Darla's expression became subdued. "Do you have to write about that? It's *so* depressing. Couldn't you do a story about the squad and our trip to compete at Nationals?"

"That's not my assignment." He saw Darla's lips start to form a frown. "But I could ask my editor about it."

Darla placed her hand on Jerry's arm. "Could you?"

Her touch was warm. Fingernails a shiny red. Jerry remembered Busby's explosion at lunch. He never liked her cynicism. Cheering wasn't his thing, but these girls seemed to be committed athletes, dedicating themselves to their passion. "I'll see what I can do."

"Outstanding." Her hand remained on Jerry's forearm.

Jerry was having trouble concentrating. With great effort, he managed to recall why he was here in the first place. "Can I ask you about the girl who was hurt, Cassie McGlaughlin?"

"Yeah, what do you want to know?"

"How about what happened?"

"We were practicing here yesterday. They tossed her for the basket catch. Four of the guys come together and launch her into the air." Darla stood and made an uplifting motion with her arms.

Jerry immediately missed the touch of her hand.

"She's actually one of our better flyers. Gets good elevation and extension. The lights flickered; it was during the thunderstorm. She came down wrong, collided with someone, and splat!" Darla made a fist and pounded it into her open hand.

"Splat." Jerry jotted in his notebook.

"At first, we thought she had the wind knocked out of her. But she was all lost up here." Darla lifted her hands to her head and wiggled her fingers. "Cassie sat out the rest of the practice. One of the trainers checked her out. Last I heard, she was blind, and they took her to the hospital." Darla sat down on the bleachers, closer to Jerry than before, her knee grazing Jerry's thigh.

Jerry stole a quick glance at the tanned leg and swallowed hard. Tom Petty's *American Girl* blared from his pocket. *Busby!* What did she want? After the display she put on in the cafeteria, Buzz was the last person he wanted to talk to. He pulled out the phone, silenced it, and jammed it into his pocket. "Sorry, I usually remember to turn off my phone when I conduct interviews."

Darla looked up from inspecting her nails. "No one important?"

"Uh, no. Probably somebody selling extended car warranties."

"Cause with that ringtone, I thought the call might be personal." Darla's green eyes bored into Jerry as if she could see the lie hidden within him.

His chest tightened and face reddened. Darla's lips twisted into a grin, and the blushing grew worse. He broke eye contact and glanced around the gym: Mike taking photos of one of the twins in a split, the rest of the squad practicing at the far end of the court, the sole championship banner hanging from the ceiling.

"Sorry if I embarrassed you." But Darla's smile made it clear she was enjoying this.

"Not a big deal." Jerry again tried to clear his thoughts. "Where was I?" He rechecked his notes. "Blind?"

Darla tilted her head. "That's what I heard. Maybe Cassie's better now. I don't know."

"I had no idea how dangerous cheerleading is."

"Well, if you're good like me and know what you're doing, it isn't so rough. But we do suffer for our sport. That's what it takes to be a champion."

"Can you tell me anymore about Cassie?"

"She lives in Hamilton Hall. I think she's a Speech Pathology major. Okay for a freshman. But it's a tough transition. You're queen of high school, then you come here and start all over at the bottom. She didn't know how to deal with that."

"How do you mean?"

"For example, yesterday on the way to practice, me and Talia and Veronica were running up the steps. But Cassie was on the other side. She split the group. And she was being a real b-word about it. If you know what I mean."

"Split the group?"

"Yeah, you know, she was on the other side of the railing. It's bad luck. And I told her so. She acted like she didn't know what I was talking about. That's probably why she got hurt." Darla stopped, her mouth a perfect oval, and covered it with her hand. "Oh my gosh, you're not going to put that in your story, are you?"

"You mean the part about how Cassie ran up the wrong side of the steps, jinxed herself, and ended up blind?"

Darla nodded, biting her lip.

Jerry shook his head. "I'll leave that part out."

"Thanks." Darla leaned in and nudged her shoulder against his.

"Hey, Jerry!" Mike shouted. "We're done with the photos and going to get pizza. You want to come with?" He sported a wide grin as Talia and Veronica flanked him.

"We're good, Michael," Darla replied. "But don't forget to email me those photos."

Jerry tapped his chest. "Actually, you need to email those photos to *me*."

"Got it. Both of you." Mike turned away and escorted the twins out of the gym.

Darla leaned forward, and Jerry was engulfed by her candy shop scent. "You seem like a really good reporter. Will you talk to your editor about doing a story on me? The struggles, challenges, and triumphs of the Assistant Cheerleading Captain? Michael can take some more photos of me: candid, action, posing. You could even come to Dallas and write a story about me competing at Nationals." She paused and dropped her voice to a whisper. "We could have plenty of fun in Texas."

Jerry knew *The Chronicle* didn't have the budget to send him to Dallas, but this didn't seem to be the time to discourage Darla. Could Vanessa be persuaded to let him write a story on her? "I'll see what I can do. What's your number? I'll text you."

"What's yours? I'll text you now."

Jerry gave her his number. She tapped her phone.

"Okay." Darla rose. "I've really got to get going."

Jerry stood. "Thanks for the interview. It was good meeting you." He offered his hand, but Darla ignored it, stepped forward, pressed her body to his, and hugged him.

Her hot breath brushed his ear. "Think about Dallas."

Darla broke the embrace. She raised her arms, and the uniform top rode up, revealing her belly button surrounded by lethally tanned abs. Bending her knees, she launched into the air, spun backward, nailed her landing, and winked at Jerry.

"Au revoir." She grabbed her gym bag, spun a hundred eighty degrees on one foot, and waved goodbye.

As Jerry watched her hips swiveling like ball bearings, he was determined to convince Vanessa to let him write a story on Darla. As she disappeared out the door, he let out a deep breath. He pulled out his phone, added Darla's number to his contacts, and checked his texts.

Busby: At the hospital. Rick's been in an accident.

CHAPTER 7

Dmitri: Where you at?

Miranda: Hospital

Dmitri: You ok?

Miranda: Busby's brother was in an accident

Dmitri: Bad?

Miranda: Dunno

Dmitri: When you stopping by?

Miranda: Dunno. Got to write a paper on Orwell for a linebacker.

Dmitri: you so smart and sexy

"The nurses won't tell anything about Rick's condition." Busby flopped onto the plastic chair next to Miranda. "Something about health privacy."

Miranda tapped her phone. "It's called HIPAA. The Health Information Portability and Accountability Act."

Busby ripped the phone from Miranda's hands. "How about a little less trivia, Sanchez? And a little more sympathy."

Miranda leaned back in her chair. "I'm here, aren't I?"

Busby pursed her lips together. Miranda was not only here keeping her company, but she was also the one who drove Busby to the hospital. Getting mad at the people closest to her wasn't going to help. She took a deep breath. "Yeah, I'm sorry. Thanks for being a good friend." She handed the phone back. "And where is Williams?" Busby's pocket buzzed. "This better be him." She pulled out her phone, saw the caller, and sighed. "Hi Mom."

"Honey, what happened? How's Rick?" Busby's mother's eastern Tennessee accent was thick as gravy on grits.

"His truck was in an accident. But the hospital won't say how he's doing. Something about privacy and hippos. Did you tell Daddy?"

"Your father's on a flight back from Singapore. I haven't been able to get a hold of him. But I'm arranging for both of us to come up."

"Mom, don't do that. You're making it sound too serious."

"But you said you don't know how Rick is."

"I promise to call as soon as I hear something." Busby spotted Jerry at the doorway, scanning the waiting room. "Okay, Mom. Got to go. Love you." She shoved the phone into her pocket.

Busby intercepted Jerry in the middle of the room. "Williams, where the hell have you been?" She could feel the frustration and helplessness overwhelming her anger. She looped her arms around Jerry and held him tight.

Jerry let Busby rest her head on his shoulder while patting her back. "Buzz, it's going to be okay."

She broke the embrace. A single tear ran down her cheek. "Why do you smell like the candy aisle at Target?"

"Long story. How's Rick?"

She took a deep breath. "All I know is that Rick was in an accident. But the nurses won't tell me anything."

"This is where having a boyfriend who works for a newspaper comes in handy." He leaned forward, held Busby's hand, and kissed her on the forehead. "I'll find out what happened. I spotted a police officer when I came in." He dropped his voice an octave. "Jerry Williams, Ace Reporter, is on the beat."

Busby's blue eyes twinkled, and her lips curled into a smile. "Thanks, Williams. You're the best."

Busby returned to her seat next to Miranda, and Jerry rushed back the way he came in.

With notebook in hand, Jerry approached the policeman. The cop was a tall blond, maybe 6'4", in a yellow rain slicker standing inside the emergency room entrance. "Excuse me, Officer."

"Actually, it's Deputy Kirk Clayton of the Stuyvesant County Sheriff's Department."

"Right. Sorry, Deputy. I'm Jerry Williams with the *Van Buren University Chronicle*. Do you mind if I ask you a few questions?"

"Aren't you a regular Woodward Bernstein?"

"What?"

"Don't they teach you anything at that college? Woodward N. Bernstein is the guy who invented the Watergate, so they could impeach Nixon."

"Right, I've heard of him," Jerry lied, figuring he wouldn't get much help if he contradicted the deputy. "Do you know anything about a traffic accident involving a Ford F-250?"

Clayton nodded. "I got called out for that one. A tractor trailer clipped the pickup, sending it into a drainage ditch. Three passengers and the driver in the pickup."

Jerry scribbled a note. "It wasn't the fault of the pickup driver?"

"I'm not in the business of assigning fault. In fact, I said too much already. You'll need to contact the department's press office for more information. Hours are Monday to Friday, eight to four-thirty."

Jerry frowned. "You really can't tell me anything else?"

Clayton shrugged. "Sorry, kid. Those are the rules. We've had trouble with the press before."

Jerry managed a half-smile. "Thanks for your time."

"If it's any consolation. I admire your drive. Maybe you'll win a Wurlitzer."

Jerry backtracked through the hospital, up and down hallways, around corners, until he found the information desk and a sour-faced nurse in blue scrubs. He put on his best disarming smile. "Hi, I'm wondering if you can give me any information on a patient named Rick Tilden?"

The nurse looked tired and overworked. She sighed and put down her coffee cup. "Are you family?"

Jerry shook his head.

"Then I can't give out any information."

"But he's my girlfriend's brother."

"*Your girlfriend's brother?* Why didn't you say so? That changes everything. What do you want to know?"

"Really?" Jerry couldn't believe his luck. "Well, first off, what's—"

"That was sarcasm."

Jerry tried to look serious. "His sister is in the waiting room. What do I tell her?"

"You don't tell her anything. When the patient is awake and aware, he can give permission to share his status. Your girlfriend can even visit him. That hasn't happened yet because the doctors are still working on the patient. When they're done, they'll speak with her."

Jerry wasn't going to get any info he could pass on to Busby, but maybe there was a story here for *The Chronicle*. "Rick was in a traffic accident. I think the ambulances brought the rest of the people in the truck here. Can you tell me about any of them?"

The nurse looked at him skeptically. "Are any of them family?"

"Not sure. I don't know who was in the truck."

"You don't even know their names?"

Another dead end. "How about a patient named Cassie McGlaughlin?"

The nurse sighed. "Are we going to do this all night?"

"Last one. I promise."

"Is Ms. McGlaughlin family?

"No." Jerry shook his head.

"Not your girlfriend's sister?"

"I don't even know her."

"Then why do you want to know how she's doing?"

"Look, I know I'm being a pain, but I'm on a deadline. I'm a reporter with the *Van Buren University Chronicle*." Jerry pulled out his press badge. "She's a cheerleader and got injured at practice. I'm writing a story about her. Can you give me her room number?"

The nurse tapped on her keyboard. "Good news. Ms. McGlaughlin shared her information in the directory. Let me see some ID."

Jerry handed her his driver's license.

The nurse squinted at it, grabbed a marker, and scribbled his name on a badge. "Wear this. Ms. McGlaughlin is in room 414. Elevators are down the hallway on the left."

"Thanks."

The nurse didn't reply. She was already back to drinking her coffee.

Jerry rode the elevator to the fourth floor, followed the signs past the nurses' station, and found room 414. Inside was one patient, a girl with a shaved head. The image reminded him of his mom going through chemo. This was the first time he'd been to a hospital since she died. He swallowed, but his mouth was dry, and ended up coughing.

"Hello?" Jerry rapped his knuckles on the open door.

"Is that you, Marcus?" The girl didn't turn her head, kept staring straight ahead.

"No, my name is Jerry Williams. I'm with the college newspaper. Are you Cassie McGlaughlin?"

"Yeah, that's me."

"I'm doing a story on you and the squad. Do you mind if I ask you a few questions?"

"I suppose it's okay. I'd like to have some company."

Jerry took a seat on the chair next to the bed. He took out his notebook as Cassie continued to stare at the wall. "So, uh, how are you doing?"

She laughed derisively. "I can't see anything, and the doctors don't know why. Aside from that, everything's peachy."

"Sorry."

"Don't be. It's not your fault."

Jerry leaned forward. "So, what happened?"

"Came down wrong. I think my foot hit someone's head, and I ended up eating mat. I've been cheering since I was in middle school, and this is the first time I've really gotten injured."

"Did it hurt?"

"I don't remember." Cassie sighed. "People say I got the wind knocked out of me."

"You said you cheered back in middle school. Where was that?"

"Port Penn, Delaware."

"How did you get interested in cheerleading?"

The interview continued for another fifteen minutes with Cassie providing background on herself and the squad.

Jerry stood. "I think I've got everything I need. Thanks for your time. I wish you a speedy recovery."

"Wait!" Cassie reached out her hand. "Do you have to go?"

"I don't need any more information."

"I'd like someone to talk to. My family is supposed to be on their way, but I don't know when they're getting here. No one from the team has stopped by, not even Marcus."

"Okay." Jerry held her hand and sat down. "I can stay for a bit. What do you want to talk about?"

"I told you all about cheering. Why don't you tell me about being a reporter?"

Jerry grinned. "Now that's a subject near and dear to my heart. My dad's the editor of a newspaper in South Jersey, not too far across the river from Port Penn. One night, one of his stringers was sick, and he needed someone to cover a school board meeting. I volunteered, did a good job, and he kept me on. Campaign appearances, traffic accidents, public meetings, football games. I loved it all. From that first story, I knew I wanted to be a reporter. When I came to Van Buren to major in journalism, it made sense to work at *The Chronicle*."

Jerry recounted to Cassie how he tracked down one of Van Buren's no-show Board of Trustee members, who would rather spend time gambling at the racetrack instead of appearing at the required meetings. "I walked right up to him and snapped a photo with my ph—"

Cassie pulled her hand back. "What happened? Did I fall?"

"Cassie?"

"I can't see! Who's there?"

"It's me, Jerry. What's wrong?"

She thrashed on her bed. "Help, I can't see!"

"Hold on, I'll go get someone."

He raced out of the room and flagged down the first person he saw, a tall man in green scrubs. "Cassie, the girl in 414. She's freaking out and needs help."

The man rushed into Cassie's room.

"Williams?"

Jerry turned to see Busby and Miranda.

"What's going on?" Busby stepped forward and poked him in the chest. "You were supposed to be finding out about Rick. Remember, *Ace Reporter?*"

"I was. I mean, I did. The cop wouldn't tell me anything, and neither would the nurse. But she did say I could interview Cassie, the cheerleader. So—"

"Cheerleader? Rick could have been dying." Tears welled up in Busby's eyes. "But they say he's okay, and we're on our way to his room now."

Jerry leaned forward to hug her, but Busby pushed him away.

"Come on, Buzz. I just—"

Busby slapped him across the right cheek with full force. "No, Jerry. This is the last time. I'm sick of your undelivered promises. We're through. C'mon, Sanchez. Let's go see Rick."

Jerry, more in shock than pain, watched Busby stomp down the hallway.

Miranda remained behind, jabbing him in the chest with her phone. "I warned you. Hopefully, she didn't really mean it. I'll see if I can fix things."

"Sanchez!" Busby waved for her to join her.

"Right there!" Miranda waved. She leaned close to Jerry. "But this only works if you try and do better by Busby."

Miranda turned and hustled down the hallway to the waiting Busby while Jerry rubbed his face in disbelief.

CHAPTER 8

Busby crossed her arms. "Sanchez, what were you saying to Williams?"

"Dispensing relationship advice."

Busby arched an eyebrow. "You're one to be offering guidance."

"I'm only trying to help." Miranda tilted her head. "Are we going to see Rick or what?"

"The nurse said he's in room 426. Shouldn't be much further."

The corridor was filled with antiseptic smells. Overhead, florescent lights flickered, creating eerie shadows on the pale blue walls. Busby imagined one day walking down this hall, or one like it, full of confidence with the earned look of respect in her colleagues' eyes.

They turned the corner and found Rick's room. He lay in the near bed, leg suspended in a cast, a pair of bandages on his face. A partition screen hid the other bed.

"Rick!" Busby raced from the door and hugged him.

"Ow, watch it, sis." Rick returned the hug half-heartedly. "They won't give me anything stronger than aspirin."

"You're okay." Tears filled Busby's eyes again. "I mean, the nurse wouldn't say anything for the longest time. Then she said *stable*, whatever the hell that means, but still wouldn't give me any details."

"I'm fine, except for the leg." He pointed at the cast. "Snapped my tibia. I'm out for the season."

"Who cares about stupid football?" Miranda plopped in the chair by the door and tapped her phone. "I'm updating Dmitri with the good news."

Rick turned his head and grimaced in pain. "Oh, hey there, Miranda, got any word on how Vince is doing?"

She rolled her eyes. "How would I know, and why would I care?"

"That's a little harsh, Sanchez," Busby admonished.

"So, no word on Vince?" Rick frowned.

"Vince was with you?"

"Yeah, him and a couple of girls. Oh man, I wonder how the Ford made out. I really love that truck."

"I wouldn't worry about that. You won't be driving for a couple of months." A knock drew their attention. In the doorway stood a man in a white lab coat with a stethoscope around his neck.

"Good evening, I'm Dr. Singh. Just coming by to see how our patient..." He glanced at the tablet in his hand. "Frederick Tilden, Jr. is doing."

"My name is Rick. And I could use something a little stronger for the pain."

Dr. Singh checked his tablet again. "I'm afraid we can't give you anything stronger until all the alcohol is out of your system."

"You were drinking?" Disappointment and disapproval replaced the concern in Busby's voice.

Rick shrugged as best he could with his leg suspended in the air. "Just a couple of beers."

"Yeah, right." Miranda rolled her eyes.

"Anyway, Frederick." Dr. Singh stepped to the bedside. "The CT scan came back negative. No concussion. Just the broken leg and some contusions. I want to check your heart and blood pressure, but we should be able to discharge you in the morning."

"It's Rick. And do you know how Vince Murphy is doing?"

Dr. Singh didn't answer. The room plunged into an awkward silence. The doctor placed his stethoscope on Rick's chest. He flinched as the cold plastic of the diaphragm touched his skin. The doctor stared at his watch for fifteen seconds, then withdrew the scope. He looped the blood pressure cuff around Rick's arm, inflated it, squinted at the dial, and ripped off the cuff. "Heart and BP are fine."

Rick grunted. "But what about Vince and Briana and...that other girl?"

Dr. Singh tapped his tablet. "They aren't my patients. I wouldn't know."

"No one knows anything." Rick sighed.

"If there are no further questions, I'll be on my way."

After the doctor left, Rick growled, "You'd think someone could tell me how Vince is doing."

"Who's Briana?" Miranda looked up from her phone.

"A girl we picked up on South Campus. Her and..." Rick paused like he was searching his memory for the name. "Her friend. Sis, can you find out something? Maybe put your boyfriend Kolchak on the case?"

"Let's not talk about Williams." Busby frowned.

Rick chortled. "Is there trouble in paradise?"

Busby slapped Rick's cast.

Rick convulsed in pain. "Jesus H. Christ, sis. That was totally uncalled for."

"Let's change the subject. Mom called and—"

"Excuse me. I'm Deputy Clayton, and I'm looking for Frederick Tilden, Jr." A tall blond man in a yellow rain slicker stood in the doorway.

"It's Rick." He slapped the bed. "Jesus H. Christ. My name is Rick."

Clayton nodded. "Is it okay if I ask you a few questions about the accident, Rick?"

"Sure, but it's all still kind of fuzzy."

"Can we stay?" Busby pointed at Miranda.

Clayton nodded. Busby took a seat next to the bed and held Rick's hand.

"I understand things might be jumbled." Clayton pulled out a notebook. "Do the best you can. What do you remember about the accident?"

"Not much. We were driving down Route 32 toward town. Rain was heavy. Pretty dark. Lightning hit nearby." He shook his head. "That's the last thing I remember."

"Do you recall what side of the road the truck that struck you was driving on?"

Rick paused for a moment. "I don't even remember the other truck."

Clayton scribbled in his notebook.

Miranda looked at the deputy. "Are you saying the other truck caused the accident?"

"I'm not saying anything. I'm trying to establish what happened." Clayton glared at her. "But if you want to stay, I'll ask that you not interrupt."

While still tapping on her phone, Miranda made the zipping her lips motion with her free hand.

Clayton turned back to Rick. "Had you been drinking?"

Rick started to speak, but Busby slapped her hand over his mouth. "Don't answer that."

Clayton glared at Busby. "And you are?"

"Busby Tilden. His sister." She removed her hand from Rick's mouth, made eye contact with him, and put a finger to her lips.

"Ms. Tilden, I'm just trying to establish the facts. The hospital drew blood from your brother when he was admitted, so he's not really hiding anything by refusing to cooperate." Clayton addressed Rick. "It's best if you're completely honest with me."

Rick looked from Busby to the cop and back to Busby, staying silent the whole time.

"That's it, Rick, Don't say anything." She pointed at the deputy. "Maybe you should leave."

"The young lady is correct," a male voice announced from behind the partition separating the room.

Busby and Rick exchanged puzzled glances.

"Who said that?" Clayton demanded.

The screen drew back to reveal a fifty-something man in a white hospital gown. He had silver-and-gray hair and a face sagging like a basset hound. "I did. Alan Berg, attorney-at-law." He glanced at Rick. "I didn't mean to eavesdrop, but the conversation was getting rather vocal. Your sister is correct, Mr. Tilden. You shouldn't answer any questions. Not until you are represented by competent counsel."

Clayton pointed at the lawyer. "Mr. Berg, are you representing Mr. Tilden?"

Berg shook his head. "Nope, just handing out some free legal advice to my roomie."

Busby sat up straighter. "See Rick? I'm right. Say nothing."

Rick frowned at the deputy. "I'm done answering questions."

The cop sighed. "I thought you'd want to assist our investigation. Help out your friends who were in the truck with you."

"What happened to them?" Miranda put down her phone.

The deputy glared at her. "Who are you?"

"What does that matter?"

Clayton flipped through his notebook. "Briana Sorenson is in stable condition with a concussion and three broken ribs. Jacqueline DiBernardo has been discharged with a broken wrist. Vincent Murphy was pronounced dead upon arrival at the hospital."

"What?" Rick's voice dropped. "Vince?"

"Vince?" Miranda's lips quivered.

"What do you care?" Rick snapped. "I thought you had a boyfriend."

"Take it easy, Rick." Busby squeezed his hand. "We're all upset."

Miranda tried to speak, but the words wouldn't come. She burst into tears, stumbled out of the chair, and scrambled out of the room.

"Now you can understand why we want to get as much information about the crash as possible." Clayton snapped his notebook shut.

"Rick, it's more important than ever not to say anything until such time that you've secured representation." Berg cleared his throat. "Everyone's emotions are running high right now. It's better to wait and deal with this rationally."

"If you're not his attorney, you can leave." Clayton pointed at the door.

Berg grinned. "But this is my room."

"I still think *you* should leave." Busby waved her hand at Clayton.

"It's up to you, Rick." The deputy held up his notebook. "Do you want to cooperate?"

Rick looked from Busby to Berg to Clayton. "No, I think I'll talk to you guys later."

"Suit yourself." Clayton tipped his cap to Busby and left the room.

Berg sat on the side of his bed. "Ooh. Shouldn't have gotten up."

Rick looked at him for an explanation.

"Hemorrhoids." Berg grimaced.

Busby struggled not to laugh. "Thanks for the advice, Mr. Berg. Is Rick in real trouble? Could you be his lawyer?"

"Slow down." Berg raised a hand. "First of all, I specialize in Civil Rights law. Employment discrimination. First Amendment and such. I don't do criminal law."

"Criminal law?" Rick replied. "I'm no criminal."

"I didn't say you are. But from what I gather, one of your passengers was killed in the accident and there may have been alcohol involved. This is a tricky area, and even if you are innocent, you require a competent, experienced attorney who specializes in these kinds of cases."

"*If you are innocent.* What is that supposed to mean?" Busby scowled.

"Settle down, sis. He's just explaining the situation."

"Thank you, Rick. Yes, Busby, I didn't mean anything by it. That's how lawyers talk."

"If you can't defend Rick, can you recommend someone who could?"

Berg's eyes lit up. "I can. My wife, Allison." He rose from his bed, shuffled to the closet, retrieved a wallet from his slacks, and pulled out two business cards. He handed one to Busby and one to Rick. "She's the best in Stuyvesant County, and I'd say that even if we weren't married."

Busby inspected the card; the scales of justice filled the upper left quadrant. *Alison Adams, Attorney-at-Law, Criminal Law, DUI, Traffic Cases.* Underneath that, the phone, email and website addresses were listed. "Thanks, Mr. Berg."

"You're quite welcome." Berg winced. "I better return to bed." He shuffled across the room. "Remember if the police, or anyone else for that matter, ask about the accident, don't say anything. Give Allison a call in the morning. Good evening." He closed the curtain.

Rick's chin sunk to his chest.

Busby sighed. "What's wrong?"

"What's wrong? Are you kidding, sis? Vince is dead. The cops are looking to pin it on me. And now I need a lawyer? I can imagine calling up Dad and asking him for the money to hire one."

"Actually, I don't think you'll have to call."

"Why not?"

"I was talking to Mom earlier. She and Daddy are coming up."

Rick groaned. "Why? It's only a broken leg."

"Yeah, but I didn't know that at the time."

"Call them back and tell them I'm okay." He paused for a moment. "No, it's probably best that they come."

"What about the accident?"

"The lawyer told me not to talk about it with anyone."

"Not funny." Busby made a fist and pounded him on the shoulder. "Seriously, Rick. How much did you have to drink? Was it more than a couple?"

He let out a weary breath. "Maybe. But I was *not* drunk. Just a little buzzed. And you heard the cop's questions. Sounds like the other truck is the one at fault."

"Possibly, but you're not sure."

Rick shook his head. "No, I can't remember at all."

CHAPTER 9

J erry sat at his desk in *The Chronicle's* newsroom, finishing his story on Cassie, her injury, and the cheer squad. He attached the shots that Mike sent him, grabbed a couple of photos from Cassie's Instagram account (she gave permission for their use), added the image he took of her with his phone at the hospital, included captions, and emailed the entire package to Vanessa.

The newsroom was mostly deserted. Besides Jerry, the only reporters who remained were Noah, working on his story about the groundbreaking for the new football stadium, and Fallon, completing her theater review. Wind gusts and fierce rain continued to slam the windows. Every couple of minutes, the low rumble of thunder drowned out the downpour.

Jerry powered off his PC, stood, and walked to Fallon's desk. She leaned left, letting him read her review.

According to authorities, Bernie Madoff's investors were defrauded of some fifteen billion dollars, which is a fate infinitely more palatable than having to endure the VBU Drama Club's latest crime against musical theater, Ponzi Scheme: The Rise and Fall of Bernie Madoff.

The cringe begins with the opening number "Roll Over" sung by junior Cliff Clark (in the eponymous role) to the tune of Greg Kihn's "The Breakup Song." The insipidity of senior Allison Cole's lyrics is surpassed only by Clark's off-key performance.

But the wincing doesn't end there. Sophomore Daphne Conrad's role of Mrs. Ruth Madoff contains nothing but the worst stereotypes about overbearing Long Island Jewish mothers. I wouldn't be surprised to learn that the ADL will picket future showings, in the unlikely event that the production doesn't close after one night.

No doubt director George DeMaris's curious decision to dress the SEC and FBI investigators in Roman-style togas is an attempt to make some profound statement. But by that point, this reviewer simply no longer cared, and prayed for a quick and merciful end to the so-called musical.

The dramaturgical nightmare concluded with a big song and dance number as the entire cast spasmodically boogied and caterwaulingly crooned "Too Good To Be True", another of the uninspired tunes penned by Cole.

Zero Stars. Rather than attend this travesty, you'd be better off using the ticket money you saved to invest in some dubious multi-level marketing scheme.

Jerry chuckled. "Scathing, but I think it might be too much."

"Pfft. Actors, singers, playwrights, and directors all need to develop a thicker skin." Fallon tapped her keyboard. "Done."

"I was thinking more about Vanessa. No way she runs that."

"We'll see." Fallon turned off her monitor.

"How about you, Noah? Almost finished?"

"Just about." He stuffed the last bit of cinnamon donut into his mouth, chewed, and swallowed. "How does this sound? Groundbreaking for Van Buren University's new, seventy-five-million-dollar football stadium took place on Th—"

"Seventy-five million!" Fallon pounded her desk. "Can you imagine all the good the Gender Studies Department could do with that money?"

Jerry sighed. "The boosters and alumni who made contributions for the stadium probably aren't interested in making a donation to your favorite programs. But you could always ask."

Fallon jabbed her finger at Jerry. "The donations don't cover the full cost of construction. The rest of the money's coming from student fees, the general operating budget, and the endowment. That's money that should benefit the entire university. Not crypto-fascist football fans."

Jerry shrugged. "You want to write an Op-Ed, go ahead."

"What I want is for money to be spent on forward-thinking, progressive causes, not some reenactment of the worst horrors on the Eastern Front with a side order of toxic masculinity and premature dementia."

"Can you guys please keep it down to a dull roar?" Noah raised his arms, then lowered them in a calming motion. "I'm trying to finish this up."

"We can argue over here." Jerry walked to the break room, poured the last two cups of coffee, and cleaned the pot.

"I'm not interested in arguing. I want genuine change." Fallon stirred almond milk into her mug.

"Go occupy an administration building or something. Football's popular. Get over it. I'm not a fan. Busby's brother is on the team, and he's the biggest jerk around." *Busby!* Jerry rubbed his cheek. Was she really dumping him, or would she cool off and give him a chance to apologize? Hopefully, Miranda could talk some sense into her.

"Jerry? You there?"

"Huh? What?" He became aware Fallon was speaking to him.

"I said: Then shouldn't you be on my side?"

Jerry replayed the conversation in his head. "No, it's not about sides."

"That's an odd take for a journalist."

"No, Fallon, it's the best take. I don't advocate. I report and dig for the truth, and I'll bring down anyone who has it coming. Even if I happen to agree with them."

"You're deluded if you think there's an objective truth, Jerry. There's only competing narratives and manufactured consent. Read your Chomsky."

"Guys, I'm done." Noah poked his head in. "You want to get out of here?"

"About time." Fallon rinsed out the rest of the cups in the sink.

They grabbed their rain jackets and assembled at the entrance. Outside, a bolt of lightning illuminated the campus for a fraction of a second.

"This is some storm." Jerry pressed his nose against the glass doors. "Maybe we should wait it out."

"The Weather Service put out a Thunderstorm Warning and Flash

Flood Watch for Stuyvesant County until midnight." Fallon held up her phone. "Wind gusts up to sixty miles per hour."

"You don't need an app for that. Just look." Jerry pointed outside.

"I'm going to risk it." Noah pushed his way through the door and attempted to open his umbrella. A gust of wind pushed the ribs past the locking mechanism and the cover inverted. Noah struggled to fix the umbrella, but the wind was too strong. He grabbed the door handle, dragged it open, and hauled himself inside. "It's worse than it looks."

"Climate change caused by increasing levels of carbon dioxide in the atmosphere is resulting in more frequent and destructive thunderstorms." Fallon flashed a smug expression.

Jerry sighed. "Does everything have to be political with you?"

"Who's being political? It's a scientific fact. Don't you care about the enviro—"

"Ugh, you know what?" Noah wrestled the umbrella closed. "I changed my mind. I'm not waiting for it to let up. Rather take my chances out in the storm than in here with you two trying to recreate The Hundred Years' War." This time, he opened his umbrella inside.

Fallon pointed. "You know that's bad luck, right?"

"Bite me, Fallon." Noah used his foot to brace the door open wide enough for him and his umbrella to squeeze through and stepped outside.

"That was totally uncalled for." Fallon watched Noah struggle in the downpour.

"Fallon, did you ever think that maybe you—"

A bolt of lightning stuck outside the building concurrent with a deafening crush of thunder. Noah's body flew through the air like a beanbag in a corn hole competition. The umbrella slipped from his hand, blowing away in the wind.

"Noah!" Jerry rushed into the pouring rain.

Fallon followed. Noah lay face down in a puddle next to the pavement. Jerry flipped him over. Singe marks on Noah's jacket. His eyes closed.

Jerry shook his shoulders. "Noah, are you okay? Wake up!"

Fallon knelt beside him. Over the storm, she shouted, "Is he breathing?"

Jerry leaned close, rain stinging his eyes. "I can't tell. Grab the door. I'm bringing him inside."

Fallon ran to the door and battled the wind to hold it open. Jerry, still crouching, slipped his hands under Noah, lifted, and stood up shakily. He took one tentative step toward the entrance and a gust almost knocked him over. Catching his balance, Jerry staggered through the door, took three steps inside, dropped to his knees, and laid Noah on the floor.

"Is he alive?" Fallon crowded Jerry.

Jerry put his hand under Noah's nose. Nothing. He placed his thumb and index finger on Noah's carotid artery. No pulse. "Get the AED!"

"The what?"

"The defibrillator. It's on the wall outside Vanessa's office. And call 9-1-1. I'll start CPR." Jerry unzipped Noah's rain jacket, pulled his penknife from his backpack, and cut away Noah's shirt. Jerry tilted Noah's head back, opened his mouth, checked for obstructions, but didn't see any. He placed his hands together in the middle of Noah's chest and pressed down.

Crack.

Jerry winced. In the excitement, he pressed way too hard, breaking Noah's ribs. Jerry took a deep breath to compose himself. *Steady mind, steady hands. Noah's counting on you.* He continued with the compressions.

Fallon pulled out her phone and raced off for the AED. Jerry heard her rapid-fire call to the 9-1-1 operator. "Noah's been hit by lightning. He's not breathing, I'm getting the defibrillator. Jerry's giving him CPR."

Come on Fallon, keep it together.

"Van Buren University Gleason Building come quick please!"

Jerry counted the compressions. "Eleven...Twelve..."

Fallon returned with the defibrillator and knelt.

"Fallon, if we're going to help Noah, we have to keep calm." Jerry stopped the compressions, lowered his head to Noah's, pinched his nose and blew two rescue breaths into Noah's mouth. Lightning flashed outside the building again and thunder followed a half second later.

"I'm trying Jerry, but this storm is crazy. Everything is crazy!" She closed her eyes and took a deep breath, then put the phone on the floor. "Okay, 9-1-1 lady, you're on speaker. I'm with Noah. He has the defibrillator."

"What's his status?" The operator's voice crackled from the phone's speaker.

"Twenty...Twenty-one...Twenty-two...I'm performing chest compressions...Fallon, open up the defibrillator and attach the electrodes. Twenty-nine...Thirty..." Again, Jerry stopped compressions and blew two deep breaths into Noah. He checked for a pulse. Nothing.

"The ambulance is three minutes away," the operator announced.

Lightning struck again with thunder, and this time, the building shook.

"What the hell is going on with this storm?" Fallon fumbled open the box. "What do I do?"

"Four...Five...Pull the covers off the electrodes. Attach one to under his right collarbone and the other under his left armpit. Fourteen...Fifteen..."

"Was the victim outside?" The operator's voice remained calm. "Is his chest wet? You'll need to dry it off."

Fallon spotted Laurie Inverso's sweater draped over her chair. She dashed over, grabbed it, returned to Noah, and mopped the water off his chest. She tossed the sweater aside. Jerry paused the compressions.

Fallon attached the electrodes. "Now what?"

"Don't touch Noah. Press the yellow analyze button on the AED."

"Make sure everyone is clear of the body," the operator instructed.

"Analyzing," the device announced. "No shock advised."

"What does that mean?" Fallon's voice filled with panic.

"It means we keep up the CPR." Jerry resumed compressions. "One...Two...Three..." He could feel his arms getting tired.

"Where's that ambulance?"

Another lightning bolt struck outside the building. The thunder was deafening. The office lights flickered for a moment before the office was plunged into darkness.

"Hello?" Fallon picked up the phone. "Line's dead."

The emergency lights over the entrance clicked on, casting an eerie glow on the three.

"No bars." Fallon glared at her phone. "This is nuts."

"Doesn't matter. We can't give up. Nine...Ten...Eleven..."

Fallon activated the flashlight app on her phone and shone it on Jerry and Noah.

Jerry felt his arms weakening. "Fallon, I'm getting tired. Three...Four...Five...Get ready to take over."

"What? How? I don't know CPR."

"Don't panic. I'll tell you what to do. Watch where I placed my hands."

Two paramedics, a man and a woman, carrying a stretcher and a med kit, burst through the doors.

The female EMT knelt next to Jerry. "What happened?"

"Noah got hit by lightning. Dragged him inside and started compressions." Jerry glanced at his watch. "That was four minutes ago."

The male EMT crouched next to Noah. "Good job. We'll take over. Miller, let's get him intubated." Jerry and Fallon stepped back and let the EMTs do their work. Another pair dressed in firefighting rubber uniforms rushed in. The four engaged in a quick discussion. One held a portable container and hooked an oxygen mask over Noah's mouth and nose. Fallon cringed at the sound as they ripped the patches from Noah's skin.

The EMTs strapped Noah to a board and lifted him onto the stretcher. Jerry scrambled to the door, holding it open as they wheeled Noah into the rain. Jerry stood in the downpour as the first responders loaded his friend into the ambulance.

Lightning struck again, narrowly missing the ambulance as it drove away.

Fallon put her hand on Jerry's shoulder. "Noah will be okay. I know it."

CHAPTER 10

Darla held the phone, framing her roommate in the background and the Red Solo cup in the foreground. She tapped record. "Go."

Lucy faced the camera, smiled, and curtsied. She held a golf ball in one hand and a nine iron in the other. She wore a long-sleeved navy-blue top, white leggings patterned with gold diamonds down the sides, and white New Balance sneakers with pink laces. Her dark hair was up in a ponytail, poking through the back of her Titleist branded visor.

"Lucy Davenport here, and welcome to my latest fabulous trick shot." She turned ninety degrees. With the ball in her left hand and club in her right, she dropped the ball, caught it with the clubface, and began bouncing the ball to eye level.

After five bounces, Lucy lifted her right leg and swung the club underneath. *Click. Click. Click.* She switched the club to her left hand and maneuvered the club beneath her left leg. *Click. Click. Click.* She gave the ball some extra oomph and tossed the club in the air, sending it spinning. She grabbed the grip of the twirling club in time to catch the ball before it struck the floor. *Click. Click. Click.* Lucy bounced the ball higher and dropped the club on the floor of the dorm. As the ball plummeted, she lifted her right foot and kicked the ball with the side of her sneaker. The ball arced through the air, coming within inches of the ceiling. The ball began its downward trajectory toward Darla and plopped into the Red Solo cup with a satisfying splash.

"Yes!" Lucy raised her hands in victory.

"*Hors pair.* That is some lucky landing."

"Not luck, D. All skill." Lucy winked for the recording.

"Whatever. Outstanding, Lucy! I'm uploading it now—"

Darla's phone emitted a nails-on-chalkboard screech. Lucy's phone lying on her desk emitted the same disturbing noise.

"What's going on?" Lucy covered her ears.

Darla squinted at the phone. "It's the U app." She furrowed her brow. "Due to the tragic events that have occurred, all classes have been canceled for Friday, October 6th."

"What tragic events?"

"It doesn't say." Darla scrolled through the notifications. "But grief counselors are going to be made available."

"What the hell happened?"

"I have no idea. But I know someone who might."

In *The Chronicle*'s newsroom, the mood was restrained. Half the desks were empty. The staffers that were present spoke in whispers. The loudest sound was the clacking of the keyboards.

Noah's desk had been converted to a makeshift shrine. Photos, flowers, and a couple of stuffed animals surrounded a box of unopened Krispy Kremes.

Jerry, bleary-eyed from lack of sleep, slumped in his chair. He had cranked out Cassie's obituary and spent the last twenty minutes staring at a blank Word document and blinking cursor. He couldn't believe he talked to Cassie and Noah yesterday and now they were both dead.

"Jerry, are you okay?" Laurie looked at him with concern.

"I'm fine." He wasn't fine, but didn't know what else to say. "What's up?"

"Vanessa wants to see you in her office."

Jerry shrugged, locked his desktop, and stood. He shuffled across the newsroom and poked his head into Vanessa's office. "Laurie said you wanted to see me?"

Vanessa clicked her mouse, then looked up from the monitor. "Yes, Jerry. Come in and close the door."

Jerry did as instructed and took a seat.

"I heard about yours and Fallon's efforts to save Noah last night. You're both heroes."

"Nope." Jerry looked down at the front of her desk, not making eye contact. "It didn't make any difference. He's still dead." The words caught in his throat.

"But you tried."

Jerry said nothing and continued to avoid her gaze.

"I'm sure you understand why I can't let you or Fallon write Noah's story. You're part of it. I'm giving it to Laurie, and she'll interview both of you."

"That's fine."

"As for Cassie, we'll run the obit you wrote for now. You can interview her family later, and we'll do that feature on her."

"Yeah." Jerry remembered Cassie sitting in the hospital room. All alone and putting on a brave face one moment, then freaking out the next. "She was a nice kid."

"What I'd like you to do is delve into the history of the university. When has Van Buren ever been through such a loss? Three students in one day. I don't—"

"Three?" Jerry lifted his head and made eye contact for the first time.

Vanessa nodded. "Didn't you hear? One of the football players, Vince Murphy, was killed in a car accident last night."

"I knew Vince. He was at our lunch table yesterday." Jerry stared at the wall.

"Jerry, I was going to give you this assignment, but now I'm thinking you should go back to your room or visit the grief counselors. They're stationed at Student Health and the Orange Building."

He crossed his arms. "No, I want to be here."

"Okay. I appreciate it since we're short-handed with...you know. First, you've covered sports before, right? Can you take the football game tomorrow?"

"The game's still on?"

"You know football." Vanessa rolled her eyes. "They played the Sunday after JFK was shot."

"Yeah, I can do it."

"Here's the credential." She handed him an envelope. "But for today, with these deaths, the campus needs us to put it into perspective. I want you to check the archives and see what kind of deaths and tragedies struck the campus in the past."

"Sure, I'll do it. But that will take like a five-minute computer search."

"Only the last twenty years of *The Chronicle* are online. I want you to go all the way back. There's over a century of history to mine. And I can't think of anyone better to do it." She paused. "If you're up for it."

"Whatever you want." He stood and silently left the office.

The musty smell in the basement of *The Chronicle* resembled that of old newspapers, but that was a coincidence. No stacks of yellowing past issues, only rolls and rolls of microfiche.

Jerry grabbed a random spool, not even bothering to check the year, inserted it in the reader, and flicked it on. He squinted at the small print and turned the dial to increase the magnification. He stood, walked to the wall, turned out the lights, and returned to his seat. The darkness made it easier to read. It also felt like a thick, black blanket that he could curl up under and hide from his friend's death, Busby dumping him, the rest of the world.

He scrolled through weeks' worth of issues, scanning the headlines until he found a story about a junior who left the school in 1915, traveling to Ontario, then on to Great Britain, where he joined the Royal Air Force. After completing training, the pilot was assigned to the continent. Shot down over Belgium and presumed dead, his body was never recovered.

Jerry jotted down the relevant details, pulled out another spool, browsed the archives, and stumbled upon a story of two students who died after drinking what turned out to be methyl alcohol at an off-campus party in 1924. More pointless deaths.

Another twenty minutes of scrolling brought him to a story of Peggy Johnson, a student who died on campus in 1984, but the details of her death weren't in the article. He'd look for a follow-up story in the next issue.

"Hello?" a female voice called. "Jerry, are you down here?"

"Busby? Is that you?"

The lights flicked on. At the base of the steps stood Darla. She wore a yellow blouse, turquoise mini skirt, gray ankle boots with a matching gray purse slung over her shoulder. For most girls on campus, their wardrobe consisted of T-shirts and jeans or sweats, but Darla looked like she stepped out of the H&M website.

"Who's Busby?" Her green eyes narrowed at Jerry.

"Uh, nobody." Jerry unconsciously rubbed his face where Busby slapped him. "What are you doing here, Darla?"

"The U sent out that message about classes being canceled, but it didn't say why. All mysterious and grief counselors and stuff. I figured you'd know." She frowned. "But you didn't answer my texts."

Jerry pulled his phone from his pocket. "I turned it off to concentrate."

Darla stepped forward, and Jerry was engulfed by her scent. She didn't smell like a candy shop this morning. More like a botanical garden. Her eyes were greener than remembered. The tightness in his chest returned.

She grabbed his phone, powered it up, and thrust it back into his hand, brushing her fingers against his. "You'll want to keep it on at all times." Her lips curled into a smile. "In case I need to get in touch with you."

"Okay." Jerry was still puzzled by her presence. "How did you find me, anyway?"

Darla gave a noncommittal wave of her hand. "I was talking with your editor, and she said I could find you down here. You forgot to ask her about doing a story on me, didn't you?"

"Yeah, sorry. With everything that's been happening, it kind of slipped my mind."

"That's okay. I suggested it to Vanessa. That's her name, right?"

Jerry stifled a laugh. "You told Vanessa you want me to write a story about you?"

"Uh huh."

Jerry marveled at Darla. He didn't think he'd ever met anyone so lacking in humility. "What did she say?"

Darla huffed in frustration. "She blew me off. Something about the focus being on the tragedies on campus. I didn't even get a chance to talk to her about sending you to Dallas with the team."

Thank God for small favors.

"Anywho, she said I could find you down here."

"I don't understand. You were looking for me because you wanted to know why they canceled classes. But after talking with Vanessa, you must know. So why are you here?"

Darla stepped closer and picked an invisible piece of lint off Jerry's shoulder. "I had a delightful time chatting with you yesterday. I thought you felt the same way."

"Uh, yeah, I did."

"I thought we'd do it again. Also, *Jerry,*" she pronounced his name like a third-grade teacher lecturing a problem student, "when a young lady takes the effort to look nice, it's customary to compliment her appearance." She posed with her hands on her hips.

Jerry's face burned bright red. "Darla, you, uh, look absolutely amazing."

She tilted her head. "That will do for now. But I'm sure you'll improve with practice."

Practice? Jerry gulped.

She looked around at the microfiche machines. "So, what's all this? What does Vanessa have you doing down here in this dusty old basement?"

"These are all the old copies of *The Chronicle* on microfiche. They took photographs of all the pages and shrunk them down and put them on film, and you use these machines to read them."

"Why not put it all online?"

"Cost? Guess it makes little sense, since no one really wants to go back and read what happened over a hundred years ago. Here look." Jerry sat and slid his chair to the side.

Darla took a seat and rolled next to Jerry, her knee brushing against his. Jerry stole a quick glance at her legs, then made eye contact.

"What were you going to show me?" She seemed positively delighted with his interest.

Jerry cleared his thoughts and forced himself to look at the microfiche screen. "I've been looking up deaths of students. Found a guy who was a pilot in World War I and got shot down. Couple of kids drinking antifreeze during Prohibition. This is the latest one I found from 1984."

Darla squinted at the screen. "Friday the 13th? No wonder she's dead."

"What?"

"Look." With a shiny red fingernail, Darla traced the date beneath the paper's masthead. "Saturday, July 14th. The article says she died the day before. That makes it Friday the 13th and that's super bad luck."

"Bad luck." In his mind, Jerry heard Fallon mocking Noah for opening the umbrella indoors. Saw Vince knocking over the salt at the table in the student center. Remembered Darla recounting the story about Cassie splitting the group.

"Bad luck," Jerry repeated, trying to process it all.

"I just said that."

"Noah, Vince, and Cassie. They all broke a superstition. Now they're all dead."

"You promised not to mention Cassie splitting the group." Darla wagged her finger. "If you have to report it, leave my name out."

Jerry ignored that. "I'm not sure what I'm going to do. This is all so insane. Can it really be true? Could bad luck have killed them?"

"Bad luck is bad. That's why it's called bad luck."

Jerry blinked his eyes like waking up from a long nap. "I think there's a story here."

"A story that I helped you get started on, right? I was the one who made the bad luck connection."

Jerry grinned. "Yeah, Darla. I doubt that I would have put it together without you."

"Okay, I see you're going to be busy doing whatever reporters do. Do you have a car on campus?"

"Yeah, why?"

"I'm going to let you take me to dinner. You did say you wouldn't have this story without me. Seems fair. I'm in 214 Clinton Hall. Pick me up about eight." She put her hand on his chest, pinched a wrinkle in his blue-and-white rugby shirt, and rubbed the material. "And Jerry, be sure to dress to impress." Darla rose, crossed the room, paused at the door, and winked.

She spoke in a perfect French accent, "*Jusqu'à ce que nous nous retrouvions.*" Darla flipped the light switch, leaving Jerry alone in the dark.

CHAPTER 11

Jerry sat in *The Chronicle*'s dark basement, Darla's flowery scent hanging in the air. Both times they talked, she sucked all the oxygen from the room, becoming the absolute focus of all his thoughts. And now they were going to dinner? Being honest with himself, Jerry found her interest in him surprising and unexpected. They didn't appear to have much in common. But she was cute. No, more than cute; Darla was a knockout. And her lack of self-awareness? Jerry found that amusing, almost charming.

And Busby really shouldn't have slapped him. Yeah, Jerry got sidetracked trying to find out what happened to Rick, but in the last month, Buzz had become more erratic and less fun. Did she do him a favor by breaking up with him? Jerry doubted he would have the guts to dump her.

His thoughts returned to Darla. What were her parting words? *Jusqua seekay new new retrovision?* He typed the phrase and variations into Google Translate but came up with nothing.

He powered off his phone. Back to work.

The Chronicle didn't publish on Sundays. The next paper after Peggy's death was Monday the 16th, where he found her obituary. Peggy was a townie from East Stuyvesant, but no information on how she died. He scrolled through the rest of the week but learned nothing.

Jerry booted up his laptop and checked the website of the local newspaper, *The Stuyvesant Whig*. But their free archives only went back six months.

Jerry used his phone to take a photo of Peggy's obit, and an idea occurred to him. He checked the 1984 calendar. The year had *three* Friday the 13ths: January, April, and July.

He grabbed the microfiche roll covering March and April 1984 and inserted it in the machine. He scrolled to the April 14th edition. His heart skipped a beat. Another death!

Franklin "Frank" Hearst, a junior and business major, died on campus the previous day. Again, no details on his death. Frank's obituary appeared in the following Tuesday paper. Another local who had lived in Fulton County, the next county over.

Jerry swapped out rolls, moving onto the January. He scrolled to the 14th. His throat tightened as he read about yet another death. This time it wasn't a student: Wayne Copeland, 52, an employee of the university's physical plant, who lived in Stuyvesant. Jerry scoured the next three editions of the paper, but no more information on Copeland's death was forthcoming.

Three deaths, all on Friday the 13th, and no details. Surely, Vanessa would approve the cost of subscribing to *The Whig's* archives. Or he could see if the U library had a subscription or copies.

Jerry scanned the microfiche for 1983 (May) and 1985 (September and December) but he didn't find any additional Friday the 13th deaths.

He had two, maybe three stories. The article Vanessa wanted: a historical look at the deaths at Van Buren. But he had discovered, with Darla's help, the connection between superstitions and the recent deaths on campus, and the three deaths from 1984. He began composing one massive article that covered all his research.

Jerry was deep in thought, typing away, when a voice called out, "Williams, you down here?"

"Darla, is that you?" Jerry kicked himself mentally. She wouldn't call him Williams. The voice was Busby's distinctive eastern Tennessee drawl.

The lights flicked on. Busby stood at the bottom of the stairs wearing a gray Van Buren sweatshirt, jeans, and sneakers, her hair up in a messy bun.

She crossed her arms. "Who's Darla?"

"Uh, nobody."

Busby eyed him suspiciously. "And why are you hiding down here in the dark?"

"I'm not hiding. I'm working on a story for *The Chronicle*. Why are you here, Buzz?"

She blew out her breath. "I wanted to apologize about last night. I overreacted. Sanchez, of all people, helped me see that. But you aren't easy to find. You're not answering your phone or replying to my texts."

Jerry held up his phone. "I turned it off, so I could focus."

"What else is new?" Busby frowned. "Anyway, last night I was upset and with good reason. I was worried about Rick, but I shouldn't have slapped you. Or said what I said. I lost it, and I wanted to apologize for my behavior."

Jerry absentmindedly rubbed his cheek. "That's okay, Buzz. I understand. It was a stressful situation."

"No," Busby snapped. "It's not okay. Normalizing violence is *never* okay."

Jerry wasn't going to argue. "You're right. I accept your apology."

"Is there anything you want to say to me?"

Jerry studied Busby's demeanor. Her lips were pressed tight, head tilted, arms still crossed. She wanted to hear the same from him.

He shrugged elaborately. "I'm sorry that I got caught up in the story. I should have been more attentive to your needs."

Busby grinned. "That's my Williams."

She stepped forward and started to loop her arms around Jerry, but he put up a hand and stopped her. "I forgive you for slapping me, but when you said we were through—"

"It was in the heat of the moment."

"I get that, Buzz. But you can't expect me to hear that and it not have an effect."

Busby crossed her arms. "You're saying you want to break up?"

"I don't know what I want at the moment, Buzz. I'm dealing with a lot. Noah and Cassie and—"

"And Vince." Her voice became small. "Yeah, I get it."

Busby's phone buzzed. "That's my parents. They want me to meet them at the hospital. Rick's getting discharged, and we're taking him back to his dorm. I'll text you later?"

"Sure." Jerry shrugged.

Busby dashed toward the door, stopping at the stairs. "Do you want the lights on or off?"

"Off is good." Once again, Jerry was plunged into darkness.

In *The Chronicle* newsroom, Jerry watched the faces of the staffers huddled around his terminal, reading his story. Fallon furrowed her brow. Laurie squinted through her glasses; her blue eyes filled with disbelief. At 6' 6" Brandon towered over the others. He suppressed a smirk.

"Well?" Jerry looked at his colleagues.

Fallon laughed. "Remember when you said that you didn't think Vanessa would publish my review? Well, your chances are a hundred times worse."

Jerry scowled. "Are you saying there's something wrong with my writing?"

Fallon shook her head. "Of course not. You're the best writer on staff. Except for me." She used her feet to push her roller chair back to her desk. "The historical research about World War I and Prohibition is a significant find and would make for an interesting sidebar. But that other stuff..."

"Other stuff what?"

Fallon puffed up her cheeks and blew.

"What about the rest of you?" Jerry counted on his fingers. "Three deaths on Friday the 13th? Doesn't that pique your interest?"

"It's a coincidence." Brandon shrugged. "People die every day. It would be weird if no one died on Friday the 13th."

Laurie shook her head. "And it's a shame about Noah. But it's not bad luck to carry an umbrella with a metal shaft in a thunderstorm. It's common sense."

Jerry spread his arms wide. "What about Cassie, the cheerleader? She split the group and now she's dead."

Fallon arched an eyebrow. "Split the group? What does that even mean?"

"It's some cheerleader superstition, I think. Anyway, it's bad luck. Then there's Vince."

"What about Vince?" Brandon replied.

"He spilled salt on the table when we were at lunch yesterday. Then he didn't pick up a pinch and throw it over his shoulder."

Laurie bit her lip. "Are you listening to yourself, Jerry? You sound like you should be on *The Alex Jones Show* ranting about chemtrails."

"This is all true. I can't explain it, at least not yet. But the facts are clear. These incidents preceded these deaths. There may be more. I'm going to keep checking the archives."

Vanessa stepped into the newsroom. "Jerry, can I see you in my office?"

The newsroom fell silent. Fallon pretended to look at her monitor. Laurie stared at her phone. Brandon leaned over to tie his shoe. Jerry stood and followed Vanessa into her office, where she closed the door, and they sat.

"Jerry, I appreciate all the hard work and research you put into this article, but I can't run this in its current state."

"Fix it up. You're the editor."

"This is beyond a little tightening and word choice."

"Why?"

Vanessa let out a weary breath. "Bad luck? It's not real. This is superstitious nonsense. How can you even ask?"

"But it's all true. The three cases from 1984 were all documented by *The Chronicle* itself."

"And from a historical context, that's fine, exactly what I wanted. But in your rewrite, drop all references to Friday the 13th."

"Vanessa, that's the day that they all died."

"And it's not relevant to the story. It's titillating and sensationalizing, and that's not the sort of newspaper that I'm running. We do real journalism. *The Chronicle* has a storied history. We're not some clickbait BuzzFeed wannabe."

"And what about the material I uncovered about Noah, Cassie, and Vince?"

"That also has to go." Vanessa waved her hand. "I'm a little disappointed with you. That's not reporting. You've inserted yourself into the story."

Jerry raised his voice in frustration. "I didn't insert myself. I was a witness. But not the only one. Fallon was there when Noah opened his umbrella. A bunch of us saw Vince spill the salt. Plus, I wasn't even there when Cassie split the group."

"This is one level above the chain emails my great-uncle Claude forwards me." Vanessa drummed her fingers on the desk. "I changed my mind. Obviously asking you to do a rewrite is problematic. Give Brandon your research, and I'll have him tackle it."

"Brandon?" Jerry leaned forward in his chair. "This is a solid story. It doesn't need a rewrite. It has to be published. Not only that, it requires more investigation. I want you to expense a subscription to *The Stuyvesant Whig*. Their free archives only go back six months. I need to see what they wrote about the 1984 deaths."

"No, Jerry. You're not going forward with this, and I'm certainly not spending any money chasing down ghost stories." She paused and looked at him with concern. "This morning you came in here all depressed, and that's understandable. But now you're all manic and wild-eyed. Talk to one of the grief counselors. You don't need to make an appointment."

"What does that have to do with my story or anything else?"

"The story is over, Jerry. Forget it. If you don't want to talk to someone, I can't make you. But I think you need some time off. Clear your head. Enjoy the weekend. Come back on Monday, and we'll talk."

Jerry stood, placed his hands on her desk, and leaned forward. "There's nothing to clear." He couldn't believe that Vanessa was killing another of his stories. He remembered what Sam claimed about his article on the fast-running parking meters. "Did the administration tell you to kill my story on the parking meters because they were afraid another scandal would hurt fundraising?"

Vanessa's eyes filled with rage. "You know what? Take next week off too. Come back a week from Monday with a better attitude and *maybe* I'll find you an assignment."

Jerry opened his mouth to object.

Vanessa jabbed a finger at him. "Do you want to take the entire month off?"

Jerry closed his mouth. He glared at Vanessa and silently exited the office.

Once Jerry closed the door, Vanessa waited twenty seconds to make sure he wouldn't pop back in. Jerry was a gifted reporter, and she admired his tenacity. But when he was aimed in the wrong direction, Jerry could be nothing but trouble. Vanessa had an obligation to the paper, the college, and to her future career to make sure things didn't spiral out of control.

She picked up the phone and hit #3 on the speed dial. "This is Vanessa Howley at *The Chronicle*. I need to speak to the chancellor."

CHAPTER 12

J erry trudged into his dorm room, dumped his spare change in the giant Budweiser bottle bank sitting in the corner, and plopped himself on the sofa. The coins filled about a quarter of the bottle. The plan was to finance a blowout party at the end of the semester, which seemed like an eternity away.

"Hey, man." Mike emerged from his bedroom. He wore a blue T-shirt with an Adidas logo and jeans. "I thought I heard you come in." He crossed the room and grabbed a can of Coke from the refrigerator. "You want one?"

Jerry grunted.

Mike took a seat at the far end of the sofa. "How are you doing?"

"Still kind of in shock. I was there when Noah got hit by lightning. Tried to save him, but..." Jerry's voice trailed off. He wanted to change the subject. "Where were you last night? You weren't here when I came in or when I woke up."

Mike beamed. "I was with the twins."

"Oh?"

Mike raised his hands. "Not like that."

Jerry arched an eyebrow. "Not like what?"

"It was all business. Well, maybe not *all* business."

"Business? Is that what you kids are calling it these days?"

"Jerry Williams, get your mind out of the gutter! Talia and Veronica's dad is a venture capitalist."

"So?"

"So, Talia is going to introduce me to him when he visits for homecoming."

"I'm not following. Introduction for what? You're not thinking about getting married, are you? You met her yesterday."

Mike sipped his Coke. "An introduction so we can show off the jammer. Talia's also an EE major, and she's going to help me spiff it up. Her dad invests in all sorts of emerging technologies. The idea is to get him to finance a larger prototype and when our demo wows him, we'll go into production."

"Is dating one of his daughters part of the plan?"

"It's part of *my* plan." Mike took another swig of his soda. "Once I'm in the family, it's a done deal. I can hold back a small percentage if you want in, but you'll need to let me know soon."

"I'm going to pass."

"Suit yourself." Mike shrugged. "What's going on with you? With classes cancelled, I'd expect you to be at the paper."

Jerry's shoulders slumped. "Vanessa gave me the week off."

"Why?"

"She had me doing research on previous tragedies that struck the campus, and I found something interesting." Jerry recounted the entire story in the basement with the archives and the confrontation with Vanessa. "What do you think?"

"Dude, you've got a date with Darla!" He made the high-five motion. But Jerry didn't respond, and Mike's hand hung awkwardly in the air.

Jerry huffed. "One: that is not the point of what I told you. And two: it's not a date. We're, uh, just going to dinner, because she helped me see the patterns in the story."

"Did you tell Busby you're going to dinner with Darla?"

Jerry hesitated. "The subject didn't come up. I told Buzz I wanted some time to think."

"Time off to think about Darla?" Mike waggled his eyes.

"No!" Jerry saw the reaction on Mike's face and realized he'd spoken too harshly. "Sorry, dude. Things have been rocky with Buzz for the last month. And she actually said we were through last night, but she tried to take it back this morning. But can we get back to the part about the bad luck? What do you think?"

Mike furrowed his brow. "I guess I don't understand how it works."

"Understand how what works?"

"All of it. For example, what does 'split the group' mean? I've never heard the expression."

"It's some sort of cheerleader tradition or superstition. I'm sure Talia can fill you in."

"But that's what I don't understand. Does it apply only to cheerleaders, or people who know about this? Or is anyone anywhere on campus who's in a group and then splits off in danger?"

"I'm not following you."

Mike pressed his lips together. "Ok, here's an example: What's the unluckiest number you know?"

"Thirteen."

Mike finished his Coke and tossed the can into the recycling. "Right. In Western Culture. Hmm. Maybe not the entire west, but certainly in the United States. But in China, four is considered unlucky. In fact, when my parents bought our house, it was a big to-do. My mom loved the place, but the street number was 424. My dad wanted no part of it, but my mom was insistent."

"What happened?"

"We bought the house, and my dad made a generous campaign contribution to the guy running for town council from our district." Mike made the money gesture. "Once he was elected, our address was legally changed to 559. Wrong block, opposite side of the street, totally out of order. Drove the Domino's Pizza drivers nuts."

"That's fascinating. But what's the point of your little anecdote?"

"My point, or rather my question, is: Is everyone on campus who somehow has any interaction with the number four at risk, or only those of Chinese descent or who are aware of the number's implications?"

"I'm not saying anyone's at risk. I observed the connection between bad luck and tragedy, then attempted to report on it."

"What you really need is some tests with control groups to see if you can replicate."

Jerry laughed. "Spoken like a true engineer. You realize people are dying from this, don't you?"

"It's all a coincidence. It has to be. There's no way it can be real. If you—"

A pounding on the door interrupted Mike.

Jerry looked at Mike. "Are you expecting anyone? Talia, maybe?"

Mike checked his watch. "Not yet. She's coming by later."

Jerry rose and opened the door to reveal Sam.

She pointed at Jerry. "We need to talk."

Miranda gulped her Diet Sprite as she sat in the far corner of the student center cafeteria. With the library closed for the day, she commandeered a table, which was now covered with books and notes. She lucked out that the cafeteria was mostly deserted and much quieter than the library normally was.

She squinted at her laptop, reran the spellcheck, took two sentences and combined them with a semicolon, then jazzed up a metaphor about eighteenth-century English workhouses.

Satisfied with the result, she emailed the file to the school's second-string quarterback with the note: *This will cost you one-fifty. Two hundred if it gets an "A".*

She clicked send, and her phone buzzed.

Dmitri: Where you at?

Miranda: SC

Dmitri: Plans for tonight?

Miranda: There's a new Italian place in town. Let's try that

Dmitri: Whatever my smart and sexy girl wants

Miranda: Love you

Dmitri: Love you too

Miranda put down her phone and checked her email. A new request had arrived from the team's place kicker. He needed a six-thousand-word paper on Mary Shelley for next Wednesday. She smiled to herself. In her senior year at Coral Gables High, Miranda had written such a paper. Rework a few sentences and swap out fifteen or twenty words with synonyms, then run it through a plagiarism checker. Her older brother was a TA at Florida Atlantic University, and she'd used his credentials in the past. If it didn't throw up any flags, she'd have a quick two hundred dollars for fifteen minutes of effort. She opened up Google Drive, found the appropriate file, and went to work.

"Who is it?" Mike poked his head around the door.

Jerry pulled the door all the way open so Mike could see.

Sam wore the same navy-blue beret as the other day, plus ripped jeans and work boots. This time her T-shirt was green with an image of Hermione waving her wand.

"Oh, it's you." Mike frowned.

"Hi, Mike." Sam stepped into the room.

"At least you got my name right this time."

Sam looked at Jerry. "Let's go for a walk."

"No need, I'm out of here." Mike grabbed his jacket. As he stepped past, he bumped deliberately into Sam.

"See you later, *Mike.*"

Jerry closed the door. "Why are you trying to antagonize him?"

"Hey, I apologized. Sincerely. And I already told you that's something I rarely do. Your friend needs to get over it."

"You want a Coke or a beer?"

Sam shook her head. They took seats on the sofa.

"What's up? I'm sure you didn't stop by to talk about Mike."

"I'm here because I was concerned about you. How are you doing?"

"As well as expected." Jerry blew out his breath. "It's not every day that three people you know end up dying."

"And getting suspended from the paper can't be much fun."

"Suspended? Where'd you hear that?"

Sam chuckled. "I told you there are no more secrets."

"That's not what happened. Vanessa asked me to take some time off."

"Do you want to take time off?"

"No, not really," Jerry grumbled.

"Vanessa's making you take time off that you don't want to take? Sounds like a suspension to me." Sam nodded solemnly.

"I guess."

"What did she say to you about the story?"

"Which story?"

"Which story do you think?" Sam rolled her eyes. "The one that got you suspended. The one about the bad luck."

Jerry was wide-eyed. "How can you even know about that?"

She reached out and rapped her knuckles on his skull. "Hello, McFly? No more secrets."

Jerry smiled smugly. "If there are no more secrets, then why don't you know what she said to me?"

"Jerry, I'm trying to help you here."

He blew his breath. "Vanessa had no interest in my work at all, except for the historical sidebar stuff. Said it didn't meet her standards. Compared my work to clickbait. She demanded a rewrite, and I said no. She gave the story to Brandon, and here I am."

"Which leads to why I am here. Thought anymore about writing for *The Underground?*"

"How much do you know about my story?"

"I've read the whole thing."

Jerry opened his mouth to ask how that was possible and caught himself. "You don't think it's insane or beneath the standards of your publication?"

"You've assembled the facts. You're not making any assertions. Let the readers draw their own conclusions."

"Yes!" Jerry pumped his fist. "Finally, somebody understands."

"So you're joining us?"

"Does that mean leaving *The Chronicle*?"

"Probably." Sam shrugged. "I mean, if we publish your story, Vanessa will recognize it. Doubt she's going to want you on staff after that."

The corners of Jerry's lips curled downward. "You're right."

"But it's not like you're getting to write for them now. Even after your suspension, she'll have you on a tight leash."

"What kind of stories could I write for *The Underground?*"

"Write anything you want." Sam pointed at Jerry. "You're a solid reporter. We don't give out assignments. Occasionally, we might get wind of something and ask if you want to look into it, but you can say no."

"And if I wanted to write a profile on one of the cheerleaders, could I do that?"

Sam squinted at Jerry. "Profiling a cheerleader? Yesterday you said writing about them was a way for Vanessa to punish you."

Jerry's face burned red. "I have a different perspective now."

"Sure. Cheerleaders are fine. Like I said, write whatever you want."

"And photos?"

"Photos are fine too."

Jerry was silent for a moment. "I don't suppose *The Underground* has a travel budget?"

"Travel to where?"

"Dallas. There's a national cheerleading championship that Van Buren will be competing in."

Sam laughed. "I don't know why you've got cheerleaders on the brain all of a sudden, but no, I'm not paying your way to Texas."

"Worth a shot."

"Back to business." Sam handed him a USB stick. "This has all the instructions you need, plus a kick-ass cryptography program. It will allow you to securely upload your articles to our server. And it will even fake your MAC address, but nothing is one hundred percent. The NSA could crack it if they were inclined. You can connect using the U network, and you're probably fine. If you're super paranoid, walk to the McDonald's off campus and use their Wi-Fi."

Jerry stared at the thumb drive. "Anything else?"

"Please spell-check and self-edit. I do my best, but we're a shoestring operation compared to *The Chronicle*."

"Got it." Jerry shoved the drive into his pocket.

"Don't tell anyone you're writing for *The Underground*. And you don't know me."

"But I *don't* know you. At least I don't know your real name."

"That's the way I like it. And remember if anybody, Vanessa or whoever, asks if you are writing for us: deny, deny, deny. They can suspect but can't prove a thing." Sam stuck out her hand and shook Jerry's. "Welcome to *The Underground*."

CHAPTER 14

THERE'S NO CHAPTER 13... IT'S BAD LUCK

FRIDAY 4:11PM

Jerry sat in a corner booth at McDonald's making a few minor changes to his story. If Vanessa confronted him, he could plausibly deny it was his. He saved his work, stuffed a handful of fries into his mouth, and connected to the Wi-Fi. Once on the Internet, he inserted the USB stick that Sam gave him. He double-clicked the executable, and a page of instructions loaded. An image that looked like a beach ball appeared on his screen and started spinning faster and faster until the laptop beeped, and a pop-up message informed him that he was connected to *The Underground* server.

Jerry followed the prompts and created an account. He uploaded his story and was required to give it a description. He typed, "Coincidence or Bad Luck? The Shocking Details of the Recent VBU Student Deaths." Would they use that as the title? He wondered who *they* were. He still wasn't sure what Sam's role was: editor, publisher, both?

The laptop chimed, announcing the file successfully uploaded. Jerry logged off, ate the rest of his fries, and headed back to campus. On the way to his dorm, he detoured by the library to see if they held the archives of *The Whig*. He mentally kicked himself for asking Sam about traveling to Dallas, but not about money for archive access. And he realized he had no way of contacting her.

As he approached the four-story brick building, Jerry felt something was amiss. No one was going in or out. He reached the library and stared at his reflection in the glass. He pressed his face to the window and squinted. The interior was dark, and he didn't see anyone. He pulled the door: Locked. A hastily scribbled note taped to the inside announced that the library would reopen Saturday morning.

Back in his room, Jerry found Mike and one of the twin cheerleaders from Thursday afternoon hovering over the jammer, circuit boards, and various electronic parts. The girl wore a white long-sleeve top, black leggings, and blue Nikes. Safety goggles covered half her face. She held a soldering iron in her left hand.

Mike looked up. "Jerry, this is Talia Decker. I don't think you two were introduced the other night. Talia, this is my roommate, Jerry Williams."

Jerry nodded. "Nice to meet you."

Talia finished soldering a USB port and slid the goggles on top of her head. "Excited about the big date with Darla?"

"I'm not sure it's exactly a date. She helped me with an article. Taking her to dinner is my way of saying thanks."

Talia waggled her eyebrows. "Trust me. It's a date. Darla's been blowing up Snapchat all afternoon."

"Told you." Mike smirked.

Talia looked Jerry up and down, studying him like a critic at Fashion Week. "What are you wearing tonight?"

"Not sure." Jerry tugged at his shirt collar. "Darla did say, 'Dress to impress.' "

"Let me see what you have."

"Really?" Jerry furrowed his brow.

"Really." Talia crossed her arms.

Jerry looked at Mike for help. Mike responded with a "can't help you" shrug.

"Come on." Talia spun Jerry by the shoulders and marched him into his bedroom. She rifled through his closet. "Not a lot of possibilities here." She grabbed a few button-up shirts and slacks, tossing them on his bed. A look of confusion crossed her face as she picked up a green sports jacket. "Did you win The Masters or something?"

"A gift from my grandmother." Jerry snatched it from her hand.

She returned to searching the closet. "Don't you have any t—Yech!" Talia's lips twisted into a disgusted frown. She held a gold clip-on at arm's length like a dead rat. "How did this get in here?"

"What? It's just a tie."

"No, it's not." She dumped the clip-on in the tiny trash basket beside Jerry's desk.

"Hey!"

"Another gift from grandma?"

"I don't remember how I got it."

"No loss." Talia walked up to Jerry, looped her arms around his neck, and pulled close.

Jerry was perplexed. Was she coming on to him? With Mike in the next room? He wasn't sure what to do. He went limp, keeping his arms at his side.

"Stand up straight."

Jerry complied. "What are you doing?"

She released him without answering. "Try on the pale-yellow shirt with the khakis."

"Now?"

"Relax, I'll give you some privacy. Let me see what I can do about a jacket." She walked out of the room.

As Jerry dressed, he considered Talia holding him. She was definitely one of the hotter girls on campus, but being around her wasn't at all like being around Darla. Easy to breathe, no commanding focus of attention. Whatever was special about Darla, it wasn't just because she was a knockout cheerleader. He finished dressing and stepped into the living area.

Jerry looked about the room. "Where's Talia?"

"Dunno. She was on her phone, then left. Said she'd be right back. Have you gotten around to telling Busby about your non-date?"

"No. At the time Darla asked, we were technically broken up."

"Technically?"

"Didn't I say this before? Buzz said we were done. She tried to take it back this morning, and I—"

"You thought you'd see how things go with Darla before you decide on getting back with Busby."

Jerry sighed. "I wouldn't put it exactly like that, but yeah."

"You're playing a dangerous game, my friend."

"I know, and I'm torn. I've had great times with Buzz. She's scary smart, but she also has this sarcastic streak. It's quite annoying."

"True." Mike nodded.

"On the other hand, Darla is hot. Scorching hot."

"Don't have to tell me. I took her photograph."

Jerry sighed. "But sometimes she comes off too self-absorbed."

"Well, she is a cheerleader."

"I'll be sure to tell Talia you said that."

"What are you going to do?"

"I don't know." Jerry shrugged.

"Decide quick. Because if you don't, worlds will collide." Mike brought his fists together and made explosion sounds.

"That's not helpful, but there is a favor I need from you."

"Me?"

"Yeah, you." Jerry pointed at Mike. "Don't slip up and mention anything about Darla to Busby or Miranda. And don't say anything about Busby to Talia."

"Relax. I've got Talia covered."

"What about me?" Talia walked through the door.

"I was wondering where you went."

"To get this." She held up a blue sports coat.

Jerry squinted at the jacket. "Where did you find that?"

"I borrowed it from Ted. You're about his size. I also grabbed some ties."

"Who's Ted?" Mike narrowed his eyes.

"A guy I know who lives on the fourth floor."

"A guy you know?"

Talia gave Mike a hard stare. "We only met yesterday, so there's a lot you have to learn about me. One important lesson: I'm not a fan of jealousy."

Mike, looking humbled, nodded and returned to fiddling with the jammer.

It dawned on Jerry what happened in his room. He looked at Talia. "You were measuring me."

"You'd make one heck of a reporter. Now for the ties. We won't mention what I found in your closet. Your secret is safe with me." She held them one-by-one against Jerry's chest. First, a solid black tie, then the green with gold stripes, and finally a solid burgundy tie. "This is the one. Put it on."

He struggled with the tie, and Talia grabbed it from him.

"I've got this." She flipped up his collar, knotted the tie, and pulled it tight. "Can you breathe?"

"Yep."

"Now the jacket."

Jerry slipped on the jacket.

"Spin around."

Jerry spun.

"Looking sharp. I'll be honest, I'm not being altogether altruistic. When Darla is happy, cheer practice runs much smoother. I've done what I can. The rest is up to you."

"Talia, I'm thankful for all your help. Mike, what do you think?"

Mike squinted at Jerry. "I'm not even sure who you are anymore. Where's my roommate?"

"Hilarious." Jerry mock laughed.

Talia licked her fingers and slicked down a few stray hairs on Jerry's head. "Where are you taking Darla?"

"Am I too well-dressed for Planet Pizza?"

"Yeah." Talia giggled.

"Actually, I think Darla has a place picked out."

"Sounds like her." Talia glanced around the room. "Where are the flowers?"

"Flowers? What is this, 1955?"

Talia blew out her breath. "Darla is very traditional. We all tease her about it. But she *is* expecting flowers."

"But Darla asked Jerry out," Mike observed. "How is that *very* traditional?"

Talia narrowed her eyes at Jerry. "Would you have asked Darla out?"

Jerry considered the question. Even if Buzz weren't a factor, he didn't think he would. Darla and he seemed to be from different worlds. "I don't think so."

"Right. Darla knows most guys are intimidated by her looks. So she'll ask, but she's still old-fashioned and expecting flowers."

"But Darla didn't mention that."

"Of course not. Get yellow roses. They're her favorite."

Jerry sighed. "Where am I going to get flowers?"

"There's a florist on Montcalm across the corner from the bank."

"Probably less expensive at the supermarket." Mike shrugged.

"Do not cheap out on Darla." Talia wagged her finger at Jerry.

Jerry nodded. "Is there anything else I need to know?"

"You'll do great. Be charming. And chivalrous. And funny. And relaxed. And don't try too hard. And for—"

Mike cleared his throat. "If you're done with Jerry's makeover, can we get back to our million-dollar idea?"

She slid her goggles back into place and picked up the soldering iron. "Why settle for millions? I want billions."

Jerry walked down the second-floor hallway of Darla's dorm, a dozen yellow roses in hand. The flowers set him back $65, plus tax, and he worried about having enough money to cover the evening. Darla asked *him* out, but she didn't seem like the type who would pick up the check or go Dutch. Depending on how expensive the restaurant was, he might have to use the emergency credit card his father entrusted him with. Jerry took minor pride that he made it through the third month of his sophomore year without resorting to using it.

He stopped outside room 214 and paused, hoping to quiet the butterflies in his stomach. With the flowers in his left hand, he took a deep breath and knocked with his right.

A tall, thin, barefoot brunette wearing a gray VBU Women's Golf Team T-shirt and navy shorts opened the door.

"Flowers? For me?" She grinned and grabbed the bouquet from Jerry before he could object. Holding the flowers to her nose, she inhaled audibly. "Thanks, these are awesome."

Did he get the number wrong? "Is this Darla Jaggard's room?"

The brunette laughed. "I'm just having fun with you. Jerry, right? I'm her roommate, Lucy Davenport. D's getting ready. Come in."

Darla and Lucy's dorm looked nothing like Busby and Miranda's. The latter was a mishmash of Wayfair clearance sales and third-hand items from Craigslist. But the room Jerry stepped into looked like it belonged in the pages of *Town & Country*. The sofa and chairs matched. The tables were made from a dark wood. Expensive-looking bookshelves filled with reading material and knickknacks lined one wall. A mammoth high-def screen was mounted on a second wall. A pair of neatly organized work desks were placed against another wall with a framed poster of Nelly Korda hanging between them. A couple of maroon throw rugs covered part of the living room floor.

"Where are you going for dinner?" Lucy set the flowers down.

Jerry shrugged. "I think Darla's picking it out."

"Sounds like her. Did she tell you yellow roses are her favorite?"

He held his hand to the side of his mouth, imitating a conspiratorial whisper. "No, but I had inside information."

"You're on the paper, right? D said you're writing an article about her. Ever think about profiling the women's golf team?" Lucy pantomimed swinging a club. "We've got a chance to win the conference this year."

Jerry didn't want to get into all the complications with *The Chronicle* where he never covered sports, and he wasn't sure if he still worked there, so he lied. "I'll see what I can do." Maybe it wasn't a lie. Sam said he could write whatever he wanted. Would Darla appreciate it if he did a story on her roommate?

"Lucy, have you seen my white clutch?" Darla appeared at the hallway entrance to the living room. She wore a sleeveless turquoise dress, cinched with a silver belt, that ended above her knees, paired with sparkly, strappy high heels. Her honey-blonde hair was piled high with wispy strands curling down to her ears. Emerald stud earrings magnified the green in her eyes, and a silver necklace hung around her neck.

Jerry's chest tightened. Once again, he felt like all the air was being sucked from the room. His jaw dropped open. He hoped it wasn't too noticeable. "Darla, you look spectacular."

She half-turned one way, then the other. "Thanks, Jerry. I was sure you would approve. Also, I'm happy to see my training is working."

"Training?" Lucy arched an eyebrow.

Jerry's face burned a little red.

"Yeah, I've been drilling Jerry on compliments." Darla walked over and ran a finger along the lapel of his jacket. "And you're looking crisp yourself." Her scent engulfed him. She smelled like the florist's shop he had come from.

"D, Jerry brought these for me." Lucy pointed to the flowers. "But I'd feel better if you take them."

"Yellow roses!" Darla's eyes grew wide. "Someone's been doing his homework." She kissed Jerry on the cheek, grabbed the flowers, and disappeared into the kitchen.

Lucy winked at Jerry, giving him a thumbs up.

Darla returned a moment later with a clear vase full of the flowers, set it on the coffee table, and inhaled. "Perfect. Now all I need is my clutch."

"On your desk." Lucy pointed.

Darla grabbed the white purse. "I think that's everything. Don't wait up for us!" She looped her arm through Jerry's and guided him to the door.

Lucy saluted. "No worries about me. I planned an exciting evening at the range, hitting bucket after bucket, until I perfect my drop fade."

"That's my car." Jerry pointed across the lot at a black-and-white Ford Crown Victoria. The gas cap door hung askew, and Jerry kicked himself for not having fixed it. He hoped Darla wouldn't notice.

She looked it over. "Kind of like an old police car."

"It is. I picked it up at auction. Two hundred bucks. The cops beat the hell out of it, but the engine and transmission were solid. I replaced all the belts, hoses, and shocks."

"Fixed it yourself? I like a boy who's handy." Darla grinned and pressed her shoulder to his.

Jerry's heart quickened. Why was he trying to kid himself? This was a date. And starting out perfectly.

As they approached the car, Talia's words echoed in Jerry's head: *Darla is very traditional.* He led her to the passenger side and opened the door.

"I like a boy with manners." Darla arched an eyebrow as she slid into her seat.

Jerry hustled over to his side, got in, and started the engine. "Where are we going for dinner?"

"Cascata. It's a new Italian place that I've been dying to try out. Head into Old Stuyvesant and take a left on Burgoyne."

"Got it."

Darla pointed at the dashboard. "That's not a cop radio."

"No, they took that out, and I installed this one and the speakers."

She powered it on, and the gravelly voice of George Thorogood blasted from the speakers. "95.3. Classic rock, huh?"

"Some of it is interesting." *Was his choice in music a problem?*

"Let's see what else we have here." Darla cycled through the presets. "NPR. Top Forty. Sports Radio. Best of the sixties, seventies, and eighties." She killed the volume. "You can tell a lot about a boy based on his car radio."

"Really? What does mine say about me?"

Darla pursed her lips, like she was in deep thought. "I think your love of classic rock comes from road-trip family vacations where your parents played *their* favorite music." She looked at Jerry. "How'd I do?"

Jerry was stunned. She nailed it. And apparently, the music wasn't a problem. "You are remarkably perceptive."

"Yes, I am." Darla smiled smugly.

"What about the rest of the stations?"

"NPR: you're open-minded and intelligent. Sports talk?" She frowned. "I'll let that one slide. Top Forty—slow down, you're going to miss our turn."

Jerry braked, signaled, and turned left.

"Now turn right at the next light, and Cascata will be three blocks further down."

Jerry followed her directions. Outside the restaurant, a valet station was set up. "I bet I can find a spot a couple of streets over."

"Uh, uh. I'm not walking all over town in these heels. Use the valet."

Jerry was already out the money for the flowers. Now there was the valet, plus a tip, and from the outside, Cascata looked expensive. He glanced at Darla, and she looked so damned amazing. This was certainly an emergency worthy of using the credit card, but he wasn't sure how to explain that to his dad.

"Okay." Jerry pulled in front of the restaurant. He handed the valet the key, twenty to park, and a five-dollar tip. He escorted Darla inside to the hostess station.

The hostess, Jennifer by her name badge, greeted them with a smile and a nod. "How may I help you?"

"Jaggard. We have an eight-thirty reservation."

Jennifer grabbed two menus. "Please follow me."

Jerry was a third of the way across the dining room when he froze in horror. Busby! She was walking toward him with an older man and a woman. Had to be her parents. The three of them headed for the exit and would pass right by him.

"Uh, Darla, I'll be right back. I left my wallet in the car."

"Jerry?" She turned, but he was gone.

Jerry hurried back to the hostess station, but there was no place to hide. No potted plants or cloakroom. He rushed to the street, glancing in every direction, looking for cover. He ran to his left and hid in the shadows of the recessed doorway of a closed barbershop.

Jerry peeked around the corner. Busby and her parents exited the restaurant. If they walked in his direction, there'd be no way they could miss him.

Busby's father approached the valet station, and Jerry breathed a sigh of relief. But he needed them to get their car and leave quickly. Who knew how Darla was handling his disappearance? The valet jogged off while the three stood on the sidewalk, chatting. Busby pulled out her phone and started tapping.

"C'mon, hurry up," Jerry whispered to himself. His phone buzzed. He pulled it out. Busby! He powered down the phone and shoved it in his pocket.

A black Lincoln Navigator arrived. The valet hopped out, and Busby and her parents got in. Jerry relaxed and stepped out of the doorway.

"Excuse me, sir?"

Jerry turned to the voice and saw a man in the khaki uniform of the Stuyvesant County Sheriff's Department.

The cop aimed a flashlight in Jerry's face. "Why are you hiding there, sir?

"Please, officer, it's my ex-girlfriend." Jerry pointed at the car as it sped away. "It ended badly. I didn't want to upset her or her parents. I was waiting for them to leave."

"It's deputy. And let's see some ID."

Jerry fished out his wallet and produced his driver's license.

The deputy illuminated the license with the flashlight. "New Jersey?"

Jerry handed over his student ID. "I'm a sophomore at Van Buren."

The deputy looked over the card and compared it to Jerry.

Jerry shifted his weight back and forth.

The deputy flashed the light in Jerry's face. "You in a bit of a hurry?"

"My date is inside waiting for me."

"Ex-girlfriend and a date?" The deputy smiled and handed back the ID and license. "Okay, you can go."

Jerry rushed inside. He scanned the dining room, spotted Darla at a table along the far wall, and threaded his way over to her.

Jerry made a theatrical display of holding up his wallet. "Sorry about that." He took his seat.

"I thought you bailed on me. But then I realized that couldn't be. Because no one would ever bail on me." Darla smiled and seemed to relax. "I didn't order any wine. I have ID, but I wasn't sure about you. So, I got us sparkling water and a calamari appetizer."

He wasn't sure what calamari was, but wanted no more disruptions, so he lied. "Sounds good."

Jerry looked over the menu. No wine was helpful, but the prices of the entrees left no doubt that he'd be using the credit card. He'd have to remember and call his dad. He didn't want the charge to come as a surprise. In the end, he ordered the *veal parmigiana* while Darla went with the *pollo marsala*.

"Jerry, I have a little something for you."

"Really? What?"

"It's a surprise. Hold out your hand."

Jerry stretched his right arm across the table and held his palm up.

"And close your eyes."

He hesitated for a moment.

Darla flashed a smile. "Come on, close your eyes."

Jerry complied.

"Now stick out your tongue."

"Darla!"

"Okay. Good enough."

Something soft dropped into Jerry's hand.

He opened his eyes. A small furry orange object rested in his hand. "What's this?"

"It's a rabbit's foot. You know, for luck."

"It wasn't lucky for the rabbit."

"Har, har! Seriously, with what you uncovered about bad luck and students dying, I thought we could use a little protection."

"We?"

"Uh, huh." Darla pulled a mint green rabbit's foot from her purse. "Promise me you'll keep it with you at all times."

"I promise." The foot had a metal ring attached, and he hooked it to his keys. "Where did you find this?"

"Five Below. Good luck was never so affordable."

Jerry gazed at the foot one more time. He didn't believe it could really provide good luck. But Darla seemed enthusiastic, and it was a sweet gesture. "Thanks, Darla." He rubbed the foot for show, then shoved it in his pocket.

"You are quite welcome." Darla placed her elbows on the table and her hands under her chin. "So, tell me all about Jerry Williams."

"I'm from a little town in South Jersey called Mullica Hill. My dad's the editor of the *Gloucester County Times*. In high school, he hired me as a stringer, covering local government meetings, sporting events, parades, and such. I loved it so much I followed in his footsteps. So, here I am majoring in journalism and writing for the school paper."

"Ambitious, I like that. Any brothers or sisters?"

"One brother, Brian. He's older. Working on his PhD in Chemistry at the University of Washington."

"Chemistry? That's a coincidence. I'm majoring in chemical engineering."

"Really?"

Darla narrowed her eyes at Jerry. "Is that such a surprise? You think cheerleaders are all airheads who can't handle a challenging major?" She pointed an accusatory finger.

"What? I mean, of course not, you can do—"

"Because I'm getting sick and tired of everyone treating me like a life-sized Barbie doll." She tilted her head and, in a high-pitched voice, mimicked, "Math is hard."

"Please, Darla, I didn't mean anything by it."

Darla balled up her napkin and tossed it on her bread plate. "I think you should take me back to the dorm." She stood, hands on her hips, her green eyes staring right through him.

Jerry's stomach was in knots. The world was crashing all around him. He tried to stand, but his knees buckled.

"Got you!" She flashed a wide grin and plopped back down. "I should have taken a pic of the look on your face." She giggled and sipped her water.

"Oh." Jerry was confused, then a wave of relief flowed over him. "That was a bit?"

Darla nodded. "Keep on your toes around me."

Jerry forced a smile. Maybe Darla was more than he could handle. Busby would never pull a stunt like that. "So you are, or aren't, majoring in chemical engineering?"

"An exothermic reaction releases heat, while endothermic one absorbs it. The job market looks promising. There's always a shortage of qualified employees, so wages are rising." She frowned for a moment. "The same can't be said for journalism."

"I know. My dad tried to warn me off, but I think I've got it in my blood. I'm thinking the chemical engineering bit will be a good hook for your story. Cheerleader smashes stereotype."

The waitress delivered the calamari along with an assortment of sauces.

Darla dipped a piece in tartar sauce. "This is delish."

"I'll confess that I'm not familiar with calamari. Is it onion rings?"

Darla laughed. "It's squid, silly."

"Squid?" He stared at Darla's face, trying to read her expression. "Are you joking with me again?"

"Nope, it's really squid. Have some."

Jerry was cautious. He smothered his in marinara and popped it in his mouth. "Hey, this is pretty good."

"Told you."

When the main course arrived, Jerry reached for his knife, but Darla grabbed both of his hands. Before he could react, she closed her eyes, lowered her head, and spoke, "Bless us, O Lord, and these thy gifts, which we are about to receive from Thy bounty, through Christ, Our Lord. Amen."

Jerry recovered from his shock in time to simultaneously say Amen.

Darla opened her eyes and released his hands. She observed Jerry's puzzled look. "Yeah, it's always weird when to say grace in a restaurant: when they bring out the bread, or the appetizers, or the main course." She shrugged. "But I figure as long as we let God know we're thankful, it doesn't really matter when we say it."

"Good point." Jerry was relieved that she misinterpreted his expression. He turned the conversation on Darla. "What about your family?"

"My dad runs a hedge fund, which he's super good at. My mom stayed at home to raise us four kids. Corey is the oldest. The Brewers drafted him in the third round. Shortstop. He hasn't made it to the majors yet. He's going to play Mexican ball this winter. Terry is gorgeous. He's a model in Los Angeles and trying to break into acting. He was on one of the *NCIS*s. Can't remember which, but he didn't have any lines. He played a corpse."

Jerry chuckled. "I never heard a guy called gorgeous before."

"Trust me. He's got Mom's cheekbones and skin to die for."

"And your sister?"

"Ashlee." Darla rolled her eyes. "Such a teenager."

For dessert, Darla suggested they split a cannoli, which they enjoyed with coffee.

Jerry offered to let Darla have the last bite of the pastry, but she shook her head.

"Darla, this was an outstanding meal. Thanks for picking this place. The only Italian my mom ever made was spaghetti and meatballs."

"What's your mom do?"

Jerry was quiet for a moment. "She was a bookkeeper. She died. Cancer."

"*Je suis désoleé.*" Her green eyes filled with empathy, she reached across the table, entwining her fingers with his as if to try and absorb some of his pain.

"It's been a few years. Didn't mean to sabotage the mood."

"Nonsense." Darla continued to hold his hand. "I'm having a wonderful time."

When the bill came, Jerry almost choked at the total. He added a 25% tip. He delivered pizzas one summer and worked hard for those tips and never forgot to return the favor.

When they stood to leave, Darla pointed around the room. "We're the hottest couple in this place. We didn't get a chance to show off when we arrived, but we're going to let everyone know. Let's work our way across the dining room in a big circle giving them all a chance to gawk, okay?"

Jerry was almost certain the evening was going well, but the idea that Darla wanted people to see them together cinched it. He looped his arm around her waist, and they began their march around the room.

In the far corner of the Cascata dining room, Miranda's phone buzzed. She picked it up and frowned.

Dmitri set down his wine. "What is wrong?"

"Fitzgerald wants a paper on Dumas. Says he's willing to pay double." She groaned. "I've made it clear to these knobheads that I only do English Literature."

"But there is nothing my smart and sexy girl can't do."

"Yeah, but I don't want to make it a habit. I start doing French and the next thing I know; they'll be asking for Garcia Marquez or Tolstoy." She made a face and pinched her nose.

"Demand they pay more."

"I could do that. It would be awesome if we could afford to go to St. Bart's for winter break. I'll offer to do it for triple." She tapped on her phone, looked up, and frowned again.

"Tolstoy?"

"No. Jerry is here."

Dmitri turned to see the couple walking across the room. "That girl he is with is not Busby."

"I know." Miranda held up her phone, switched to burst mode, and focused on the couple. "And I've never seen him so dressed up before."

Darla maneuvered Jerry around a busboy clearing a table. For a moment, their faces turned toward Miranda.

She snapped the photo and checked the results. "Gotcha!"

Jerry pulled his car over to the curb outside Darla's dorm.

"Walk me to my room." Darla's tone was more command than question.

Jerry rushed around to open her door. Darla emerged from the car, holding her shoes in one hand. She walked across the grass, cool on her bare feet. She held Jerry's hand while he pointed out constellations in the sky.

Darla let her head rest against his shoulder for a moment. Jerry had proved to be an almost perfect date. He was a smart, funny, ambitious boy. And cute too.

They rode the elevator to the second floor and walked down the hallway to 214. Darla paused in front of the door, let his hand go, and turned to face him.

"Jerry, I had a wonderful evening. I was a little worried when you disappeared, but that was just a little bump in the road on the way to a perfect evening."

"No reason it has to end now." He leaned in to kiss her.

"Actually, it does." She put a hand on his chest, stopping him. "I do want to see you again. But even though they cancelled classes, I have a ton of homework. Plus, I need to get up early and workout, and there's an extra cheer practice for the game tomorrow. With all that going on, I'm afraid I can't invite you in. I need sleep." *The big test.* How would he react?

"Okay." His tone told her this wasn't the ending of the evening he was hoping for. And Darla could see the disappointment on his face. "You look like a lost puppy." She dropped her shoes, looped her arms around him, pulled close. As her nails caressed the back of his neck, she kissed him solidly on the lips.

He slipped his arms around her and squeezed tight.

When her breath grew short, she broke the embrace. "Better?"

"Much. Maybe I could come in after all?"

"Were you even listening to me?" She bopped him on the nose. "Why don't you come to the game tomorrow? Mike's going to be taking photos of us."

"He is?"

"Yeah, he got a credential from our coach. I don't know if you can get down on the sidelines where he'll be. But you can watch me from the stands."

"I have a pass too, so I'll be able to get down to the field."

"Really? Great." She kissed him one last time. "Text me when you get home, so I know you're okay."

She grabbed her shoes, stepped inside, winked, then shut the door.

Lucy lay on the couch under a blanket, watching TV, cup of hot cocoa in her hand.

Darla dropped the clutch on her desk. "You look comfy."

Lucy sat up and paused the show. "Binging *Rizzoli & Isles*. You need me to clear out?"

Darla returned to the door, pressed her eye to the peephole, and watched Jerry. He sported a huge grin. Excited, eager, not angry. *Perfect.* "You're good, Lucy. We're done for the night. You know my motto: Always leave boys wanting more."

CHAPTER 15

Jerry walked back from the gym. It occurred to him that Darla said she'd be working out this morning, but he didn't see her. He didn't think he'd ever seen any of the cheerleaders at the gym. Maybe they had their own workout facilities, like the football and basketball teams.

He powered on his phone and checked his texts. Darla wished him a good morning. That brought a smile to his face, and he replied in kind. Mike suggested breakfast at the Student Center. Jerry texted that he'd meet him there. He showered and dressed back at the dorm, then found Mike in the breakfast line at the cafeteria.

"There you are." Mike grabbed a set of utensils. "You were up early for a Saturday. Things didn't go well with Darla?"

Jerry grinned. "*Au contraire*. We had a most amazing evening. I was so jazzed up, I hardly slept."

"Really? I want details. Now!"

"A gentleman never tells. What about you and Talia?"

Mike grimaced. "Ha, ha, very funny. Actually, the next-level jammer prototype is almost done. Some minor adjustments and we'll be ready to field test."

"Sounds romantic."

Mike's phone buzzed. "It's Talia. She wants us to sit with her." He scanned the room, spotted her, and waved.

The line moved forward. Mike filled his tray with a plate of pancakes, a side of bacon, and four slices of toast. Jerry grabbed a granola bar, a banana, and a carton of whole milk. The line advanced, and they paid for their breakfasts.

Mike grabbed his tray. "Follow me. The twins are this way."

"We're having breakfast with both of them?"

Mike nodded. "Yeah, I expect they're going to be part of our new social circle. Maybe even the entire squad. And we're going to need some new friends."

"How so?"

"Since things went well with Darla, I'm guessing that means no more Busby. Then Miranda won't hang out with us anymore. Rick too."

Jerry shrugged. "Rick's not much of a loss. But I don't think it will be that bad."

"When Busby learns you're going out with a cheerleader, she'll go nuclear."

Jerry and Mike navigated the tables and found Talia and Veronica near the center of the room. Mike sat opposite Talia, and Jerry across from Veronica. The twins wore their auburn hair up in ponytails, no make-up, and identical desert camo T-shirts that read: *Statesmen Cheerleader Boot Camp*.

Talia grinned, displaying perfect white teeth. "Jerry, you were never introduced to my sister Veronica."

Jerry peeled his banana. "Nice to meet you."

"Likewise," Veronica replied.

Mike drenched his pancakes in butter and syrup. "Those are some big breakfasts." He pointed with his fork at the twins' plates loaded with scrambled eggs, bacon, sausage, and hash browns.

Veronica raised her right arm, slid back her sleeve, and flexed a tan bicep. "We need the calories. We've got a long day of being on our feet: practice, then the game. Five-Hour Energy can only take you so far." She gulped a glass of grapefruit juice.

"Jerry, I heard it went pretty well with Darla last night." Talia waggled her eyebrows.

Jerry glared at Mike. "Big mouth."

"Mike didn't say a word. It's Darla." Veronica held up her phone. "She's been blowing up Snapchat all morning."

"Really?" Jerry thought the evening went well but welcomed the confirmation.

"I bet it was the way I knotted your tie." Talia laughed.

"That had to be it," Mike agreed. "It certainly wasn't Jerry's winning personality."

"You're such a good friend." Jerry grabbed a packet of grape jelly from the condiment tray and tossed it at Mike, bouncing it off his forehead.

Veronica slid her phone across the table. "Jerry, look at these photos."

Jerry picked up the phone and squinted at the image: an antique car from the 1930s. He scrolled through photos of more cars: antiques, sports cars, high-end imports. After the cars, a blonde in a red one-piece swimsuit wearing a sash proclaiming her Miss Michigan USA. The caption read: *Jennifer Johnson*. More photos: Jennifer in an evening gown, in a cocktail dress, in a green bikini.

Veronica leaned over the table to look at the screen. "Notice a resemblance?"

Jerry didn't. He had no idea what she was showing him. "No. Why don't you just tell me what's going on?"

"Last summer, Talia, Darla, and I coached cheer camp in Michigan. Afterward, we stayed at Darla's house. That's her dad's car collection and her mom."

"Actually, the house is more like a mansion." Talia spread her arms wide.

"Castle." Veronica made a circular motion with her glass. "It had those round things. Gables?"

"Towers?" Jerry replied.

"Turrets?" Mike suggested.

"Yes, turrets!" Veronica pointed with her fork for emphasis. "Her room is at the top of one."

"Darla lives in a castle?" For a moment, Jerry imagined Darla as a fairy-tale princess protected by a moat and drawbridge.

Talia nodded. "Yeah, her dad's somebody *real* important in finance or business. I think he might be the boss of the secretary of the treasury or something."

"That would make him the president," Mike explained. *"Of the United States."*

"Whatever. The point is: the house is amazing."

Jerry munched his banana. Darla's family was rich. Did she expect lots of fancy dinners at places like Cascata? That would break him pretty quickly. He kept scrolling. Darla's mom behind the wheel of a red BMW. He squinted. No, this photo was Darla herself. "This is Darla's car?"

Veronica nodded; her mouth full of scrambled eggs.

Mike looked at the photo. "Her parents bought her a convertible."

Talia shook her head. "Darla bought it. Actually, I think it's a lease. She does part-time work as a model. Local department stores. Cheer University. That sort of thing."

"There's a university for cheerleaders?" Mike laughed.

"It's a brand. For uniforms, equipment, and such."

"How about that, Jerry?" Mike slapped him on the shoulder. "She's rich *and* a model."

Jerry was becoming increasingly uncomfortable with the direction of the conversation, and the coming realization that Darla was probably out of his league. He slid the phone back to Veronica. "Can we change the subject?"

Mike checked the weather on his phone. "I hope the storm holds off until after the game. I don't want to risk the water damaging my camera equipment."

"And it's no fun for us cheering in the rain." Talia made an exaggerated frown.

"Huh." Veronica tapped her phone. "This is wild."

"What's that?" Talia leaned over to peek.

"This article on *The Underground*. You know the three students that died? It claims the deaths of those students are tied to some kind of bad luck. Like when Cassie split the group."

"Let me see." Talia grabbed the phone and scrolled through the article. "This *is* creepy."

Mike pulled up the story on his phone and stared wide-eyed at Jerry. "You're writing for *The Underground?"*

"What?" Jerry's heart skipped a beat. *"The Underground?* Don't be crazy. I work for *The Chronicle.*"

Mike pointed to his phone. "But this is *your* story. Exactly as you described it to me. It has to be you."

"It could be Fallon. She was with me when Noah opened his umbrella."

"But how would Fallon know about the salt that Vince knocked over?" Mike pointed to the shaker on the table.

"Or that Cassie split the group?" Veronica added.

"What does that even mean? Split the group?"

Talia rolled her eyes. "The group needs to stick together. We were running up the steps leading to the gym and Cassie was on the other side of the railing from us."

Mike scrunched up his face. "And that's bad luck?"

You don't have to believe us." Veronica tapped the phone. "It says so right here in Jerry's article."

Jerry's stomach flip-flopped. Writing for *The Underground* was supposed to be a secret. He fought to remain calm. "Look, I don't know who wrote that article. Anyone could have done a bit of investigating and learned the facts. Please don't suggest to anybody that it could have been me."

Mike eyed Jerry suspiciously. "All right."

"Okay," the twins agreed in unison.

"We've got to head off for practice." Veronica stood.

Talia leaned across the table and kissed him on the cheek. "Bus our trays for us?" She winked at Mike.

Mike blushed and nodded. The twins waved goodbye and headed for the door, causing necks to crane at nearby tables.

"Did you see that?" Mike pointed at the twins as they disappeared out of the cafeteria.

"What?"

"How all the guys watched Talia and Veronica walking to the door? We've finally arrived."

"Funny, I thought I was already here."

Mike punched Jerry in the arm.

"Hey! Remember, it was because of me you even met Talia."

"Yeah, I suppose you're right." Mike shrugged.

"So what now?"

"I spent so much time working on the jammer, I'm falling behind. I'm going to the lab to work on my 2250 project. Then I'll probably knock out some homework before the game. What about you?"

"Going to check to see if the library has reopened. I need to find out if they have archives for the local paper. I'm looking for more exa..." Jerry's voice trailed off.

"Looking for what? More examples of fatal bad luck?"

"Keep your voice down." Jerry frowned and leaned close to Mike and whispered, "Okay, yeah. That's my story in *The Underground.*"

Mike grinned. "I knew it. But why all the secrecy?"

"That's how *The Underground* works. Sam said that—"

"Sam? She's part of this?"

Jerry groaned. "Keep that quiet too. You know nothing. You don't know I'm writing for them. You don't know her."

"But I *don't* know her. I don't even know her real name."

The sound of throat clearing caused Mike and Jerry to look up. A campus policeman, tablet in hand, stood at the end of their table.

"Gerald Williams?" the officer inquired.

Jerry and Mike exchanged glances.

"Yeah, I'm Jerry Williams."

The officer swiped his tablet. "The chancellor has asked me to escort you to her office on a matter of extreme urgency."

Jerry sat next to the cop in one of the campus police golf carts as it sped across the quad. "What's this all about?"

"Don't know." The cop shook his head.

"Kind of weird she wants to see me on a Saturday."

"Maybe they want to talk to you about trying to save that kid's life with CPR. You might even get some kind of award."

Jerry didn't want to think about Noah and stayed quiet for the rest of the brief trip. Two minutes later, the cart pulled to a stop outside the Administration Building.

The cop pointed at the front entrance. "The chancellor's office is on the third floor. Room 310."

"Thanks." Jerry waved as the cop drove away.

Jerry entered the building, climbed two sets of stairs, and walked down the hallway until he came to 310. The door was open, and he stepped inside. The room looked to be more like a waiting room: an unoccupied desk and empty seats against the walls. He spied another open door, knocked on the frame, and poked his head inside.

A Black woman, probably in her early forties, in a green blouse, with gold hoop earrings, sat behind a mahogany desk writing on a notepad. A white man in his fifties sat in one of the two chairs opposite the desk. His cheeks were scarred from what looked like a severe bout of acne as a teen. And the man was severely overweight, barely fitting into a uniform covered with medals and ribbons.

"Yes?" The woman put down her pen.

"Hi, I'm Jerry Williams. There's no one in the outer office, but I think you're looking for me."

She nodded but didn't smile. "Come in, Mr. Williams. Please close the door and take a seat."

Her lack of a smile and the tone of her voice made Jerry uneasy. "Sure thing, Ms. Thort—"

"*Doctor* Thornton-Gaston." She looked at the man in uniform. I suppose you know Chief George Characopus, head of the Campus Police."

Police? Maybe Jerry *was* getting an award. "And both hard at work on a Saturday. Van Buren is fortunate to have such dedicated staff." He smiled and slipped into the empty seat.

"Mr. Williams, what do you know about this?" The chancellor looked at the chief and nodded.

Characopus handed Jerry an iPad. On the screen was his story from *The Underground*.

Jerry deflated. He wasn't getting an award. "The name says it all. It's the school's underground newspaper."

Thornton-Gaston harrumphed. "I was specifically referring to the article on the screen. The one about the recent deaths of Van Buren students."

"Oh." Jerry scrolled down, pretending to read the article. "Interesting."

"You took a long time to read that." Characopus pointed at the iPad.

"Didn't want to miss anything. It's pretty solid reporting."

"You've never seen this before?" Thornton-Gaston demanded.

"I don't have *The Underground* app on my phone."

"I'll come straight to the point, Mr. Williams. Did you write that article?"

Jerry swallowed hard. Sam cautioned him against telling anyone he wrote for *The Underground*. He didn't feel guilty about hiding the truth from the twins or trying to fool Mike. But lying to someone in the administration was a whole other level. "What makes you think it was me? I'm on the staff for *The Chronicle*."

"Your editor, Ms. Howley, informs me that you're on an extended leave."

"That was her idea, not mine."

"You didn't answer my question, Mr. Williams. I have plenty of experience with students who are trying to hide something."

"And you didn't answer mine, Doctor. What makes you think I wrote it?"

Thornton-Gaston grabbed the pen from her desk and pointed the tip at Jerry. "According to Ms. Howley, you submitted this same article to her yesterday. Being the responsible editor that she is, Ms. Howley refused to publish such outlandish accusations. Can you provide me with an alternate explanation of how an article that you wrote could end up in *The Underground*?"

"Hackers?" Jerry forced a smile. "The security on *The Chronicle*'s server is pretty lax."

Characopus guffawed. "That's your best explanation?"

"Actually, it's not even my article. Sentences have been rearranged and words changed." Jerry pretended to be in deep thought. "I showed the article to some of *The Chronicle* staffers before I submitted it to Vanessa. Any of them could be behind it."

The chancellor let out an exaggerated sigh. "Is that what you really expect us to believe?"

Jerry was careful. He had dodged direct questions and not told any lies. "You can believe whatever you want. Plus, I don't know why the administration even cares what some random website posts. There are a thousand conspiracy sites on the Internet. What's the big deal about this article?"

Thornton-Gaston jabbed the pen at Jerry as she spoke. "The big deal, Mr. Williams, is that it puts the spotlight on Van Buren in an unfavorable way. That's bad for all of us. Administration. Faculty. *And* students. There's even a rumor that Channel 37 in Albany is sending a reporter to investigate."

Jerry sat up straighter. "Maybe someone should ask questions. Three students are dead. Including my friend."

"Each death is a tragedy. And Van Buren is committed to providing the resources necessary for the student body to face these challenges in such a troublesome time, but the school has enough negative coverage. It doesn't need sensational accusations with no basis in fact. Really? Bad luck?"

Jerry studied the face of the chancellor. He couldn't read any emotions. But her tone made her sound more concerned with her own well-being. He flashed on the memory of Sam talking about Vanessa killing his last story. "Negative coverage? You mean like fast running parking meters so the U can make money on fees from tickets and towing?"

Thornton-Gaston flinched, and Jerry knew Sam was right. The chancellor killed his story. Vanessa couldn't be trusted. She was practically an arm of the administration.

The chancellor ignored Jerry's accusation. "My goal, the university's goal, is to provide a safe and secure environment where all students can learn."

Jerry leaned back. "Then we're on the same side."

"Are we?" The chief shifted in his chair. "What about Noah Chen?"

"He was my friend. What about him?"

"It's possible that in your efforts to save him, you might have accidentally killed him."

Jerry jumped out of his chair. His face red with anger. "That's bullshit. The EMTs said there was nothing more I could have done."

The chief shrugged. "EMTs aren't medical examiners. They don't know. A thorough autopsy might bring additional information to light."

Fear overtook Jerry's anger. Was that a threat? Would they try somehow to blame him for Noah's death? That was crazy. Or was it? As he looked from the chancellor to the chief and back to the chancellor, he figured there was no good reason to keep talking with them. "I have nothing left to say." He slammed the door on the way out.

Thornton-Gaston glared at the shut door, then fixed her gaze on Characopus. "What was the point in bringing up Chen?" Mixed in her anger was a hint of her long suppressed Southern accent.

"You weren't getting anywhere with the kid. I thought I'd shake him up a bit."

"You certainly did that, Chief. What do you think?"

"He wrote the article."

"Christ! Of course, he wrote the article. Do you think we scared him off?"

Characopus shook his head. "I doubt it. He seemed more angry than afraid."

"I agree." Thorton-Gaston picked up her phone. "I think it's time to get the committee involved."

CHAPTER 16

J erry stormed across campus, his head down and his heart racing. Despite the cool fall breeze, he was drenched in sweat.

He replayed the conversation in the chancellor's office in his head. He never lied, never admitted to being the author of the article on *The Underground*. And he was certain he did nothing wrong.

The administration was trying to rattle him, and his trembling hands were a sign they were succeeding. But blaming him for Noah's death was going too far. The chancellor wanted the timid schoolboy to cower and fold in the face of pressure. But he hadn't. And he wouldn't.

His anxiety turned to resentment. In his head popped thoughts of John Peter Zenger, Seymour Hersh, Julian Assange, even Larry Flynt. People who weren't afraid to speak out, regardless of the cost.

Sam needed to know what was happening. Jerry grabbed his phone, opened up the dialer, and stopped. He didn't have a number for her. Or an email address. The USB stick she gave him didn't include any instructions on how to contact her.

Back at his dorm, Jerry booted up his laptop and searched Facebook for students at Van Buren. He scrolled through page after page, searching for Sam, but couldn't find anyone who looked like her. But to Jerry's eye, when a girl changed the style or color of her hair, she seemed like an entirely different person. He probably looked right at her photo, failing to recognize her. On the other hand, would someone as concerned about anonymity as Sam be on Facebook?

Jerry launched *The Underground*'s website and clicked on the "Contact Us" link. A new window appeared. He composed a message, then stopped. The connection from the laptop to the server was being transmitted over the university's network. Was the administration able to monitor any message he sent? Mike could supply the answer if he were here.

Jerry shut down the laptop, switched to his phone, and disabled Wi-Fi. On Verizon's network, the college shouldn't be able to monitor him. He navigated to the "Contact Us" page and typed.

Sam

It's Jerry. We need to talk. Call me.

No good. He couldn't use his name. Sam emphasized that *The Underground* was operating under complete anonymity. If someone other than Sam retrieved and forwarded the messages, that person would learn Jerry's name and might crack under questioning from the chancellor. He couldn't take that chance. He backspaced over the line, thought about their conversations, and grinned.

It's the guy thinking about adding photos of his non-existent cat to his Substack.

Only Sam could know Jerry was behind this message.

Need to talk to you. Urgent.

He clicked send. It failed. A pop-up message informed him an email address was required. Why would a site dedicated to anonymity need an email? Jerry grimaced, filled in a fake Gmail address, and clicked submit. This time, the message sent successfully. Did Sam have his number or email? Somehow, she located him walking on campus and in his dorm room. He installed the Underground App on this phone. Made sense to do so now that he was writing for them.

Jerry checked his watch. Still plenty of time before the football game, giving him a chance to study. He hadn't cracked a book since Wednesday. He grabbed the hefty volume on Imperial China, flopped on the couch, and opened to the chapter on the Ming Dynasty.

Jerry's eyes flowed over the words, and he reread the same page three times before slamming the book down. The inner workings and intrigues of the Emperor's Court held no interest. He should be researching the bad luck story. If the administration wanted to scare him off, then he'd fix them by digging deeper. Grabbing his laptop bag, he headed for the library.

The library was open, but more deserted than usual for a Saturday morning. Jerry counted three students in the stacks as he navigated his way to the periodical section. A quick investigation revealed that the library did have access to the digital archives of *The Whig*. Jerry breathed a sigh of relief. No more scrolling through roll after roll of microfiche.

He booted up his laptop and tethered it to his phone. With the USB stick, Jerry connected to *The Underground*'s server and uploaded his story on the fast-running parking meters. That would show the chancellor that she couldn't push him around.

He reviewed his notes on the bad luck deaths. Margaret "Peggy" Johnson was the student who died on July 13, 1984. A search of *The Whig*'s archives returned links to eight articles containing her name.

Peggy was quite the scholar-athlete. From the first six articles, Jerry learned she set the school record for three-pointers in her senior year, earned a National Merit Scholarship, and was Valedictorian of East Stuyvesant High. She led E.S.H. to the Group III section of the NY State playoffs. Her team lost in overtime to a school from Brooklyn in the semi-finals.

The next-to-last article concerned Peggy's death and was written by a *Whig* staff reporter named Paul Wysocki. Her body had been found in the pool at Van Buren's gymnasium. Jerry was puzzled; the university's pool wasn't in the gym. But that was close to forty years ago, so things must have changed. No foul play was suspected. The coroner ruled her death an accidental drowning. Jerry's pulse quickened. A broken mirror was found in the girls' locker room.

The last link led to Peggy's obituary. She was nineteen, born in Stuyvesant, and survived by her parents and a brother, Mark.

Mark Johnson. The name rang a bell. He typed in the name into Duck-DuckGo. Over five hundred thousand hits came back. Mark Johnson was the name of an All-Pro cornerback for the Houston Texans. He figured that was why he recognized the name.

Jerry printed out the obit and the story concerning Peggy's death. He moved on to Franklin Hearst, the junior who died on April 13, 1984.

Hearst wasn't the scholar-athlete that Peggy Johnson was. Before this death, he appeared in only one article in *The Whig*: an entry in the crime log for underage drinking.

A second article reported the circumstances of his death. Franklin had been stuck by the campus circulator bus. Witnesses claimed he stepped off the curb without bothering to look in either·direction, walking directly into the path of the bus. He was taken to John Jay Hospital, where he was pronounced dead. The authorities didn't charge the bus driver. Paul Wysocki was again the reporter.

The last link was to an obituary. Frank was born in Albany, an only child, and grew up in Ticonderoga.

The third death from 1984 was Wayne Copeland, the physical plant employee who died on January 13th. Copeland appeared in *The Whig* archives three times.

The story of his death, again written by Wysocki, explained that Copeland was working on construction for the new gymnasium—Aha!—when a trench collapsed.

Jerry shuddered. There was no pleasant way to die, but the image of being buried alive made his throat tighten.

Copeland's obit mentioned no living family. He was originally from Greenville, South Carolina, and had worked at VBU for seven years. The last article, six months after Copeland's death, reported that OSHA had fined the university $250,000 for the unsafe work practices that led to Copeland's death. This final article was also written by Wysocki.

Jerry wondered about the broken mirror found near Peggy Johnson's body, and if there was anything associated with bad luck at the other death scenes that didn't make it into the paper. Maybe the details were killed by a gun-shy editor at *The Whig*, the same way Vanessa spiked his story?

He pulled up *The Whig*'s website on his laptop and checked the "Staff" page. No listing for Paul Wysocki. He went back to the archives and did a search solely for articles by Wysocki. Hundreds of links were returned, but the most recent story was from six years ago.

Jerry sighed. Did the reporter move? Retire? Die?

Jerry grabbed his phone. He despised people who talked in the library, but he was too eager to wait to walk outside. Besides, he was the only person in the periodical section.

No word from Sam. Only one text.

> Darla: looking forward to seeing you at the game

He was looking forward to seeing her too. Especially in that cheerleader uniform.

> Jerry: wouldn't miss it for the world!

He found the number for *The Whig* on the website and called.

"*Stuyvesant Whig.* Collins," a bored woman's voice answered.

"Hi, I'm trying to track down a reporter who used to write for your paper. His name is Paul Wysocki."

"There's no one here by that name."

Jerry scowled. *Pretty sure I just said that.* "Yeah, that's what I figured. His last story was six years ago. Is there anyone who could tell me how to reach him?"

"Hold on. I'll get Mr. Grant, the editor, for you."

A click, then the muzak version of "The Safety Dance" played. While waiting, Jerry continued to explore *The Whig*'s website. He found a photograph of Mitchell Grant: 50s, bald, friendly smile.

"Editor's desk, Grant."

"Hi, Mr. Grant. My name is Jerry Williams, and I write for..." Technically, he was still on staff. "*The Chronicle* over at Van Buren University. I'm trying to track down one of your former reporters."

"Jerry Williams, did you say?"

"That's right, sir."

"The same Jerry Williams who wrote that story about the no-shows on Van Buren's Board of Trustees?"

"Yep, that was me."

"A solid bit of reporting, young man."

"Thanks. I'm surprised you even knew about it."

Grant sighed. "Before all the cutbacks, we used to have a full-time beat reporter for Van Buren. These days, I'll check out *The Chronicle* and if a story piques my interest, I assign someone. What can I do for you, Mr. Williams?"

"I'm trying to track down a former reporter for *The Whig*, Paul Wysocki."

Grant chuckled. "Ah yes, Paul."

"You know him?"

"Sure, I worked with Paul for ten years. He had the Van Buren beat for a while. What do you want to talk to Paul about?"

"He wrote some stories about the school back in 1984, and it's connected to something I'm working on."

"Nineteen eight-four? That's way before my time. I admire your tenacity."

"Thanks, sir. About contacting Mr. Wysocki?"

"I'm sure Paul would be happy to talk with you. He always loves to reminisce."

"Do you have a number for him?"

"No number. He's a resident at the Shady Pines Retirement Village over in Saratoga. Paul doesn't hear well these days, so he's no good on the phone. You'll need to visit in person."

"Thanks for all your help, Mr. Grant."

Jerry ended the call, pulled up the webpage for the retirement home, and plugged the address into Waze. The drive to Saratoga would take close to an hour. No chance he could get there, interview Wysocki, and return in time for kickoff. As much as he wanted to follow up, he did promise Darla.

The Shady Pines website listed visiting hours for Sunday. Jerry would go tomorrow. He packed up his laptop and notes. Time to watch Darla cheer.

CHAPTER 17

Under a partly cloudy sky, Jerry and Mike stood on the plaza at the north end of the football stadium. Van Buren fans in green and gold outnumbered their Fillmore counterparts decked out in black and red. Kickoff was thirty minutes away.

Mike wore a blue T-shirt and cargo pants with his camera backpack slung over one shoulder. A lanyard with his photographer's credential hung around his neck. "What happened with the cop? What did the chancellor want?"

Jerry let out a weary breath. He didn't want to think about the confrontation with the Chancellor. He was here for Darla but recounted the events to Mike.

"The grid's melting down, Jerry. What are you going to do?"

Jerry related his attempt to contact Sam, the research he uncovered at the library, and his plans to interview the reporter Wysocki on Sunday.

"Yes!" Mike pumped a fist in the air. "Sticking it to *The Man!*"

"Not exactly. The chancellor is a woman."

"Then let's smash the system!" Mike slammed his fist into his open palm.

"Can we put that on pause for the moment, Comrade Lenin? We've got the girls and the game to watch."

"Okay, but I've never been much a football fan."

"Me neither. I'm more of a hockey fan." Jerry pantomimed taking a slap shot.

"It's baseball for me."

"You know, Darla's brother plays minor league baseball." It seemed like a random thing to bring up, but Jerry liked the chance to say Darla's name. He thought back to last night's dinner. "Larry? Barry? No wait, it's Corey."

"Corey Jaggard? Never heard of him. But there are thousands of players in the minors."

Jerry looked around the plaza. "Where do we get in?"

"Media gate is on the East Side." Mike led the way.

As they circled the stadium, Jerry caught a flash of red hair in the crowd. Busby? He left Mike behind, trying to push his way through the throng of students and fans. Another glimpse. She was walking away, so he could only see her from behind. But it sure looked like her. Next to the redhead, a brunette turned around. Miranda! She was saying something to Dmitri in that black duster he always wore.

"Buzz!" Jerry shouted.

But she didn't hear. Or pretended not to. Jerry pressed forward. He and Busby were through, might as well make it official and avoid any complications.

The crowd grew thicker, and the distance between Jerry and the trio increased.

"Buzz!" he yelled again.

Something clamped on Jerry's shoulder. He turned to see Mike.

"Where are you going?" Mike held up his camera bag. "Media entrance is the other direction."

"I saw Busby and figured might as well make it official that we're over."

Mike laughed. "You wanted to officially break up with Busby in public? Not just in public, but in front of thousands of strangers, some of who would be certain to record and post it on social media, so that you can relive the experience forever."

Jerry frowned. "You're right. What was I thinking?"

Mike punched him in the shoulder. "Cheer up! We're going to watch Darla and Talia."

Down on the field, Jerry leaned against the wall separating the stands from the field. Mike knelt a few feet away, adjusting his camera's shutter speed and aperture for the increasingly overcast sky.

"Please welcome today's opponent, the Millard Fillmore College Black Bears," the announcer's voice boomed from the speakers.

Fans jeered as the Black Bears, wearing white jerseys with black trim and red pants, rushed onto the field. A bear mascot in a red sweater and cheerleaders dressed in red-and-black uniforms took up positions on the far sideline.

Mike grinned. "More cheerleaders! I'll have to work my way over to the other side and snap some photos. Maybe in the second half."

"I thought you were here to shoot Talia and her teammates."

"I am. But no reason not to take advantage of this opportunity." He paused for a moment. "When I make my fortune, I think I'll buy an NFL team. That's what all the hip billionaires do. Then I could give myself a photographer's pass to every game. Heck, if I'm the owner, I can help pick the squad at auditions."

Jerry dropped his voice an octave. "College sports photographer shares his delusional fantasies, but first a check on the weather."

"And now your Van Buren University Statesmen!" the announcer roared.

Fans stood, clapped, and whooped. The Statesmen in green jerseys, gold pants, and black armbands raced to midfield before moving to their sideline. Martin, the Statesmen mascot, and the cheerleaders, also wearing black armbands, bounded down the running track that lined the perimeter of the stadium. The cheerleaders were in uniforms similar to the outfits Jerry saw Thursday night, but this version sported long sleeves.

Darla raced down the sideline, then sort of leapt and threw herself at the ground at the same time. As her body neared the ground, she extended her arms. She hit the track with her hands, her feet high in the air. Darla spun, her feet touching down for the briefest of moments, then back in the air. She twirled tighter and faster, her arms recoiling like springs, launching her straight into the air. Arms and knees tight to her body, Darla completed two flips, then stuck her landing. She raised her hands high and flashed a dazzling smile for the crowd.

"Wow!" Jerry clapped furiously. "Did you get all that?"

Mike checked his display and nodded.

The cheerleaders broke into two equal-sized groups and took up positions between the goal line and the twenty-yard line. Darla and Talia—and Veronica—were in the group near the north end zone. Jerry and Mike stationed themselves between this group and the stands.

Jerry squinted and spied a tiny version of the Martin mascot painted on Darla's left cheek. The letters "VBU" in green adorned her right cheek. She carried poms now, holding them high, leaping in the air, and waving to Jerry.

The announcer's voice boomed, "We ask that you please rise for the playing of our national anthem to be performed by Van Buren University senior Martha Gracehart."

The fans stood. Jerry placed his hand over his heart. The players and cheerleaders turned to face the giant American flag fluttering high atop the south end of the stadium.

The scoreboard video screen showed the image of a young woman in a Western get-up, complete with cowboy hat. She stood at midfield before a microphone, holding an acoustic guitar, and began to perform.

While her guitar work was adequate, her singing was improbably off-key.

Mike covered his ears. "It's like one of those *American Idol* rejects."

Jerry and Mike exchanged pained glances and stifled smiles. The performance lasted a terrifying two-and-a-half minutes.

At the conclusion, someone in the stands shouted, "Hey, it's Enrico Pallazo!" This was followed by mild laughter and a round of sarcastic applause.

"Please remain standing," the stadium announcer instructed. "Tragedy struck the Van Buren University community this week with the heartbreaking and untimely deaths of three of our students: Vincent Murphy, Cassandra McGlaughlin, and Noah Chen. Vincent was a member of the Statesmen football team. Players will wear a black armband with his number, eighty-one, for the remainder of the season.

"Cassandra was a member of the Statesmen cheerleaders, and the squad will also wear black armbands for the rest of the season. Please honor our losses with a moment of silence."

Jerry and Mike bowed their heads. Predictably, a group of half-in-the-bag frat boys used the opportunity to whoop it up, chanting, "Beat Fillmore!"

"And now let's play some football!" the announcer boomed.

The crowd roared in approval. Fillmore won the toss and elected to defer to the second half. Their kicker sent the ball sailing through the end zone.

Starting on their twenty-five, Van Buren rushed for no yardage first down. On second down, the running back was tackled for a three-yard loss. The quarterback dropped back on third down, but all his receivers were covered. His protection broke down before he could dump the ball, and he was sacked for an eight-yard loss.

Van Buren brought out the punt team. Fillmore overloaded the left side. Attackers swarmed through Van Buren's line and blocked the punt. One of the Black Bears scooped up the loose football and rumbled into the end zone for a touchdown. Fillmore easily converted the extra point.

Mike glanced at the scoreboard. "At this rate, we're going to lose by more than a hundred and forty points.

"Always the optimist."

While the players prepared for the kickoff, three of the VBU male cheerleaders lined up. Talia and Veronica scrambled onto their shoulders and stood, becoming the middle of a pyramid. Jerry watched in amazement as Darla scaled her way on top of the twins. A cheerleader at ground level tossed a giant cardboard megaphone to Darla. With a foot on each of the twin's shoulders, she led a round of cheers.

After the kickoff, Darla dropped the megaphone, searched for Jerry, spotted him, and gave him an exaggerated wink. She crossed her arms over her heart and fell backward off the pyramid. Jerry flinched. But Darla landed safely in the waiting arms of two male cheerleaders.

Mike reviewed the latest images of Darla. "She's exceptional."

Jerry faked a smile but was secretly worried. Cassie went blind, then died from a cheering accident. Darla appeared to know what she was doing, but those stunts looked dangerous. He was surprised how concerned he was with her well-being. He must be really falling for her.

Again, Van Buren started on their twenty-five.

Talia grabbed the megaphone. "Offense!" she chanted.

The girls shook their poms. The boys raised their fists.

Their exhortations didn't help. Another three and out for the States-men. They got the punt away this time, only to have the Fillmore deep man return it sixty yards for a touchdown.

Boos spilled down from the crowd.

Jerry leaned against the wall. "This is going to be a very long day."

"Might as well forget about the game and focus on the girls at this point."

The Statesmen mascot, dressed in an eighteenth-century black suit and a similarly styled hat atop his comically oversized head, approached one of the cheerleader twins, flowers in his hand.

"Uh, Mike. It looks like Martin is trying to make time with your girl."

The cheerleader theatrically refused the flowers.

Mike squinted. "Nope, that's Veronica."

"How can you tell?"

"Oh man. Don't let either of them hear you say that."

Martin dropped the flowers in his pile of props and retrieved a box of candy. He chased after Veronica, offering her the sweets. Veronica dismissed Martin and his gift, swaggering away from him. Martin swapped the candy for a ukulele. He raced over to Veronica, dropped to his knees, and pantomimed playing the instrument. Veronica, appearing to be won over, leaned down and kissed the mascot on the cheek. Martin clutched his chest like he was having a heart attack, rolled over, and played dead. The crowd laughed and cheered at the spectacle, eager to have a distraction from the game.

Mike glanced at the scoreboard, which now read 20-0. "Fillmore scored again? This has to be some kind of record for futility."

As Fillmore lined up for the extra point, raindrops fell. By the time they were set to kick off again, the wind picked up, blowing hot dog wrappers and empty cups all over the stadium.

Jerry found shelter from the rain under a slight overhang extending forward from the stands. From his refuge, Jerry waved at Darla, who mock frowned at him. As the rain intensified, Mike joined Jerry under the ledge. He slipped his camera equipment back in his bag.

"Not going to take any more photos?"

"Only if it stops raining. Do you know how much this stuff costs?" Mike glanced at the cheerleaders, their soggy uniforms clinging in all the right places. "I will say one thing; the girls may be miserable out there, but the drenched look is *hot.*"

Powerful gusts of wind buffeted the stadium. Was it Jerry's imagination or were the light towers starting to sway? The rain fell almost sideways. Even in their mini-shelter, Jerry and Mike were getting soaked.

Jerry shielded his eyes from the downpour. "I wonder if they'll stop the game."

Mike raised his voice over the wind. "No way. This is football. They'll only stop if we get some—"

A bolt of lightning struck the nearest light tower. A bulb exploded, showering sparks onto the crowd below.

"That was too close!" Jerry shouted.

Mike pointed to the referees conferring at midfield. "Maybe they *will* stop the game."

A gust of wind blew the cheerleaders' megaphone down the field, and Darla chased after it. The lights and scoreboard flickered for a moment, then went dark. Another gust of wind slammed the stadium from the west.

Jerry focused on the damaged light tower. A few sparks still tumbled down. Fans seated under it scrambled to get away. Each time it swayed in the wind, the tower leaned a little farther. One big gust at the wrong time could send it falling. Falling right on an oblivious Darla still racing after the megaphone.

Jerry dashed across the field. "Darla! Move! Watch out!"

CHAPTER 18

Pelting rain stung Darla's eyes, making it almost impossible to see. Another gust of wind blew the megaphone toward the end zone. Did someone call her name? She couldn't hear anything over the storm, the rain, the crowd. As she raced after the megaphone, her sneaker slid on the wet turf, twisting her ankle. *"Merde!"* She struggled to regain her balance but failed and slammed headfirst into the turf.

Her uniform soaked, a dazed Darla pushed herself up, and her foot erupted in pain. She fell, but someone caught her by the shoulders. *Jerry!* She took a step, but her ankle wouldn't support the weight.

"I can't walk. My ankle."

Jerry nodded. "I got you."

He lifted Darla into his arms: one about her back, the other under her knees. She looped her arms around his neck. Jerry staggered through the rain and wind to the sideline. Players raced off the field. Fans in the stands crowded for the exits. Jerry paused, seemingly uncertain where to go.

"The tunnel." Darla pointed toward the entrance in the wall.

A tremendous crash came from behind. Over Jerry's shoulder, the light tower lay on the field. Bulbs exploded and electricity sparked. Darla closed her eyes and squeezed Jerry tighter.

He carried her into the tunnel. "Least we're out of the wind and rain."

"Pretty sure we can get out the other end."

An eerie red glow from the emergency lights illuminated the way. Jerry's feet sloshed through inches of accumulating water as he carried Darla the length of the tunnel. At the end stood a pair of metal doors. He kicked open one side, and they emerged on the plaza. The rain and wind had eased a bit. Fans and students hurried from the stadium. A pair of ambulances, red lights spinning, sirens blaring, pushed slowly through the crowd.

"Over there." Darla nodded toward a covered bus stop.

Jerry carried her into the unoccupied shelter, setting her on the bench. "Are you okay? Do you need to go to the ER?"

Darla shivered and shook her head. "But I can't walk, and I don't think the bus will come by anytime soon. Can you carry me back to my dorm?"

Jerry sat next to her and lowered his head. "Sure. Give me a second to catch my breath."

Darla flicked wet grass off her uniform and winced at the stains embedded in the fabric. "My uniform is ruined." Tears streamed down her cheeks. A silly thing to be upset over, but she couldn't hold back.

"Hey, it's okay." Jerry hugged her. "The important thing is you're safe. You can always get a new uniform."

Darla buried her face in his chest until the tears stopped. She knew she was a mess but raised her head and kissed Jerry. "Thank you."

"No problem." Jerry used his thumb to wipe away a last tear. "Time to get going." He knelt on the concrete base of the shelter.

"What are you doing?"

"As light as you are and appealing as it is, I can't carry you in my arms all the way to your dorm. You need to get on my shoulders."

"This could be fun." Darla climbed into position. As they left the shelter, she leaned sideways to avoid hitting the top of the entryway.

Jerry carried Darla, careful to avoid slipping on wet leaves or pavement, through the drizzle toward Clinton Hall.

Two-thirds of the way to the dorm, Darla could feel Jerry fading. His pace slowed. His steps less certain. She ran her fingers through his hair and caressed his ears. "You can do it."

"Not helping."

Upon reaching the vestibule of her dorm, Jerry set Darla down in a wooden chair and leaned over, his hands resting on his knees.

"Made it." Jerry exhaled and stretched his arms.

"I hope Lucy's home. My keys are in my purse back in the locker room."

Jerry glared at her.

Darla smiled. "Relax, it'll be okay. If my room is locked, the RA can let us in."

"Okay, final push. But we'll have to do it piggyback style. The elevator entrance is too low."

Darla climbed onto Jerry's back. They rode the elevator to the second floor.

As they stumbled into Darla's room, Lucy dropped her book and leapt from the couch. "What happened?"

Darla pointed to her foot. "Ankle."

Jerry nodded. "She fell."

He set Darla down. She stood on her good foot, leaning against the wall.

"You guys are drenched. Jerry, grab a towel from the bathroom and dry off." Lucy pointed down the hall. "In my bedroom closet, you'll find some of my boyfriend's clothes. You're both about the same size. I'll help Darla out of her wet things."

Jerry, somewhat drier, stood in the living room wearing a borrowed, slightly too large Buffalo Bills sweatshirt and jeans. "Is there anything I can do?"

No answer.

He wandered about the room, stopped at Darla's desk, and picked up a framed photo. This was a seriously good-looking family. Darla, her parents, brothers, and sister, all styled and decked out in their Christmas best, posed in front of a twelve-foot tree, sporting grins worthy of an orthodontist's website. Jerry swallowed hard. He missed Christmases like that with his family.

He set the photo down and inspected the two others. In one, Darla and her mom were in matching pink wetsuits, goggles propped on their heads, on a dock surrounded by crystal blue water. Darla's mom barely looked older than her daughter. He needed to remember to work that in, if or when, they ever met. *Darla, you didn't tell me you had a second sister.*

The last photo was from winter. Darla, bundled up, was hugging a Welsh Corgi frolicking in the snow. Each trying to out-smile the other. He looked at the shelves above the desk. The first held half a dozen cheerleading trophies. The next filled with books: *Madame Bovary, Candide,* and *The Man in the Iron Mask* all in French, *Macbeth,* textbooks on differential equations, organic chemistry, Russian history, and a thick blue book with what looked like a griffin on the cover. He reached for that last book.

"D's purse is back at the stadium."

Jerry turned to see Lucy emerging from Darla's room. "I'll get it."

"You might have trouble getting into the girls' locker room."

Jerry chuckled. "Guess you're right."

The sounds of a running shower filled the room.

"D's getting cleaned up. Stay here and take care of her. There's drinks in the fridge, but please use a coaster. Be back as soon as I can." Lucy grabbed her umbrella and hustled out the door.

Jerry opened the fridge and frowned: Mike's Hard Lemonade, White Claw Seltzer, Coors Light, and Diet Coke. He shrugged and grabbed a beer. At least it was cold. He sat on the couch, popped the top, and placed a coaster on the glass coffee table.

On the table between the vase of yellow roses and a green-and-gold backpack sat a closed MacBook and a stack of magazines. Jerry leafed through the titles: *Golf Digest, Golf for Women, American Cheerleader, Chemical Engineering Monthly, Golf Course Architecture.* He grabbed one of the golf magazines, looking for something to distract his thoughts from Darla in the shower.

An article entitled "Confessions of a Drink Cart Girl" caught his attention. He was two-thirds of the way through it when Cheap Trick's "Surrender" blared from his phone.

"Hey, Dad."

"Jerry? Are you okay?"

"Yeah, why wouldn't I be?"

"I'm watching CNN. They're showing what happened at your football stadium."

"CNN? Really?"

"Actually, they're replaying videos from TikTok."

"I was at the game, but nowhere near the light tower. Never in any danger." Jerry didn't like lying to his dad, but it was better than having him worry. "I'm at...uh, a friend's now."

"I'm relieved that you're okay."

Jerry suppressed a grin. That was the most emotion he could expect from the old man.

"I haven't heard from you in a couple of weeks. How's school?"

"Classes are fine. My favorite is the course on the Freedom of Information Act that Professor Goetter is teaching. For my class project, I'm using FOIA to compile a database of all officer-involved shootings in the five-county area."

Jerry considered telling his dad about the suspension from *The Chronicle*, writing for *The Underground*, and the confrontation with the chancellor. But if he got into that, he'd have to explain his article tying the deaths to bad luck. He wasn't sure how a traditional newspaperman like his dad would react.

Instead, it was time to confess. "Actually, I'm glad you called. I used the emergency credit card. Thought I should let you know before you get the bill."

"Maybe I should enroll in automatic notifications?"

Jerry sighed. Best to get it over quick, like ripping off a bandage. "It's for a hundred and twenty-five dollars. From an Italian restaurant called Cascata."

"What kind of emergency happened at an Italian restaurant? Busby's birthday?"

"No, someone else."

"A new girl you wanted to impress?"

Jerry chuckled. "That wasn't the plan. Her name is Darla. She asked me out. I had no idea she would pick somewhere so expensive. Dad, she's so hot. She's a cheerleader, but no flibbertigibbet. She reads Voltaire and Dumas in French."

"I get the picture and can appreciate the circumstances. Your mother initially asked me out. But that card is for emergencies only. No more fancy Italian dinners."

"Okay, Dad. Thanks for checking on me. Love you." Jerry shoved the phone back into his pocket.

In an exaggeration of Jerry's Jersey accent, Darla mocked, "She's a cheerleader, but no flibbertigibbet."

He turned to see Darla hopping on one foot across the room. She wore a bright pink, fitted T-shirt and pale-yellow shorts. Hair wet, a silver bracelet on her left wrist, a comb in one hand, and a rolled-up bandage in the other. She plopped herself down at the far end of the sofa. He'd figured Darla for about 5'4" or 5'5" but the way her legs stretched across the cushions; they looked as long as the lanes of the Garden State Parkway.

"First, I don't sound like that. And second, a flibbertigibbet is someone who—"

"I *know* what it means, Jerry. Do you want to compare SATs?" Darla laughed. "And you sound like an extra from *The Sopranos*. Hey Tony, I say we rub dese guys out, if dey don't give us da dough."

Jerry burned red.

"Oh look, the boy is blushing. Again. So cute. Can you wrap my ankle?" Darla tossed him the bandage.

Just out of the shower, Darla smelled clean and fresh. With her make-up scrubbed off, her complexion resembled that of a Danish milkmaid. Jerry leaned forward, unrolled the bandage, and looped it around her ankle. For the first time, he really noticed her even tan running all the way to her toes.

"Make it nice and tigh—Ow!"

"Sorry!"

Darla pressed her lips together. "Don't worry. Been through this before. It can't be helped."

He finished wrapping and velcroed the end of the bandage. "All done."

"Good job. I can't flex it at all. Maybe you should go pre-med instead of journalism."

"I took a Wilderness First Aid course. My dad and I do plenty of outdoors stuff, hiking and camping."

Darla scrunched up her nose. "Outdoors? It's full of bugs and bears. And you can't wear heels on the hiking trail."

So much for snuggling with Darla around a campfire while toasting marshmallows. But that wasn't a deal breaker.

"I do like boats, though." She held up her hands like she was steering as she raced across the water. "My dad has a fifty-foot cabin cruiser we take out on Lake Michigan. And jet skis are plenty of fun. Vroom!"

Jerry said nothing. He wasn't a fan of cacophonous two-stroke engines. Maybe he and Darla were from different worlds?

"There's ice in the freezer and Ziploc bags in the second cabinet from the left. Can you fill a bag for me?"

Jerry stood and bowed. "It would be my pleasure. Do you want something to drink?"

"I'm good."

Jerry returned with the bag to find Darla combing out her wet hair. He propped the bag of ice on her bandaged ankle.

"You called your dad to tell him about me?" Darla's tone hinted that she always expected to be the subject of conversation.

"No, he called me. Saw video from the tower collapse at the stadium on CNN."

"Really?" Darla leaned to grab the MacBook off the coffee table. The ice slid off her ankle.

"Stay put. I'll get what you need." Jerry put the bag back in place.

"My own private butler? I love it." Darla powered up the machine, searched for videos, and frowned.

"What's wrong?"

"This guy on Fillmore who scored the last touchdown. He's dancing around the end zone like a five-year-old who ate an entire bag of M&Ms. Act like you've been there before, dude. Do stuff like that and you'll—" The blood drained from Darla's face.

"You'll what? Darla?"

"Jinx yourself," she whispered.

"Wait, you can't think that had anything to do with the tower?"

Darla continued to scroll through videos and her eyes went wide, her body shook, goose bumps covered her legs.

"What now?"

"Th—this video. Y—you saved me. The light tower would have totally flattened me if it wasn't for you."

"It's probably just the angle of the camera."

"No, Jerry. The tower came down on the megaphone I was chasing. You risked your life to save me." Darla closed the MacBook and set it on the table. She scooted toward Jerry but yelped in pain.

"Darla, please don't move." Jerry put the bag back on her ankle. "Let me check out your other foot."

"My other foot? It's fine."

"Trust me." Jerry edged down the sofa, lifted Darla's left foot, and let it rest on his knee. He used both thumbs to massage the ball of her foot and her heel.

"What are you d—Oh my gosh! That feels amazing."

"That's the idea." Jerry cracked the knuckles of her toes. "Lie back and enjoy it."

Darla scrunched down on the sofa, put her head on the armrest, and closed her eyes. Jerry continued to knead the muscles in Darla's foot in silence. A smile of contentment crossed her face. Her chest rose and fell slightly with each even breath. It reminded him of watching a sleeping kitten.

"I have to stop. My hands are getting tired." He lifted Darla's foot, slid his leg from under it, and set it on the couch.

Darla didn't react or answer.

Jerry lowered his voice. "Are you awake?"

Darla's eyes fluttered open. "Yeah, and I'm definitely keeping you around." She flexed her uninjured foot. "That was outstanding. Where d'you learn to—"

"Hey guys, I'm back! And I brought friends!" Lucy burst through the door.

Mike and Talia followed Lucy into the room. Talia had changed out of her uniform and wore a red polo shirt and jean shorts.

"There's the hero!" Mike grinned at Jerry.

"Here you go, D." Lucy handed Darla the purse.

"Thanks, Lucy." Darla retrieved her phone from the purse.

"Don't thank me. I couldn't get close to the stadium. They only let in one person, Veronica, to grab all the girls' stuff."

"Then yay for Veronica. Where is she anyway?"

Talia pointed in the direction of her dorm. "Went back to our room with Greg."

Darla rolled her eyes. "Oh, boy."

"What?" Mike furrowed his brow.

"*Sylvilagus heftris*," Lucy announced.

Jerry spread his arms wide. "I have no idea what that means."

"For those of you who aren't planning on a career in Wildlife Management, that's the genus of the Adirondack forest rabbit." Lucy put her hands to the sides of her head, stuck out her index fingers, and wiggled them.

"Still not getting it."

Talia blew out her breath. "Ronnie and Greg go at it like rabbits. Only much louder."

Mike covered his ears with his hands. "That is more information than I needed."

"Speaking of rabbits." Darla rifled through the purse, pulled out the mint green rabbit's foot, and hooked it to her bracelet. "That's much better."

Mike squinted. "What's that?"

"Rabbit's foot." Darla rubbed the fuzzy oval. "You know, for luck. I got them at Five Below."

"Wasn't lucky for the rabbit," Mike observed.

"Har, har." Darla groaned. "Does Jerry write all your material? He said the same thing. Anyway, I didn't have mine, and I hurt my ankle and almost got clobbered by the light tower. But Jerry had his, and he rescued me."

"Jerry?" Mike looked at his roommate in disbelief. "You've really bought into this nonsense? It goes against common sense and all we know about science."

Jerry pulled out his keys and dangled from the orange rabbit's foot. "I'm not saying I believe it one hundred percent, but I'm not going anywhere without it."

Talia nodded. "A lot of the squad were talking about that article with the bad luck on *The Underground*. They're taking it seriously."

Mike rubbed his chin. "I still say it's nonsense." He turned to Talia. "If we can't go back to your room, what are we going to do?"

"Work on the jammer?"

Mike nodded. "But we need to pick up an RF modulator, some capacitors, and more solder over at Electrical Supply Hut."

"Let's go. I'll drive." Talia pointed at Jerry. "You want a lift?"

Jerry patted Darla's leg. "I'm going to stay here and minister to the wounded."

"Shotgun!" Mike called.

As they walked out, Talia looped her arms through Mike's. "You don't need to call shotgun if you're the only one riding."

After the door closed, Darla laughed. "It's scary how much those two are right for each other."

"Spooky." Jerry leaned back.

Lucy flopped into the chair across from the sofa and spied the bag of ice resting on Darla's ankle. "You going to be okay, D?"

"I think so. We'll see how my ankle feels in the morning. If it's still bad, I'll stop by Student Health." She adjusted the bag. "So, what are you up to?"

"Dunno. Guess I could catch up on my reading for biology."

"What about Jim?"

"He went home to Cape Vincent for the weekend. It's his mom's birthday."

Darla suppressed a frown. "How's your drop fade?"

"Perfected. We've got a match against Franklin Pierce on Tuesday morning over at Oak Valley. The seventh hole is this par-five dogleg to the right." Lucy stood and pantomimed swinging a golf club. "I'm going to cut the corner, land the ball past that no-longer-intimidating fairway bunker, and make the green in two. Then on the tenth hole, I'll use my..."

Darla's head subtly tilted toward Jerry, her eyes communicating a silent plea.

"You know what?" Lucy glanced out the window. "The rain's stopped, and my short irons could use some work." She disappeared into her bedroom and emerged wearing a green-and-gold visor, her golf bag slung over her shoulder. "After the range, I'll hit the SC for an early dinner. Figure I'll be gone at least three hours." She winked at Darla and walked out the door.

"Alone at last." Darla grimaced as she inched down the sofa toward Jerry.

"You stay put."

"Nope."

The bag of ice fell from the sofa to the floor.

"I need to duct tape that thing to your ankle."

Darla climbed into Jerry's lap.

"What are you doing?" Jerry was surprised, but not displeased with her actions.

Darla leaned close, nibbled on Jerry's earlobe, and whispered, "Thanking the boy who saved my life." She looped her arms around his neck and kissed him on the lips.

The kiss continued until the need for oxygen proved too strong.

"You're welcome." Jerry gasped for air. He licked his lips. Darla tasted like fresh cherries.

"I'm not done. I barely started." She slipped her hands under Jerry's borrowed sweatshirt.

"Ah, cold!" Jerry's body jerked.

Darla's lips twisted into a mischievous grin. "Guess we'll have to do something to warm them up." She pressed her body against Jerry and kissed him again.

CHAPTER 19

Darla sat on a bench in the shade of a sugar maple and checked her phone. She wore lavender overalls over a purple turtleneck with matching New Balance sneakers. Her hair was up, secured by a purple-and-white polka dot scarf. Her eyes hidden behind orange-rimmed Dior shades. She snapped three selfies, slipped the glasses to the top of her head, squinted at the images, selected the cutest (her pout was unarguably adorable), and uploaded to Instagram. The likes and comments poured in as Jerry pulled up in his ex-police car and honked.

Darla approached the passenger door, favoring her left foot. The swelling in her ankle decreased overnight, but still hurt to put weight on it. Forget heels anytime soon. She slipped into the seat. Jerry wore a red-and-gray striped rugby shirt and khakis. Darla fastened her seat belt, leaned over, and kissed her boy.

Jerry returned the kiss enthusiastically. He licked his lips. "Frosted Flakes?"

"Close, Frosted Cheerios."

Jerry maneuvered the car onto the road and headed toward the north-east campus exit.

Darla pointed at the windshield. In front of her, a crack ran half the length of the glass. "Was that here before?"

Jerry nodded. "I have to get it fixed."

"Safelite repair, Safelite replace," Darla sang the jingle.

"Or we could take your car."

"Who told you that I—Oh the twins. But you asked me to come, so it's your responsibility to drive."

"I could drive your car." Jerry grinned.

"Nope. It's not just you, Jerry. I don't let any boys drive it."

Any boys? A twinge of jealousy struck Jerry. "No problem. How was your morning?"

"Productive. Lots of studying. I couldn't work out because of my ankle. Not hopeful about cheer practice tomorrow night. And I went to church."

"Church, huh?"

"Yep, Missouri Synod Lutheran. Old school. And you?"

"And me, what?"

Darla narrowed her eyes. "Did you go to church this morning?"

The ends of Jerry's mouth pulled down into a slight frown.

"Jerry." She poked him in the ribs, causing him to smile. "I'm not judging. It's not like we're getting married. But I want to know more about you."

"Uh, I'm a Quaker."

"Like the oatmeal?"

"Yes, Darla. I come from a long line of grain worshippers. My parents had a mixed marriage. My mom's family were barley cultists."

"Funny, Jerry. Seriously, tell me. I don't know anything about Quakers."

"Well, there aren't any Meeting Houses in Stuyvesant County. I find a quiet place on campus and sit for thirty minutes to an hour and do some deep thinking and contemplation."

"You mean like the library?"

They exited the campus, and Jerry turned left on the state highway. "Sometimes. Or it could be on the quad or under a tree. Not much noise or people on a Sunday morning. If it rains, I stay in my room."

"And you sit in silence?" Darla searched for Quakers on her phone.

"That's pretty much what we do. But not this morning. I was working on an article about the light tower collapse." Jerry paused. "I think you're right about that jinx. Muller, the guy who scored that last touchdown for Fillmore and danced that jig, was killed by the falling tower. And three students hurt in the stampede were still in the hospital as of this morning."

Darla bookmarked the Wikipedia article on Quakers and put her hand on Jerry's forearm. "It's crazy what's happening. We have to stay safe, whatever it takes." She pulled her rabbit's foot from her purse. "Still got yours?"

"Yeah." Jerry pointed to the steering wheel. His rabbit's foot dangled from the key chain.

"Good boy. Now, how about a smile? I don't enjoy seeing you down."

"Okay." Jerry grinned and looked her over. "I like your outfit. It's cute. Rosie the Riveter?"

"You mean I look like a strong, patriotic woman who did her part to help the Allies defeat Nazi Germany and Imperial Japan?" Darla rolled up a sleeve and flexed her bicep.

Jerry chuckled. "That's exactly what I meant: Strong, patriotic, and...cute."

"I'll accept that. Where are we headed?"

"Saratoga. There's a retired reporter I want to interview."

"A reporter interviewing a reporter? Sounds pretty meta. Are you sure the universe won't collapse in on itself or something?"

"I certainly hope not. I hate it when that happens." Jerry chuckled. "Paul Wysocki, that's the reporter, wrote articles for the local paper on the VB students and staff who died back in 1984."

"They died on Friday the 13th. Remember I pointed that out?"

"I'm not likely to forget since you bring it up at every opportunity."

Darla shrugged. "Just trying to help."

"And your help has been invaluable."

"So why don't you call him? Not that I mind. It's a beautiful day for a drive." Darla glanced out the window at the changing leaves and the blue sky interrupted by puffy white clouds.

"His old editor told me Mr. Wysocki doesn't hear too well. Phoning wasn't an option. And the bonus is: you get a behind the scenes look at the life of an unheralded newspaper reporter."

"When I was in ninth grade, I saw Unheralded Newspaper Reporters open for NSYNC at the Saginaw Civic Center." Darla pulled a hairbrush from her purse. Holding it like a microphone, she belted out "This I Promise You."

"Number one rule for riding in my car: No boy bands." Keeping one hand on the steering wheel, Jerry grabbed the brush from Darla and tossed it in the backseat.

"Fine." She turned to watch the passing scenery. Outside, pastures full of cows whizzed by. Darla rolled down the window. "Moo!"

"I see you've got a case of bovilexia."

"What's that?"

"The uncontrollable urge to say *Moo* when you see a cow."

Darla narrowed her eyes at Jerry. "Is that an actual word?"

"Still want to compare SATs?" He laughed. "Of course it's real. Being a reporter means developing a wide vocabulary."

"Ok, Mr. Unheralded Reporter with a Wide Vocabulary, what's the status of the story you're doing on me for *The Chronicle?* Did you talk to Vanessa?"

Jerry gripped the steering wheel tighter, his knuckles turning white.

"What's wrong? Did she say you can't write the story?"

Jerry stayed silent, eyes on the road.

"Jerry, tell me."

"I'm not working for the paper anymore."

"You're not? Then why were you writing that article this morning? And why are we going to Saratoga?"

Jerry blew out his breath. "Okay, but you have to promise to keep it a secret."

"*Oui.*" Darla crossed her heart.

He recounted his confrontation over the bad luck story with Vanessa, his meetings with Sam, posting the story to *The Underground*, and being called into the chancellor's office.

Darla's eyes grew wide. "I'm dating a rogue journalist, under fire from the college administration, who won't back down in his quest for the truth. How exciting!" She tapped her phone. "I'm texting my mom. I wonder if she'll approve."

"We're dating?"

"You don't want to?"

"We've only known each other a couple of days. And last night was amazing for sure. But—"

"Boys!" Darla poked him in the ribs. "Are we going out or not?"

"Stop that. I'm ticklish."

She poked him again. "Answer the question."

"Yes, okay. We're officially dating."

"Outstanding!" Darla kissed him on the cheek. "Now, did you talk to this Sam about doing a story on me for *The Underground?*"

Dr. Janelle Thornton-Gaston, EdD entered the conference room late, her standard power move. Around the elongated oak table sat the athletic director, the university's legal counsel, the head of media relations, and the campus police chief.

"Where's Case?" Thornton-Gaston looked around the room. Rodney Case was Van Buren's chief information officer.

"Fishing in Vermont." Characopus pantomimed casting a reel. "According to his wife, there's no cell service at the cabin. He should be back tomorrow."

Thornton-Gaston sighed. The situation required all hands on deck. She was in the last round of interviews for the president's job at South Georgia Coastal College. If she landed the position, she'd be back to living near her family in the land of *real* grits and peach cobbler. No more blizzards and ice-cold winters. But the campus chaos of the last three days threatened to derail her triumphant return home.

"I guess we'll get started." Thornton-Gaston took her seat at the head of the table. "Thanks to everyone for coming in on a Sunday. I called this meeting to develop options for dealing with the articles in *The Underground*, but first I'd like an update on the stadium and the light tower."

Characopus read from his tablet. "One dead, a player for Fillmore, crushed by the tower. Twelve injured, ten VBU students and two staff. All from the stampede. We were lucky the tower didn't fall on anyone else. Three still in the hospital as of an hour ago. All broken bones and expected to make a full recovery. The Physical Plant is inspecting the stadium and will begin removing the downed tower later this afternoon. Don?" Chara-copus nodded toward Don Gehring, the athletic director.

Muscles bulged beneath Gehring's green VBU sweater vest. Despite being fifty-two, the AD maintained the physique he had from his college wrestling days. He cleared his throat. "The game with Fillmore has been declared a no-contest. With no common open weekends for the rest of the season, the game won't be rescheduled. Kind of fortunate since we were well on our way to getting thumped." The AD half-smiled. "We're sched-uled to play Calvin Coolidge for homecoming on Saturday. I've talked to my counterpart at CC, and we can shift the game to their campus if our field isn't useable. But unless the Physical Plant comes up with some surprises, I expect the stadium and the team to be ready. Maureen?" He glanced in the direction of the university's legal counsel.

Maureen Stepanian swept back a lock of her jet-black hair and consulted her notes. "I've been in touch with our insurance carriers. They hope to settle all claims quietly and quickly. But with everything that's happened in the last week, expect to see a significant increase in our premiums when we renew."

Thornton-Gaston nodded. If things worked out, skyrocketing insurance rates would be a problem for the *next* chancellor.

"Julie?"

At twenty-five, Julie Fredericton, head of media relations, was the youngest member of the committee. The blonde wore a black blazer over an off-white blouse and drummed her long, red fingernails on the table. "I've sent releases to TV, radio, print emphasizing Van Buren's dedication to the safety and health of our students and our commitment to trans-parency. Parents and alumni got a similar email blast. I scheduled a memo-rial service for the students who died this week. It's at six tonight on the Quad. I hope you can all attend." She glared at Gehring. "And I would suggest for the time being that the Athletic Department ceases sending out fundraising appeals describing the current stadium as *crumbling infrastructure.*"

"Yes, that's not making my job any easier either," the counsel added.

Gehring jabbed his pen at Julie. "We're under a tight schedule. We need the donors to respond to the urgency of the request if we want the new stadium ready for next season."

Thornton-Gaston raised a hand. "Mike, I'm sure you can raise your money in a way that won't make the school a target for plaintiff's attorneys. Ask Julie if you want help."

The AD grunted. He wasn't about to take advice from some kid with a public relations degree who should be making espressos.

"Anything else on the stadium or what happened yesterday?" Thornton-Gaston inquired.

The group shook their heads.

"Good. Let's get to the original reason I called this meeting. George?"

The chief dimmed the overhead lights. A giant video monitor on the far wall lit up and displayed the homepage of *The Underground*. The top headline read: "Stadium Light Tower Collapse Results in Fourth Death Tied to Bad Luck."

"They don't take the weekend off," the chancellor grumbled. "We don't know who's behind this scandal sheet, but we have a good idea of the identity of one of the reporters. What we need are ideas on how to counteract or suppress the fear and disinformation being spread."

"Is this really such a big deal?" The AD pointed at the screen. "Why worry about the nonsense that some website is peddling?"

Thornton-Gaston couldn't reveal her true concerns: that any additional negative news about Van Buren would affect her chances of landing the Georgia Coastal job. "Mike, with the way the silliest story can go viral these days, it's imperative we shut down any gossip or rumors that could adversely affect Van Buren. Kids are flighty. Who knows what could cause them to go to another college? And athletes can be pretty superstitious. You wouldn't want to lose a top recruit over something as ridiculous as a fear of bad luck, would you?"

The AD shook his head. "I suppose not."

The chief scrolled down to reveal more articles: the fast-running parking meters, a list of which local bars didn't card, and a review of *Transformers vs. Predators 2*.

The counsel squinted at the screen. "Parking meters?"

The chief nodded. "It went up yesterday about an hour after we met with Williams."

"That settles it." The chancellor slammed the table. "He's definitely working for them. Any suggestions about what we can do?"

"See if Case can have IT block *The Underground* from the campus network?" Fredericton suggested.

The AD leaned forward. "Will that work?"

"I'm no tech expert, but I don't see why they couldn't." Fredericton shrugged. "Students might get around it by using the data on their phones, but it's something."

"I want to remind everybody that as a state-supported institution, Van Buren is bound by the First Amendment." The counsel tapped the table with the eraser end of her pencil. "We can't selectively block websites because we don't like what they're saying. An action like the one proposed would place the university at risk for a lawsuit."

"I don't want to hear what I can't do," the chancellor growled. "Tell me what I *can* do."

The lawyer rubbed her chin. "I suppose a public safety emergency, narrowly tailored for a limited duration, might work. If it ever gets litigated, we'll probably lose, but most likely we'll be told not to do it again. The PR hit might be worse than any actual damages."

"I'll take that risk. This is a short-term solution while we get things under control. I doubt a bunch of students will sue us because they can't read a website for a week."

The AD added, "If they can block the site, maybe Case can also tell who is uploading files to *The Underground*. And we can identify their reporters that way."

The counsel nodded. "I see no problem with that. The IT department has the right and responsibility to monitor network traffic for performance and security issues."

Thornton-Gaston smiled. "Good. Maureen, you tell Case what we want. Do it in person. No emails. And make sure he doesn't leave a paper trail with his staff."

Maureen nodded and scribbled herself a note.

"Maureen! No paper trail!" Thornton-Gaston scolded.

The counsel looked sheepish and tore up the paper.

Thornton-Gaston continued, "With *The Underground* blocked, we'll build our own narratives. I'll chat with the editor of *The Chronicle*. Get her to publish a story explaining a few parking meters had glitches, a manufacturing defect or software bug. And it's being taken care of. We can even report that a few students received refunds."

"I've been thinking about how to undermine the 'bad luck' stories." Fredericton tapped her phone. "What if I talked to some STEM professors, and we did a VBU version of *Mythbusters?*"

"Excellent idea," Thornton-Gaston agreed. "Get a few communication majors to film it and upload to YouTube."

"Tik-Tok would be even better." Fredericton held up her phone open to the app.

"I can't keep track of all these new websites. Do what you think is best. And how do we handle Williams, or any other reporters that Case might give us? George and I tried scaring him yesterday, but it obviously didn't work."

"What if a couple of football players were to *express* their displeasure with this Williams kid?" A menacing grin spread across the AD's face.

"Are you suggesting what I think you are?" The counsel shook her head.

"Relax. Kids get into fights all the time." The AD pounded a fist into his open hand.

"Yeah, in grade school. What you're suggesting is a felony. I want to be clear I can no longer ethically be a part of this discussion. I'll pass along the instructions to Case, but I'm out of here." The counsel stood and left.

After the door closed, the chancellor pointed to the AD. "We'll keep your idea in reserve, Mike. I'm thinking we convene an investigatory committee empowered to determine all the facts related to these deaths. And if Mr. Williams, or anyone else, refuses to cooperate and share what they know, we'll threaten to suspend or expel them."

Characopus shifted in his seat. "Can we do that?"

"With Maureen gone, I'm not sure. But I think if we really pressure these kids, maybe even get their parents involved, they'll stop spreading this nonsense. And it won't come down to taking any formal action on our part. Any objections?"

The four remained silent.

"Anything else?" Thornton-Gaston looked around the table.

The AD sighed. "There's the matter of Rick Tilden. He's the student who was driving the truck that Vince Murphy was killed in."

The chief leaned back in his chair, visibly relaxing. "I think we're going to be okay there. I talked to the sheriff this morning. As far as he's concerned, the driver of the tractor trailer that struck the pickup is at fault. The student is in the clear."

"Great." Fredericton tapped her phone. "We'll play that up in *The Chronicle*. The tragic death was the responsibility of an outsider. The idea that one of our students was drunk and at fault will dry up."

Thornton-Gaston scribbled herself a note. "I think we're done here. We'll meet again tomorrow at nine. Someone be sure to tell Maureen and Case. Plan on meeting every morning until the crisis is over."

The chancellor rose and left the room, followed by Fredericton.

The chief stopped the athletic director on his way out the door. "Mike, we need to think about what happens if this thing explodes in our faces."

"What do you mean?"

"I mean, if all these grand plans don't work, someone has to take the blame. It's not going to be me. I'm making sure of that. You should be ready to duck and point at someone else."

"Someone like who?"

"Dr. Janelle Thornton-Gaston, EdD."

Jerry pulled into the visitor's lot of the Shady Pines Retirement Village and killed the engine. "Not sure how long this will take, but I'll be back as soon as I can."

Darla furrowed her brow. "What do you mean? I'm coming with you."

"You'll be bored."

"What was all that about a behind-the-scenes glimpse of the exciting life of a newspaper reporter? A *rogue* newspaper reporter?"

"I said unheralded, not exciting."

"Jerry, I didn't come all the way to Saratoga to count cows on the side of the road. You saw me cheer. I want to see you do reporter stuff." She crossed her arms and pouted.

"Darla, please."

She pushed out her lower lip and made the saddest eyes possible.

"Darla, I'm telling—Okay, fine. You can come along."

"Yay!"

"But you have to let me do all the talking."

"You're the reporter. What am I going to say, anyway?" She flipped down the passenger visor, checked her make-up in the mirror, and touched up her lipstick.

They stepped out of the car.

Darla inhaled deeply. "Love that pine fresh air."

"Thought you weren't big on the outdoors?"

"Relationships are about compromise. You're letting me come along on the interview. Maybe we could do something outdoorsy together."

"Camping?" Jerry again flashed on the image of snuggling up to Darla, in her hiking shorts, around a fire.

"Maybe not camping." Darla widened her eyes. "But what about *glamping*?"

"That seems fair." He wrapped his arm around Darla's waist and they headed toward the main building.

Inside the entrance, they approached a harried fifty-something woman behind the reception desk.

Jerry cleared his throat. "I'm here to see Mr. Paul Wysocki. Can you direct me to his room?"

"Are you family?"

"No."

The woman shook her head. "Then I'm sorry, but you won't be able to see him. Sundays are for family visits only."

Jerry paused for a moment, attempting to construct a reply.

"He's not family, *yet*." Darla entwined her fingers with Jerry's. "We just got engaged and we're here to tell my grandpa the big news."

"That's wonderful." The woman smiled, displaying coffee-stained teeth. "Congratulations!"

"Thanks, I'm thinking Paris or Rome for the honeymoon. But Jerry has his heart set on Niagara Falls." Darla poked him in the ribs."

The woman frowned at Jerry. "You only get one honeymoon, young man, and it should be memorable. Listen to your fiancée. Europe can be so romantic."

"Yes, ma'am." Jerry glared at Darla, who returned a "who me?" smile.

The woman looked at Darla. "What was the name of your grandfather again?" Panic flashed in Darla's eyes. "Uh, Grandpa? His name is...Paul...Wysocki." She glanced at Jerry, who barely nodded. "Right. Paul Wysocki."

The woman tapped on her keyboard. "Your grandfather is in 179 west. It's down that far hallway." She pointed across the room. "Follow the signs and you'll find it."

"Thanks again." Darla led Jerry across the lobby and down the hall. "Did you still want me to stay in the car?"

"I appreciate the save." He kissed her on the forehead.

They continued down the hallway, following the signs. They turned right once, left twice, passing two residents and a member of the staff before arriving at a door marked 179-W.

"Remember, let me do the talking." Jerry knocked on the door.

No answer.

"Maybe louder." Darla made a fist. "He doesn't hear too well, right?"

Jerry banged on the door. "Mister Wysocki?"

Still no answer.

"What should we do?" Jerry frowned. "What if he's in there, but can't hear the knocking?"

"*We?* You're the unheralded newspaper reporter."

"Can I help you?" An old man in a flannel robe and using a walker, stood in the open doorway across the hall.

"We're looking for Mr. Wysocki. I'm not sure if he's in his room." Jerry wrapped his arm around Darla. "This is his granddaughter, Darla. We're here to tell him the good news that we're getting married."

The old man scowled. "I don't remember Paul saying anything about having children, let alone grandchildren."

Jerry blinked rapidly. "W—well it's like this—"

"Grandpa and Mom have been estranged forever." Darla frowned. "It's been so long, I'm not sure they remember what started it. We're hoping that the wedding will spur them to reconcile."

The old man's scowl became a smile. "That's nice to hear. Families should stick together. Congratulations."

"Thanks! I'm thinking of doing something different. Like a wedding on a farm. Maybe in one of those big barns we saw while driving here. But

Jerry just wants to go to Justice of the Peace and have a sit-down dinner with our families."

The old man pointed a bony finger at Jerry. "Listen to the young lady. Your wedding should be a memorable and special day."

"Yes, sir."

"Do you know if Mr. Wys—I mean, if my grandpa is in his room?"

The old man shook his head. "He's out on the terrace. Go back down the hall and take the first left all the way to the end."

"Thanks." Darla waved goodbye.

They backtracked halfway down the hallway, then Jerry stopped. "You sure are thinking a lot about weddings."

"Should I still let you do all the talking?"

"If you gave me a moment, I would have come up with something."

"Maybe." Darla smirked. "But I would think an unheralded newspaper reporter could think faster on his feet."

"Being a reporter isn't about making up lies on the spot. It's about digging for the truth and asking the right questions."

"Whatever." Darla held up two fingers. "Anyway, that's twice you owe me."

"Do you recall me saving your life about this time yesterday?"

"Yes, I do. You're a brave boy." Darla looped her arms around Jerry's neck, pulled herself close, and kissed him. "How about we call it even?"

"Deal. Now let's find Mr. Wysocki."

They exited the building and stepped onto an elevated terrace that ran the length of the building. The terrace overlooked a freshly mowed lawn gently sloping to a creek. A dozen or so white metal tables shaded by umbrellas were scattered across the terrace. A staff member stood at the railing, staring at his phone. Four women shared a table, playing cards. Two men sat by themselves. One was nearby reading a book, the other at the end of the terrace.

Darla's eyes flicked between the two men. "Which one?"

"Don't you know what your own grandfather looks like?"

Darla stuck her tongue out at Jerry.

"C'mon. Fifty-fifty chance." Jerry walked up to the closest man and cleared his throat. "Excuse me, Mr. Wysocki?"

The man put down his book, a large print edition of the latest Lee

Child. "No, I'm Barry Chasteen. That's Paul down there." He pointed at the other man.

Darla apologized, "Sorry to have disturbed you."

Jerry and Darla maneuvered through the tables to the far end of the terrace. The man sat in a wheelchair, oxygen tank at his side, looking out at the creek, not appearing to be doing anything else. He wore a gray sweat-shirt and sweatpants. Full head of snow-white hair. Age spots dotted his face.

Jerry stood at the man's side. "Excuse me, Mr. Wysocki?"

The man didn't respond.

"Not so quietly," Darla whispered in Jerry's ear.

"Excuse me, Mr. Wysocki?" Jerry raised his voice.

The man turned slowly. "Yes?"

"My name is Jerry Williams." Jerry kept his volume high. "And I write for *The Chr*—I mean, I'm a journalism student at Van Buren University." Jerry watched Wysocki's gaze flick from him and linger on Darla. "And this is Darla Jaggard, my, uh, associate."

"Girlfriend," Darla announced with pride.

Wysocki smiled. "I like her."

Jerry took out his notepad. "I wanted to ask you a few questions about some stories you wrote for *The Whig*."

Wysocki nodded and chuckled, but the chuckle devolved into a coughing fit. Jerry and Darla watched awkwardly as Wysocki struggled for a full minute to get his cough under control. He grabbed his glass of water with a shaky hand and took a sip.

"Sure, it would be nice to talk to someone. Have a seat. I warn you that my memory's not all that great anymore, but I'll do my best."

Darla and Jerry pulled up chairs.

Jerry flipped through the pages of his notebook. "Do you remember a man named Wayne Copeland? He worked for Van Buren and was killed when a trench collapsed on him. You wrote the story about him that appeared in *The Whig*."

Wysocki looked away from the two, once again staring in the direction of the creek.

"Mr. Wysocki?"

"I'm sorry? What were we talking about?"

"Wayne Copeland. He worked at Van Buren and was killed in an accident in 1984."

"Nineteen Eighty-Four." Wysocki shook his head wistfully. "Geraldine Ferraro. They never gave her a chance."

"Wayne Copeland, sir? Do you remember anything?"

Wysocki shook his head. "I'm sorry, Gary. I don't remember."

"That's okay. How about a student named Franklin Hearst? He was struck by a bus. Also in 1984."

Wysocki shifted his gaze from the creek to Darla. "You are an exquisitely beautiful young lady."

"Thank you." She smiled, all dimples.

"Mr. Wysocki? About Franklin Hearst?"

"That name means nothing to me. Sorry you came all the way out to talk to a forgetful old man."

"No problem, sir. Just one more name. Peggy Johnson? She drowned in the pool in the college gymnasium on July 13th, 1984."

Wysocki looked back to the creek. "Geraldine Ferraro."

"No, sir. Peggy Johnson. She was a student. In the story you wrote, there was mention of a broken mirror in the girls' locker room."

Wysocki closed his eyes. "A broken mirror," he mouthed silently.

"Mr. Wysocki?"

"Peggy Johnson. I almost forgot. I wish I had. And now it's coming back. Peggy. Hearst. Copeland. The football players..." His hands trembled.

"Football players?"

Wysocki grabbed his glass with shaky hands and drank the rest of the water, spilling some on his shirt. "Three nasty and vicious brutes. The school covered it up as best they could. Nothing on their record. Got off scot-free."

Jerry jotted in his notebook. "Do you remember the players' names? What did they do?"

"Poor Peggy. She didn't ask for what happened to her."

"What happened? The coroner ruled she drowned accidentally."

"We didn't have a choice. Such a sweet girl." His gaze returned to Darla.

"Mr. Wysocki, can we talk about Peggy? Are you saying her death wasn't an accident?"

Wysocki shook his head. "Peggy was smart too. And quite an athlete. Professor Harding suspected."

Jerry scribbled furiously. "Professor Harding?"

"Ellen. If it weren't for her, we could have never stopped it."

"Stopped what?" Darla leaned forward. "Was it bad luck?"

Jerry glared at her, and she shrugged back at him.

"All of us swore never to tell. I wrote the story, but it was a coverup. Just as bad as the college. Lied to the public, to her parents, to her brother Mark." Wysocki launched into another coughing fit. "Maybe it's time everyone knows the truth."

"Yes, sir. I'd love to help you get the truth out. But your story's a bit jumbled. Let's start with Peggy. What really happened to her?"

Wysocki coughed again and his face turned bright red. His arms flailed, knocking his glass off the table. The glass shattered on the concrete floor.

"It's okay, Mr. Wysocki." Jerry reached for the largest shards and scanned for a trash can.

A staffer appeared from nowhere. "Come on, Mr. Wysocki, let's go back to your room."

Wysocki, still coughing, nodded his head.

Darla and Jerry exchanged looks of puzzlement and concern.

Another staffer approached the table. She pointed at Jerry and Darla. "Mr. Wysocki is returning to his room to rest. You must leave now."

Jerry started to object, but Wysocki was already whisked off the terrace and inside the building.

CHAPTER 20

> Mike: Where you at?

> Jerry: hot dog king

Jerry waited for the next text. After thirty seconds, he gave up and put the phone down.

"Geraldine Ferraro?" Darla drummed her fingers on the wood grain surface of the table.

"She ran for vice president." For the first time, Jerry noticed Darla's nails were painted lavender, matching her overalls.

"I *know* who she was, Jerry. I got a five in AP US History." She tapped her phone and read. "On July 12, 1984, Walter Mondale announced Congresswoman Geraldine Ferraro would be his running mate. That's one day before Peggy Johnson died!"

"It's a coincidence. Ferraro was on Wysocki's mind because she was in the news when whatever happened with Peggy...happened."

"Are you sure, Jerry? You don't think it's the disembodied spirit of Geraldine Ferraro, still bitter over her crushing loss to Reagan and Bush, killing off the student body?" Darla raised her hands and wiggled her fingers. "Oogedy, boogedy!"

"I'm so glad I brought you along."

"Here you go." Bev, the counter girl, slid two plastic red trays onto the table. Three hotdogs, a bag of barbeque chips, Coke for Jerry, and lemonade for Darla.

Bev wore a Hot Dog King T-shirt and a denim skirt. Jerry kept his eyes forward on Darla. Last month, Busby blew up at him when his eyes ever so briefly lingered on Bev's legs. Jerry didn't want to screw things up with Darla. Or was he actually—*gulp*—maturing?

Jerry ripped open the bag and spread the chips across the tray. "These hot dogs are great, I promise you."

"It's not Cascata, but I guess it will do."

Jerry's stomach tightened. Darla was obviously used to finer dining options than he could afford. He thought she might have overheard the conversation he had with his dad about the emergency credit card but guessed not. If they were really going out, she needed to understand the state of his finances.

"Darla, I need to tell you something."

She focused her big green eyes on Jerry. "Please don't tell me you're in love. We've only been going out for like five hours."

Jerry almost choked on his hot dog. "What? No!"

"Gotcha again!" Darla smiled all teeth.

Jerry's face burned bright red.

"Wow, I really did get you."

"Darla, please be serious. This is important."

"Okay." Darla made a somber face and folded her hands on the table. "Go for it."

"Darla, I think you're great."

"Don't say the *L* word."

Jerry glared, and Darla stifled a smile.

"But I need you to understand that my finances aren't as robust as I'd like. I enjoyed taking you to Cascata, but that can't be a common occurrence. That's what I was talking about with my dad. I used the credit card he gave me for emergencies to pay for dinner."

"*The Chronicle* doesn't pay you?"

Jerry shook his head.

"Or *The Underground?*"

"Afraid not."

"We talked about the job prospect for journalists before. It's not too late to change your major to chemical engineering. We could be study buddies."

Jerry laughed. "I'll keep that in mind."

"What about social media?" Darla tapped her phone and held it out to Jerry, displaying her Instagram. "Brands pay me to promote their clothes and products."

"I think the market favors blonde assistant cheerleading captains over rogue college newspaper reporters."

"I suppose." Darla pulled back her phone. "Can't you make money by doing other writing? It feels like we're living in a Stephen King movie. And he's loaded. You should write a book."

"That is not an altogether bad idea. But it would be quite a while before the money comes rolling in. In the meantime, are you okay with more chili dogs and less calamari?"

"Mom did warn me it was as easy to fall for a poor boy as a rich one. I suppose I can rough it." She grinned. "For a little while."

"I appreciate your sacrifice."

"But think about writing that book. A bestseller. Book tour. Movie rights. A gala red-carpet opening. I'd be fab in a Tom Ford gown, mingling with the A-listers."

"Tom who?" Jerry didn't pay attention to Darla's answer. He was too busy imagining her in a sparkly sequined gown with a plunging neckline and slit to her hip.

Darla reached for the ketchup bottle.

Jerry adopted a raspy voice. "Nobody, I mean nobody, puts ketchup on a hot dog."

"Huh?" Darla's head flinched.

"You know, Clint Eastwood? *Sudden Impact?*"

Darla narrowed her eyes. "Are you quoting movie lines at me?"

Jerry hesitated. "Yeah."

"Don't. First, Clint Eastwood? Ew! He's all wrinkly and like a hundred years old. Second, why would I know or care about some dumb cowboy movie? Third, what's the point? Do you wait all day for someone to grab the ketchup and spring that quote on them, like one of Pavlov's puppies?

Ketchup, Quote. Ketchup, Quote."

Jerry chuckled nervously. "I had no idea you felt so strongly."

Darla tapped the side of her head. "Why do some boys fill their skulls with movie lines? Talk to me, not at me."

Jerry held up his hands defensively. "As you wish."

Darla's eyes softened, and she broke into a grin. "That's the *one* movie you're allowed to quote." She slathered her dog in ketchup and bit into it. "This is pretty good."

"The rollers make all the difference. Like at the ballpark. Today everyone microwaves their hot dogs." Jerry devoured his first hot dog. "Anyway, back to Wysocki. What do you think?"

"He's a nice old man. But he seemed a few yards short of the end zone, if you know what I mean."

Jerry pulled out his notebook. "Three football players. No names. I don't have even a hint of what they did. I could dig up a team roster, but then what? Chase down eighty or ninety players from almost forty years ago. I don't even know what I'm looking for." He flipped the page. "Then there's Professor Ellen Harding." He tapped his phone. "Aha! She still teaches at Van Buren. Sociology."

"Are you sure it's the same woman?"

Jerry scrolled through her bio. "PhD from NYU in 1981. Former President of the VBU Faculty Senate. It must be her. She has office hours tomorrow from one to three."

Darla frowned. "I have Differential Equations at one, back-to-back with Thermo. I can't ditch. Both grade on attendance. Does she have hours on Tuesday?"

Jerry checked his phone. "Yeah. But I don't want to wait, and you really don't need to go with me on every interview." He flipped the page in his notebook. "I should talk to Peggy's family. Parents. Her brother Mark. If we can locate them."

"There's a football player named Mark Johnson. Texans, I think."

"Pretty sure that's not him. But that points out the problem. It's such a common name, the *right* Mark Johnson is going to be almost impossible to track down." Jerry finished the last bite of his second hot dog. "You done with this?" He pointed to the remaining few chips on the tray.

Darla nodded.

"You want dessert? I'm getting a scoop of ice cream."

"Why not? Chocolate for me."

Jerry departed with the trays and returned with two bowls of ice cream. He set the chocolate in front of Darla.

She squinted at Jerry's bowl. "Is that French Vanilla?"

"Nope, banana. This is the only place around that I can find it."

Darla scooped a spoonful, slipped it into her mouth, and closed her eyes. "Mmmm...this *is* good. Maybe the second-best ice cream I've ever had."

"What's the best?"

She opened her eyes and took another scoop. "From a place called *Crèmerie Dalla Rosé.*" She pronounced the name with a perfect French accent.

"Crimoria Della Rosy?" Jerry butchered the name.

"*Crèmerie Dalla Rosé.* They use the milk from their own cows to make the ice cream. The decor is all nineteenth century, and they have this amazing cuckoo clock. It's a charming little shop in St. Moritz. That's Switzerland."

"Switzerland?"

Darla nodded. "I love Switzerland. The architecture. The culture. The scenery. But especially the skiing. Everyone raves about Vail and Aspen, or even Telluride, but I think Colorado is totally played out, don't you?"

Jerry half-nodded. He held no opinion, having only been skiing once. His memories of that drunken weekend in the Poconos were spotty.

"I know." Darla's eyes lit up. "We should totally go to Switzerland for Christmas break! Imagine: we're in the lodge, a roaring fire in the fireplace, snuggling with a glass of schnapps—the drinking age is eighteen. Wouldn't that be romantic? I already mentioned the skiing. And you can see for yourself about the ice cream."

Jerry bit his tongue. Had Darla already forgotten their conversation about his finances? For a few minutes, he actually thought he could make things work with her. Was he wrong?

He made a serious face. "Darla, I can't go to Switzerland."

"Why not?" She licked the back of her spoon.

"I told you. I can't afford it."

"It can't be that much. Dad used to take us almost every year."

"The airfare alone—"

"Got you again!" She burst out laughing.

"What? Darla!"

"Jerry! Oh my gosh! The look on your face. You're always so serious. No, what's the word? Earnest. That's it. I can't help myself. You're so easy to tease."

Jerry was relieved, but annoyed. "Maybe next time I'll take a shot at you."

"Have at it. I'm a firm believer that if you dish it out, you need to be prepared to take it."

"Was anything in your story true?"

She slurped on her lemonade. "Parts."

"Which parts?"

"The part about this being good ice cream." She scooped up the last of her chocolate.

"Huh?" Jerry spotted Sam walking through the front entrance of the restaurant. She stopped at their table, still in her blue beret and this time in a red T-shirt with a picture of Elon Musk.

Jerry gave a small wave. "Hey Sam."

"The famous Sam?" Darla arched an eyebrow.

"She knows who I am?" Sam looked Darla over. "Let me guess. This is the cheerleader? It all makes a kind of twisted sense."

"Darla Jaggard. That's one J and two Gs. I'm the assistant captain."

"Sam, why are you here?" Jerry spread his arms wide.

"You tell me. You sent a message that we needed to talk. Your roommate said I could find you here."

"Oh, right." Between the light tower yesterday and visiting Wysocki today, Jerry forgot he reached out to Sam for help.

Darla sucked on her straw, slurping the last of her lemonade. "I had my fill of reporters for the day. I'm heading back to my dorm. You guys can huddle up about the story Jerry's writing on me." She leaned across the table and kissed him. "Let's meet for breakfast in the SC at seven-thirty."

Jerry licked his lips. Chocolate. "But what about your ankle?"

"I'll manage. Plus, it will give me a chance to walk off the ice cream."

Sam looked on with incredulity as Darla limped out of the door. "Please tell me I'm not here to talk about a story on Miss *Bring It On*."

"No. And her name is Darla." Jerry recounted his confrontation with the chancellor.

Sam waited until the end of the story to ask, "Where did the campus police officer who took you to the chancellor find you?"

"I was at the Student Center eating breakfast."

"But *how* did he know *where* to find you?"

Jerry shrugged. "I didn't think about it."

"They're tracking us somehow," Sam muttered. "How did you pay for breakfast?"

"VBU Card."

"Could be it. Do you have the U app installed on your phone?"

Jerry nodded.

"That's two possibilities. Think about uninstalling it. I'm also hearing rumors that cameras in the buildings are tied into a new facial recognition system being run by campus police. This surveillance is getting out of control. I need to dig deeper."

"That's all very interesting, Sam. But what about my problem with the chancellor?"

"What about it? The administration can't prove you wrote the article. You tell anyone else you're writing for *The Underground* besides the cheerleader?"

"Her name is Darla. And Mike figured it out."

"Figured it out? Jerry, what happened to deny, deny, deny?"

"I'm not used to lying to my friends."

Sam blew out her breath. "Okay, but don't tell anyone else. Like I said, I don't think there's anything to worry about with the chancellor."

"What if you're wrong? Since I got hauled into her office, I posted two more stories that won't make her happy. And I have more to follow up." Jerry told Sam about what he learned from Wysocki.

"Even if the university knows it's you, they can't really do anything. Van Buren is a state institution. That means you're protected by the First Amendment."

Jerry sighed. "You're saying after the college screws me over with an expulsion that I can look forward to tens of thousands of dollars in legal fees before I eventually win in court five years later?"

"Jerry, I appreciate what you're doing. Your stories are top traffic generators. Even more than our article about how to buy fake IDs from China. I got you into this, and I have your back." Sam paused, like she was contemplating something. "I'll bring out the big guns to protect you. Even if that means revealing my identity."

"Who are you? I looked for you on Facebook."

"Facebook? Yeah, that's a good one." Sam laughed. "I'm a student here at VBU. You don't need to know more. That's protecting both of us."

"Thanks for the support." But Jerry wasn't entirely convinced. "What if I need to contact you?"

"Use this email address: TheUnderground@NeutrinoMail.com. But don't send from your campus account."

"NeutrinoMail.com?"

"Yeah, it's a totally unbreakable encrypted server run by a bunch of privacy-minded scientists at CERN in Switzerland."

"Switzerland?" Jerry furrowed his brow.

Sam looked puzzled. "You got a problem with Switzerland?"

"Uh, no."

"Good. If the college tried dropping a Stuyvesant County subpoena on them, they'd just laugh. Plus, they deliberately don't keep any server logs." Sam checked her phone. "I've got to be somewhere. Is there anything else?"

Jerry shook his head.

"We're really glad to have you on board *The Underground*. Keep up the good work and try not to get too distracted by Diana."

"Her name is Darla."

"Sure it is." Sam laughed and walked out the door.

The college student glanced around the suburban street. She didn't see any nosy neighbors walking dogs or peering through windows from the row of identical houses. With a paper grocery bag in one hand, she headed up the path, climbed the steps, and knocked on the front door.

The door opened to reveal Professor Mark Johnson in a gray sweater and jeans, a touch of gray in his thinning hair. "Didn't expect to see you tonight."

The student held up the paper bag. "I had some free time. Thought we should catch up."

"Excellent." Johnson smiled and pulled back the door.

They settled in the living room: Johnson on the sofa, the student on an overstuffed recliner. She pulled a six-pack from the bag, offered one to the professor, and popped the top on her can.

"You'll be interested in this." Johnson held up his phone. "The University's Media Relations Department sent out an urgent email asking for volunteers to film examples of bad luck superstitions in an attempt to debunk them."

The student arched an eyebrow. "You're kidding."

"Not at all. I already answered in the affirmative, assuming you would approve. They'll be setting up to record for my Introduction to Geology class tomorrow morning."

Miaw! A gray-and-white cat entered, crossed the room, and rubbed against the student's legs.

She scratched the cat's ears, then swigged her beer, stood, and took a seat next to Johnson. Her lips curled into smile, and she leaned close. "How can I ever thank you?"

CHAPTER 21

Jerry ran four miles, showered, dressed, and was on his way to the Student Center for breakfast when his phone rang.

Busby!

His first instinct was to let it go to voicemail. She slapped and dumped *him*. What was to be gained by talking to her? But they'd be on the same campus for the next two-plus years. He was going to run in to her from time to time. Better to be mature and talk to her.

"Hey, Buzz."

"What the hell, Williams? You didn't wait twenty-four hours before going out with some cheerleader, but apparently that's not enough, so you decided to destroy my whole family?"

"Slow down, Busby. I have no idea what you're talking about."

"Spare me the lies. Sanchez saw you at dinner. She has photos and everything."

"*You* broke up with *me*, Buzz."

"At the hospital, I was upset. I copped to that. But let's skip Miss *Teen Vogue*. Why'd you write that article about Rick?"

"I really have no idea what you're talking about."

"Right. You have no idea how that story about Rick drinking before his accident ended up in *The Underground*."

Jerry was genuinely confused. "Rick was drinking? What story?"

"Do not pretend this isn't you. You write for *The Underground*. I saw the story about *bad luck*. Like you told it to me. And there's that bit about the parking meters that you would not shut up about."

Jerry sighed. Sam made it clear not to tell anyone else he was writing for *The Underground*, but Busby figured it out.

"Yes, Buzz. I wrote *those* stories. But I swear I don't know anything about an article on Rick."

"For your own good, take it down and print a retraction. Daddy's very protective of the family. When he finds out, I don't know what he's going to do."

"I'm telling you I didn't write it. I'd be happy to look—"

Busby hung up.

"What a great way to start the day," Jerry muttered.

He launched *The Underground* app and found the article. A video attributed to Priya Modi, Class of '28, showed Rick arguing, leaving a crushed beer can on a car hood, and getting into a pickup truck. The story quoted an anonymous source stating that Rick imbibed multiple beers in the truck before the accident. A copy of the sheriff's report on the accident accompanied the article.

Jerry never considered who else might be writing for *The Underground*. They had some genuine talent and real go-getters on staff. He walked the rest of the way to the Student Center in a funk.

Inside, he found Darla waiting for him near the cafeteria entrance. She wore a black blazer over a white blouse, a black skirt just above the knee, and black flats. Her hair was tied back in an elaborate braid. Glasses with oversized frames magnified her green eyes. A string of pearls hung around her neck.

Darla's eyes lit up when she saw Jerry. She looped her arms and kissed him. She smelled like the candy shop again.

"How is the boy this morning?"

"Much better, now. And you look terrific, like—"

"Like the CEO of a Fortune 500 integrated chemical company that focuses on intelligent solutions and innovative products?"

"That's exactly what I was going to say."

Darla winked. "Dress for the job you want." She fiddled with the collar of his rugby shirt. "On the other hand, do you have a closet full of these?"

"What? I like them."

Darla patted his chest. "Clearly, I need to take you shopping."

Jerry wasn't thrilled with that idea, but no sense in bringing down Darla's mood. They stepped inside the cafeteria, grabbed trays, and moved down the line. Darla loaded up with eggs, bacon, two slices of toast, and orange juice. Jerry grabbed a banana, a granola bar, and a milk.

"That's all you're getting?"

"I'm not that hungry."

They carried their trays toward the center of the room, where Mike, Talia, and Veronica sat. As Jerry approached their table, a student he didn't recognize handed Mike some money. Talia handed the guy a plastic bag. He waved and left.

Jerry and Darla took seats at the table across from the three.

Jerry looked at Mike. "Please tell me you're not dealing pot in the Student Center cafeteria."

Mike shook his head.

Darla leaned forward and asked in a conspiratorial whisper, "Adderall?"

Mike laughed. "Far from it. Show him, babe."

Talia held up a plastic bag containing a turquoise blue egg-shaped object.

Darla squinted at the baggie. "You're selling rabbit's feet?"

Talia slipped the bag back into her purse. "Yep, bought out the complete inventory. They gave us quite a deal: seventy-five cents a unit. We're selling them for ten bucks apiece. Jerry's latest article in *The Underground* is really driving business."

"Uh, I don't write for them. Remember?"

"Sorry, dude." Mike looped an arm around Talia and squeezed. "I couldn't keep a secret like that from my business partner."

Veronica rested her head on Talia's shoulder. "And a good sister couldn't keep that secret from me."

"Great." Jerry slumped in his seat. "Is there anyone who doesn't know I'm writing for *The Underground*?"

"There you are!" a voice behind Jerry shouted.

He turned to see a red-faced Miranda shaking her finger at him. "Miranda, what's wrong?"

"I get you and Busby are on the outs. But why do you have to ruin my life too?"

"What are you talking about? I told Busby I didn't write that story about Rick."

"Who cares about stupid Rick? I'm talking about this." She thrust her phone in his face. *The Underground* app was open to a headline that read "Sophomore Writing English Papers for Football Team."

"Let me see that." Jerry reached for the phone.

Miranda pulled the phone back. "You don't need to see it. You already wrote it. Why Jerry? What did I ever do to you?"

"Miranda, honest, it's not me."

"Bull. Busby told me you write for *The Underground*. You knew about the papers. Don't lie to me."

"Miranda, please, I'm telling you that's not my article."

"If the administration comes down hard on me, it will be ten times worse for you. You think Dmitri's joking about having relatives in the Russian mob? You'll see." Miranda stormed off.

Jerry twisted his head around. Not only were his friends all wide-eyed, but the students at the neighboring tables were staring at him. "The article isn't mine."

Talia shrugged. "Doesn't matter. If she's really writing papers for the football team, she should get in trouble. The integrity of the university is at stake."

Jerry narrowed his eyes at her.

"I'm serious, Jerry. Just like the football team, all of us on the cheer squad," she pointed at Darla and Veronica, "we have to worry about practice, competitions, and travel on top of our classes. Why should the players get a break? Why allow that girl to devalue the degrees we're all working so hard for?"

Jerry nodded. "You make a good point. But I can't take credit for the story. It wasn't me."

Mike looked at Jerry. "Really?"

"Have I ever lied to you?"

"How about two days ago when you swore you weren't writing for *The Underground?*" Veronica crossed her arms.

Jerry's face burned red. "Yeah, the girl who runs it asked me not to tell anyone." He pointed at the surrounding tables. "Now everyone knows. All I can do is ask you two," he glanced at the twins, "to forgive me."

Veronica shrugged. "I don't care. I was trying to score debating points."

"I'm more interested in who this Busby is." Darla scrunched her nose. "I've heard that name before."

"That's Jerry's ex," Mike clarified.

Darla arched an eyebrow. "Really? Is she the *American Girl?*"

"Huh?" Confusion covered Mike's face.

"Darla means the ringtone," Jerry explained. "Yeah, that's Buzz."

"Interesting...I wonder..." Darla tapped her phone, then held it to her ear. "Voicemail? Jerry, turn on your phone."

"Huh, why?"

Darla widened her eyes, pressed her lips into a thin line with a "just do it" look on her face.

"Okay." He powered it up.

Darla tapped again. "And She Danced" by The Hooters blared from Jerry's phone.

"Oh my God, that sounds so old." Veronica mock shuddered. "Is that the Beatles?"

"I think it's Glenn Miller." Talia covered her ears with her hands.

"I can certainly shake the paint off the wall." Darla hummed the tune. "I'll accept that."

Jerry silenced his phone. "Buzz called me this morning and said—"

"She's regretting letting you go and wants you back?" Darla poked Jerry in the ribs. "Well, she can't have you."

"Not exactly." Jerry recounted Busby's rant.

"Sounds like someone on *The Underground* has it on for you. I bet it's that Sam. She has the worst fashion sense."

Mike held up a pair of fingers. "Make that two votes for Sam. I never liked her."

"That's crazy." Jerry shook his head. "Sam wouldn't screw me over. Plus, how would she even be aware of my connections to Busby and Miranda?"

"Dunno." Mike shrugged.

"But I will ask her right now who wrote the articles. Hopefully, I can get this cleared up before Busby's dad or Dmitri's cousins have me whacked." On his phone, Jerry typed out a message and sent it to Sam's NeutrinoMail address.

"On a lighter note, we're doing a test run on the jammer this afternoon." Mike pointed around the table. "Can I count on everyone's help?"

Jerry nodded. "I can do it after three-thirty."

Darla checked her phone. "Three-thirty is good for me. But we have cheer practice at six."

"We'll be done way before then," Mike assured her.

Veronica shook her head. "I've got pirate duty this afternoon."

"Pirate duty?" Mike furrowed his brow.

"Yeah, Captain Morgan promotion. I'm one of the Morganettes."

"She dresses up like a sexy pirate to encourage guys to get drunk." Talia pantomimed downing a shot.

"To raise brand awareness of Captain Morgan Spiced Rum among the targeted demographic," Veronica corrected.

"Should that really take priority the jammer?" Mike frowned.

"What are you paying?" Veronica held out her hand, palm up.

"You want to be paid to be part of a historical scientific achievement?"

"Of course." She smiled.

"Can't help you." Mike pounded the table. "I really wanted to get this done today."

"Let me ask Lucy." Darla tapped her phone. "Good news. She's in."

"Great, everyone meet in my room at three-thirty."

A girl in a pink T-shirt and jeans stepped to the table. "You're the guy with the rabbits' feet, right? I'll take three." She handed her money to Mike and grabbed the purchase from Talia.

"We're going to make a fortune this week." Mike stuffed the bills into his wallet.

"Yeah, Friday the 13th is just four days away." Talia exhaled.

Busby spotted Miranda, checking her phone and leaning against an oak tree near the entrance to the Physical Sciences Building.

"Sanchez!" Busby waved to her.

Miranda picked up her backpack and hustled over. "Where were you this morning?"

They walked into the building and headed down the hall.

"Stuyvesant. I had to drive Rick to the lawyer's office." Busby frowned. "I'm looking forward to two months of chauffeuring him around."

Miranda shrugged. "Make him take Uber. What did the lawyer say?"

"I don't know. She met with him alone. Attorney-client privilege."

"What did Rick say?"

"Some macho stuff about nothing to worry about. But I know when he's lying. Daddy talked with the sheriff, even gave him a campaign contribution. Everything seemed all right. But now with Williams's story in *The Underground*, everything's blowing up. Rick is concerned. Maybe even scared."

Busby and Miranda filed into the lecture hall, took their traditional seats in the back row, and whipped out their notebooks.

Busby looked around the hall. "What's going on?"

A video camera was mounted in front of the lectern. A table had been brought on to stage. On it sat an animal carrier, three horseshoes, and a couple dozen small mirrors. A pair of trash cans flanked the table. Elsewhere on the stage were a pair of rocking chairs and at the far end stood an aluminum ladder.

At precisely five minutes past eleven, Professor Johnson, in his standard tweed jacket, took his position behind the lectern. In a booming voice, he announced, "I've prepared something different from my normal lecture today. But you're still responsible for *Chapter 8: Synclines and Anticlines.*"

A few students groaned.

"Now for today's unexpected treat. With the help of Beth Powers, President of the Van Buren University Skeptics Club," He nodded toward a blonde in a white sweatshirt and white jeans, "we're going to put on a little demonstration challenging our notions of superstitions.

"A website popular with some members of the campus community and specializing in the worst forms of yellow journalism has suggested that recent tragic events are the result of *bad luck*. What we hope to achieve today is to put a rest to such non-scientific thinking."

In the front row, Vicky Tran raised her hand. "Is this going to be on the midterm?"

Johnson let out an over-exaggerated sigh. "No, Ms. Tran, let me assure you and your classmates that you will not be burdened in such a manner."

Three students on the left side of the hall gathered their belongings and stood.

"However," Johnson pointed at the three, "failure to remain for the entire presentation will count as an unexcused absence. And I might remind the class that starting with your second unexcused absence, each missed class will drop your final grade one letter."

The students muttered to themselves and sat down.

"Ms. Powers and her skeptics have assembled for us a group of items that can be associated with bad luck: an umbrella to be opened indoors, a ladder to be walked under, a black cat to cross your path, and so on. Over the next fifty minutes, we will experience and challenge these superstitions, and explore why human irrationality has given these objects such power over ourselves and our lives. Today's first example: *felis catus*, the common house cat. Ms. Powers, if you please."

Beth opened the carrier. A black cat poked his head out cautiously. He flopped on the table and stretched out. She rubbed the cat's tummy.

The professor left the lectern and picked up the cat. The feline went limp in his hands. He inspected the name tag. "Some unimaginative jokester, who no doubt watches too much television, has named this mouser Salem. How could such a lovely and delightful creature crossing your path result in misfortune?"

"Because it's bad luck!" shouted someone.

The class laughed.

Professor Johnson scowled. "Actually, that's my point. Should you be out and about, and a black cat crosses your path, then something untoward happens in your life that day. You'll remember that and blame the black cat for your misfortune.

"But what if a calico, or Siamese, or Norwegian Forest Cat crossed your path, and the same adversity befell you? Would you attribute your *bad luck* to one of these other felines?

"Or consider the opposite? A Persian cat with one blue eye and one green crosses your path, then your significant other announces she won the lottery. Would you attribute this good fortune to the cat in question? Doubtful."

Vicky sat up in her seat. "What are you saying, Professor?"

"I am saying that the luck, either bad or good, isn't created by these objects, but by our expectations. They are social constructs, and their only power comes from the power that we attribute to them, for either good or bad."

Johnson released the cat on the floor. "We'll let Salem waltz around the hall. By the time lecture is over, none of you will be able to leave without crossing his path."

Salem meandered toward Vicky. The cat sniffed her sneaker, then leapt into her lap. She stroked his fur.

"Ms. Tran, please do not monopolize dear Salem. He has a task to perform."

The cat flipped onto his back and purred loudly.

"I don't think he wants to be disturbed." Vicky scratched his ears.

"I am reminded of the story of The Prophet, a cat, and a sleeve. Moving on." Johnson grabbed a red-and-blue pack of cigarettes from the table, removed one for himself, and offered one to Beth. "Who would like to be third?"

"Third what?" someone called out.

"The third cigarette. A popular superstition informs us that lighting three cigarettes on one match will result in severe calamity."

Vicky raised her hand.

"You are volunteering, Ms. Tran?"

"No, but isn't this a tobacco-free campus?"

"These are marshmallow root." Beth sighed. "I borrowed them from the Theater Department."

Johnson glanced about the lecture hall. "No one wants to assist in the advancement of knowledge?" He paused. "What about for extra credit?"

Miranda's hand shot into the air.

"Ms. Sanchez? Splendid. Please join us down in front."

Busby glared at her. "Seriously?"

Miranda intoned *sotto voce*, "I know. I'm such a grade-slut." She squeezed through the aisle, descended the steps, and took the proffered cigarette.

Professor Johnson produced a matchbook from his pocket. "Quickly, we don't want to ruin our experiment." He lit his cigarette, Beth's, then Miranda's.

Miranda inhaled deeply, held her breath, and blew three perfect smoke rings.

"Very impressive, Ms. Sanchez."

"The rewards of a misspent youth."

Johnson grabbed an ashtray and ground out his cigarette. "I think we've satisfied the conditions of the legend."

Beth stubbed hers out.

Johnson held out the ashtray for Miranda. "Ms. Sanchez?"

"Hold on." Miranda inhaled deeply. A look of concentration on her face, she puffed up her cheeks and exhaled. Smoke in the form of a heart emerged from her mouth and floated across the room.

The class gave her a round of applause.

"Thank you." Miranda stubbed out her cigarette, took a bow, and returned to her seat.

"That's not proof." A guy seated near the front griped. "We have to wait and see if anything bad happens."

"Or if something good happens." Johnson grabbed one of the hammers from the table. "Who would like to break a mirror?"

No response.

"Surely someone in attendance would relish the chance to relieve the frustrations of Monday morning by smashing something?"

Mike Wimmer in the second row stood and walked toward the aisle.

"Mr. Wimmer, excellent. First, put on the eye protection. Then slip this make-up mirror inside one of the trash bags and break it over the garbage can so we don't risk shards of glass all over the floor."

The student did as instructed, grabbed the hammer, and swung. The sound of shattering glass filed into the lecture hall. A roar went up from the students. Salem leapt from Vicky's lap, dashed up a few rows, and hid under an unoccupied seat.

"That's the spirit!" Johnson encouraged the student.

With a grin on his face, Mike smashed another mirror.

"That's fourteen years of misfortune!" Johnson yelled. "Who else would like a turn?"

Students formed a line and took turns with the hammer. When there were no more mirrors to smash, the students returned to their seats.

Beth swept a few shards that had slipped out of the bags. "It wouldn't be bad luck if someone hurt themselves on broken glass. Only poor house-keeping."

The demonstrations continued with students opening the umbrella, spilling salt, rocking the empty chairs, and so on.

When the wall clock read 11:45, Johnson pointed to the twenty-foot aluminum-folding ladder with an open can of paint with a stir stick on the shelf. "We're almost out of time, but we still need someone to walk under the ladder."

Busby raised her hand.

"Ms. Tilden? Excellent. Come on down."

Busby shook her head. "I'm not volunteering. Not because it's bad luck. It's common sense not to walk under a ladder. Especially with that paint can up there."

"Ordinarily, I might be inclined to agree with you, Ms. Tilden. But the order of the day is to dispose ourselves of these antiquated superstitions. Some minor risk is required."

Professor Johnson glanced about the room. "Still no takers? Then I shall perform the service myself." He approached the ladder, bowed his head slightly so as not to hit the spreaders, and passed through.

"No problem at all." Johnson reversed direction. As he stepped under the ladder, the hall was plunged into darkness. The emergency lights did not flick on. Startled screams came from a couple of the students, followed by a terrible crash, like the ladder falling. Students put their phones in flashlight mode, dimly illuminating the lecture hall.

"Professor?" Beth cried. "Professor Johnson, are you all right?"

Students murmured and shuffled toward the exit.

The lights flicked on. The ladder lay on its side, the can tipped over, and red paint spread across the floor. But Professor Johnson was nowhere to be seen.

CHAPTER 22

J erry stood at the entrance to the Whitmore Building, one of the older buildings on campus: stone façade, high ceilings, and hallways lined with radiators.

He rechecked the info on his phone. Professor Harding's office was room 228, and her office hours ran for another forty-five minutes. The photo in her bio showed a smiling woman with intelligent brown eyes and white hair. Jerry guessed she was in her late sixties or seventies.

Jerry pushed open the double doors. He located the stairway, climbed the steps two at a time, and entered the second-floor hall. He followed the ever-increasing room numbers to the far end of the hallway. The door to room 228 was open. Taped to the door was a cartoon of a witch scowling at her smartphone. The caption read: *Oh, it's in flying broom mode.*

He knocked on the doorframe and poked his head inside. Professor Harding, glasses hanging from a silver chain around her neck, sat behind an overflowing desk. Plants filled the windowsills, and the walls were lined with packed bookshelves.

"Professor Harding? Are you available?"

The woman gave him a grandmotherly smile. "Of course, young man. That's what office hours are for." She squinted at Jerry. "I'm sorry, I don't recognize you."

"My name is Jerry Williams."

"Come in, Mr. Williams, and take a seat."

Jerry slipped off his backpack and maneuvered himself across the cramped office to the sole chair.

"Which of my classes are you in?"

"Actually, I'm not in your class."

Professor Harding sighed. "This time is specifically set aside for my students."

"I appreciate that, but this is really important. If one of your students comes by, I'll be happy to leave."

"Fair enough. Now why are you here?"

Jerry grabbed a pen and his notebook from his backpack, flipping to a page where he had prepared some questions. "I'm a reporter for—er here on campus. And I'm writing a story about some deaths that happened at Van Buren back in 1984."

Professor Harding shifted in her seat. "I was here in 1984. And I vaguely remember a death or two on campus. But I don't remember any details. Why would you think I'd have any information about this? You're probably better off asking the campus police or checking old issues of *The Chronicle*."

Was she pretending not to know? Wysocki said what happened to Peggy was covered up, and he said it was time to tell the truth. Maybe Professor Harding didn't feel the same way. Or was it so long ago that she truly forgot?

"Paul Wysocki gave me your name." Jerry watched the professor's face for any hint of reaction. "He was a reporter for *The Stuyvesant Whig*."

Her tone turned icy. "Your reporter friend is mistaken. I don't know any Mr. Wysocki or anything more about 1984 than I've already told you. I think you should go, Mr. Williams."

"But I just—"

"As I stated, my office hours exist for my students to come for guidance and assistance, not to answer random questions from strangers about topics that I have no knowledge of. Good day." She slipped her glasses on, turned to her monitor, and typed.

Jerry was certain from her reaction that the professor knew something. "Professor Harding, I understand you have good reasons for not wanting to talk about 1984." He took a deep breath. "But I think the four deaths on campus this week are related to whatever happened back then. And it's not over. If I don't figure out what's going on and how to stop it, more people will die."

The professor stopped typing and stared over her glasses at Jerry. "What do you mean, the deaths are related?"

"The students who died this week are all tied to bad luck: spilled salt, opening an umbrella indoor, and such. The deaths in 1984 were all on Friday the 13th. I'm afraid of what's going to happen *this* Friday. Not only does the administration not believe me, they're actively suppressing the news."

Professor Harding rested her elbows on her desk and tented her fingers. She whispered, "It's happening again." She opened a drawer, retrieved a plastic *Do Not Disturb* door hanger, and gave it to Jerry. "Put this on the knob and close the door."

Jerry did as instructed, returned to his seat, and pulled closer to her desk.

"Mr. Williams, tell me all you've learned. Start from the beginning."

Jerry recounted the circumstances of the deaths of Cassie, Noah, Vince, and Muller, the football player from Fillmore. He relayed his suspension from *The Chronicle*, the publication in *The Underground*, and the confrontation with the chancellor.

"You've been quite busy. What's this *Underground* you speak of?"

"It's a web-only alternative school newspaper." Jerry gave her the URL.

Professor Harding typed the address into her browser and hit enter. She squinted at the screen. "That's odd. It appears to be redirecting to *The Chronicle*."

"Sounds like the chancellor and the administration are working overtime to suppress the story." Jerry continued to fill in Professor Harding about the research from the library that led him to interview Wysocki at the retirement home.

"What did Paul tell you?"

"Not much. His memory isn't that great. He implied Peggy didn't drown. Or at least not accidentally. Also, something happened with players on the football team. A cover-up that he was a part of. What can you tell me?"

Professor Harding pulled open a desk drawer and retrieved a bottle of Blue Grass Bourbon and two tumblers. She filled the glasses with the brown liquid and offered one to Jerry.

He held up this hand. "No thanks."

Professor Harding shrugged and downed Jerry's drink. "Peggy was brutally raped by three Van Buren football players. The athletic director and the head football coach, with the help of a few wealthy boosters, covered it up."

"That's the cover-up Wysocki was talking about?"

"Partly. Van Buren is the county's number one employer. Stuyvesant's entire economy is dependent upon us. Easy enough to persuade the Sheriff's Department not to investigate."

Jerry scribbled away.

"When no one would listen to Peggy, when she couldn't get justice anywhere else, she came to me."

"If the college and the sheriff wouldn't do anything, what could you do?"

"I showed her how to fight back. That was a mistake. But I was young and foolish, burning with rage at the way institutions that should have protected her ended up betraying her." Professor Harding stared at the empty glass. "From before the dawn of history, women who have been wronged by men have been challenged with how to fight back. Lacking the physical strength or political power, they developed...other methods."

"What kind of methods?"

Professor Harding stood, searched one of the crowded bookshelves, retrieved a blue volume, and handed it to Jerry.

Curse Tablets and Binding Spells: Women's Magic from the Ancient World. Above the title was a drawing of what Jerry supposed to be a griffin. He turned the book over in his hands. He couldn't place it, but the book seemed familiar.

"You've got to be kidding. Magic isn't real."

"Mr. Williams, you're the one who told me bad luck caused these deaths. What you call bad luck is one way that magic manifests itself in our world."

Jerry leaned forward, confusion on his face. "I always thought I'd find a logical explanation of how bad luck could be responsible for everything that's happening."

"Magic is what's responsible. This book *is* the logical explanation. It opened a door for Peggy. She stepped through and gained the power to fight back. The result was three dead football players."

"They're dead? Wysocki told me they got away with it."

"They most certainly did not. Maybe Paul doesn't remember clearly. You did say he was having memory issues."

"How did it happen? How did she do this?"

"December 1983. The three players, and no one else, died in a car accident. The roads were icy. Alcohol was involved. There wasn't much for the sheriff to investigate. After that, I thought it was over. Then a student who worked part-time for the Athletic Department died. Hit by a bus."

Jerry nodded. "Franklin Hearst."

"Three months later, a construction worker at the new football stadium was killed. People who had no connection to what happened to Peggy were dying. I confronted her that week. She had changed. The hurt and fearful girl I knew had become angry, spiteful, contemptuous. The power corrupted her soul. I tried to talk to her, help her. But she would have none of it. She threatened me."

"How does Wysocki fit in?"

"I guess he was much like you with a reporter's instinct. He wouldn't stop digging. I don't remember how he figured it out. He barged in while we were deciding how to take action against Peggy, so we asked him to join in."

"We?"

"My coven."

"You're an actual witch?" Jerry's head spun. "This is a lot to take in. Then what happened?"

"We stopped Peggy."

"You killed her?"

Professor Harding grabbed the other glass and downed the shot. She looked at her window, at the leaves changing for the fall.

Jerry sensed she wouldn't answer. "You and Wysocki and the coven stopped Peggy, then what?"

"The deaths ceased. I guess the good guys won." She laughed bitterly.

"My actions haunted me for a long time, but over the years, the guilt faded. At times, I'd go semesters without thinking about her."

"Why is this happening now? Is Peggy, or her spirit, somehow back?"

"No, her soul has gone to the Realm Beyond Ours. I know of no way for it to return. Even if she were back, I would sense it. It's someone else. Someone new."

"Who?"

"I don't know. Tell me more about the recent victims."

"Two were football players: Vince and Fuller." Jerry raised his voice as the pattern became clear. "Cassie was a cheerleader. She performed on the sidelines at games. And there's Noah. On the day he died, he wrote a story on the groundbreaking for the new football stadium. All the deaths are football related. It's got to be someone with another grudge against the team."

"Maybe."

"Maybe? It seems pretty obvious."

"It's possible, even likely, that whoever has tapped into the power isn't in complete control yet. I would expect that with a neophyte with no guidance. The power may act out its previous pattern, targeting those connected to the institution that wronged Peggy. But given time, it will grow so strong that everyone, whether connected to the football team or not, will be at risk."

"Will this protect me?" Jerry held up his key chain with the rabbit's foot.

Harding smiled. "It may for the moment *if* you're not a specific target. But in time, all the good luck charms in the world won't protect any of us."

"How do we find out who's behind this?"

"In the spring, I had a student. She was quite enthusiastic about learning the potential of magic, specifically manifesting luck. With most of my class, it's a struggle to keep them awake. She asked me for guidance, wanted to tap into the power. But I learned my lesson with Peggy. I lied. Said it was nonsense."

"What was her name?"

The professor squinted at Jerry, like she was racking her brain. "I'm sorry. I don't remember." She typed on her keyboard, and the printer roared to life. She grabbed the sheet, put on her glasses, and looked it over.

"This is a list of all the students who signed up for A Survey of Magic Systems this past spring. None of the names ring a bell. All I can remember is it was a young woman."

"I know someone who might be able to help." He folded the printout and shoved it in his backpack. "I'm also going to look for people who might have a grudge against the football team. When I do find who's behind this, how do I stop her? Or him? Can the coven help?"

Professor Harding shook her head. "No. They're all dead or retired to Florida. I was the kid of the group. There's a new coven in the area, but these ladies are more focused on politics. Their interest lies in placing hexes on Supreme Court nominees and such. I'll ask if they can assist, but I'm not hopeful."

"What can *we* do?"

"Evacuate the university? At a minimum, anyone with even a tangential connection to the football team should leave. I suspect the magic is grounded to the campus, more than a couple of miles away, and its power will fade to nothing."

"No way Dr. Thornton-Gaston will agree to that. She won't do anything that could damage the college's image." Jerry frowned. "Getting back to how to stop this. How did you stop Peggy?"

Professor Harding let out a long sigh. "Witchcraft is transmitted along lines of force. The ancient practitioners didn't know about electromagnetism. They only knew when magic worked and when it didn't."

"Like radio waves?"

"In some senses, yes. Water blocks most of the ways the power radiates, which is why in the olden days, suspected witches were often dunked. I asked Peggy to meet me at the gymnasium, and the coven ambushed her. It proved to be quite the supernatural struggle. One of the older members broke her leg. I suffered a concussion. But eventually, we forced Peggy into the pool, cutting her off from the power."

"And what? She melted, sank?"

"We had to drown her. The life drained from her body. You can tell yourself it's not murder. That she was a force, not a person. But it's not an easy lie to swallow. But I kept lying. Lied to the school, Peggy's parents, her brother Mark."

"Is there another way?" The cold reality settled in Jerry's mind. Stopping the threat meant taking another life. He wasn't sure he could do that. "You said you tried to talk to Peggy. What if we convince whoever's behind this round to stop?"

"I would always advocate for non-violent solutions, but that might not be possible. If the power has corrupted their soul, all the talking in the world won't help."

Jerry looked over his notes. "Peggy killed the football players in December, and your...confrontation with her was seven months later. Whatever's going on now has been happening for a short time. Maybe it's not too late to settle this with words."

"One can only hope."

Jerry and the professor exchanged contact information and promised to keep each other informed of any fresh developments.

He stood. "Wish me luck."

"I would, but I'm afraid that won't be enough."

CHAPTER 23

"I texted Jerry again. Still no answer." Darla frowned. "I'm worried."

Mike, Talia, Lucy, and Darla sat around the kitchen table in Mike and Jerry's dorm. Lucy wore a red top with *Van Buren Golf* in block letters running down her right sleeve, jeans, and a white bucket hat. Talia had changed from her school clothes into a green tank top and gold shorts for cheer practice. Darla wore a white button up Detroit Tigers jersey with navy blue trim, navy shorts, and sneakers with no socks. The copper-cased jammer lay at the center of the table.

Talia put her hand on Darla's shoulder. "I'm sure he's okay."

"Jerry turns his phone off all the time," Mike grumbled. "It gets pretty annoying."

"And I told him to stop that." Darla pouted.

Lucy pointed at the jammer. "Can we start, or is Jerry required?"

"We need someone to walk in each of the four cardinal directions while I stay here and monitor things," Mike explained.

"If we have to wait, then I need to study before practice." Talia stood, grabbed her backpack, and flopped on the couch. From the pack, she retrieved a thick textbook. "Ah, Maxwell's equations. I do love how God ordered the universe."

"What do you want to do?" Darla looked at Lucy.

"Dunno."

Mike opened a drawer and produced a deck of cards. "There's always Uno."

Darla groaned. Lucy covered her eyes.

The door opened, and Jerry walked in.

"We're saved." Lucy raised her hands high.

"About time, dude!" Mike pointed to his watch.

Jerry shrugged and tossed his backpack on a chair.

"Jerry!" Darla raced across the room, hugged him, then frowned. "You didn't answer my texts."

"You know that I turn my phone off for interviews."

Darla batted Jerry on the nose. "Turn it on now and don't do that again. Where were you?"

Jerry pulled out his phone and powered it up. He adopted his radio announcer's voice. "College newspaper reporter make startling break-through in baffling case." He resumed his normal voice. "I met with Professor Harding. Then I stopped by the library to do some follow-up on what I learned." He went to the fridge and grabbed a Coke.

"Who's Professor Harding?" Talia shrugged.

Jerry popped the can. "She's in the Sociology Department. Teaches comparative religions, folklore, stuff like that."

"You're not taking any of those courses," Mike pointed out.

"This isn't about class. This is about bad luck. She was teaching here in 1984."

Darla's eyes widened. "Did she tell you anything about the first super-stitious deaths?"

"Yeah, you're not going to believe—"

"Hey, hey, Mulder and Scully." Mike waved his hands. "Can you talk conspiracy theories later? Right now, it's *jammer* time!"

Talia looped an arm around Mike's waist. "You've been waiting all day to say that, haven't you?"

"Think of the marketing possibilities. I bet we can get MC Hammer to endorse us pretty cheap."

Jerry chugged his Coke and tossed the can in the recycling bin. "What do you need us to do?"

"Everyone get their phones out." Mike fiddled with the controls. He flipped a pair of switches. Green lights flashed, and the machine beeped. "Okay, how many bars?"

"Zero," the girls replied in unison.

"Four bars here." Jerry raised his phone.

"Wait for it." Mike watched the readout on the jammer. "It can take a few seconds to update."

Jerry squinted at the screen. "Yep, no bars."

Mike flipped two more switches. "Now check your Wi-Fi."

Jerry tapped his phone. "No networks available."

"Same here." Darla tapped her phone screen.

"Ditto." Talia nodded.

Lucy stared at her phone. "There it is: no networks. Mike and Talia, you guys are geniuses!"

"This I know." Mike bowed.

"And he's so modest." Talia looped an arm around his waist and kissed him on the cheek.

Jerry leaned closer to look at the jammer. "Can it block all frequencies?"

"Not all. Visible light is EM radiation," Talia explained. "The same with microwaves. The jammer can't make things invisible or stop you from microwaving popcorn."

"And we wouldn't want it to. A jammer that operated on those frequencies would end up killing someone." Mike clutched at his throat like he was strangling himself. "Why the sudden interest?"

Jerry shrugged. "Just curious."

Mike flipped more toggles and depressed a series of buttons. He pulled out a Boy Scout compass and rotated the jammer almost ninety degrees. "Now the big test: range and direction. I want each of you to go outside and walk away from the dorm. Slowly, like a step every ten seconds. That will give your phones time to update. Jerry goes west. Talia to the east. Darla north, and Lucy south. Count how many steps before you regain a signal."

"Which way is north?" Talia looked out the window.

Darla pointed. "North is toward Knox Hall. East is straight out the main entrance. West is the other end of the building and takes you to the football stadium. South is toward the Student Center."

Talia gave her a puzzled look. "How do you know all that?"

"Didn't I ever tell you guys that my dad was an Army Ranger? He taught me all about orienteering. And he's got his very own qualifying course for boys who date me." Darla entwined her arm with Jerry's and pulled him closer.

"Really?" Jerry gulped.

Her eyes twinkled. "Prepare yourself for a week of backcountry camping in the snows of the Upper Peninsula. Hope you can start a fire with no matches."

Lucy pointed at the TV. "Isn't this the premise of a reality show?"

Darla burst out laughing. "Got me. The closest my dad ever came to serving was weekend marathon sessions of *Call of Duty 4*."

Jerry wagged his finger at Darla. "Someday, that sense of humor is going to get you in trouble."

"What kind of trouble?" Darla stepped forward, pressing her chin into his chest.

Jerry faked a serious look. "I'm sure I can think of something."

"Hey, hey." Mike waved his hands. "Knock it off with the weird flirting until after the test."

Lucy stared at her phone. "How far do we have to walk?"

"I set the jammer to block different distances depending on the direction. I don't want to influence you by telling you how far to expect. But it's quite a bit. I want to jam an area as large as all the lecture halls in the Gursky Building."

Jerry looked around the room. "Is there anything else we need to know?"

"Nope." Mike shook his head. "And thanks again for being part of technological history."

Lucy rolled her eyes. "Yeah, this is like being at Kitty Hawk with the Wright Brothers."

"Let's bounce." Darla led Jerry out the door, Lucy and Talia trailing them.

At the main entrance, Talia announced, "Time to split up. Keep a straight line as much as possible. Jerry, you'll have to loop around to the other side of the building, and approximate where the line runs. Like Mike said, take it slow. Ten Mississippis then another step. When you get both bars and Wi-Fi, head back to the room, and give the info to Mike."

Darla kissed Jerry. "Try not to get lost."

"I think I can manage." Jerry headed west around the north side of his dorm. He took a step. Counted ten Mississippis. Checked his phone. Another step. Another ten Mississippis. Deca-Mississippi? Check the phone. Step, Mississippis, phone.

When he reached the far side of the dorm, he moved south to where he guessed he was lined up with the jammer, then proceeded west. His path took him across Roosevelt Lane. As he stood in the middle of the street counting Mississippis, the circulator bus roared around the curve and screeched to a halt. The bus driver leaned on the horn. But Jerry stuck to the plan, not getting out of the way: step, count, phone.

When Jerry reached the other side of the street, the bus driver shouted a departing expletive. Gears ground, and the tailpipe coughed a cloud of black smoke.

Jerry was up to one hundred and twenty-seven steps. Mike wasn't kidding about jamming a wide area. Once Jerry figured out who was behind the bad luck, he hoped he could use the jammer to block their power at a distance. He'd need to ask Professor Harding more about how the magic worked and consult with Mike to see if he could make the technical changes.

Jerry glanced ahead and frowned. Miranda was approaching, phone in one hand, soft pretzel in the other. He didn't want to get into it with her again, and shielded his face, hoping she wouldn't recognize him.

Miranda scowled, annoyed at her phone. Jerry smiled; the jammer was hard at work. She took a bite from her pretzel, still staring at the phone, and stumbled.

Miranda held out her hands, dropping the phone and pretzel. She hit the ground hard. Jerry stood, watching, unsure what to do. Slowly, she climbed to her knees, a look of distress on her face. Something was wrong.

Jerry forgot about the jammer test and ran to her. "Miranda, are you okay?"

Miranda's face registered recognition, then anger. She opened her mouth to speak, but no words came.

"Miranda?" Jerry's heart raced. "Are you choking?"

Panic filled her eyes. She nodded aggressively, pointing to her throat.

Jerry punched 9-1-1 into his phone. The call didn't go through. No bars.

"Come on, stand up." Jerry lifted Miranda to her feet and dragged her to a bench. He propped Miranda against the back of the bench, stood behind her, and slipped his arms around her waist. With his hands under her rib cage, he made a fist and jerked his hands violently, twice, three times.

"Call 9-1-1!" Jerry yelled at a passing student.

The girl tapped on her phone.

"No!" Jerry shouted. "Phones don't work here. You have to get away, then call for help."

The girl responded with a puzzled look on her face and kept tapping her phone.

"What's going on?" A campus policewoman stopped her car, half on the street, half on the curb. She got out, leaving the door open.

"She's choking!" Jerry continued the Heimlich maneuver.

The cop looked at Miranda's face. "You've got to stop. She's unconscious. Lay her down." The cop pressed a button on her chest-mounted radio. "Dispatch, this is Charlie-Three. Request an ambulance to Roosevelt Lane near Darlington Dorm. Twenty-year-old female choking."

The radio crackled. "Roger, Charlie-Three. Ambulance to Roosevelt near Darlington."

Jerry laid Miranda on the grass.

"Back up," the cop ordered. She tilted Miranda's head back, checking for obstructions in her airway.

"I think it's the pretzel." Jerry pointed to the half-eaten snack on the sidewalk.

"Right." The cop gave two rescue breaths and began compressions.

Jerry counted the compressions out loud. When he reached thirty, the cop gave two more rescue breaths, then started compressions again.

Passing students gathered in a circle.

"What's wrong?"

"Did she have a heart attack?"

"I think that's the girl who's writing papers for the football team."

A few used phones to record the efforts of the policewoman.

The color drained from Miranda's face. Her lips now tinged blue. Two more rescue breaths. Thirty more compressions, but Jerry wasn't conscious of his counting. He felt like he was outside his body, watching himself, the policewoman, and Miranda on a video screen. His mind filled with images of Noah, unconscious and singed, on the floor of *The Chronicle*, Fallon's panicked cries, thunder roaring, the lights going out.

"Get back." The cop pushed Jerry, who fell backward onto the grass.

Two EMTs crouched over Miranda. Their ambulance parked diagonally on the street, red lights flashing. Another campus cop had arrived, and he ordered back the gaggle of students.

"You too," the second cop pointed his baton at Jerry.

Jerry stood halfway before his knees buckled. He fell to the sidewalk, jamming his shoulder.

From his vantage point, Jerry watched the EMT's cut away Miranda's shirt. A white bra contrasted against her deep tan. One of the EMTs swabbed the area between her neck and chest with a cotton ball. The other EMT used a scalpel to cut Miranda's skin. A trickle of blood ran down her neck to the grass.

Jerry's chest tightened. His hands felt odd, numb. He wanted to look away, be anywhere else, but found himself compelled to watch.

The second EMT pulled a plastic tube from a med kit and inserted the tube into the hole he had created.

Jerry's gag reflex kicked in. Chunks of bacon cheeseburger and French fries spewed from his mouth. His Coke too, the CO_2 bubbles fizzing on the sidewalk. His throat burned. He spit to rid the acid taste from his mouth.

His stomach convulsed again. More undigested lunch, followed by yellow fluid dripping from his mouth. His body shuddered. The heaving continued. The yellow fluid ran dry; he vomited up air.

The EMTs lifted Miranda onto a stretcher and loaded her into the ambulance. Sirens roared, tires squealed, and the ambulance raced away.

"You all right?" The lady cop put a hand on his shoulder.

Jerry rose to his knees and tried to speak, but he had no breath. He gave the cop a nod. His abdominal muscles ached. His head dizzy. He needed to calm down and get his breathing under control or he'd hyperventilate. With great effort, he crawled a few feet to a patch of grass and collapsed.

CHAPTER 24

"Where is Jerry?" Darla pulled back the blinds and peeked out the window.

"It's like *déjà vu* all over again." Mike threw up his hands.

Talia blew a purple bubble the size of a grapefruit and popped it with her fingernail. "And we can't call or text him, cause the jammer is doing its thing."

"Can't we kill the jammer, then call him?" Darla pointed at the copper box. "Jerry must have reached the edge of its range by now?"

Mike shook his head. "I will not risk invalidating my results just because Jerry is slacking off."

Lucy stood. "Do you guys still need me?"

Mike shook his head. "Your data checked out."

"Then I'm out of here." Lucy pantomimed addressing a golf ball, took a full swing, and shaded her eyes against an imaginary sun. "Three feet from the pin. Franklin Pierce is in for a world of hurt tomorrow morning."

"Good luck." Talia gave Lucy a thumbs up.

"Can you pick up more beer?" Darla mimicked chugging a can. "I think your boy Jim drank the last of it."

"You got it." Lucy saluted and walked out the door.

"Now what?" Mike sat at the table, watching the jammer.

"While we're waiting, I should check out Jerry's bedroom." Darla glanced in the direction of the hallway.

"Under the roommate code, I can't allow that."

"Why not?" Talia shrugged. "I was in there."

"That's completely different. You're not dating Jerry."

Darla peered down the hall. "Is there anything I need to prepare myself for?"

"Do you have a hazmat suit?" Talia shuddered.

"That bad?"

"See for yourself." Talia pointed. "Room on the left."

Mike held his hands in the air. "If Jerry objects, I'll say you two over-powered me."

Darla stood at the door to Jerry's room and closed her eyes. He had yet to disappoint her. She could handle a messy bedroom, but if he were an out-and-out slob, she'd rethink their relationship. She pushed opened the door, took one step in, cracked open her left eye, and breathed a sigh of relief. "Hilarious, Talia!"

A navy-blue blanket covered a well-made bed. No piles of dirty clothes or empty pizza boxes on the floor. The desk was neat and organized, a few yellow Post-it notes stuck to the monitor. Posters, mostly related to the Philadelphia Flyers, covered the far wall.

In the center hung a single framed movie poster: *The Outlaw Josey Wales*. Darla sighed. More Clint Eastwood. Hanging next to Clint was a top-heavy blonde spilling out of her orange bikini.

Darla inspected the only bookcase. Textbooks and required reading filled the top three shelves. The next shelf was devoted to paperback science fiction. The bottom shelf was filled with hardcover books on World War II, acquired mostly from used bookstores, judging by the stickers on the books' spines.

On the nightstand, Darla found a photo of Jerry and a woman. Darla couldn't help but grin. Jerry had to be twelve or thirteen, and he was posi-tively adorable. The woman had dark hair and friendly eyes. This must be Jerry's mom. Darla's heart sank.

How could Jerry deal with such a loss? If Darla lost her mom, she knew she couldn't keep it together.

Darla lay on the bed, staring at the ceiling, and recounting the last four days. Jerry was certainly cute. He had proven to be funny, clever, brave, and ambitious. Plus, he was a joy to tease. And he gave the most amazing foot rubs. Definitely a keeper. She nodded to herself, stood, and walked back to the common area.

Talia grinned. "Did he pass?"

"Uh huh. But I'm thinking a conversation about that Kate Upton poster is in order."

"If it solves the problem, I'll hang it in my room," Mike suggested.

Talia glared at him.

"Or maybe not." Mike smiled sheepishly.

Jerry burst through the door, red-faced and out of breath.

"Jerry! Where—"

"Turn it off! Turn it off!" Jerry ran to the jammer and flipped switches randomly.

Mike shoved him away from the table. "Dude, what are you doing?"

Jerry grabbed the jammer's electrical cord and yanked it out of the wall socket.

"Stop!" Mike shook Jerry by the shoulders.

Talia yelled, "Hey, this is a delicate piece of machinery! You can't just kill the power like that!"

Jerry broke Mike's grasp. "It's jamming all the calls."

"That's the idea," Mike agreed.

"*All* the calls. Including 9-1-1."

Mike frowned. "Oh, I hadn't considered that. But what are the odds that—"

"About one thousand percent. I was with Miranda. She was choking. But I couldn't call for help."

"Miranda? Our Miranda? What happened?"

"She tripped. I thought something was wrong. She couldn't speak. I gave her the Heimlich. But it didn't work. A campus cop came by and called for help. Then Miranda started turning blue..."

Darla grabbed Jerry's hand. "Come sit with me." She led him to the sofa.

Jerry held his head in his hands. "The EMTs had to stick a tube in Miranda's throat. They took her away in the ambulance."

"Someone should tell Busby," Mike suggested.

Talia and Darla looked at Mike.

"I guess that someone is me." He pulled out his phone. "I should go to the hospital. Talia, can you give me a lift?"

"Sure, let's roll." Talia grabbed her purse and backpack. "Darla?"

She put her hand on Jerry's shoulder. "I'm staying here."

Mike and Talia raced out the door.

Jerry's body shook. "I tried to save her, but I couldn't."

"It's okay, Jerry." Darla put an arm around him.

"It's *not* okay! Don't you see? I can't stop my friends from dying. No one believes me. No one's safe. I don't know what to do."

"We're safe. We have our rabbit's feet. Nothing is going to happen to me or you."

"According to Professor Harding, it's not enough." Jerry blew out his breath. "Everyone's going to die, and I don't know how to prevent it. Noah, Cassie, Vince, Miranda." He seemed on the verge of tears, but sucked in his breath and held it back.

Darla looped her other arm around Jerry and pulled close. In his ear, she whispered, "Don't talk or think about that stuff. Just hold me. That's all you need to do right now."

"Okay." He squeezed her and buried his face in the crook of her neck.

"It's going to be all right." She ran her hands up and down his back.

Darla held him for five solid minutes before he broke the embrace. Jerry made eye contact and forced a smile. "Thanks, I needed that."

"I said you'd feel much better. Go clean yourself up. And brush your teeth."

"Huh?"

"Your breath."

"Oh yeah. When they stuck that tube in Miranda, I threw up."

"Better than me. I would have passed out. Now go." She waved him away.

Jerry went to the bathroom, and Darla grabbed a Coke from the fridge and a glass of ice water for herself. She set them on the coffee table and waited on the sofa for Jerry.

He came back, sat down, and kissed Darla.

"Minty fresh. Much better." She handed him the Coke. "To settle your stomach. Don't guzzle. Tiny sips."

"Thanks again. I'm re-energized. Wait till you hear what I learned from Professor Harding."

"No." Darla crossed her arms.

"No?"

"Jerry, you're pushing yourself way too hard. You're emotionally and physically exhausted. How much sleep did you get last night?"

"Not much. I stayed up late doing research, and I had an early breakfast date with this hot cheerleader."

"Oh sure, blame it all on me." Darla pushed him in the chest. "Lie down."

"What?"

She pushed harder. "I told you to lie down."

Jerry gently reclined.

"All the way." She tossed the end cushions on the floor.

Jerry stretched out. His head and feet were propped uncomfortably on the sofa arms.

Darla shook her head. "Such a tall boy. Get up."

Jerry sat up. "Now what?"

She took him by the hand. "We'll have to use your bed." She pulled, but Jerry remained seated.

"You can't go into my bedroom."

Darla shrugged. "I've already been. Mike said it was okay."

"He did?"

"Come on." Darla pulled harder, and this time Jerry stood.

In the bedroom, Darla gathered up the blanket and hung it over Jerry's chair. They sat on the edge of the bed. Darla glanced at the photo on the nightstand. "Your mother was a lovely woman."

Jerry's eyes welled up. He fought back tears. "I miss her so much. Sorry."

Darla hugged him. "Don't ever apologize for loving your mom."

Jerry composed himself. Grabbed a tissue from the nightstand and blew his nose. He balled it up and launched it across the room; it bounced off the side of his desk into the trashcan. "Two points." He smiled weakly.

"Better?"

Jerry nodded.

She reached down, then tried to untie his shoelace. "Great, it's knotted."

"No problem." Jerry used the toe of each sneaker to slip off the heel, his shoes now half on. "Watch this." He flicked his right foot, and the sneaker tumbled through the air and landed on an empty spot on his bookshelf. He repeated the same motion with his left foot and the sneaker landed next to the other one.

"How much time did you waste practicing that?"

"It won me twenty bucks from Mike the first week we roomed together."

"Fantastic." Darla rolled her eyes, then slipped off her shoes. She put her hand on his chest and gently shoved. "Lie down."

"Darla, if you're suggesting what I think, now is not the proper time."

"Down." She pushed harder.

Jerry lay back, his head resting on the pillow, stretched out on the bed. He crossed his hands and placed them over his stomach.

"Nope. Arms at your side."

He lifted his head. "Why?"

"You'll see." Darla crawled onto the bed, pressing her body against Jerry. She looped one arm around his waist and rested her head sideways on his chest, ear over his heart. "I love tall boys, they're the perfect size."

"This is nice. Now what?"

"Now nothing. We're going to lie here. Not moving. Not talking. Not even thinking. No worries and no troubles. They don't exist. Just you and me. I can hear your heart. Feel it beating in your chest. We're going to be so still and silent that you can feel mine."

"Is this some kind of meditation?"

"This is what my mom did with me when I got frustrated with gymnastics. Take it from a family full of overachievers. Sometimes you have to zone out, or the stress will kill you."

"That makes sense."

"Good. Now stop talking."

The room became silent. The only noise was the occasional rattle from the heating vents or the passing shouts of students outside the window.

Darla lay there, her eyes closed, focused on the rhythm of Jerry's heart. Strong and determined. Jerry was full of ability and able to accomplish great things. And she'd be right there beside him to help.

Twenty minutes passed. Jerry's breathing became shallower, more relaxed. Darla lifted her head. The tension gone from his face and neck muscles, replaced with a hint of a smile.

"Jerry?" Darla whispered. "Are you awake?"

No answer.

Careful not to disturb her sleeping boy, Darla eased off the bed. She grabbed the blue blanket and tucked him in. She padded to the common area and grabbed her phone.

Darla texted Coach Nightlinger that her ankle would keep her out of practice. An acceptable white lie under the circumstances. Her phone chirped.

> Talia: miranda's alive. they're checking for brain damage

> Darla: i'll say a prayer for her

She returned to the bedroom. Darla couldn't help but smile at the peacefully napping Jerry. She framed the bed with her phone, snapped a photo, uploaded to Instagram, and captioned it: *My Sweet Sleeping Boy.*

Three sharp raps at the door. Darla rushed to answer before the pounding woke Jerry. She opened the door to a campus police officer.

The cop's eyes flicked down for a moment, taking in Darla's legs.

Ugh, really? The ends of her mouth turned down into a frown.

"Gerald Williams?" the cop inquired.

"Jerry?" Darla answered in a loud whisper. She raised a finger to her lips. "He's asleep."

The cop didn't modulate his voice. "Give him this when he wakes up." He thrust a folded piece of paper into Darla's hand.

Before she could berate him, the cop turned and departed. Darla closed the door and unfolded the paper.

From the Office of the Chancellor of Van Buren University
The University's Emergency Management Committee

requires the presence of
Gerald K. Williams SID# 556-42-0826
to give testimony and information on matters concerning the safety and well-being
of the student body and staff. The Committee Meeting will take place in Room 202
of Landon Hall on Tuesday, October 10th at 11am. Your appearance is mandatory.

CHAPTER 25

Jerry climbed the marble steps to the second floor of Landon Hall. Both Mike and Darla offered to accompany him for moral support, but he told them no. If things didn't go as Jerry planned, he didn't want his friends to suffer retribution.

He pushed open the heavy oak door and walked down the deserted hallway. Outside room 202, a solitary figure sat on a bench. At the sound of Jerry's approaching footsteps, she lifted her head.

Fallon!

She wore an unbuttoned flannel green-and-red checkered shirt over a black tee, jeans, and Timberlands. She glared at Jerry over the rims of her glasses. Fallon was the last one Jerry expected to sell out. All her talk about sticking it to the establishment was empty rhetoric.

She read his original article connecting Cassie, Noah, and Vince's deaths to bad luck. And she was here, no doubt, to tell the committee all about it. Jerry glanced around for Vanessa. He suspected she'd arrive shortly. But the committee playing was an old game. Whatever Fallon and Vanessa had to say was irrelevant. Jerry was ready to drop the world's biggest reverse card.

He powered up his phone. Last night, he emailed Sam about his appearance before the committee. Still no reply.

Jerry: ready to face the fire

Darla: good luck! i'm so proud of you

Jerry's throat tightened. He'd only known Darla five days. Four-and-a-half, really. But in that time, she'd proven that she knew him better than he knew himself. She'd been supportive in a way that neither Busby, nor any other girl he'd dated, had been. He was determined to prove Darla's faith in him was not misplaced.

Perhaps the most improbable part of their relationship was that her looks really didn't matter to him. Jerry chuckled to himself. Let's not go overboard, Darla was a knockout. He recalled the way she pulled her body tight against his, her soft kisses on his neck, the way she slid her tongue—

"Hey!" A campus police officer held the door to room 202 open. "They're ready for you."

A single table with two folding chairs and two microphones were set up at the far left end of the room. On the far right was a dais where the six members of the committee sat. Jerry had met the chancellor and the police chief. The athletic director he knew. He didn't recognize the other three.

Jerry looped his backpack over the empty chair and sat. He ignored Fallon, refusing to make eye contact.

Dr. Thornton-Gaston gaveled the meeting to order. "Mr. Williams and Ms. Ahern, so nice of you to join us today." Her voice, amplified by her microphone, echoed through the conference room.

"As if we had a choice," Fallon protested.

Jerry suppressed a smirk. Fallon: Always bringing the attitude.

"Let's skip the formalities. Ms. Ahern, could you please tell us what you know about the website called *The Underground*?"

Fallon pointed at the dais. "May I at least know who my inquisitors are?"

Dr. Thornton-Gaston sighed. "I assume you know who I am. To my left are Captain George Characopus, Campus Police Chief; and Don Gehring, Athletic Director. On my right are Maureen Stepanian, University Counsel;

Julie Fredericton, Director of Media Relations; and Rodney Case, Chief Information Officer."

Fallon stood. "Fallon Ahern, Class of '26. Arts and Entertainment Critic for *The Chronicle* and winner of this year's Adirondack Area Golden Reviewer Award. All press, not only college media, are eligible. And I beat the lot of them." She bowed and sat.

"Congratulations, Ms. Ahern." The chancellor's voice was filled with undisguised contempt. "What can you tell us about *The Underground*?"

"I check it out from time to time. They have decent movie reviews. But I'm having trouble accessing their website." Fallon held up her phone. "Does anyone here know about that?"

Jerry chuckled at Fallon's theatrics. But what was she up to? She wasn't playing the role of friendly witness.

"We'll be asking the questions this morning, Ms. Ahern. Do you write for *The Underground*? Movie reviews or otherwise?"

"I already stated that I'm the Arts & Culture Critic for *The Chronicle.*"

"Which doesn't answer my question and doesn't prevent you from writing for *The Underground*."

Fallon let out an exaggerated sigh. "I'm not sure why your question is relevant. Van Buren is a state school and constrained by the First Amendment."

"The First Amendment is not absolute," the chief argued. "It doesn't give you the right to shout *'fire'* in a crowded theater."

"I can't believe you actually made that reference." Fallon groaned. "Does anyone here know the actual case behind that?" She glared at the University's Counsel. "It's *Schenk v. The United States*, which isn't even relevant law any longer. The controlling case is *Brandenberg v. Ohio*. But getting back to Schenk, here's the too-long, didn't-read version. Schenk distributed pamphlets encouraging people to resist the draft during World War I. For some crazy reason, he thought it was a bad idea to conscript young men and ship them overseas to be killed or horribly mutilated in the no-man's-land of a misguided war of imperialism whose true purpose was to line the pockets of the munitions' manufacturers. And for the audacity of trying to save these men's lives, the government locked him up.

"This was not about a false claim of danger in crowded conditions that could result in bodily harm or death. And the articles that appear in *The*

Underground aren't threatening to create the conditions of an out-of-control stampede. They are responsible reporting that upset the powers-that-be, as all good journalism should."

"Thank you for the history lesson, Ms. Ahern." The chancellor looked to her right. "Rodney, do you want to take over?"

The CIO cleared his throat and read from his laptop. "Ms. Ahern, at ten forty-seven yesterday morning, routine monitoring of the campus network detected a secure file transport protocol connection from your laptop to a host that we've tentatively identified as belonging to *The Underground*. Would you care to comment?"

Jerry's jaw slipped open. Fallon wasn't here to rat him out. The university was after her.

Fallon shook her head in mock disbelief. "You're tracking students like you're the Stasi, and we're living in East Germany during the sixties?"

Case sat up straighter. "The university has the right and responsibility to manage its network. Our proactive scans serve to enhance the student experience and protect their privacy."

Fallon laughed. "You're good. You sound like you actually believe that."

The chancellor leaned toward her microphone. "Answer the question, Ms. Ahern."

"Computers make mistakes all the time." Fallon shrugged. "Last month, my grandfather turned sixty-five. The government mailed him one hundred and eleven Medicare cards. Not one of them had his name on it."

"We are quite sure about our results." The CIO tapped the side of his laptop. "We've checked and double-checked."

"Look, even if your spying *is* legal, and your scanning program *is* accurate, that doesn't mean *I* connected to this mystery server. My girlfriend uses my laptop. So does my roommate."

"Enough with the obfuscations, Ms. Ahern," the chancellor demanded. "Are you writing for *The Underground*? Yes or no?"

Fallon crossed her arms. "You don't have the right to ask that question, and I'm certainly not going to answer it."

"Very well. We can only conclude from your lack of denials that you are contributing to *The Underground*."

"I think we need another history lesson. This time on the McCarthy Era."

Jerry stood. "Can I say something here?"

"You'll have your chance, Mr. Williams." The chancellor glared at him.

"You want to know who's writing for *The Underground*? It's me. I admit it freely."

The chancellor relaxed in her seat. "That's quite a turnaround from Saturday."

"The circumstances have changed."

She consulted her laptop. "To be clear, Mr. Williams, you admit to being the author of the articles entitled: 'Three Student Deaths Tied to Bad Luck', 'Fast Running Parking Meters: The Administration Cover-up', and 'Stadium Light Tower Collapse Results in Fourth Death Tied to Bad Luck'?"

"Yes, all mine."

"Very mature of you, Mr. Williams. We'll want you to write retractions for all three articles. They'll be published in *The Chronicle*, on the university's website, and distributed to local media."

"Hold on!" Jerry raised a hand. "I'm not retracting anything. I stand by all I've written. Friday the 13th is three days away, and we can expect more deaths related to bad luck unless we find the perpetrator. That's the reason I'm here, why I admitted to everything. I can't do it alone. I need the university's help."

"You cannot be serious." Fredericton rolled her eyes.

Jerry pounded the table. "It's all documented. Read my stories. It all goes back to a series of deaths that happened on campus in 1984. I've done the research, interviewed witnesses. It's all real."

"This is exactly the kind of fear-mongering that will cause a panic on campus. Mr. Williams, you have one last chance to change your mind." The chancellor glared at him.

"I've laid out the facts. I'm willing to help, share all that I know. But the administration has the ultimate responsibility to keep students, faculty, and staff safe. That won't happen if you ignore what I've discovered."

"George, cut his microphone."

Jerry's voice stopped booming. He picked up Fallon's mike. "You can't silence me!"

The chief cut the other mike.

"We've heard enough." The chancellor wrote on her notepad. "I make a motion that Ms. Ahern and Mr. Williams be placed on suspension, effective immediately. They'll be allotted six hours to gather their personal belongings and depart campus. They're not to return until reinstated by this committee."

"You can't do this!" Fallon yelled.

Jerry cupped his hands to his mouth. "You're going to get more people killed!"

"Do I hear a second?" The chancellor glanced around at the committee.

"Seconded." The athletic director raised his hand.

"Maureen, please call the yeas and nays."

The counsel grabbed a pen. "Mr. Gehring?"

"Aye."

"Ms. Fredericton?"

"Yes."

"Chief Characopus?"

"Aye."

"Mr. Case?"

"Yes."

The counsel scribbled on her sheet. "I vote in the affirmative. Dr. Thornton-Gaston?"

"Aye."

"By a vote of six—"

"Stop, stop, stop! You must halt these proceedings immediately!"

All eyes turned to a fifty-something man who stood at the open door. He had salt-and-pepper hair, a droopy face, and wore an ill-fitting suit.

"This is a closed meeting," the chief snapped.

"Certainly not closed to legal counsel." The man shuffled into the room.

"Whoever you are, there is no need for counsel." The chancellor glared. "This is not an adversarial process. It's a fact-finding committee."

"The name is Alan Berg. And a fact-finding committee that's about to suspend my clients? Sounds pretty adversarial to me."

"You're too late, Mr. Berg. You can have a conversation with the university's counsel after the meeting concludes. But your clients' fates are sealed."

"Not so fast." Berg shuffled toward the dais. "Forgive my slow gait, I'm recovering from hemorrhoid surgery."

The chief information officer's face scrunched up in disgust.

"Oops, was that too much information?" Berg dropped a sheaf of papers in front of each member of the committee.

"What is this?" Case squinted at the pile in front of him.

"Copies of a temporary restraining order issued by Judge Lois Huberty of the United States District Court for Northern New York prohibiting Van Buren University, its officers, employees, contractors, or anyone else in a position of authority from taking any disciplinary actions against my clients."

The chancellor looked to the counsel. "Maureen?"

The counsel glanced at the papers. "It appears legit."

Dr. Thornton-Gaston drummed her fingers. "The judge says we can't zig, then we'll zag. A conversation with Mr. Williams and Ms. Ahern's instructors wouldn't result in any *disciplinary* action but could prove most unfortunate for their GPAs."

"I would advise against such threats." Berg tapped his briefcase. "Judge Huberty is notorious for enforcing not just the letter of her orders, but also the spirit."

"Janelle, this only holds things up until I can get into court." The counsel shuffled the papers. "I'll work on a brief this afternoon. I'm sure I can convince the judge that the university has to be permitted wide latitude when dealing with disciplinary issues."

Berg sized up the counsel. "You seem a worthy adversary, Ms..."

"Stepanian."

"I look forward to meeting you in court, Ms. Stepanian. Nothing like a good legal battle to get the old ticker wound up." Berg thumped his chest, then addressed the chancellor. "Since the purpose of the committee's meeting is now moot, I'll collect my clients." Berg trudged to the table where Jerry and Fallon stood in wide-eyed amazement.

"What just happened?" Fallon shook her head in disbelief.

Jerry pointed at Berg. "Why are you helping us?"

Berg leaned forward. "Not here." He shuffled out of the room with Fallon and Jerry in tow.

In the hallway, Berg stopped. "Can we take the elevator? I'm really not in condition for the steps."

Fallon shrugged. "Sure."

"Mr. Berg, please—"

"Patience, young man. All will be revealed."

The three rode the elevator to the first floor. The doors slid open to reveal a waiting Sam. Same blue beret, but this time in an orange T-shirt with Alex Jones's face.

"Sam!" Jerry pointed at her. "This was all your doing?"

"Sam?" Fallon furrowed her brow. "She told me her name was Gretchen."

"Hi Rachel." Berg smiled.

Fallon and Jerry exchanged puzzled glances.

Sam/Gretchen/Rachel stepped forward and hugged Berg. "Hi Dad."

CHAPTER 26

TUESDAY 12:17PM

Darla: How did it go?

Jerry: Not suspended

Darla: Yay!

Darla: Meet for lunch?

Jerry: Can't. I'm in stuyvesant

Darla: ?

Jerry: At salad co-op

Darla: ?

Jerry: Fallon's a vegan

Darla: Who's Fallon?

Jerry: Long story. Tell you later

Jerry powered off his phone and shoved it in his pocket. He returned to the sidewalk table where Fallon, Rachel, and Alan Berg were sitting.

Fallon set down her water glass. "I want to say thanks one more time, Mr. Berg, for helping us out."

"Yeah, we appreciate the save." Jerry offered his hand, and Berg shook it.

"Not at all. It is I who should be thanking you." Berg removed his glasses, took out a handkerchief, and cleaned his lenses. "I can only defend crusaders for the First Amendment when someone is actually crusading. Fallon, Jerry, you are both to be applauded for your efforts at uncovering truths, fighting the system, and not backing down. I am honored that I could be of assistance."

"Well said, Dad." Rachel put her hand on his forearm.

"Wow, when you put it like that." Jerry straightened up in his seat.

Fallon looked around like someone might be eavesdropping, then lowered her voice. "How long will this restraining order protect us?"

"Ms. Stepanian, the University's Counsel, looks like she's spoiling for a fight. I would guess we'll be in court early next week. And now I really must run." He gulped the last of his coffee. "I'm due at the courthouse in fifteen minutes. Rachel, your mother would like it if you could come for dinner on Sunday evening."

She nodded. "I'll be there."

Berg stood, waved goodbye, and trundled to his car.

"Is your name really Rachel? Or did you give your dad a phony one too?" Fallon raised an eyebrow.

"Ha, ha. After your experience with the committee, I'd expect you'd have a greater appreciation for the benefits of anonymity."

Jerry leaned forward. "Speaking of anonymity, who wrote *The Underground* exposés about Miranda Sanchez writing papers for the football team and Rick Tilden being drunk when he had his accident?"

Rachel's eyes flicked to Fallon, then back to Jerry. "I can't answer that. All my reporters' identities are secret."

"Could you at least confirm to my friends that I'm not the author? They feel like I betrayed them."

Rachel sighed. "I don't want to get into the habit—"

"I did it," Fallon confessed. "Those articles are mine."

"You? Thanks a bunch, Fallon!"

"What's your problem, Jerry? Thursday night in *The Chronicle's* break room, you told me that a good reporter goes where the story leads and doesn't let their personal opinions or circumstances get in the way."

"Yeah, but—"

"But when it looks bad for *your* friends, then getting the truth out isn't so important, is it?"

Jerry looked at Rachel. "Fallon's admitted to being the author. Can we please tell my friends and clear this up?"

"Actually, I'm thinking at this point our anonymity is shot. The chancellor isn't stupid. She knows you two write for us. Now that my dad stepped in, they'll figure out I'm involved. With the protection of the restraining order and the likely risk of bad PR to Van Buren if they move against us, it might make sense to reveal ourselves to the world at this point."

Fallon beamed. "Like one big coming out party."

"I'll check with the other contributors, but you guys have no problems if I slap bylines on all your work?"

"I'm on board." Jerry nodded.

"Go for it," Fallon agreed.

The waitress dropped off their orders: a Greek salad with almond cheese instead of feta for Fallon, nine vegetable soup for Rachel, and a garden salad for Jerry.

Jerry picked through his lunch, eating all the tomatoes first. "You know, Fallon, we could have gone to Hot Dog King. They have tofu dogs."

Fallon jabbed her fork at Jerry. "Which they would have cooked on the same rollers as your regular hot dog. Do you want me to explain in nauseating detail the manufacturing process for turning pink slime and meat slurry into what they claim is food?"

"Hey, I'm trying to eat here," Rachel protested.

"Or how much energy and water are required to raise a pound of meat? A salad is much better for your health and the health of the world."

Jerry held up his hands defensively. "Forget I mentioned it."

Fallon checked her phone. "Huh, *The Underground* is back up."

"It's always been up." Rachel set down her fork.

"Then why couldn't I get it to load this morning at the committee meeting?"

"The U is blocking access via their network. Inserting their own DNS records so it redirects to *The Chronicle*. If you switch to your data plan while on campus, you're good. My dad's looking into a separate lawsuit. In the meantime, my nerds are executing a workaround."

"Nerds?" Fallon picked at her salad.

"*The Underground* technical staff. A couple of guys, or rather one guy and one girl, who can out whiz whatever campus IT throws at them."

"Gender equity." Fallon grinned. "That's excellent."

Jerry dropped into his radio announcer's voice. "Another blow against the patriarchy, but first, the stock report." He raised a clenched fist. "We should focus on the bigger problem. The administration doesn't believe me or what's happening. Can I count on you two? I need all the help I can get if I'm going to stop this by Friday."

"Friday?" Rachel repeated. "What's so special about Friday?"

"Friday is the 13th. No one on campus will be safe."

Fallon furrowed her brow. "Safe from what? I'm still not sure what's happening."

"Here's what I know." Jerry leaned forward. "Back in 1984, a justifiably angry and hurt student named Peggy Johnson sought out a witch who taught her how to tap into magic or bad luck, which she used for her revenge. But the power proved too great, spinning out of control. People died. The same thing is happening again."

"Witches? Magic? That's wild." Rachel shook her head in disbelief.

"Not at all." Fallon leaned forward. "It's a natural result of marginalized women trying to fight back against their oppressors."

"Can we put a hold on the politics until after the crisis is averted?" Jerry stabbed a piece of lettuce.

Fallon poked a banana pepper with her fork. "Funny how there's always a reason the fight for justice has to be delayed."

"Let's focus." Rachel dabbed her mouth with her napkin. "Jerry, what did Peggy want revenge for?"

"She was raped by three football players. The team, the school, and the Sheriff's Department all covered it up."

Fallon huffed. "Why am I not surprised?"

"And now?" Rachel pointed. "Peggy Johnson is back?"

Jerry shook his head. "No, she died back in '84, but the pattern is the same. We have to figure out who it is. I'm thinking it's someone who has a grudge against the football team. Everyone who's died so far has a connection to the team."

"Someone who hates football?" Fallon rolled her eyes. "That will *really* narrow down the list."

"Another angle, but a long shot, is Peggy's younger brother Mark. I'd like to track him down and see what he can tell me about his sister."

"There's a Professor Mark Johnson here at VBU." Fallon's eyes filled with excitement.

"Wait, what?"

"Yeah, he teaches geology. My girlfriend is in his class, and she told me that yesterday he did this big production with superstitions in class. Black cat, broken mirrors, the whole bit."

Jerry scribbled in his notebook. "That's too much of a coincidence."

"And get this. At the end of the class, no one would volunteer to walk under a ladder. So, he did it himself. Lights went out. There was a gigantic crash and when the lights came back on: No professor."

"What do you mean, *no professor*?" Rachel furrowed her brow.

"The lights came back on and like that...he's gone." Fallon raised her fingers to her lips and blew.

"Really, Kevin Spacey?" Jerry rolled his eyes.

"Then what happened?" Rachel leaned forward.

Fallon shrugged. "She said it was the end of class. Most of the students shuffled out like the drones that they are."

Rachel stared at Fallon and sighed.

"Let's be real, that's what most of them are. The only reason Vicky's in that class is 'cause she needs three science credits."

Jerry pointed at Fallon. "What do *you* think happened to Professor Johnson?"

"To be honest, when I heard about this, I thought it was a gag. I sat in for a lecture once. Professor Johnson is a real eccentric. Overexaggerated pronunciation. Overworked vocabulary. The whole bit. But now, I'm not so sure. Class is Mondays and Thursdays. Guess, we'll find out in two days."

Rachel tapped on her phone. "According to his Van Buren bio, this is Professor Johnson's first semester teaching here. Before that, he was at Oregon State and Central Oklahoma University. Did his undergrad and got his doctorate at McGill." She showed Fallon and Jerry a photo of the professor, an average looking white man in his fifties with a touch of gray in his thinning dark hair.

"Doesn't prove if it's him one way or the other." Jerry said.

"No, it *is* him." Rachel tapped away at her phone. "This Mark Johnson. Mark C. Johnson to be exact, was born in Stuyvesant and had an older sister named Margaret, or Peggy. And he lives in East Stuyvesant."

Fallon pointed at Rachel's phone. "You figured all that out just sitting here?"

"Databases. The world's full of them. Why do think I'm so paranoid about privacy? The professor lives at 226 Wolfe Street."

Jerry gulped the rest of his Coke. "Let's finish up lunch, then we can swing by and do some investigating."

Fallon shook her head. "It will have to be the two of you in the Mystery Mobile. I've got Gender, Power, and International Development class at one."

"Yeah, wouldn't want to miss that."

Rachel typed the address into Waze. "That actually works. We can drop you off. The U is on the way to the professor's place.

Jerry pulled his car into the Student Center parking lot.

Fallon opened the rear door. "Thanks for the lift. After class, I'll swing by Professor Johnson's office, then text you anything I learn."

"Good luck." Rachel waved bye.

Fallon slipped out of the car and walked toward East Campus.

Rachel turned to Jerry. "What about your other theory? Someone who hates the football team?"

"The problem is where can we find a list of s—Damn!" Jerry reached for his backpack.

"What?"

"The list! I forgot that Professor Harding gave me this list of students who signed up for her class."

"Who's Professor Harding?"

"Didn't I tell you? She's the witch. She gave me the info about Peggy and introduced her to magic."

Rachel shook her head. "You skipped where you got the information."

"Anyway, this past spring, Professor Harding taught A Survey of Magic Systems. One student, a girl, asked her about learning about luck and real magic. The professor didn't remember her name but gave me a list of students who took the class. Maybe between your nerds and your data-bases, you can narrow it down. Cross off anyone who graduated, dropped out, transferred, or is studying abroad." Jerry fished the paper out of his backpack and handed it to Rachel.

"There's got to be fifty names here."

"We can knock out the half who are guys."

Rachel scanned the list. "More like a quarter. Looks like interest in magic skews female."

"Fallon would be pleased."

"You can say that again."

"What do you mean?"

Rachel held up the list and pointed to the first name.

AHERN, FALLON G. - SID #247-91-9715

CHAPTER 27

J erry drove down the street of identical looking houses. "I still can't get my head around the idea that Fallon could be behind this. It's nuts. Or is it? She certainly has it in for the football team."

Rachel squinted at the house numbers. "She's one possibility. Assuming whoever approached Professor Harding is responsible for all the deaths."

"Maybe." Jerry rubbed his chin. "It's weird that Fallon didn't act too shocked when I brought magic up at lunch."

"And she *did* bring up Professor Johnson. Is he a red herring? Are we off on a wild goose chase?"

"Nice mixed metaphors. But there's one way to find out."

"This is it." Rachel pointed to a two-story white house with a front porch and detached garage. The white paint looked fresh, possibly less than a year old. The lawn was free of weeds, but the grass needed mowing.

Jerry pulled over and leapt from his car. "Come on." He led the way up the walk to the front door.

Rachel pressed the doorbell.

Jerry opened the screen door and slammed the brass knocker three times. "First thing they teach you about delivering pizzas: Don't use the bell, you never know if it's broken."

"Have you thought about what you're going to ask Professor Johnson?"

"I'm not going to accuse him of anything. Just inquire about the recent events on campus and judge his responses. See if he's helpful or if it appears that he's hiding something." He banged the knocker again.

Rachel pressed her face against the sidelights to the left of the door and shielded her eyes. "I don't think anyone's home."

Jerry peeked in the black mailbox to the side of the front door and pulled out a flyer for Comcast. "One piece of junk mail. Probably delivered today."

"Careful. Taking someone else's mail is a federal offense."

Jerry returned the flyer. "Let's try around back."

They followed the asphalt driveway past two trash cans, one half-filled with recyclable plastic bottles, to the garage.

Jerry peered through a garage window. "Lawn mower, but no car. And nothing magical. At least nothing that looks magical to me."

Rachel climbed two brick steps to the nine-light back door and knocked. "Door leads to the kitchen. Don't see any dishes on the breakfast table or the counter."

"Hello, there!" Jerry tapped on a window to the left of the door.

A gray-and-white cat sleeping on the sill woke, yawned, and stretched.

"Aren't you a pretty girl?" Jerry continued tapping, but the cat leapt to the floor and disappeared from view. "This has proven worthless."

Rachel shrugged. "Not completely. The cat proves the professor, or someone, lives here."

"I guess. But I wanted something, anything, that would tell us if we're on the right track. If I could see what books he owns or sneak a look at his computer, that might help." Jerry jiggled the doorknob. "I wonder if we could—"

"Stop right there." Rachel held up her hand. "You're not thinking about breaking in, are you? Because I don't have 'commit felony burglary' on my to-do list."

"No." Jerry lied. He was already contemplating returning tonight, alone. If Professor Johnson were home, great, Jerry would ask his questions. Otherwise, he'd slip inside and poke around.

"If we're done here, let's get back to campus. I need to talk to the rest of *The Underground* about the bylines and get my nerds to run down that list of students you gave me."

They headed back to the front of the house. Jerry ripped a page from his notebook and scribbled a note, asking the professor to contact Jerry. He included his number and email and slipped the note under the knocker.

"What are you kids up to? You need a permit to solicit in this town."

Jerry and Rachel turned to see an older man, maybe in his seventies, wearing a dark-blue sweatshirt and matching sweatpants on the sidewalk. The man held a leash with a Jack Russell terrier struggling at the other end.

"We're not selling anything." Jerry raised his hands to show they were empty. "We're looking for Professor Johnson. Have you seen him?"

The man sniffed. "And who are you?"

"Students from Van Buren."

"You kids should stay on campus. You come into town and cause nothing but trouble."

"This isn't going well," Rachel muttered to Jerry. She walked up to the pup, knelt, and patted his head. "Who's a good boy? What's your name?"

"It's Milo." The dog owner softened his tone.

"Such a good boy, Milo." Rachel continued to pet the dog. "Is he named for the Jack from *The Mask?*"

The old man smiled. "That's very good. I'm surprised you know that reference."

"I'm a big fan of Jim Carrey, the early years anyway. I'm sorry I don't have a treat for such a handsome boy."

"Well, we don't want to spoil him, do we? I'm Tom Rodgers, by the way."

"Nice to meet you, Mr. Rodgers. I'm Rachel Berg, and that's my friend Jerry Williams. Have you seen Professor Johnson lately? He hasn't been on campus."

Rodgers shook his head. "I haven't seen Mark much at all since he came back."

"Came back?"

"Yes, he's been gone ever since high school. This was his parents' house. They retired to Florida this past summer, and Mark moved in early

August. I talked to him once or twice. Terrible about what happened to his sister. Even after all these years."

Rachel nodded. "Thanks for your time, Mr. Rodgers."

"Not at all." He gave the leash a jerk, pulling Milo down the walk.

Rachel waved goodbye to the dog.

Jerry walked up to her. "Nice job. At least we learned something."

"You just have to know how to talk to people."

"Or talk to dogs, but I'm more of a cat person." Jerry spun three-sixty, taking in the neighborhood, making mental notes for his return that night. "I'll take you back to Van Buren."

Jerry pulled off the state highway onto the campus and headed toward his dorm.

"Actually, I'm in Buckley Hall." Rachel pointed to the right.

"We should swing by my place first." Jerry continued to drive.

"Why's that?"

"Rabbit's feet."

"Rabbit's what?"

"Rabbit's feet. You know, for luck." He pointed to the furry orange oval hanging from his keys. "My roommate has a whole supply. Professor Harding said they'd provide limited protection for now. We should get you one to be safe."

"Thanks. I've published a lot of weird stuff in *The Underground*. I guess believing in magic and bad luck isn't all that crazy."

Jerry parked, and they walked to his room. Inside, they found Mike and Talia fussing over the jammer. Mike wore a gold polo shirt and khakis. Talia had on a long-sleeved, white crop-top, aqua leggings, and black sneakers.

Mike pointed an accusing finger at Jerry. "Stay away from the jammer. We've almost fixed all the damage that you've done."

"Yeah, I wanted to talk to you about that." Jerry sat on the couch, and Rachel took a seat next to him.

"What did you want to talk about?" Talia crossed her arms and stared down at Jerry. "Something along the lines of an apology would be nice."

"Look guys, I *am* sorry about yesterday. I was a bit out of control, but I think it's understandable considering the circumstances."

"*A bit?*" Talia raised an eyebrow.

"Knowing Jerry, that's probably the best apology we can expect." Mike looked at Jerry. "What's up? How did the meeting with the committee go?"

"Rachel's dad got a restraining order against the school. They can't touch me for a week. Hopefully, I can solve everything before then."

Mike high-fived Jerry. "That's great. But who's Rachel?"

Rachel raised her hand. "I am."

Mike scrunched up his face. "Oh, right. The made-up name."

Jerry pulled out his keys and let the rabbit's foot dangle. "The reason I brought Rachel by is to pick up a rabbit's foot for her. She's a friend, so please don't price gouge her."

"Can't help you." Mike shook his head. "We're all out."

"But you bought Five Below's entire inventory."

"And people are freaked." Talia made a frazzled face. "Especially with what happened to Miranda yesterday. We got mobbed in the SC at breakfast. Should have raised the price to twenty-five dollars."

Mike wrapped an arm around Talia's waist, pulled her close, and kissed her on the cheek. "That's my entrepreneurial gal."

The image of Miranda choking flashed in Jerry's mind. "How is she?"

"They let her out of the hospital this morning. No brain damage, but according to Dmitri, she's going to have a nasty scar where they tubed her."

Jerry shuddered at the memory of the tracheotomy. "Back to the jammer. I wanted to ask you about its capabilities."

"What does it matter?" Mike let out a deep breath. "You pointed out the flaw in the plan: emergency calling. No business will risk installing one. It's a mega-lawsuit waiting to happen. I'll have to make my billions elsewhere."

"Our billions." Talia hugged Mike. "For now, it's going to serve as my class project for Electrical Engineering 3010."

Jerry pointed at the jammer. "Yesterday, you talked about all the frequencies you can block. Is there a way to block the maximum amount of frequencies?"

"Maximum amount of frequencies?" Mike furrowed his brow. "I'm not sure what

"You're the engineer. I don't know the lingo." Jerry shrugged. "Professor Harding says that magic is propagated along lines of force, something similar to electromagnetic radiation. Water seems to block it. That's why they used to dunk witches. Yesterday, whatever you were blocking wasn't enough. Miranda was in range of the jammer. Her phone wasn't working, but the bad luck still got her. And the cop's radio worked. What I'm asking is if you can try to block as many frequencies as possible, to protect us from the bad luck?"

"A magic-jamming jammer?" Talia laughed. "*That* should be my class project!"

Rachel looked at the others. "This is the most bizarre conversation I've had in a while."

Mike tapped the jammer case. "We can certainly broaden the range of affected frequencies. But I have no idea if that would help. It sounds so fantastical."

Talia nodded. "And I'm not sure I really believe in magic and bad luck, but whatever is going on, I doubt it's operating between nine hundred million and three billion cycles per second like microwaves or we'd have reports of nearby burns when people died."

Mike looked at Talia with awe. "God, I love your brain."

She kissed Mike on the cheek. "Jerry, did you see anything weird when Miranda was choking?"

"I don't think so. And I don't remember anything odd when Noah died."

"I'm thinking about what Professor Harding told you about water and magic. Water is transparent to light. Pretty sure whatever is happening, it's not operating along the visual light spectrum. But we couldn't block it, anyway. If we came up with a method, they'd give us a Nobel Prize. Did the professor give you any more information on how this magic supposedly works?"

Jerry shook his head. "I didn't ask her any specifics because I didn't get the idea of using the jammer until we ran the test yesterday. After I drop Rachel off at her dorm, I'll swing by the professor's office and find out all she knows."

Talia nodded. "Tell us what you learn, and we'll make the adjustments."

"Is that thing portable?" Rachel pointed at the jammer.

"No." Mike shook his head.

Rachel sighed. "Too bad. 'Cause unless whoever is behind this decides on a confrontation in your dorm, I'm not sure how helpful the jammer will be."

Mike flipped a pair of switches. "We can block some frequencies up to two hundred and fifty feet. But you have a good point."

Talia's eyes danced back and forth as she puzzled out the problem. "We could add an inverter. Run it off direct current, like a car's USB port. Add a battery."

"Sounds like another trip to Electronics Supply Hut." Mike pulled out his wallet, looked into it, and frowned. "I'm almost out of start-up capital. I hope this is worth it."

Talia caressed the copper case. "A magic-jammer could be the answer for making money. We could sell to people who think their house is haunted or that they're under some sort of curse. Even use it for ghost hunting and star in our own cable reality show."

"I like the way you think." Mike kissed her again on the cheek.

"I'll drive." Talia grabbed her purse. "Jerry, let us know as soon as you talk to Professor Harding."

Jerry nodded. "Will do."

Mike and Talia were a few paces short of the door when Darla, out of breath, wearing a maroon blouse and gray slacks, burst in.

Mike jabbed a finger at her. "I know you're dating Jerry and all, but do you want to knock first?"

Darla ignored Mike. "Jerry, I've been trying to get a hold of you. Is your phone off again?"

"Sorry." Jerry shrugged, pulled out his phone, and powered it on. "What did you need to tell me?"

"It's Professor Harding." The blood drained from Darla's face. "She's dead."

CHAPTER 28

Yellow police tape, guarded by uniformed officers, cordoned off the Whitmore Building. Vehicles from the Stuyvesant County Sheriff's Department, the Coroner's Office, VBU Campus Police, and the local ambulance company were scattered like confetti across the sidewalk. Fifty students milled about, recording the spectacle on their phones.

Jerry spotted the chancellor and the police chief near the building entrance. Dr. Thornton-Gaston was sitting in the passenger seat of a golf cart. She pointed at Jerry. Characopus nodded and spoke into his radio mic.

"Let's find out what's happening." Jerry motioned for Rachel and Darla to follow. He walked away from the crowd and picked out a young campus cop, maybe twenty-five, far from the action. "Excuse me, Officer. I'm Jerry Williams with the school newspaper. Can I ask you a few questions about what happened?"

"Keep on that side of the tape, and I'll see what I can tell you."

"Thanks!" Jerry retrieved his notebook from his backpack. "What happened in there?" He motioned toward the building.

"It's still pretty preliminary, but it appears we have one deceased. White female in her seventies. The—"

"Kerkorian! Shut your trap!" Chief Characopus appeared out of nowhere, his belly bulging under his white dress shirt, and stepped between the officer and Jerry.

"Uh, sure. Sorry, Chief." Kerkorian lowered his head and stepped back.

Jerry adopted a conciliatory tone. "Chief Characopus, all I want—"

"Mr. Williams, this is your first, last, and only warning." The chief puffed out his chest and moved into Jerry's personal space. "Do not bother any of my officers or any other law enforcement, or I'll have you arrested for obstruction."

Jerry scrunched up his nose as he was engulfed by the chief's garlic breath.

"Is that clear?" The chief jabbed his finger into Jerry's chest.

Rachel stepped forward. "You try that, and we'll slap Van Buren, the campus police, and most importantly you, with a multi-million-dollar lawsuit so fast it'll make Usain Bolt look like a turtle with arthritis."

Characopus looked down his nose at Rachel. "And who is *we*, young lady?"

"My parents. They're both lawyers. You met my father, Alan Berg, earlier today. You saw what he can do. And my mom's twice as tough. I'm not bluffing."

Characopus frowned at Rachel. "Fine." He sneered at Jerry. "I'm watching you." He jabbed his finger at Kerkorian. "Don't say anything and keep them outside the line. If they cross the tape, arrest them." The chief glared at the trio of students, then shuffled off toward the chancellor in her golf cart. Jerry looked at Rachel. "Thanks for the save."

"Way to go, Sam!" Darla slapped her on the back.

"Actually, my name's Rachel."

Darla squinted at her. "Nope, you definitely look like a Sam to me."

Rachel ignored that. "Glad I could help, but it doesn't sound like we're going to get much official cooperation in finding out what happened."

"Let's spread out, talk to some students, and see if they heard anything." Jerry spotted Laurie Inverso from *The Chronicle* chatting with a deputy. "I may have a lead."

Laurie, in a white blouse and an olive ankle-length skirt, finished her conversation and walked in the opposite direction.

Jerry rushed after her. "Hold up, Laurie!"

She turned, shook her head, and laughed. "No way, Jerry. Vanessa told us you went over to the Dark Side."

"Relax Laurie, I'm not after a story for *The Underground*. I want to know what happened. The cops won't tell me anything."

"You're *persona non grata*. Vanessa would have my head if she knew I was even talking to you."

"You can't let Vanessa boss you around like that."

"Vanessa *is* the boss, Jerry. I think your problem is you never really understood that."

"Forget Vanessa, we're friends."

"We weren't friends; we were colleagues. Emphasis on *were*. Want to know what happened? Pick up a copy of tomorrow's paper." Laurie's phone buzzed. She tapped twice. "I've got to go." She walked off in the direction of *The Chronicle*'s offices.

Jerry milled about the crowd and talked to a couple of students, but they were in the dark as much as he was. Jerry was about to give up when he spotted an older man who he thought he recognized but couldn't remember where. The man had a bullet-shaped bald head and wore a blue sports coat over an open-collar white shirt and khakis. He spoke briefly with a deputy, then walked toward Jerry. As the man passed by, Jerry spotted a press credential hanging around his neck. Something clicked in Jerry's mind. He'd seen the man's photo on *The Stuyvesant Whig* website.

"Mr. Grant?"

The man stopped and stared at Jerry. "Do I know you?"

"We've never met, but I'm Jerry Williams. We talked on the phone the other day."

"Mr. Williams, a pleasure." Grant offered his hand, and Jerry shook it.

"I'm surprised to see you out here."

Grant's smile was replaced with a subdued look. "It's the first murder in the county in eighteen months. My few remaining reporters were out on assignment, that left me."

"Can I ask you what you learned? Campus police isn't cooperating with us."

"I'm having the same issues with the Sheriff's Department." Grant flipped open his notebook. "One deceased. Professor Ellen Harding. White. Female. Seventy-one. That's all they would give me. Nothing about cause of death or any suspects." Grant checked his watch. "Great talking to you, but I've got to get back. I have a newspaper to run."

Jerry waved goodbye. He spotted Darla leaning back against a tree across the street. Rachel was walking toward her.

Jerry jogged over to them. "You guys learn anything?"

Rachel groaned. "Those rubberneckers are less than worthless. One guy told me he heard this was an attack by radical Islamic terrorists. Another girl wanted to know if it's an automatic 'A' if your professor dies."

"Aside from confirming it was Professor Harding and that it's only her who's dead, I struck out too."

Darla grinned. "I learned something."

"Really?" Jerry and Rachel replied in unison.

"Yup, I talked to this cute deputy." Darla pulled a business card from her purse. "Corporal William Brick. He invited me to the gun range."

"He did?" Jerry's face burned red.

"Relax. I'm not going. My mom would flip if I went out with a cop. But I did lead him on enough to learn that Professor Harding was shot three times by what appears to be a small-caliber handgun. Multiple witnesses report hearing the shots at about one-forty. But no one saw anything, according to Billy."

"*Billy?*" Jerry narrowed his eyes.

"That's some fine investigative work." Rachel smiled at Darla.

Darla laughed. "You guys make this reporting stuff sound hard, but it really isn't. I'd like to see you try a back flip sometime."

Jerry rubbed his chin. "Shot to death? That doesn't sound like bad luck, just plain old murder. Maybe Professor Harding's death isn't related to all the others. Could be some sort of domestic situation? Or a student upset over a perceived unfair grade?"

Rachel pointed at the entrance to the building. "On the other hand, after we dropped Fallon off, she had plenty of time to go to her dorm, pick up a gun, then go to Professor Harding's office."

"You told me I didn't mention the professor's name at lunch. But if Fallon is the student who asked about magic, she might have figured out from our conversation that the professor and I talked. I said stuff that only Professor Harding could have known."

Darla frowned. "There's that name again. Fallon. I asked before, but I never got an answer. Who is she?"

"She worked with me on *The Chronicle,* and she also writes for *The Underground.* Fallon was on a list of suspects that Professor Harding gave me. *And* she hates football."

"How could anyone *hate* football?" Darla shook her head. "Not liking it is one thing. I don't understand it, but I can accept it. But hate?"

"We're drifting off subject." Rachel pointed out.

"I don't know this Fallon, but I don't think it's her. She's vegan, right? That's why you had lunch at Salad Co-op? Fallon the Vegan is the killer? If she won't eat eggs, or even drink milk, how can she murder someone?"

Rachel sighed. "Murder is rarely logical."

"Thanks, Mr. Spock." Jerry held up his fingers in the form of the Vulcan greeting.

Darla shrugged. "Just trying to help puzzle it out."

"Why don't I talk to Fallon? See if I can find out where she was at one-forty." Rachel looked at Jerry.

"Don't tip her off," Jerry said.

"I think I can manage that. Let's exchange numbers so we can keep up." Rachel pulled out her phone.

Jerry gave his number to Rachel, and she texted him.

"I should get going. I still have a lot to do at *The Underground.* Jerry, if you could work on a story about Professor Harding, not only the murder but also about her career, that would be great." Rachel faced Darla and offered a hand. "And Darla, good work, I mean that sincerely."

"Thanks." Darla ignored the hand and hugged Rachel.

Caught off guard, Rachel went limp in Darla's arms, a mixed look of surprise and distress on her face. "Okay guys I'm off." Rachel headed toward East Campus.

Jerry put a hand on Darla's shoulder. "Look at you making new friends."

"Yeah, that was a sweet move she pulled on the chief, but she has questionable fashion sense. I mean those T-shirts?" Darla poked a finger in her open mouth. "And berets should be reserved for Special Forces and mimes."

"We're done here. Go back to my place?"

"On the way, you can fill me in on your day."

Jerry entwined his fingers with Darla's and recounted the committee meeting, what Fallon said at lunch about Professor Johnson's disappearance, and the visit to Johnson's house. "I was on the fence about going back tonight, but with Professor Harding's murder, I need to ask him some questions."

"You can't do that. It's too dangerous. What if he's the murderer? What if he tries to shoot my sweet boy?" Darla stopped, looped her arms around Jerry's neck, and kissed him. "Tell the police about Professor Johnson."

"Tell the police what? I have no evidence that Professors Johnson and Harding even talked in the last forty years. And if I try to explain about bad luck, I'm the one the cops will lock up. In a mental institution."

"I still don't like it."

"Relax. He's probably not connected to this. I just need to eliminate him from consideration."

Darla pressed her lips into a thin line. "I approve, but on one condition."

"I wasn't aware I needed your approval."

"Who got you the details on Professor Harding's death?"

Jerry sighed. "Fine, what do you want?"

"I'm coming with you."

"What? Out of the question."

"Why?" She crossed her arms.

"It's too dangerous."

"But you said he's probably got no connection to any of this."

"*Probably*. What if I'm wrong?"

Darla pushed out her lower lip. Her green eyes boring in on Jerry with laser-like focus. "You should know that I'm used to getting my way."

Jerry held up his hands. "Okay, you can come. But you have to do everything I say."

"Of course." Darla poked Jerry in the ribs.

"And none of that."

"But I want to play. When are you planning on going to the professor's?"

Jerry looked at the sky. "Maybe eight. I want to wait until after sunset."

"Outstanding. That gives us plenty of time."

"Time for what?"

Darla slipped her hands under Jerry's shirt.

"Ah, cold!"

She winked. "Time for another round of 'warm things up' back at your place."

CHAPTER 29

"Two beef tacos, one chicken taco, chips and salsa, medium Coke, and a lemonade." The Taco Mondo employee, Ray by his nametag, set the red plastic tray on the counter.

"That's us." Jerry stepped forward.

Ray tapped a button on the register. "It's $9.45."

Jerry reached for his wallet, but Darla grabbed his hand. "I got this." She pulled an obsidian American Express Card from her purse, inserted it in the payment terminal, and picked up the tray. "Grab some napkins and straws."

"Thanks for getting dinner." Jerry was relieved that his finances wouldn't take another, albeit minor hit, but felt awkward at having Darla pay.

"Not a problem. I hope the food is good."

"I've never been here. No reason to come to East Stuyvesant before." Jerry held up his phone. "But it's got a four point eight on Yelp!"

They picked a table near the back of the restaurant.

Darla said grace, then crunched into her taco. "Not bad."

Jerry took a bite and nodded.

Don Henley's "Dirty Laundry" blared from Jerry's phone.

Darla rolled her eyes. "Are all your ringtones from the 80s?"

"It's Rachel." He answered the call. "What's up?"

"I've got news. Fallon didn't kill Professor Harding. She was on the other side of campus when the murderer struck."

"She told you this? Or you have witnesses?"

"Better than that, Jerry. We tracked her phone."

"Huh? Tracked? Who's we?"

"Remember when I asked how the campus cop found you in the Student Center, and I wondered if the U was tracking our phones? They are. Steph, one of my nerds, hacked their system. Fallon was on East Campus in or near McGrath Hall, over half a mile from the Whitmore Building, when Professor Harding was killed."

Jerry's mind reeled with possibilities. "Hey, if you can determine who wasn't near the building, you can also figure out who *was* there."

"Steph counted over three hundred phones in the area at the time of the Professor's death." Rachel said. "But the tracking isn't precise. We can't tell if they were actually in the professor's office, in the hallway, on the same floor, or walking past the building. Plus, there's no way to track anyone who doesn't have the app on their phone."

"Still, you could run that against Professor Harding's list. It might give us a lead."

"OK. Will do. What are you up to?"

"Just dinner."

"If I learn anything more. I'll let you know." Rachel ended the call.

Darla dipped a chip into the salsa. "What was that all about?"

Jerry shoved the phone into his pocket. "Rachel says Fallon can't have killed Professor Harding."

"I believe *I* came to that conclusion hours ago." Darla's eyes widened. "So that makes Professor Johnson your prime suspect?"

Jerry shook his head. "I'm not sure I would characterize him as a suspect, prime or otherwise. Just want to ask some questions."

"Is there anyone else on your list?"

"I don't even have the list Professor Harding gave me anymore. Rachel has it and is narrowing it down."

Darla finished the last of her taco. "What are you going to ask Professor Johnson?"

Jerry grabbed a napkin and wiped beef juice from his chin. "Start with what was going on with his geology class. The bad luck demonstrations and his disappearance."

Darla drummed her fingers on the table. "If he really disappeared, it will be weird to find him at his house."

"Perhaps it's a gag, like Fallon thought. Then I'll ask about Professor Harding and judge his reaction."

Darla slurped her lemonade. "Still think that's dangerous. Can't you call the cops? Let Billy handle it."

Jerry frowned. "Can we please not talk about Billy?"

"Ooh, someone is jealous. Relax, you're the only boy for me." She leaned across the table and kissed him.

Jerry licked his lips. Maybe next time he should order the chicken taco. "About done?"

"Yep."

They stood. He picked up the tray and dumped the trash. Arm in arm, Jerry and Darla walked out of Taco Mondo and into the October night.

Jerry drove his Ford down Wolfe Street. "That's the professor's house coming up on the left. The one with all the lights out."

Darla squinted through the car window. "Not encouraging."

Jerry cruised past the house, not slowing down.

"Where are you going?"

"There's a park at the end of the street. I'm going to leave the car there. I don't want it sitting outside of the professor's house."

"Why?"

"I have my reasons." Jerry killed the engine and unbuckled his seatbelt. "You don't have to come with me."

"Oh, I'm coming. Parked way down here, I'll never be able to tell if you need help. Besides, remember." Darla ticked off her fingers. "I figured out the bad luck connection. I got the info on Professor Harding's murder. *And* I paid for the tacos."

"That last one is an argument I can't refute." Jerry grabbed his backpack.

Out of the car, Darla sniffed the air and scrunched up her nose. "Skunk."

"Is that bad luck?"

"No, silly." Darla poked him in the ribs. "It smells."

Jerry rolled his eyes. "Come on."

They crossed the street to the side with the professor's house and headed down the sidewalk. A few houses had outdoor lights on. Jerry jogged up the walk and steps to Johnson's porch with Darla in tow. He checked the mailbox. Only the Comcast flyer that he saw earlier in the day.

"Tampering with the mail is a federal offense."

"Who's tampering?" Jerry retrieved the note he left under the knocker, crumpled it, and shoved it in his pocket. "My expectations are sinking by the minute." He banged the doorknocker three times. "Fallon was supposed to see if the professor was in his office today. Now that she's in the clear, I can ask what she found out, but I don't have her number. Maybe Rachel does." He texted Rachel.

Darla pressed her face against the sidelights. "Too dark. I can't see a thing."

Jerry banged the knocker again. Still no answer. "You should go back to the car."

"Me? What about you?"

"I'm going to go around back and see if I can slip inside."

"Jerry!"

"Shhh! Don't alert the entire neighborhood to the plan."

Darla leaned closer. "Breaking and entering is a crime."

"So is murder. If I can find some evidence, then I can tell the police, like your friend Billy. Or maybe the professor's innocent, and I can move on."

"I'm coming with you."

"No way, Darla."

"Don't argue. You know you can't win."

In the faint light, he could see her lips twisting into a determined smile. "Fine. Follow me."

Down the steps, around the side, up the driveway to the backdoor. Jerry tried the knob. Locked.

Darla looked around. "Now what?"

Jerry retrieved a pair of latex gloves from his backpack and slipped them on.

"That's not going to help. Your prints are on the mailbox and the knocker."

"Nothing illegal about knocking on the door. Doesn't prove I broke in." Jerry pulled out his wallet and removed the emergency credit card. "This used to work all the time on old episodes of *The Rockford Files* I watched with my dad." He forced the card into the gap between the door and the jamb. He slid the card up and down, while jiggling the knob. After thirty seconds of effort, the knob turned, and the door creaked open.

"Outstanding!" Darla pumped her fist.

"Shhh! Last chance. You can still go back to the car."

She crossed her arms. "Nope."

"Put these on." Jerry retrieved another pair of gloves from his backpack.

"For me? That's true love." She leaned her head on his shoulder.

"Actually, I know how stubborn you can be."

Darla stuck her tongue out.

"Come on." Jerry pulled out two flashlights and handed one to Darla. He pushed the door open and stepped into the kitchen.

Darla followed and closed the door. "What are we looking for?"

"Good question. Books or magazines on magic? Day planner? A computer would be nice. Check out everything and let me know if something seems odd or suspicious."

They exited the kitchen and entered the dining room. The table had place mats for four, but no settings. A breakfront filled with china stood against the far wall. On a small table lay a photo from the eighties based on the clothes and hair. Two parents and two teen-aged children. The boy looked like a younger version of Professor Johnson's photo from the VBU faculty website.

Moving on from the dining room, they entered a room with a flat screen TV mounted on the wall, a sofa, two recliners, a coffee table filled with knick-knacks and magazines, and a roll-top desk. Darla flipped through the magazines: *Time, The Economist, Sports Illustrated, Geo-Physical Sciences Monthly.* Jerry inspected the desk: stamps, envelopes, pens, and pencils. In the drawers, he found a mess of cables and consumer electronic manuals.

One more room on the first floor. Jerry poked his head in and swung the beam around. A home gym: exercise cycle, weights and weight bench, treadmill, and the floor covered with mats. In the corner was a litter box.

"This floor is a bust," Jerry observed. "Let's try upstairs."

"Lay on, Macduff."

Jerry took his time climbing the stairs, the wood creaking with every step.

"Why so slow?"

"Figured I should be cautious. I'm kind of new at breaking and entering."

At the top of the steps, Jerry flashed his light down the hallway. Two doors on each side and what looked to be the bathroom at the end. He opened the first door on the left and entered what appeared to be the master bedroom. The bed was made. The room neat. Jerry opened the dresser drawers and found underwear, T-shirts, and socks. Darla inspected a closet full of suits, jackets, shirts, and slacks. On the nightstand were a clock/radio and a paperback Lawrence Block mystery.

"Another dry hole." Jerry frowned.

The other room on the same side of the hallway appeared to be a guest bedroom. Perhaps it belonged to Peggy or Mark when they were growing up. Again, the bed was made. Dresser and closet empty.

Nothing of interest in the medicine cabinet in the bathroom at the end of the hall. Two rooms left. What about a basement? Jerry didn't remember seeing any door that could lead down. Was there an entrance outside of the house?

The next room could also have been a child's bedroom but was now a library with packed bookshelves lining the walls. A computer monitor sat on a desk in the middle of the room.

"Now we're getting somewhere." Jerry eased into the roller chair and inched forward. The tower was on, but the screen blank. He jiggled the mouse, and the monitor blinked on. A Windows 10 logon screen. "Mark" pre-populated the username field. Fingernails caressed the back of Jerry's neck; soft lips brushed his ear.

He jolted upright in the chair. "What are you doing?"

Darla giggled. "Helping."

"If you want to help, check the bookcases for titles related to magic or the supernatural. I'll tackle the desk and computer."

He searched the drawers, hoping for a list of passwords or even a sticky note, but discovered only software manuals and licensing agreements.

Jerry turned to the computer and tried: *Password*. No good. *Password123*. Again, no good. *Iloveyou*. Bzzt. This would likely be his last chance. By default, Windows 10 allowed four failed attempts.

"I'm seeing lots of dust covering thick books on geology, plus plenty of mysteries and thrillers. But nothing to do with mag—Aah!"

"What's wrong?"

"Something brushed my leg." Darla scanned the floor with her flashlight. The beam landed on a gray-and-white cat. "Kitty, you scared me."

"You're not the only one."

Miaw! The cat brushed against Darla's leg again.

"I bet he's hungry." Darla picked up the cat. "I saw empty bowls in the kitchen."

"He?"

Darla illuminated the cat's collar. "Yep, tag says Boris. I'm going to feed him."

"Feed him? Now?"

"Yes, now." Darla scratched Boris's ears. "Who knows how long the professor's been gone?"

"Darla, I appreciate your concern for the cat, but feeding him is a terrible idea. It might tip off someone that we've been in the house."

"I can't let him starve." She aimed her beam at a bookshelf. "That's as far as I got." She whispered in the cat's ear, "*Allez minou*," then walked out of the room and creaked down the stairs.

Jerry shook his head. Feeding a cat during a burglary? Darla never ceased to amaze him, but maybe she had solved his problem without even trying. He typed *Boris* into the password field and pressed the ENTER key. The computer beeped and a pop-up informed him that the account was locked out.

"Crap!" Jerry pushed back from the desk, rolling to the bookshelves. Starting with where Darla left off, his eyes flicked from title to title. After three bookcases, Jerry suspected this was all a colossal waste of time. Either Professor Johnson had nothing to do with the bad luck, or he was smart enough not to leave evidence lying around. On the next to the bottom shelf of the last bookcase, he saw a familiar griffin figure on the spine of a blue book.

He pulled the book out. *Curse Tablets and Binding Spells: Women's Magic from the Ancient World*. The same book that Professor Harding had shown him. He knew he'd seen the book somewhere else but couldn't place it. He inspected the volume. Unlike most of the other books, this one was dust free. Too much of a coincidence. Professor Johnson must be involved with the deaths on campus. Jerry returned the book and searched the last two shelves, but nothing stood out.

Back to the computer. Unlocked. Definitely Windows default settings. The account re-enabled after ten minutes. Jerry tried: *QWERTYUIOP*, *1234567890*, *Passw0rd*, and *BorisTheCat*. The last attempt locked the computer again.

He could ask Mike or Talia if they could whip up a gizmo that could decrypt passwords. But Jerry wasn't sure about pressing his luck and breaking into the house a second time. With no more bookshelves to search, he turned to the printer stand. A single sheet of paper lay on top of the printer. He grabbed and illuminated it.

I'm responsible for all the carnage on campus. And I killed Ellen. I'm sorry. May God have mercy on my soul.

Jerry's mouth went dry, and his heart pounded as he reread the note.

"Jerry! Come here!" Darla's voice was filled with terror.

"Shhhh!" He replaced the paper on the printer.

"Jerry, now!"

He raced to the hallway. Darla stumbled out of the one room they hadn't searched. She grabbed him, buried her face in his chest, and sobbed. He flashed his beam into the room.

A knocked over chair lay on the floor. A body hung from the rafters with a noose around its neck. Jerry aimed the beam at the head and gasped when he saw Professor Johnson's face.

CHAPTER 30

TUESDAY 11:56PM

"What is the holdup?" Darla pounded her fist on the aluminum table. "We've been here for hours."

She and Jerry sat on a pair of uncomfortable metal chairs in a dull gray interrogation room at the Stuyvesant County Sheriff's Department. Overhead, a fluorescent light flickered and buzzed.

"Calm down." Jerry made the irritation clear in his voice. "You were the one who said we should go to the cops."

Darla rolled her eyes. "Like we had any other choice, Jerry. We found a dead body. You think we could go back to our dorms and pretend we didn't see anything? We have a responsibility. Plus, it was your idea to break—"

"Shush! Remember I told you not to talk about that." Jerry glanced at the mirror on the wall. "They could be listening."

Darla jabbed her finger at Jerry. "Don't tell me to shush. If I have something to say, I'll say it."

"Darla, I'm sorry." He reached for her hand, but she pulled away. "Look, it's not—"

The door opened. A woman in her early fifties with frosted blonde hair stepped inside. She wore a blue suit and carried a briefcase.

Jerry stood to be polite.

"Jerry, Darla? I'm Allison Adams, Rachel's mom. And for the moment, your attorney."

"Finally." Darla blew out her breath. "I knew Rachel would come through. Can we get out of here? I have a Thermo midterm that I should be studying for."

Jerry sat and kicked Darla under the table. "Thanks for coming at such a late hour, Ms. Adams."

"Rachel explained to me that you're part of her news operation. Helping you gives me a chance to support her work." Adams placed her briefcase on the table and sat opposite the pair. "As for getting out of here, you'll have to talk to the police first."

Darla groaned. "We already told them we found the body."

"They want more. Jerry, I know you told Rachel that you didn't volunteer any additional information. That's good. You should never speak to law enforcement without an attorney present. You're going to tell me what happened, and I'll take it from there."

Jerry looked at the ceiling. "But what if they're listening in?"

"Paranoid." Darla pointed a finger at her head and twirled, making the 'crazy person' gesture.

Adams shook her head. "I assure you that no one is listening. If they were, it would make things much easier. I could get any charges against you tossed. Plus arrange for a fat settlement."

"Charges?" Darla sniffed, holding back her tears.

Adams reached out patted Darla's hand. "I didn't mean that you were going to be charged, dear. That's just a hypothetical. It's how lawyers talk. Now how about filling me in on what happened? Don't hold anything back. I'm your lawyer, and I can't divulge any of this conversation unless you expressly permit it." From her briefcase, she pulled a yellow legal pad and a pen.

Jerry recounted the events of the day starting with his first visit to Professor Johnson's house, the murder of Professor Harding, the connection between Peggy Johnson and Professor Harding, his suspicions about Professor Johnson's involvement in not just Harding's death but superstitious deaths on campus, and the break-in leading to the discovery of the body. Then Darla told her version of what happened.

Adams scribbled on her pad. "Rachel told me about your bad luck theories. To be honest, it's kind of hard to believe. And I'm sure the police will not want to hear it. We'll explain that you believed Mark Johnson might have had something to do with Professor Harding's because he blamed her for Peggy's death."

"That makes sense." Jerry nodded.

"I'm going to be with you when the police ask their questions. Don't answer immediately. Look at me, and I'll let you know if you should answer."

"But what's going to happen to us?" Darla's voice cracked.

"Everything should work out as long as you told me the truth. You reported the body. It appears to be a suicide. You didn't run, didn't take anything. I'm pretty sure there won't be any charges. Even if there are, the most you're likely to get is probation."

"*Probation?* This cannot be happening. My dad is going to kill me."

"That's the worst-case scenario. They're also going to want your fingerprints. They need them so they know you're telling the truth about not going near the body."

"*Fingerprints?* I'm going to be in the system?" Darla could no longer hold back her tears, and they streamed down her face.

Jerry shook his head. "They don't need our fingerprints. We wore gloves."

Adams sighed. "Gloves? You didn't mention that before."

"Yeah, latex gloves for both of us. Is that a problem?"

"Could be. Instead of visiting the professor's house and overzealously breaking in when there was no answer, it looks like this was premeditated." She scribbled on her pad. "Let's go over your stories one more time. I don't want any surprises coming up when we talk to the police. Darla, you go first this time."

Darla repeated the events at Johnson's house, then Jerry.

Allison interrupted twice for clarifications. She jotted one last note on her pad and stood. "Hold tight. I'm going to tell the police that we're ready to talk."

"And how did you gain entry to Mr. Johnson's residence?" Detective Richard Mercer asked Jerry. The detective had a receding hairline and wore wire-rimmed glasses and a blue-and-gold checked shirt.

Jerry looked at Adams, who nodded.

"I used a credit card to jimmy the back door."

Mercer wrote in his notebook. "And what reason did you have for breaking in?"

"I thought that Professor Johnson might have something to do with the murder of Professor Harding."

"That's what we have law enforcement for. No need to play at Hardy Boys." He shifted his gaze to Darla. "Or Veronica Mars."

"My clients are aware of that."

"They understand that *now*." Mercer looked back at Jerry. "What did you hope to find?"

"Incriminating notes, day planner, a gun?"

"And did you find any of that?"

Jerry shrugged. "The only thing I discovered was the note on the printer."

"Did you search the computer?"

"No." Which was the truth. Jerry wasn't able to crack the password.

"Who found the body?"

"I did." Darla raised her hand. "I came back upstairs after feeding Boris and poked—"

"Who's Boris?"

"Professor Johnson's cat."

"Wait? You broke into the house and fed his cat?" The detective narrowed his eyes at Darla.

"He was starving. And his bowl was empty. Is someone going to take care of him?" Darla bit her lower lip.

"I'm sure someone notified Animal Services. Now what happened when you found the body?"

"Like I said, I came back upstairs and looked in the last room and that's where I saw...it." Darla shuddered.

"Didn't touch anything?"

"Nope, I saw it...him hanging there. I was maybe one step inside the room, and I got out of the there as fast as I could."

The detective shifted his gaze to Jerry. "Mr. Williams? Did you enter the room or touch the body?"

"No, I saw him from the hallway. Didn't go in."

The detective continued to ask questions. After twenty minutes, he stood. "Counselor, you want to join me outside?"

After Mercer and Adams left, Jerry stood to stretch his legs. "It's going well, I think."

"Charges? Fingerprints? Probation? I'd hate to see what you think isn't going well looks like."

"Don't worry about it. Rachel's mom really seems to be on the ball."

"How can I not worry?" Darla slumped in her chair, her chin resting on her chest.

"Come on, smile." Jerry reached out.

Darla swatted Jerry's hand away. He started to say something, thought better of it, sat back down, and stared ahead at the mirror until Adams returned.

"Fingerprints are up next," she said as she entered the room.

Darla began to object.

"There's no way around it. The cops are entitled to them. After that, they'll type up your statements. We'll go over them together and sign them. Then you're free to go."

"Yes!" Jerry pumped his fist.

"That's all?" Darla's voice was filled with relief. "Nothing on my permanent record?"

"As long as you and Jerry told the truth. The detective doesn't think you had anything to do with Professor Johnson's death. At the scene, the coroner preliminarily classified it as a suicide. They are willing to overlook the breaking and entering. But don't plan on leaving town in the near future."

"We have an away game in two weeks at James Buchanan. And I'm competing at Nationals next month."

Adams looked puzzled.

"I'm the assistant captain of the cheerleading team," Darla explained.

The Uber dropped Jerry and Darla off in front of her dorm. Jerry five-starred the driver and added a six-dollar tip.

Darla started toward the entrance, and Jerry rushed to her side.

"What are you doing?" Darla turned away.

"Walking you to your room. Can't be too careful."

"I can manage all by myself."

"Just want to protect my girl." Jerry put a hand on her shoulder.

Darla slapped his hand away. "Don't touch me!"

"Come on, Darla."

"No, Jerry! I'm not going to *come on*. We could have gotten into serious trouble. We still might. They took my fingerprints! I might not get to compete at Nationals. All because of you and your crazy conspiracy theories."

"Remember I told you not to come, but you insisted."

"And that would have been better? You locked up in jail?"

Jerry could see he couldn't win this argument. Three in the morning wasn't the time for logic. "You're upset, I get it. I'll come by in the morning, and we can get breakfast."

"Please don't."

"Darla."

She turned and walked away.

"Can I call you?" he shouted.

Darla didn't look back and entered the building.

From a darkened window on the third floor, someone yelled, "Sounds like you blew it, dude!"

Jerry flipped the finger to his invisible tormenter and headed home.

Back at his dorm, Jerry threw his backpack across the room. It knocked over the lamp, which crashed to the floor. He expected that would wake Mike up. But no lights flicked on. The door to Mike's bedroom was open. Jerry poked his head in. The bed was empty and made.

Wonderful! Over at Talia's, no doubt.

Why did Darla have to be so unreasonable? She didn't even say good night.

Jerry went to his room, flopped on the bed, not bothering to take off his clothes, and turned out the lights. He stared at the ceiling in the faint darkness but couldn't fall asleep. Too wound up. The body. The cops. Darla.

He flicked the light back on and picked up the photo of his mom from the nightstand. He'd lost her. Now maybe was losing Darla. Which was a stupid thought. He'd known Darla for less than a week, but he couldn't stop thinking about her. Wondering if she would stay mad at him. Speculating if things were over with her. He could feel a hole tearing in his heart.

Jerry went to his closet. Hidden behind his snow boots was an unopened fifth of Jack Daniel's Black Label. He bought it the day his fake New York State driver's license arrived from Belarus. He was more of a beer guy, but it seemed like the right time to break out the hard stuff.

Jerry ripped the seal, twisted off the cap, took a swig. He almost spit it out. With great effort, he swallowed, and the whiskey burned on the way down. He went to the kitchenette, grabbed a glass, dropped in a few ice cubes, and half filled it with Coke, then added the Jack. Much more manageable. He refilled his glass and gulped it down again.

Jerry carried the whiskey and the three-liter Coke bottle back to his room. He sat on the bed, staring at the Kate Upton poster on his wall. Another drink. Jerry was pretty sure Kate would be reasonable, not angry with him like Darla. Of course, to snag a supermodel like Kate Upton you needed to be a handsome, cut, three-time Cy Young Award winning, multimillionaire. She might be out of his league.

Stupid Darla. No, she wasn't stupid. He was. He should have never let her come along. Told her there was no way he was letting her break into Professor Johnson's house.

Another drink.

Maybe Darla would be over it in the morning. She was always so upbeat. Jerry couldn't imagine her staying mad at anyone or anything for long.

Another drink. The bottle was half-empty.

He played it out in his mind. He'd run into her at the Student Center in the line for breakfast. Darla would look great: hair down on her shoulders, twinkling eyes, maybe a tight skirt. Jerry would apologize. Darla would pretend to be mad, then break into laughter. She'd fiddle with his collar, kiss him, and press her head to his chest. She'd smell like a flower garden.

Another drink. The room was spinning, and his stomach rumbled. Jerry set the bottles on the floor, lay down, and closed his eyes. The glass slipped from his hand. He lost consciousness.

CHAPTER 31

"Hey, are you okay?" Mike's voice rattled inside Jerry's head.

Jerry lifted his head from the pillow. That tiny effort sent the room spinning. "Not really. I feel like the bottom of a birdcage."

"I can see why." Mike stooped and picked up the Jack Daniels bottle. "It says right on the label it's a *sipping* whiskey. You're not supposed to guzzle the whole thing."

"I'm pretty sure I spilled about a third on the floor." Jerry's stomach rumbled ominously. "Hold on." He rolled off the bed, half staggered to his trashcan, and vomited.

"Uh, I'll let you be. Just wanted to make sure you weren't dead." Mike closed the door.

Jerry spent the next five minutes kneeling over the trashcan. This was it: he wasn't getting drunk again. *Ever.* Sure, he told himself the same thing before. But *this* time was different.

A knock at the door.

"Come in."

The door swung open. Talia, hair down, in an olive-green t-shirt, ripped and faded jeans, and sandals, entered. She held two glasses. She knelt and handed Jerry one glass. "This is water. You need to rehydrate."

Jerry sipped, then gulped.

Talia put a hand to the glass. "Not too fast."

When Jerry was done, he set the glass down. She handed him the second drink, a lumpy reddish-orange liquid.

Jerry sniffed. "What's this?"

"My grandpa's hangover cure."

He couldn't place the smell. "What's in it?"

"You don't want to know. But it works wonders. Saved Ronnie and me big time after we partied too hard the night before our SATs."

Jerry sipped. Not bad. Did he taste tomatoes? Cherries? Beets? Where could Talia have gotten beets on short notice? He swallowed the contents without taking a breath and handed it back to Talia. "Thanks, I appreciate it."

"No problem. One glass should cure what ails you but let me know if you think you need more." Talia grabbed the empty glasses, exited the room, and closed the door.

Dr. Janelle Thornton-Gaston, EdD scrolled through her inbox. Questions from the Alumni Association. Concerns from the Fundraising Committee. Updates from Media Relations. She wasn't in the mood to reply to any of them.

Her phone rang. Not the office line, her iPhone. Area code 912. Georgia.

She took a deep breath and answered. "Doctor Thornton-Gaston."

"Janelle! Hey, it's Marty Reisinger from the search committee." Reisinger's accent so thick you could almost taste the boiled peanuts.

Janelle felt her heart skip a beat. Good news or bad? "Hello, Marty. What can I do for you?"

"Janelle, I was watching CNN this morning and wanted to reach out to you."

"It's a heartbreaking situation. The entire Van Buren community is grieving. I've taken the leading—"

The intercom on the desk buzzed. "Excuse me, Dr. Thornton-Gaston. Chief Characopus is here to see you."

The chancellor held the phone to her chest and jammed the intercom button. "You tell the chief to cool his heels, I'm busy!"

"Yes, ma'am," came the chastened reply.

Back to the phone. "Sorry about that, Marty. Where were we?"

"The tragedies. Simply dreadful. I can't imagine what you're going through. But I'd be remiss if I didn't tell you that certain members of the search committee were already troubled by recent...events on your campus. And with this latest—"

"Marty, let me assure you and the committee that everything at Van Buren is completely in hand. We will overcome these challenges and emerge stronger than ever. Plus, I'm about to announce a bold new Diversity, Inclusion, and Equity initiative that is sure to attract plaudits from all the right people. I'd love to send you and the committee a copy of my plan."

"Uh, I'm not sure that's necessary, Janelle."

"Are you sure? Because I've got some groundbreaking—"

"Actually, I need to be going."

"Thanks, Marty. Keep in touch."

The abrupt end to the call worried Thornton-Gaston. She buzzed the intercom. "Bonnie, send in Chief Characopus."

"Yes, ma'am."

The chief in his black dress uniform entered the room, nodded, and took a seat. "Janelle."

"George, tell me something good."

The chief exhaled loudly. "The sheriff believes Johnson acted alone in the murder of Professor Harding, then took his own life. Classic murder-suicide."

"Do they know why? Some sort of lover's quarrel?"

The chief shook his head. "I don't think so. The detectives are still tying up the loose ends, but there's a connection between Johnson's sister, Peggy, and Professor Harding. The theory is that Johnson blames Harding for his sister's death. She died on campus back in 1984."

Thornton-Gaston frowned. "In 1984? Don't tell me."

"Yeah, that was part of what the Williams kid was going on about with the bad luck, and—"

"Stop right there." The chancellor jabbed her finger at the chief. "Don't you start with that *bad luck* nonsense. That reminds me. I have to follow up with Maureen about where we are in getting that TRO lifted." The chancellor scribbled a note to herself.

"I'm just saying Williams may have been on to something. According to my sources, he was the one who found Johnson's body. As for Professor Harding, not to speak ill of the dead, but she was a strange old bird. Who knows what's really going on? There are more things in Heaven and Earth than—"

"I don't want to hear recycled Shakespeare. I want you to restore some order on campus."

"Yes, Doctor." The chief rose with stiff formality and left the room.

Janelle tapped her pen against her desk. Things on campus couldn't be allowed to get any worse. She was certain her candidacy for the Presidency of South Georgia Coastal College couldn't take one more hit.

Jerry stood under the shower, for how long he wasn't sure, willing the water to wash away the pain and nausea. When his fingers wrinkled, he killed the water and toweled off. He shaved, brushed his teeth, and dressed in a purple-and-white striped rugby shirt and jeans. He walked into the main room, where he found Talia and Mike camped on the couch playing a video game.

Jerry plopped into an empty chair.

Talia laid down her controller and looked at Jerry. "Feeling better?"

"Actually yes. Your cure really works."

She winked. "Told ya."

Mike paused the game. "What happened last night? You never missed class before. And the only time I remember you drunk was at the Tri-Delt's Meltdown Party during Rush Week freshman year." He turned to Talia. "Jerry decided to play Superman, used a plastic tablecloth as a cape, and jumped off the roof. He landed face first in the hedge."

Talia giggled. "Is there video of that?"

"Nope. It's completely deleted from the Internet. Don't bother looking."

Mike pointed at Jerry. "You still didn't answer my question."

Jerry recounted breaking into Professor Johnson's house, finding his body, and their interrogation at the police station. "Darla was really pissed at me. And I sort of don't blame her." He pulled out his phone and powered it up. No calls or texts from her. "With all the pressure I've been under, plus finding an actual dead body, the interrogation, Darla. I felt like I needed to...I don't know, do something."

"Getting drunk isn't the answer."

Jerry turned on his radio announcer's voice. "College roommate sounds like After School Special."

Mike shrugged. "I'm just saying that whatever was bothering you yesterday will still be here today."

"I get that." He glanced at Talia. "Have you talked to Darla today?"

Talia pressed her lips into a thin line and didn't answer.

"That bad?"

Talia blew out her breath. "I don't want to get in the middle of things. And yeah, Darla was not herself at breakfast. When I mentioned your name, I thought she was going to burst into flames. But she didn't go into details. I have no idea where things stand between you two. She gave her shoulders an exaggerated shrug.

"Thanks. Maybe it'll blow over in a couple days." Jerry paused. "I hope."

Talia stood and grabbed a water bottle from the fridge.

"This is the first time I haven't seen you guys hunched over the jammer."

Mike smiled. "All finished."

"We've got a rechargeable battery that will last close to three hours." Talia held up three fingers. "And I experimented with adding more frequencies, but I guess that doesn't much matter any longer."

"What are you talking about?" Jerry protested. "We still need it to block the magic and bad luck."

"This isn't over? But you found Professor Johnson's body."

"Too many unanswered questions. And it looks like I'm the only one interested in them. I'll see you guys later." Jerry grabbed his laptop and headed to the university library.

In the periodical section, he picked up a print copy of *The Chronicle*.

Laurie's article on Professor Harding's death confirmed what Darla learned from Billy the deputy: three shots, small caliber handgun, no witnesses, about 1:40 p.m. No mention of Professor Johnson's death, which he expected. The news broke after *The Chronicle*'s deadline.

He booted up his laptop. *The Underground* had the article he'd written yesterday afternoon about Professor Harding's career, but nothing new on her death or on Professor Johnson. Jerry wondered if Rachel even knew about it. Her mom did say the conversation in the interrogation room was privileged. Did that mean she didn't tell her daughter that Professor Johnson was dead?

Jerry launched the website for *The Whig*. A headline in forty-eight-point font screamed: "Two Van Buren Profs Dead."

The story by Mitchell Grant didn't include any news that Jerry didn't already know. Professor Harding was shot to death in her office on campus yesterday afternoon. And two Van Buren students were credited with discovering Professor Johnson's body. He and Darla weren't mentioned by name, nor was their illegal break-in of the house. The article didn't cite the note Jerry found or hint at a connection between the two deaths.

Questions consumed Jerry. Were all the bad luck deaths a result of Professor Johnson's despair over Peggy's death? And if so, why target other students? What about his disappearance at the end of his class?

And what was Jerry going to do? He was banned from *The Chronicle*. If he kept writing for *The Underground*, would the chancellor ease up? Maybe if Jerry had no more stories about bad luck. But he wouldn't stop telling the truth. Something he wrote would undoubtedly incur her wrath. Could Rachel and her dad protect him in the future?

Or was best to forget about reporting for a while and focus on—

Darla!

He had mercifully put her out of his mind for the past twenty minutes, but the events of last night flooded his mind. The hole in his heart returned. He grabbed his phone and called her, but it went straight to voice mail. He didn't leave a message. Instead, he texted her.

Jerry: Hey, can we talk?

Thirty seconds. No reply.

> Jerry: Look I'm sorry. Just call me

Still no response.

> Jerry: Please

He stared at the phone, willing a text from her to appear. But it never arrived.

Jerry needed to get his mind off Darla. He contacted his friends from the classes he missed, got copies of their notes and assignments, and buried himself with homework.

After finishing his assignments, he logged into *The Whig* archives. He found the story reporting the deaths of the three football players from December 1983. None were locals. He jotted down their names. Maybe Rachel and her databases could locate their families, but he wasn't sure what questions to ask.

Close to six, he called Rachel. "I'm not sure what your mom could or did tell you."

Rachel chuckled. "Yeah, she's a real stickler for attorney-client privilege. But I saw the article in *The Whig* and pieced things together."

"Darla and I found Professor Johnson's body and a note where he confessed to Professor Harding's murder, the carnage on campus. All of it."

"Good work."

"Eventually, someone would have discovered the body and the note. It's not like anything I did made a difference."

"Feeling sorry for yourself?"

Jerry sighed. "A bit. Darla didn't react well to being arrested. We're kind of on the outs."

"You'll be fine. Plenty of other fish. Maybe we could grab dinner sometime."

Was she asking him out as his editor? Or something more? Rachel was cute, but a little nutty with the privacy. "Yeah, sure, sometime."

"Let me know. Are you going to write an article wrapping this all up?"

"I don't think it is *all wrapped up*. I have lots of unanswered questions, but I don't have anyone to ask. I could go back to Saratoga and talk to Mr.

Wysocki. You could rundown relatives of the football players who died in '83." Jerry gave Rachel the names.

"I'll see what I can do."

"Thanks." Jerry ended the call. He checked his email and texts. Still no word from Darla. But he would not let her end things like this. If they were through, she'd have to tell him to his face.

CHAPTER 32

Darla, wearing a green T-shirt and gold shorts, lay face up on the basketball court. Eighty minutes into practice, her heart pounded, and her body dripped with perspiration.

Hands flat on the floor beside her ears, Darla took a deep breath, then pulled her knees to her chest. When all her weight was on her shoulders, she kicked her legs and pushed with her hands as hard as she could. Her momentum shifted. Her body exploded into the air, head rising over her legs.

Darla landed on her feet, then raced toward the mat. Arms extended, she leaned forward and threw herself at the floor. She spun feet over hands, touching the ground for the briefest of moments. She tumbled along the mat, her rotational speed increasing, executed a cartwheel without touching the floor, and finished with a full double.

Darla stuck her landing, held up her arms in a V-shape, and smiled for the imaginary crowd.

Veronica clapped. "Great stunt."

"Love the aerial." Talia nodded.

Mike checked the viewfinder on his camera and flashed a thumbs up.

Darla moved to the sidelines, grabbed her water bottle, and guzzled. She paused, prickles on the back of her neck. She wiped away the sweat, but that wasn't it. More like someone watching her. She scanned the bleachers but didn't see an—Jerry!

What did Jerry think *he* was doing at *her* cheer practice? Jerry saw her looking and waved. Fabulous! Darla turned her back to him. Couldn't Jerry get it through his thick skull that she was mad and didn't want to see him?

Darla sighed, and her shoulders slumped. She could go to the coach and have Jerry kicked out. Cheerleading practice was supposed to be closed to outsiders. But she shouldn't give him the satisfaction of knowing he was under her skin. Ignore him, focus on her stunts, and he'll get bored and leave.

"Strike a pose!" Mike rushed up with his camera.

"No, I'm all sweaty." Darla held up a hand to block the lens.

"Not sweaty, glistening. And it's an impressive look. The hard-working, determined cheerleader giving hundred and ten percent at practice."

"Nuh uh." Darla shook her head. "If you want to take action shots at a distance, that's fine. But no close-ups now. Only when I have full hair and make-up."

"Come on, the photos would be scorching."

Darla turned to Talia. "Please explain to your boy how things work around here."

Talia put her hand on Mike's shoulder. "Come on, you can shoot Ronnie and me."

"Sweaty twins!" Mike beamed. "You got it."

"What happened to glistening?" Veronica frowned.

As the three walked off toward a corner of the gym, Darla shouted at Mike, "You might want to tell your roommate he's not welcome here!" She immediately regretted her actions. Snubbing Jerry was the best strategy.

Darla continued practicing: more kip-ups, round-offs, and Arabians. She didn't succumb to the temptation to peek at Jerry. But knowing that he was present, she pushed herself harder and harder.

At eight, Coach Nightlinger blew her whistle. "Circle up, troops!"

The cheerleaders gathered around her.

"Solid practice tonight. I'm informed that Physical Plant will have the stadium ready to go for Saturday, so we'll be playing Calvin Coolidge here. No long, bumpy bus ride to Vermont."

This produced a round of applause.

"We'll practice again tomorrow at five, then have a pre-game rehearsal inside the stadium starting at nine on Saturday. That's all."

She blew the final whistle. Cheerleaders grabbed their bags and headed out of the gym.

Darla spotted Jerry climbing down the bleachers and jogging across the court toward her. He waited all this time to talk to her? Only thinking about himself, not how she felt? Could it be any more obvious she didn't want to speak with him? And to think she once considered him smart.

Darla formulated a plan. She spotted Marcus heading toward the exit, raced to catch up, and stepped in his path. Marcus was tall, with a dimpled chin and dark, curly hair, but terribly dull with the personality of an elliptical machine and the IQ of buttermilk. But that didn't matter right now.

"Hey, Marcus. Looking good today." Darla flashed her most disarming smile.

"Really?" Marcus reflexively grinned back.

"You bet!" Out of the corner of her eye, Darla saw Jerry approach. "You know we should really do some one-on-ones together. It could be fun." She traced a finger across his chest. "You've got the muscles to launch me to the stratosphere." She squeezed his bicep.

"Sure thing, Darla. When did you have in mind?"

Jerry stepped up to the two. "Hey Darla, I..."

Darla pressed herself against Marcus and wrapped her arms around him. She turned and gave Jerry a stony stare.

Jerry turned red, stood motionless for a few seconds with his mouth open, then stormed off toward the exit.

"Friend of yours?" Marcus watched Jerry slam the door on the way out of the gym.

"He's nobody." Darla broke their embrace.

"I've got some free time now, if you want to work out." Marcus smiled at Darla, but it degenerated into a leer.

"I have to study." Darla's tone was bored and distant. "Let's talk about it after tomorrow's practice."

Jerry stormed out of the gymnasium. What was Darla's deal? He apologized. He was being reasonable. But if she wanted to hang all over some empty-headed, muscle-bound cheerleader, then let her. He continued the rant in his head, wandering across campus, not paying attention to where he was going.

Honk!

Jerry looked up to see the circulator bus. He was in the middle of the road, oblivious to the traffic. The driver leaned on the horn. Jerry scampered to the curb, shook his thoughts clear, and got his bearings. Lost in thought, he had walked all the way across campus. Ahead, Busby's dorm, lights on in her window. They hadn't spoken since her tirade about the article on Rick in *The Underground*.

Darla wanted to flirt and make him jealous? Two could play that game. Or was it a game? Busby was smart, maybe even smarter than Darla. And Buzz was plenty hot. Not cheerleader hot. But she had fiery red hair, legs longer than Darla's, and that adorable Tennessee accent. Best of all, Busby wasn't into weird mind games. Darla's antics had done Jerry a favor.

If he called Busby, she'd let it go to voicemail. Better to knock on her door, redeem himself, and make the case for getting back together.

He spotted a pair of girls heading toward the dorm entrance and sped up so he could slip inside with them. He climbed the steps to the third floor and walked down the hall to Busby's room. As he stood at the door, his stomach rumbled, and his knees weakened. He silently cursed himself; he shouldn't be anxious. Relax. On his phone, he loaded *The Underground* article about Rick's drinking, checked that it carried Fallon's updated byline, then knocked.

Busby dressed in gray sweats, answered the door. She crossed her arms. "Williams."

Jerry grinned nervously. "Hey, Buzz. I wanted to clear something up." He held up the phone. "They are listing the authors for articles on *The Underground* now. You can see Fallon wrote that article about Rick, not me. Like I said, I'd never do anything to hurt you."

She narrowed her eyes at Jerry.

"Intentionally, Buzz. I'd never hurt you *intentionally*."

Busby pressed her lips into a thin line. "Thanks for the news, but I already saw that. You're in the clear. *For the article*."

Jerry sensed the conversation wasn't going well. He tapped the phone and brought up Fallon's other article. "Does Miranda also know?"

"Jerry?" A raspy voice came from inside the room. The door pulled back, and Miranda appeared in a black turtleneck and chinos. She pushed past Busby and threw her arms around him.

"Whoa, Miranda!" Jerry didn't expect this greeting.

Miranda broke the hug. Her brown eyes were alive with delight, and she kissed Jerry on the cheek. "I know what you did. Trying to save me from choking. Thank you so much! And sorry about what I said before. You know, the article about me and the paper writing. I should have known you would never do such a thing."

"Uh sure, Miranda, no problem. I'm just happy you're okay."

"Williams, I think we're done here."

"Hold on, Buzz." Jerry raised his hand. "All I want to do is talk."

"We have nothing to talk about." Busby started to close the door. "Sanchez, in or out?"

"Out." Miranda stepped into the hallway.

Busby turned away and slammed the door.

Jerry leaned against the wall and forced a smile at Miranda. "That could have gone better."

Miranda put a hand on his shoulder. "I did make a case for you. But..." She shrugged.

"Thanks." For the first time that day, Jerry realized his car was still off campus. "Miranda, can you do another favor for me?"

"Sure, hope this next one works out better. What do you need?"

"Give me a lift. I need to pick up my car."

Miranda maneuvered her Camry through the streets of East Stuyvesant. "Jerry, how did your car end up all the way out here?"

He slumped in the seat. "Long story. Darla...the cops...Professor Johnson."

"Busby and I have his class. Uh, I guess I mean had. It's so weird that he's dead."

"I'm the one who found the body. Technically Darla found it."

Miranda turned on to a side street. "Darla? That's your new girl? The cheerleader?"

Jerry sighed. "Things didn't work out. That's why I came by to see Buzz. I thought maybe..."

"Chin up, Jerry. You'll find someone else."

"Does Dmitri have a sister?"

Miranda laughed. "No sisters, but he does have a load of good-looking cousins. But they all live in Russia."

"Figures." Jerry frowned. "Make the next left and drive all the way down to the park."

"Got it."

"I'm sorry that your paper writing exploits got into *The Underground*. Has the administration contacted you?"

Miranda chuckled. "Oh, I'm not that worried."

"Really?" Jerry was surprised. "I mean that's good, but why?"

"If the university comes after me for writing the papers, they have to go after all the football players who hired me. I heard it from a little birdie that the whole incident is going to be quietly swept away."

"That's great. Still sucks that you're losing your paper writing business."

Miranda shrugged. "I was probably going to have to give it up anyway. With Chat-GPT and all the other AIs and LLMs, no one was going to pay me a couple hundred when they can get an AI to crank out a paper for free."

"I hadn't thought about that."

Miranda pulled up behind Jerry's car and shifted into park. "But it's not a total loss. Dmitri and I are thinking of starting a prompt writing business."

Jerry laughed. "Miranda, I don't want to put you in spot. I'd still like to be friends, even though it might be weird with you know, Buzz and all."

"No problem, Jerry. We'll still be friends."

They hugged. Jerry hopped out of the car and watched her drive away in the dark as her taillights faded to nothing.

CHAPTER 33

J erry carried his tray of French toast and sausage across the Student
Center cafeteria. Mike, Darla, and the twins sat at a table near the
center of the room.

Darla wore a beige blouse and matching skirt that ended two inches
above her knees. Strappy sandals wrapped halfway up her calves. From
this angle, Jerry had a perfect view of her legs. He swallowed hard. He'd
known Darla for a week but getting over her was going to take a lot longer
than that.

Before any of the group spotted him, Jerry turned and headed toward
the far wall where, until this week, he used to eat. At his old table sat
Busby, Miranda, Dmitri, and a pair of girls he didn't recognize.

He changed direction again. Maybe he should settle for an empty table
and dine alone.

"Jerry!" a voice called out.

He spun. Fallon was waving at him. Was this better than eating by
himself? Possibly? He maneuvered through the confusion of chairs and
tables to Fallon.

She wore an unbuttoned, red-and-yellow checkered plaid shirt over a
navy-blue tee. On her tray: a granola bar, a bowl of oatmeal, and a glass of
orange juice. "You looked kind of lost, wandering around out there."

Jerry forced a smile and sat. "Thanks. Things are kind of in flux with my friends."

"Still sore at you because of my articles for *The Underground*?"

"That's resolved. It's other stuff."

An Asian girl with close-cropped hair and wearing a gold VBU sweatshirt arrived at the table, set down her tray of oatmeal and coffee, and sat across from Jerry.

Fallon nodded. "Jerry, this is my girlfriend, Vicky Tran. Vicky, this is Jerry Williams, second-best reporter on campus."

Vicky grabbed a Sweet'N Low packet and dumped the contents into her drink. "The guy behind the bad luck stories?"

"I see my reputation precedes me." Jerry folded up a half slice of French toast and crammed it into his mouth.

Fallon sighed. "It's over though, right? The bad luck?"

"I don't know why everyone thinks that. Nothing has changed."

"We're still in danger?" Vicky shuddered. "I was in the class when that creepy Professor Johnson broke all those superstitions. I thought he was dead."

"He is."

Fallon sipped her juice. "If the professor is out of the picture, but you think it's not over, what's the angle?"

"I admit I'm stumped on how to proceed. There's this old reporter in Saratoga that put me on to Professor Harding and Peggy. But he doesn't hear too well, so I can only talk to him in person." Jerry checked his phone. "The retirement home has visiting hours this afternoon. I could drive over after class and try to learn something more."

"Anything else?"

Jerry lowered his voice. "You were one of my leads, but it didn't pan out."

"Me?" Fallon's eyes went wide.

"Fallon?" Vicky laughed.

"Yeah. Fallon, you were on the list of students from Professor Harding's class. One of them asked about magic. But Rachel cleared you."

"Imagine my relief." Fallon mock-wiped her brow.

Vicky leaned forward. "What's this about magic?"

"A way for women to finally level the playing field with men." Fallon rested her elbow on the table. "We'll have to play around with it sometime."

Vicky looked unconvinced.

Jerry whipped out his phone. "Rachel claimed she was going to whittle down that list of names. I wonder if she's made any progress." He lifted the phone to his ear. "Hey, Rachel. Jerry. I'm sitting here with Fallon at the SC. How's it coming with that list that Professor Harding gave me? Or the relatives of the football players?"

"Good morning to you too."

"Heh, sorry. It's just that I've hit the proverbial brick wall doing about sixty. Not sure how else to continue."

"No problem. I admire your dedication. No leads on the families of the players. I'll check with Steph and see how she's doing with the list. Keep in mind she has other responsibilities at *The Underground*. Plus classes, like the rest of us."

Jerry sighed. "I appreciate that. But tomorrow is the 13th."

"I'll let her know it's top priority. And when she gets the results, I'll have her email them to both of us. Sound good?"

"Great. Thanks. Bye." Jerry disconnected the call. "Rachel's putting a rush job on the list. That's something."

"Tomorrow is the 13th?" Vicky furrowed her brow. "What's that supposed to mean?"

"You know, Friday the 13th. Based on what happened in '84 and in the past week, it could be bad."

"Should we leave campus?" Concern filled Vicky's eyes, and she looked at Fallon. "We could go to my parents' place in Westchester."

"I don't know what to tell you." Jerry checked at his watch. "Hopefully, I can figure this all out and stop it in the next fifteen hours."

Fallon and Vicky raised their eyebrows.

"Wow, I guess that sounded overly dramatic. I meant, I'm on the case and not giving up. Guess I should get to class. It was nice meeting you, Vicky."

"Nice meeting you too, Jerry. Despite all the gloomy talk."

"See you later, Fallon." Jerry stood and grabbed his tray.

While Professor Joslin droned on about the Taiping Rebellion, Jerry replayed the events of the past week, hoping he'd discover something he overlooked. He sat through an hour of Chemistry and couldn't recall a single word Professor Gray said. The pages of his notebook were uncontaminated with any notes. Maybe he should ask Darla for help to get up to speed?

Darla!

The thought of her name was like a kick in the balls. He really needed to push her out of his head, permanently. Or it would be his high school junior year all over again; mooning over Sara Duffy for months after she dumped him at the Halloween Dance.

After Chemistry, Jerry headed to the library. Nothing new on Professor Johnson or Harding in today's edition of *The Whig*. He spent the next two hours browsing copies of *The Whig* from 1984 but couldn't find any new leads. And still no updates from Rachel on Professor Harding's list. Maybe it was over. Whatever *it* was. If so, he might never learn what exactly happened, but that would be more than a fair tradeoff, if no one else died.

At one o'clock, Jerry was walking into the Student Center, semi-confident he wouldn't run into Darla or Busby at that hour. As he climbed the steps to the second-floor cafeteria, four girls descended. Three on the left side of the silver metal railing. One coming down Jerry's side.

Jerry mentally ranked the girls. Would this help him get over Darla more quickly? Couldn't hurt. On the left, a blonde in a white sweater and black skirt looked best. Not much competition: the other two girls were in sweats and sans make-up. The girl coming down Jerry's side wore shorts and had cute legs. She tapped her phone, not watching where she was going. Jerry moved to the side, giving her room. Her feet became entangled, and she tumbled forward.

Jerry was too far away to grab her. All he could do was watch as the girl's momentum carried her forward. The phone went flying. The girl careened down the twenty or so stairs ending on the floor at the foot of the steps.

Jerry squinted. The girl's leg looked odd. Like she had a second knee. No, it was her shinbone: broken and protruding through the skin.

The girl had managed to sit up. She didn't cry out. She stared in a daze at the jagged ends of her fractured left tibia as blood oozed onto the floor.

"Kate, are you okay?" the blonde in the skirt shrieked. She and her two companions hovered over the injured girl, paralyzed with inaction.

Jerry rushed down the steps, pushed through the trio, and knelt next to Kate. "Call 9-1-1!" He pulled the knife from his backpack, sliced off his shirtsleeve, and pressed it to the wound. "I need someone to keep this in place for me."

The trio of girls, tapping on their phones, didn't look up.

Another girl, a brunette in a leather jacket and jeans, rushed down the steps. "I've got it." She knelt next to Jerry, placing her hand over the improvised bandage.

Jerry turned his attention to Kate. Her breathing had become rapid and shallow. He snapped his fingers in front of her face. "Kate, don't look at your leg. Look at me."

Still puffing, she directed her gaze from her leg to Jerry.

"My name is Jerry, and I promise you everything is going to be okay. But I need you to get your breathing under control. Regular, slow breaths." He placed his hand on her chest. "Breath with me. One in, and two out. One in, and two out." Jerry repeated his commands. Slowly, her breathing was returning to normal. "Great job, Kate. Keep with it. Slow and normal."

A crowd of students had assembled in a circle around Jerry and Kate.

Jerry shouted at the crowd, "I need something soft to put under her head!"

"You should wait for the paramedics." The blonde's voice quavered.

Jerry ignored her and looked at the crowd. "Please, someone."

A guy pulled off his blue New York Giants sweatshirt and tossed it to Jerry.

He balled it up and placed it on the floor behind Kate, then grabbed her shoulders. "Kate, I'm going to have you lie back. Nice and slow." He eased her down to the floor.

"How we doing?" Jerry asked the girl holding the makeshift bandage.

"Fine, I'm a nursing major. I got this."

Jerry turned his attention back to Kate. "What's your name?"

"Kaitlin—er, Kate Fletcher."

"And where are you, Kate?"

"On the floor?"

Despite the circumstances, Jerry couldn't help but smile. "On the floor, where?"

"The Student Center."

"Very good, Kate. And can you tell me the day of the week?"

"It's Thursday."

"Perfect. You're doing super fine. Everything is going to be okay." Jerry held her wrist, checking her pulse. Strong. That was a good sign. Ninety-six. Fast, but to be expected. He pulled a water bottle from his backpack. "Kate, I'm going to give you a bit of water. I want you to take tiny sips." Jerry held the bottle sideways and allowed a bit of water to trickle into her mouth.

A campus cop ordered the onlookers to get off the steps, and a pair of paramedics pushed through the dispersing crowd.

The first EMT knelt next to Jerry. "What happened?"

"Kate fell. Suffered a Grade I or II compound fracture. We tried to stop the bleeding first. She's aware and lucid, knows her name and where she is. Pulse is strong at ninety-six. She was hyperventilating, but I got it under control. Probably in shock. Haven't moved her, except to rest her abdomen and head on the floor."

"We'll take over now." The EMT turned his attention to Kate.

Jerry and the nursing student stood and joined the crowd, now hovering at the top of the steps.

The guy who offered the Giants sweatshirt fist-bumped Jerry. "Very epic under pressure."

The blonde in the skirt approached Jerry. "Sorry for doubting you. We were all concerned for Kate." The other two girls nodded.

Something clicked in Jerry's mind. The girls weren't just walking down the steps at the same time as Kate. They were her friends. Three on one side of the railing and Kate on the other. Like Darla had described with Cassie.

Split the group.

Jerry's mouth went dry. He *was* right. This wasn't over. Everyone was still at risk. Less than eleven hours until the 13th.

He mumbled his way past the trio of girls and pushed his way through the rest of the crowd, taking the back steps to the first floor. He called Rachel for an update but got her voice mail.

"Rachel, some girl at the Student Center split the group with her friends and ended up with a seriously broken leg. It's not over. I really need that list." As Jerry spoke, his email notification chimed.

He ended the call. In his inbox was an email with the subject line Re:list. The message was cc'd to Rachel.

From the list Rach gave me, four female students were in the general vicinity (250 feet) of the Whitmore Building between one and two on Tuesday afternoon. That's as much as I can narrow it down. - Steph

Jerry downloaded the attachment and opened the file. As he read the names, his chest tightened, and he couldn't breathe. Was this what a heart attack felt like?

His hands shook as he reread the list:

Davenport, Allison L. – SIN# 210-96-6521
Jaggard, Darla T. – SIN# 385-80-2273
Munroe, Kris W. – SIN# 128-54-1793
Tollefson, Amanda B. – SIN# 133-23-5896

CHAPTER 34

THURSDAY 1:22PM

Jerry blinked, willing her name away, but it defiantly remained.

Jaggard, Darla T. – SIN# 385-80-2273

What was Darla doing on this list?

It made no sense.

Why hadn't she mentioned she took a class with Professor Harding?

Darla inserted herself into every step of Jerry's investigation: showing up unannounced in the basement of *The Chronicle*, arguing her way into meeting with Wysocki, insisting on coming inside Professor Johnson's house.

Johnson!

Jerry's throat tightened. His fingers shook so much it took three attempts to compose the text to Veronica.

> Jerry: Can you send me that pic of Darla's mom at the pageant?

> Veronica: I won't ask why, but here you go

The image downloaded and opened. A blonde in a red swimsuit. The photo caption: *Jennifer Johnson, Miss Michigan USA*. He did remember correctly.

Darla had shown great interest in Jerry. But once Professor Johnson was dead, and the case appeared over, she no longer wanted anything to do with him. Was he delusional to have thought that the hottest girl in school could actually be interested in him? Had she been using him all along?

Jerry called Rachel. Voicemail again. "Rachel, I got the list. Darla's on it. After thinking through all the evidence, it seems plausible that she's the one. I'm going to her room to confront her."

On shaky legs, he walked from the Student Center toward Darla's building. As he cut across the parking lot behind the dorm, he passed by a red BMW convertible and stopped. Its Michigan license plate read *FLY4VBU*.

His chest tightened. He felt empty, like his insides had been scooped out. Could Darla be behind everything that happened? And if so, did he want to know?

Jerry thought back to the conversation in *The Chronicle*'s break room where he bragged to Fallon that he'd follow a story anywhere. Then Salad Co-op, where she needled him for being upset with Busby and Miranda's reactions to the stories Fallon had written.

Jerry would pursue this lead, like a good reporter should. Maybe Darla *was* behind the bad luck and the resulting deaths. His stomach churned at that thought. Or she could have a perfectly reasonable explanation. Then he would track down the other three names on the list.

Two minutes later, he stood outside her room. He took a deep breath, swallowed hard, and rapped his knuckles on the door. A few seconds later, the door opened.

Darla wore a long-sleeved, midriff-baring, off-white top, black leggings, and green New Balance sneakers. Despite the tension, Jerry's eyes flicked to Darla's abs for a second, then met her gaze.

She frowned at Jerry with undisguised contempt, glancing at Jerry's torn sleeve. "Nice shirt. What are you doing here?"

"We need to talk."

Darla crossed her arms. "I have nothing to say to you."

"I'm not here to talk about *us*. This is about the bad luck. Cassie and Noah and Vince. Professors Harding and Johnson. All of it."

"It's over. We found Professor Johnson's body. How can you not remember? I don't think I'll forget that night for the rest of my life."

"Can I please come in? I promise it will only take five minutes."

"Fine." Darla pulled back the door. She took a seat on the couch.

Jerry started to sit in a chair.

"Nuh, uh." Darla wagged a finger at him. "I don't want you getting comfortable. Stay there. Say what you have to say then go."

Jerry shifted his weight back and forth. "Whatever is happening isn't over. I just came from the SC. A girl fell down the steps. She was lucky to get off with a broken leg. Her friends were walking down the other side of the railing. They split the group. Does that ring a bell?"

"People trip all the time. They need to be more careful. If all you came to tell me was that some hungover freshman took a little tumble, then this conversation is over."

Darla's attitude seemed odd. Before, she had been superstitious. Now she was ready to dismiss the idea? A bead of sweat trickled down Jerry's back.

"Tomorrow is Friday the 13th. And if I'm right, and this isn't over, a lot of people are going to get hurt."

"Assuming you're right, why tell me? Shouldn't you be out searching for the real killer, like OJ?"

Did Darla know he suspected her? Was she baiting him? Jerry took a deep breath. "Your mom's maiden name is Johnson."

"Wait, what?" Her green eyes filled with rage and confusion.

Jerry studied her expression. Was she upset at the accusation or worried that he'd pieced things together? "I said, your mom's maiden name is Johnson."

"How do you even know that?"

"Veronica showed me a photo of your mom back in her pageant days. Jennifer Johnson, Miss Michigan USA."

"The twins need to mind their own business." Darla stood and poked Jerry in the chest. "Yeah, my mom's maiden name is Johnson. What about it? It's like the second most popular surname in the country. Two presidents and three vice presidents have been named Johnson. Are you suggesting that I'm related to that nutbag professor? What if I am? Who cares? I never even met him. Is this what's got you all worked up?"

Raised voice. Narrow eyes. Deep breaths. If Darla was faking genuine offense, she was doing a hell of an acting job. Jerry pressed on. "There's more."

"This ought to be good."

"Last Thursday, when I was interviewing you about Cassie, you talked about how she split the group. It was almost like it slipped out, that you didn't mean to say it. Then you asked me not to put it in my story."

"No, I said not to use my name, not that you couldn't report it. I was afraid I was coming off like the b-word."

Is that the way it happened? Jerry couldn't remember.

"What about when you insisted on breaking into Professor Johnson's house?" Jerry threw his hands down at her sides. "You were awfully friendly with his cat. Almost like you'd met him before."

Darla blew out her breath. "Really? Because I like cats, I'm a suspect?"

"You also demanded on coming along to interview Wysocki."

"Nope, you got your facts wrong again. You asked me to come along."

"Yeah, *for the drive*. But at the retirement home, you were adamant about coming in. Almost like you needed to be with me when I talked to Wysocki, so you could hear everything he told me."

Darla threw up her hands. She seemed more exasperated than angry. "*C'est fou*. Because I didn't want to be bored silly sitting in your car, you think I'm behind all this? That I'm some sort of murderous witch?" Darla paused, pressing her lips together. "What about when I found you in the basement of *The Chronicle* and noticed that Peggy died on Friday the 13th? How does it make any sense for me to tell you that if I'm the evil mastermind behind everything?"

Jerry rubbed his chin. She made a good point. "I hadn't thought of that."

"Some reporter."

Jerry hadn't worked his theory completely through; he was in too much of a rush to confront Darla. He struggled for it all to make sense. "Maybe you needed me to make a connection to move things forward?" The uncertainty in his voice was obvious.

Darla's face reddened. "Which is it? Am I moving things forward or hiding them from you? Like all classic conspiracy theories, yours can't be falsified. Any evidence that appears to disprove it is only proof of a bigger conspiracy."

The door swung open, and Lucy walked in. "Hey guys." She carried her golf bag and wore a white visor, yellow polo shirt, and blue golf skirt.

"Hi." Darla didn't make eye contact.

Jerry grunted.

"Fun crowd." Lucy went to her room and emerged a moment later sans visor and golf bag. She crossed to the kitchen, grabbed a White Claw from the fridge, and popped the top.

Jerry and Darla remained silent, continuing to glare at each other.

"Tension in here is thicker than maple syrup. I'll go study and leave you two alone." Lucy returned to her room and closed the door.

Darla jabbed her finger at Jerry, her voice rising. "Are you done yet? Because if you are, you can leave. And don't come back."

"Oh, there's more. How did you know Professor Harding was murdered?"

"I told you. I got the info from that deputy I flirted with. What has that got to do with anything?"

"No, before that. You came barging into my room to tell me she was murdered. How did you know?"

"I have class in Jenkins Hall, next to Whitmore. I was heading to my dorm, and there was a crowd. So I asked someone what happened, and they told me Professor Harding was *dead*. And that's what I said to you. I didn't know she was murdered until later."

Jerry tried to recall the scene when Darla rushed in. Did she say Professor Harding was dead or murdered? His memory was fuzzy. "And who was this someone who told you she was dead?"

"Just some boy. I don't know him. This has got to be the flimsiest case ever."

Time for his ace in the hole. "I've got one more, and it's the most devastating of all." Jerry paused for dramatic effect. "How come when Wysocki mentioned Professor Harding's name, you acted like you hadn't heard it before?"

"Because I hadn't. There are a couple of hundred professors on campus. I don't know them all. How come *you* didn't recognize her name?"

"I never had a class with her."

"Neither have I."

This was it. Jerry opened his eyes wide, forcing himself not to blink. He didn't want to miss a moment of how Darla reacted. "Professor Harding told me that a student of hers, a girl, came to her last spring and asked about magic and bad luck spells."

"It wasn't me. I just told you that I never took any of her classes." No tells. No hints that Darla was lying or hiding something.

"Professor Harding didn't remember the student's name. She gave me a list of everyone who registered for the class. Rachel narrowed it down to girls who are still enrolled and were in the vicinity of the Whitmore Building when Professor Harding was murdered. Four names on that list, including yours." Jerry pulled out his phone and offered it to her. "Explain that."

Darla refused the phone. "Rachel must have her wires crossed, because I ne—Wait, I remember now. Spring semester I wanted to take French II. But it was full, and I still needed a humanities. I signed up for Magic Systems. During Drop/Add, a spot opened up in French, and I switched. So yes, I did technically register for her class, but I never went or met Professor Harding."

Darla's explanations were becoming more convoluted. He was on the right track. "Never, huh?"

"That's what I said. If you don't believe me, check at the Registrar's Office."

Jerry put his phone back in his pocket and walked to Darla's desk. He picked the thick blue textbook off the shelf and waved it in front of her. "Then why do you have this? I saw this book on Saturday while waiting on you in the shower. It's required reading for the class. The same book was in Professor Harding's office and Professor Johnson's house."

"It's not my book."

Darla's weakest excuse yet. Jerry stood straighter with the conviction he was right. "You can do better than that."

She ripped the book from his hands. "I was writing a paper on *Macbeth* and thought I could get some good stuff on witches, clever metaphors or insights or something. I borrowed it from Lucy's desk."

"Lucy."

"I just said that."

"No, I mean *Lucy.*" Jerry pointed.

Darla turned.

Lucy stood in the doorway to her room, grinning, a pistol in her hand. "I try to be a good roommate and not eavesdrop, but you guys are way too loud."

CHAPTER 35

Darla's eyes widened as she stared at the gun. "Lucy, what are you doing?"

"It's her." Jerry stepped forward to shield Darla. "Lucy is the one behind it all."

"Duh Jerry, I figured that out." Darla kicked him in the shin.

"Ow! What was that for?"

"General principle. Plus, I owed you from the night at the Sheriff's Department."

"Hey, hey! Let's not ignore the person with the gun." Lucy smirked.

Jerry took one step toward her.

"Uh, uh." Lucy waved the gun. "Back up, Jerry. Then you and D get over on the sofa."

Jerry and Darla shuffled over to the couch and sat.

"Give me your phones."

Jerry fake-struggled to pull his phone from his pocket. He wanted to delay Lucy as long as possible. Rachel knew he was here. Would she arrive? And when? Would she bring help?

"Quit stalling." Lucy cocked her hip and glared.

Jerry extricated his phone and tossed it.

Lucy snagged it with her free hand. "D?"

Darla lobbed hers, but the aim was off. It landed on the floor and skidded under her desk.

"Real clever, D. Am I supposed to get down on my knees to retrieve it while you guys try to jump me? Or did you dial 9-1-1, and the cops are listening to everything we're saying?"

Jerry cursed himself for not coming up with that idea.

"Who knows?" Darla shrugged.

"Get your phone, D."

"No." Darla crossed her arms.

Lucy pointed the pistol at Jerry. "Get the phone, or your boyfriend eats a bullet."

"Go ahead. We're broken up, anyway."

Jerry's heart pounded. Lucy's lips twisted into a sinister grin. He doubted she was bluffing. Lucy was responsible for half a dozen deaths. "Uh, Darla..."

Lucy racked the slide. "I'm serious, D."

"Fine." Darla dropped to her knees, scooted under her desk, retrieved the phone, and slid it across the floor to Lucy.

"Now get back on the sofa." Lucy, keeping the gun pointed at the pair, backed to the kitchen, filled the sink with water, then splashed the two phones.

Jerry needed to keep Lucy from whatever she planned next. "What I don't get, Lucy, is why? What did Cassie, Noah, and Vince ever do to you?"

She laughed. "Nothing. I didn't even know them."

"Nothing?" Darla furrowed her brow. "That makes no sense."

"Of course you guys don't get it. Even Professor Harding didn't get it, and she had a PhD in this stuff *and* was in a coven. It's not about the bad luck, it's about the good. I'm riding the biggest wave of good luck ever. I'm playing the best golf of my life, got a hot new boyfriend, heading toward a four-oh this semester, and cracked fifty thousand followers on Tik-Tok watching all my trick shots. Plus, I've got a top sports agent who's lining up a stack of big money NIL endorsement deals.. But the thing about the universe is that these things balance out. So, while I enjoy all the good luck..."

"Others suffer the bad," Jerry finished. "But why did you target people connected to the football team if you don't have a grudge against them?"

"I didn't." Lucy shrugged. "I suspect it's residue from Peggy's anger, randomly selecting them. And football is a misogynistic, debilitating competition that sucks up way too many Athletic Department dollars at the expense of women's sports, so it's a win-win. Whatever the reason, I don't care, as long as my luck keeps rolling."

"And tomorrow?"

"Friday the 13th is going to be a bloodbath. I shot a best-ever sixty-five against Pierce on Tuesday. Amazing lies. Never a bad bounce. Wind always behind me. Lot of people are going to have to pay the price for that."

Darla pointed at Lucy. "What does it profit a man to gain the whole world at the cost of his soul?"

"D, I'm really not going to miss your over-the-top sanctimony. But I would expect nothing less from someone coasting through life on her dad's money and her mom's looks."

Darla pouted. "That's not fair. I worked hard for everything I've achieved."

"Born eighteen inches from the pin and thinks she nailed her approach."

"Fine, you got what you wanted. Let us go. We won't tell, will we Jerry? Besides, no one would believe us. They don't believe it's happening now."

Lucy laughed. "That's the one thing I do like about you, D. You're pragmatic. Students are dying left and right, but if you can save yourself, who cares? I might even have faith that you'd keep quiet. But not Ron Burgundy here." She pointed the gun at Jerry. "He would never let it drop. He's like that reporter who was following the Hulk around. What was his plan when he finally caught up with the big green guy, anyway?"

"You're right, Lucy. I won't stop."

"Jerry." Darla punched him in the arm. "Think about what you're saying."

"I am. If Lucy's right and the bad luck is random, then what can she do? Shoot us? How's she going to explain that?"

Lucy's finger stroked the trigger guard. "The police have no idea I got rid of Professor Harding. I'll dispose of you too. Remember, I've got luck on my side. Plus, the cops around here aren't too bright to begin with. They'll swallow any half-plausible story I concoct. Maybe you were attacking Darla. Domestic violence is a national scandal." Lucy shook her head and tut-tutted. "I tried to defend her, but you both got shot."

"We have good luck too." Darla held up her wrist. The rabbit's foot dangled from a silver bracelet.

"Rabbits' feet?" Lucy howled. "Let me explain how this works. Your charm is putting out the good luck equivalent of the power of a refrigerator magnet. While mine is like one of those giant electromagnets at the end of a junkyard crane, and I'm about to drop you into the crusher. You guys are completely outmatched, outclassed, and outgunned."

Jerry needed to keep Lucy talking. "I get what happened to Cassie, Vince, Noah, and Fuller. But what about Professors Harding and Johnson? That wasn't bad luck. That was murder."

"What? I'm supposed to reveal everything to you?"

"It's the reporter in me." He hoped he sounded convincing.

"If you really must know, this is the CliffsNotes version. At golf camp a couple of years ago, some girls were talking about harnessing the power of good luck to improve their game. The power of affirmations, selfless deeds, and that sort of crap. It got me curious, so I did some research on the Internet. Turns out they had the right idea about luck but were going about it the wrong way. Bad luck is the key. However, there was so much garbage to wade through, because, you know, it's the Internet. To get the actual truth, I turned to Professor Harding. The old bat wouldn't help me. Said she still felt guilty about what happened to Peggy all those years ago.

"I asked who Peggy was, but the professor clammed up. Back to the Internet. More research, more garbage. Eventually, I found a couple of members of her coven still alive down in Florida. They were happy to teach me what they knew, and I pieced together the rest.

"When I was in your dorm on Monday, I heard you say you spoke with Professor Harding. I didn't know how much she told you, but I didn't want her talking to you again."

"So, you killed her? Or had Professor Johnson do it?" Jerry steadied himself.

"Mark." Lucy's voice dripped with contempt. "He was useful for getting students to break superstitions to fill the vicinity with bad luck."

She cackled. "There's nothing like stroking a middle-aged man's ego, *among other things*, to get him to do whatever you want."

A look of disgust crossed Darla's face. "I think I'm going to vomit."

"Go ahead. Who's stopping you?"

"That still doesn't explain why Professor Johnson disappeared from his classroom," Jerry pointed out. "Or why he committed suicide. Or was he murdered too?"

"Do you really want to know? Or is this a stalling tactic until help arrives? Who are you counting on? Your geek roommate? The Bobbsey Twins?" Lucy sneered. "Story time is over. We're going for a little walk."

"What about a lunar mining drill?" Mike lay on the sofa, the back of his head resting in Talia's lap.

"Good one." Talia stroked his hair. "You'd need to operate in both extreme high and low temperatures. And figure out how, in a vacuum, to radiate away all the waste heat the drill would generate. You also—"

A knock at the door.

Mike rose from the sofa. "Keep going."

"I was going to say that you want to construct it out of the least dense material—"

Mike opened the door, and Rachel burst in, panting. "I'm worried about Jerry. He's not answering his phone."

"He's not here, but he's always turning off his phone. What's up?"

"I had my nerds run down that list of Professor Harding's."

Talia stood. "What list?"

"One of her students asked about magic and bad luck, but she couldn't remember which one."

"But I thought this was over." Mike stared at her.

"It's not. Jerry told me a girl fell at the Student Center, messed her leg up really bad. Said she split the group, whatever that means."

"Split the group?" The blood drained from Talia's face.

"One of my staff compared the names on the professor's list against people who were in the area of the Whitmore Building when she was murdered."

"You can do that?" Mike was wide-eyed.

"Yeah, the surveillance state is scary. Anyway, Steph crunched the data and came up with four names. She sent it to me and Jerry. I was in class, so he saw it first. Now I can't reach him, and I'm afraid of what's happened. Darla's on the list. Jerry said he was going to confront her." Rachel held up her phone.

Davenport, Allison L. – SIN# 210-96-6521
Jaggard, Darla T. – SIN# 385-80-2273
Munroe, Kris W. – SIN# 128-54-1793
Tollefson, Amanda B. – SIN# 133-23-5896

"Let me see that." Talia reached for Rachel's phone.

"Darla? She's the one?" Mike shook his head. "That's crazy."

Talia squinted at the phone. "Oh no! If Jerry went to Darla's, we have to get there quick. Mike, grab the jammer."

"What? You mean it really is Darla?" Mike unplugged the jammer from the wall.

"Of course not. Darla wouldn't hurt anyone." Talia rolled her eyes. "But Lucy is on the list."

"Lucy?" Rachel grabbed the phone back. "Who's Lucy? I don't see any Lucy."

Talia pointed to the screen. "Allison L. Davenport. Lucy is her middle name. That's Darla's roommate."

CHAPTER 36

Darla and Jerry walked down the dorm steps. Lucy trailed a few feet behind, a folded green jacket over her hand concealing the gun.

"Head outside, then turn right," Lucy ordered.

"Where are we going?" Jerry pushed open the door. Could he surprise Lucy? Slam the door into her, then grab the gun? He glanced at Darla. She wasn't looking in his direction. No way to give her a heads-up. The moment was over; they were outside. The sun was blocked by dark clouds. He needed to find a way to communicate with Darla so they could act in unison. Either fight or run.

Lucy continued to stay a few feet behind them. "Keep walking toward the stadium."

Darla turned her head. "Using magic for good luck isn't any different from cheating. It's not fair to the other golfers."

"Fair?" Lucy howled. "This is America. It's never been about fair. It's about what you can get, and what you can get away with."

"That's pretty cynical, even for you."

"Ever wonder how your dad made his millions? Don't answer, I'll tell you. Outsourcing American jobs to the third world countries where workers are lucky if they make a dollar a day and stripping profitable companies of their productive assets, leaving behind bankrupt shells and broken communities. That's what hedge funds do. That's what they did to my dad."

"You can't seriously blame my dad for—"

"Jeez, D. Why so defensive?" Lucy laughed. "No, it wasn't specifically your dad who screwed my dad. Doesn't really matter. The point is, there's a parasitic upper class in this country getting rich at the expense of everyone else. I'm just emulating the elites. We were so broke after my dad lost his job that if I hadn't landed the golf scholarship, I'd be paying for college with Only Fans."

"Better a camgirl than a cheater," Darla sneered.

"Watch your mouth, D. Or I'll end things right now."

Jerry again tried to catch Darla's eye but failed. *Keep it up, Darla. Anything to distract Lucy.* He looked ahead for some way to create a commotion. Or a campus cop rolling by. Lucy's luck couldn't stay good forever. Could it?

A scattering of raindrops fell as Talia, Rachel, and Mike, holding the copper-colored jammer, headed down the sidewalk toward Darla's dorm.

Rachel put the phone on speaker. "That's right, Steph. See if you can track the phones for Davenport and Jaggard from that list. Plus, Jerry Williams."

"That's Gerald Williams," Mike said loudly.

"Maybe we should call the campus police?" Talia wrung her hands.

"And tell them what?" Mike spread his arms wide. "We're chasing down The Bad Luck Killer? They won't believe us. Hell, I don't even believe it."

"Make something up." Talia shrugged. "Terrorists. Active shooter. A UFO landed on the Quad and little green men with laser rifles are marching out. Anything to get help."

Steph's voice crackled from the phone's speaker. "No signals for Jaggard or Williams. But Davenport is heading east along Wolfe, moving away from Clinton Dorm."

Talia raised her hand to shield her eyes and looked down the road. "I don't see them."

"Should we be following Lucy?" Mike glanced in the direction of Clinton Dorm. "Or should we go to the Darla's room and look for her and Jerry?"

"Jerry may turn off his phone, but not Darla." Talia shook her head. "If hers is off, that means trouble. I say we follow Lucy."

"Unless Darla's battery ran down. Or the killer is one of the two other names on the list."

Rachel raised her hand. "Another vote to follow Lucy."

"Fine." Mike started jogging. "Let's pick up the pace."

Darla, Jerry, and Lucy walked into the shadow of the football stadium.

"Head through that gate." Lucy motioned with the gun.

"The stadium is closed." Darla pointed at the sign.

"Trust me." Lucy smirked.

Jerry came to the white metal gate and pushed. It creaked open. "Why did you bring us here?"

"Keep going." Lucy ignored the question. "Head up to the second deck."

Darla and Jerry climbed the steps, crossed the concourse, and passed through a tunnel coming out in the upper deck stands. The rain was falling harder. Down on the field, a couple of girls running laps around the track that circled the field raced for cover. In the far corner, an empty crane stood next to the replacement light tower.

A couple of times, Jerry caught Darla's attention. Her eyes were alert. Her lips were pressed into a thin line. But he couldn't read what she was thinking. Couldn't figure a way to let her know what he was planning.

"You'll have to quit using magic when you turn pro." Darla stared at Lucy. "If people around you keep dying, someone's going to get suspicious and figure it out."

"No one's going to figure anything out, D. I'm unstoppable. Head toward the fifty, then go up again."

They reached midfield and climbed the steps toward the announcers' booth. The white concrete structure occupied what would have been the top ten rows of seats.

"Around to the left." Lucy ditched the jacket and motioned with the gun.

The three came to the back corner of the booth. In front of them stood the ten-foot-high outer wall of the stadium. To their right, a narrow set of steps, roped off with a yellow plastic chain, led to the roof of the booth.

"Step lively."

Jerry allowed Darla to go first. Maybe if he pretended to stumble, he could catch Lucy off guard and smash into her before she could react. But Lucy lingered back, out of reach.

Antennas on top of the booth swayed in the increasing wind. Unlike the rest of the stadium protected by the ten-foot concrete wall, only a black two-foot metal railing guarded the edge.

Lucy motioned with the gun. "Over the fence."

"Davenport is at the football stadium." Steph's voice crackled over the phone.

"Oh my God!" Rachel pointed at a pair of figures at the top of the stadium. "Is that Jerry and Darla?"

Mike squinted through the rain. "I think I see a third person."

"We need to notify the cops *now*." Talia stared at Mike. "Then turn on the jammer."

"Good work, Steph. I'm hanging up." Rachel called the campus police. "There's people on top of the football stadium. I think someone is going to jump."

The dispatcher's voice crackled. "Which side of the stadium?"

"Roosevelt Lane. Send help fast!"

"Are they—"

The line went dead.

"Jammer's on." Mike pointed to the three flashing green lights.

"Great! It can jam phone calls, but is it going to help with this?" Rachel looked at the trio on top of the stadium.

"Jerry thought so. It's a matter of if we chose the correct frequencies. We didn't know which." Talia shrugged. "We guessed."

"Are we close enough?"

Mike spread his arms wide. "In theory, it can block at distances of up to three hundred feet. We might be in range, but we should try to get as close as possible to maximize the signal."

A campus police car pulled up and parked on the sidewalk outside the stadium. The officer, in a yellow rain slicker, emerged and pointed at the three, making a motion with his hand to keep back.

"Whose bright idea was it to call the cops?" Rachel glared at Talia.

"We're the ones who made the call!" Talia shouted.

"Get back over there." The cop pointed across and down the street.

"We can't go back," Mike muttered. "We need to get the jammer as close to Lucy as possible."

A second campus cop arrived. He placed cones in the street to block traffic. The siren of a firetruck wailed in the distance.

"Distract them." Mike motioned to Talia and Rachel. "And I'll run into the stadium."

"Give it to me." Talia pointed at the jammer. "No offense, Mike, but I'm the athlete here. If anyone should the do the running, it's me."

"But cheerleaders aren—"

"Stop right there." Talia ripped the jammer from his hands. "We're not having that conversation. Especially now."

Mike's chin slumped. "Okay. Get ready to make your move." He grabbed Rachel by the hand and dragged her toward the police.

With her free hand, Rachel pointed to the roof and yelled at the cops. "They're up there!"

"We got it. Please keep back." The first cop tapped the radio mounted on his chest. "Bravo-17, requesting backup at Murray-Baldridge. Possible jumper and crowd control." No reply. He tapped the device and repeated himself. Still no acknowledgement from dispatch. "Raynor!" He shouted at the other cop. "Call for backup. Something's wrong with my radio."

The second tapped his radio, made a frustrated gesture, and re-entered his vehicle.

Mike and Rachel stopped a few feet in front of the first cop.

"Up there." Mike and Rachel pointed at the top of the stadium.

"Please, you need to get back on the other side of the street." The officer raised his hand.

While Mike and Rachel occupied the cop, Talia dashed through the stadium gate.

"You're going to make us jump?" Darla peered over the railing.

Despite the wind, Jerry could hear the fear in her voice. If he could only get close to Lucy and grab the gun. But she kept her distance. And if he tried, would her good luck ensure that he would fail?

Lucy shook her head in feigned sympathy. "Suicide is the leading cause of preventable deaths among young adults." She mocked Jerry's radio announcer voice. "Two more deaths rocked the Van Buren campus community this week. A pair of tragic suicides. One was Darla Jaggard, the popular assistant captain of the VBU cheer squad. Why would she end her own life? What twisted secrets did she take to her grave?" Lucy laughed and resumed her normal voice. "And the enterprising school newspaper reporter? The purveyor of crazy conspiracy theories? That will be an easier sell. Or maybe it was a pact between star-crossed lovers?"

"We broke up. Remember?" Darla shouted.

"You don't have to do this, Lucy." Jerry hoped he could get through to her.

"I don't have to, I *want* to." Lucy waved the gun. "Enough talk. Get over there."

Jerry and Darla climbed over the metal railing. A few inches of concrete were all that separated them from a hundred-foot fall.

Lucy grinned. "I'm trying to decide who will go first. Who wants to watch the other die? Or should both go at the same time?"

Jerry peered over the edge. Three figures rushed toward the stadium. In one of their hands, he saw a flash of copper. Mike and the jammer? He squinted. Yes! Was he in range? Jerry hoped so. A pair of cop cars pulled up. Help was here, but was it in time? He looked at Darla. He couldn't tell if she was crying, or it was rain on her cheeks.

Her voice rising over the wind and the rain, Darla prayed, "The Lord is my shepherd; I shall not want. He maketh me to lie down in green pastures: he leadeth me beside the still waters..."

Lucy shook her head. "So melodramatic, D."

"He restoreth my soul: he leadeth me in the paths of righteousness for his name's sake..."

Careful not to lose his balance, Jerry depressed the back of his left sneaker with the toe of his right. Darla's eyes met Jerry's with a look of recognition. Did she understand?

"Yea, though I walk through the valley of the shadow of death, I will fear no evil: for thou art with me; thy rod and thy staff they comfort me..."

Jerry's sneaker was loose. Now to flick it at Lucy. All that practice better pay off. He turned one hundred eighty degrees.

"Uh, uh." Lucy pointed the gun at him. "Face forward. Or your girl-friend gets it." She aimed at Darla.

"Thou preparest..." Darla turned. "I told you: We're broken up!"

"And I'm through fooling around D, you're first. I want to see the look on lover boy's face when you go splat!"

Darla winked at Jerry as she refaced the street. But what did that mean?

"Thou preparest a table before me in the presence of mine enemies: thou anointest my head with oil..."

"No more stalling, D! Over the edge!"

Darla bent her knees and launched herself into the air.

Jerry flicked his ankle. His sneaker soared directly at Lucy. She dodged the oncoming shoe and pulled her aim from the airborne Darla to Jerry and fired, the bullet whizzing past his head.

"That was a gunshot!" Rachel shouted.

Mike squinted. "I can't tell what's happening."

"I need you to get back, now!" The cop pointed.

Sucking wind, Talia raced up the steps to the second level and out of the tunnel into the pouring rain. The crack of a gunshot startled her. She slipped and skidded, her momentum slamming her into one of the seats. The jammer flew from her hand and crashed onto the concrete. The cover popped off, revealing a loose green circuit board.

"No!" she screamed.

Darla spun in a back flip. As she descended, her left foot caught the railing. Her landing spoiled, she crashed, shoulder first, onto the wet concrete.

Jerry was on top of Lucy before she could fire again. He grabbed her arm. She twisted out of his grasp and stumbled, the gun dropping from her hand. She reached for it, but Jerry stepped forward and kicked it. The gun slid across the wet roof, into the stands.

Darla, still down, moaned and rubbed her shoulder.

Jerry raised his fists. "It's over, Lucy."

"I don't need a gun. I've got my luck." She curled her fingers, beckoning him. "Come on, Jerry. Let me kick your ass."

Jerry hadn't been in a fight since the ninth grade when John Postelwaite sucker punched him. But athletic as Lucy was, she was still a girl. He had reach and weight on her. Did she still have the luck? He got the gun away from her. Maybe the jammer was working.

Jerry advanced on Lucy. He led with his left, she moved to block it, and he threw a roundhouse right aimed at her jaw.

Lucy easily sidestepped his attack. Jerry's foot slipped on the slick roof. As he tried to prevent his fall, he dropped his hands, and Lucy landed a blow to his chest. He staggered backward, wiping the rain from his eyes.

On Jerry's right, Darla started her kipping motion, rolling onto her shoulders, then yelped and her body slammed back down.

Lucy snickered as Darla writhed in pain. "Take another run at me." She motioned for Jerry to come to her.

Jerry raised his fists. Maybe the jammer wasn't working. He'd have to be clever in fighting Lucy. Let her make a mistake. He danced left and right, keeping his distance.

"Coward!" Lucy edged over to Darla and delivered a kick to her ribs.

"Argh!" Darla grabbed Lucy's leg.

In the distance, a lightning bolt flashed. Three seconds later, a roar of thunder rolled over the stadium.

"Come at me Jerry. Or I'll break all her ribs." Lucy kicked Darla again.

Darla groaned and squirmed on the wet concrete.

Jerry couldn't stay back. Wouldn't let her hurt Darla. "Stop it." He advanced on Lucy.

Talia pushed the circuit board into the slot. It clicked into place. She slid the cover back on and flipped the power switch. Nothing. She cursed under her breath and popped the cover off. She scanned the electrical innards. A dipswitch in the wrong position? She toggled it while whispering a prayer. The jammer chirped and three green lights blinked. Talia snapped the cover in place and resumed racing up the steps.

Jerry approached on Lucy's right, trying to draw her away from Darla.

Lucy turned, not allowing Jerry to get behind her.

Darla clutched Lucy's ankle.

Lucy looked down and kicked Darla away. That was enough to allow Jerry to land a right cross on her jaw.

Lucy staggered backward and spit blood. "Lucky shot." As she said the words, a look of concern crossed her face. She took three steps back, widening the space between her and Jerry.

Jerry stood taller. "Not so confident now, huh?"

Rolling back on both shoulders, Darla grunted, then kipped up, slamming into Lucy's side.

Lucy held her ground and grabbed Darla by the neck, wrestling her toward the railing. "Back off Jerry, or I'll toss D over the side."

Darla kicked at Lucy's feet, tried to pull her hair, but couldn't stop Lucy from dragging her to the railing. Darla was fit, minus her injured shoulder, but so was Lucy, and she was taller, stronger.

"Jerry, it's Talia. I'm coming with the jammer!" a shout came from below.

Lucy's eyes filled with rage. "That's what happened to my luck? Goddamn geeks always interfering." She lifted the struggling Darla over the fence.

Darla looped her feet around the top metal bar and locked her legs. Rain bombarded Lucy as she leveraged her weight, trying to push Darla off the fence, over the edge.

While Lucy was preoccupied wresting Darla, Jerry charged with open hands and slammed Lucy from behind. The impact vaulted Lucy over the fence, and she lost her grip on Darla.

Lucy stutter-stepped to a halt at the roof's edge. She grinned, raising her voice over the storm. "You still don't have a chance. All I need—" A gust of wind buffeted her. The grin contorted into a look of horror. She scrambled to regain her balance, her sneakers slipping over the side, and disappeared from sight.

Jerry helped Darla to her feet. He supported her as she limped to the edge of the roof. Lucy's lifeless body lay splayed on the sidewalk below.

Darla trembled at the sight. "The wages of sin is death."

She turned to Jerry and buried her face in his chest. He wrapped his arms around her and stroked the back of her head as icy rain continued to pelt them.

CHAPTER 37

*FRIDAY, OCTOBER 13*TH

From *The Stuyvesant Whig*:

Murder-Suicide Ruled in VBU Professors' Deaths
by Mitchell Grant

At a Thursday evening press conference, Stuyvesant County Detective Richard Mercer announced the conclusion of the investigation into the deaths of Van Buren University Professors Ellen Harding and Mark Johnson.

Mercer explained that Johnson shot Harding three times, killing her in her VBU office Tuesday afternoon, then hung himself later that day.

Mercer theorized that Johnson mistakenly believed that Harding was responsible for the death of Johnson's older sister, Margaret "Peggy" Johnson. Peggy Johnson was a student of Harding's back in 1984. The same year she died in an accidental drowning in the VBU gymnasium pool.

Johnson's body was discovered late Tuesday evening in his East Stuyvesant home by two unidentified Van Buren students. Mercer did not explain how the students came upon Johnson, only that they faced no criminal charges.

Harding taught sociology and folklore at Van Buren for the last forty-two years, coming to the university immediately after earning her doctorate at NYU. She served as VBU Faculty Senate President from 1991-95.

Mark Johnson grew up locally in East Stuyvesant. He moved from the area in his early twenties and only returned to teach geology at VBU this semester.

Harding's murder is the first in the county in eighteen months since Larry Branco, a clerk at Buy-Rite Liquors in Katskill Falls, was shot and killed during a botched robbery attempt...

From *The Chronicle:*

Chancellor Resigns; Athletic Director to Fill Interim Post
by Laurie Inverso

Dr. Janelle Thornton-Gaston, Van Buren University's 13th Chancellor, abruptly announced her resignation late Thursday evening.

In an email to the Board of Trustees, Thornton-Gaston expressed a desire to take a break from university administration and spend more time with her family.

VBU Board of Trustees Chair Rance Snead announced a committee headed by Vice Chair Selma Whitaker would begin the search for a new chancellor immediately. In the interim, Athletic Director Don Gehring will serve as Acting Chancellor while continuing his responsibilities overseeing Statesmen Athletics.

While educational observers had generally given Thornton-Gaston's tenure as chancellor positive marks, the past few months of her administration were marred by a shortfall in fundraising, a parking meter scandal, and a recent string of campus deaths.

Thornton-Gaston arrived at Van Buren five years ago after serving as the Provost of Central Vermont Polytechnic where she was credited with instituting...

From *The Underground:*

Student Killed in Football Stadium Fall:
Seventh Campus Death in Past Week
by Fallon Ahern

Allison "Lucy" Davenport, a top-ranked member of the Lady Statesmen Golf Team, was killed early Thursday afternoon when she plummeted from the top of

Murray-Baldridge Stadium. VBU Campus Police, alerted to the presence of a possible suicide attempt, were present when Davenport fell. Campus EMT Services responded, but Davenport was declared dead at the scene at 2:31 p.m. Authorities have yet to rule her death, accident, suicide, or homicide.

What Davenport was doing inside the stadium wasn't clear. Technically, Murray-Baldridge is closed to the wider college community, except for sporting and campus events. But students have long made unauthorized use of the football stadium's steps and track for exercise.

Two other students, whose names were not disclosed, were present with Davenport at the time of her fall. The pair were questioned by Campus Police and detectives from the Stuyvesant County Sheriff's Department and released. At this time, no charges have been filed.

On Friday, Acting Chancellor Don Gehring announced additional measures to tighten security at the stadium, including reinforced gate locks and frequent police patrols. Gehring also stated grief counselors would continue to be made available to students, faculty, and staff.

VBU Head of Media Relations Julie Fredericton announced that a candlelight vigil would be held on the Main Quad on Friday at 7:00 p.m. The vigil would honor not just Davenport, but all recent campus deaths.

Davenport, a wilderness management major and junior from Binghamton, rose to the number one ranking among Presidential Conference women golfers after shooting a seven-under-par sixty-five at Oak Valley Country Club in a match against Franklin Pierce College on Tuesday.

VBU Lady Statesmen Golf Coach Jan Catlin recalled Davenport as a fierce competitor...

CHAPTER 38

As Jerry shuffled through the breakfast line, students stole glances at him, turned, and whispered to their friends. Even the cafeteria workers seemed to be watching him. What were they saying?

Jerry spent late Thursday and most of Friday being interviewed by Stuyvesant County detectives concerning Lucy's fall. They questioned Darla in a separate room. At one point, he glimpsed her in the hallway. She glared but said nothing. For the few moments after Lucy fell, when he was holding Darla in his arms, he thought he might have one last chance with her. But that look she gave him at the sheriff's ended all hope and plagued him for the last twenty-four hours. He had no desire to see her again.

The police recovered the gun from the stadium. Only Lucy's prints were on it. Campus video footage showing Lucy marching Jerry and Darla across campus confirmed their claim of kidnapping. With the assistance of Rachel's mom, it appeared there would be no charges, and Lucy's death would be ruled an accident or self-defense. But who knew what bizarre rumors were being passed around campus?

Jerry shook it off and filled this tray with pancakes, sausages, and toast. He grabbed two cartons of milk, paid, and maneuvered his way toward the six-top table where Mike, Talia, and Veronica were eating.

Mike and Talia sat on one side: he in a blue polo shirt and she in a white

T-shirt that read *Niagara County BirdQuest 2022*. Veronica sat opposite her sister and wore a green-and-gold warm-up jacket and jeans.

"Hey." Jerry took the open seat next to Veronica. Talia looked at Mike. "You're right. Jerry needs cheering up."

"I'm fine." Jerry grabbed the maple syrup and drenched his pancakes. "Which is pretty good considering all I've been through."

"Battling supernatural evil?" Mike held up his fingers to make a cross.

"Stopping a murderer?" Talia pantomimed a stabbing motion.

"Getting the chancellor fired?" Veronica drew her finger across her neck.

"I don't think you can give me credit for that last one. She resigned." Jerry shrugged.

"That's a little more to it than that." Rachel set her tray down and took a seat at the end between Veronica and Talia.

"What do you know?" Mike narrowed his eyes.

Rachel grinned. "I may be in possession of a series of particularly illuminating emails between the Board of Trustees and Dr. Thornton-Gaston. She resigned to avoid the humiliation of being fired. Definitely check out Fallon's article coming up later today in *The Underground*.

Jerry buttered his toast. "The chancellor was difficult, but I didn't want her to lose her job."

Talia grunted. "Isn't she the one who tried to suspend you for trying to uncover the truth behind all the deaths on campus? I say good riddance."

Mike and Veronica nodded their agreement.

"I guess I'm in a forgiving mood this morning." Jerry slumped in his chair.

"I know." Talia's eyes lit up. "Jerry, come watch us at the football game this afternoon. That'll raise your spirits."

Mike nodded. "Calvin Coolidge is terrible. They might be the one team we can beat."

"Really?" Rachel rolled her eyes.

"Maybe we could at least score on them?" Mike looked around the table hopefully.

"You think?" Veronica laughed.

Mike shrugged. "It's something to do."

Jerry speared a sausage link with his fork. "I appreciate everyone's efforts, but I'm not in the mood."

Veronica punched him in the arm. "Don't be such a Gloomy Gus. It'll be fun. Martin and I have this hilarious new routine worked out. He's playing Don Quixote, and I'm Dulcinea."

Jerry sighed. "I'm sure it will be great. But I want to stay away from the stadium. I did almost die there. Plus, I'd like to avoid running into—"

"Darla!" Talia smiled.

Darla in a peach top, arm in a sling, and her hair tied back in a high ponytail set her tray at the last empty spot, the end between Mike and Jerry. She sat, closed her eyes, bowed her head, and whispered grace. She looked up and grabbed a sugar packet for her coffee. "Michael, are you coming to take more photos of the squad at the game today?"

"You can't cheer with your injury." Mike pointed to her sling.

"I can still hold the megaphone." Darla raised her good arm.

"Wouldn't miss it." He mimicked taking a shot.

"Veronica, can you pass me the salt?" Darla reached past Jerry without making eye contact.

Jerry's stomach rumbled. He wasn't going to take Darla's bait. He pressed his lips into a thin line and remained silent.

"Rachel, I wanted to tell your mom that I love her style, but the sheriff's office really wasn't the proper venue." Darla held up her phone with an image of Rachel's mom. "Is her red outfit Karl Lagerfeld?"

Rachel laughed. "I'll pass along your compliment, but I honestly have no idea about brands or my mom's clothes."

"We should totally go shopping sometime. All four of us." Darla pointed to the twins. "We need to spiff up your wardrobe. I mean, why are you wearing a T-shirt with Steve Irwin on it?"

Rachel looked down at her shirt. "That's not the Crocodile Hunter. It's Hunter S. Thompson."

"Who?" Darla furrowed her brow.

Jerry bit his tongue.

The four girls continued their discussion about fashion, mixed in with comments about the cheer performances at today's football game. Jerry grew increasingly frustrated. What was Darla's point, sitting here and ignoring him? He considered getting up and leaving, but Mike was *his* roommate. Rachel was *his* editor. And the twins, especially Talia, were fast becoming *his* new friends. Why should he leave because Darla was acting like a jerk? He cut another triangle of pancakes and shoved it into his mouth. He made eye contact with Mike, who gave an almost imperceptible shrug of his shoulders. No help there.

Talia nodded. "And Ted is pretty funny."

"Don't forget his blue eyes," Darla swooned.

Jerry, completely fed up with Darla's cold shoulder treatment, thrust himself into the conversation. "You look very nice this morning, Darla."

She continued like Jerry hadn't spoken. "We should definitely introduce Ted to Rachel."

Jerry's cheeks burned red. "Darla, if you're going to sit with us, can you at least be civil and not pretend that I don't exist?"

The table fell into silence.

Darla cocked her head. "Michael, did you hear something?"

He held up his hands. "No way am I getting in the middle of this."

Jerry took a deep breath. "Look Darla, you're mad. I get that, and I don't blame you. But can we move on? All—"

"Move on?" For the first time, she faced Jerry, her green eyes filled with rage and contempt. "What should I move on from, Jerry? The time when you got me arrested? Or the part where you accused me of being a serial killer?"

Jerry's chin slumped to his chest. Stupid mistake to engage Darla. No hope for the two of them. Even surface pleasantries were out of the question. He should go. He put the milk cartons on his tray, pushed back his chair, and prepared to stand.

"What are you doing?" Darla continued with the hard stare.

"You're right. I screwed up. Nothing left for me to say. I'll finish my breakfast elsewhere."

"Gotcha!" Darla burst out laughing and poked him in the ribs.

"W—What?" Jerry's mind couldn't process what was happening.

"Oh my gosh, Jerry! You have to be the most serious person, *ever!*"

"We're still together?" Confusion and uncertainty flooded Jerry. "But you told Lucy we were broken up."

"Duh Jerry, she was holding a gun on us."

"But what about that guy at cheerleader practice?"

"I was still mad at you then. You really should have given me space."

Jerry shook his head, still trying to convince himself this was real. "But this bit now? It was all a gag?"

"Yeah." Darla flashed a smile that was all teeth. "I'm over being mad. And you're so easy to tease. Plus, where am I going to find another boy as cute as you who gives the most amazing foot rubs?" She leaned forward to kiss him.

Kissing Darla was all Jerry wanted for the past few days, so he surprised even himself when he put up a hand to block her. "Uh, uh."

"What's the problem?"

What's the problem? Jerry could no longer contain his frustration. He exploded like a Fourth of July fireworks display. "The problem is, I can't deal with all your mind games. I get that I screwed up and maybe even let you down. And it's okay to be angry at me. That's what happens with couples. But when you play with my head like this, it isn't funny. It hurts. And I don't want any part of it. Or you." Jerry stood and grabbed his tray.

"Okay, you're dishing it out. I told you I can take it. Sit back down."

"I'm serious, Darla. I'm done." Jerry headed away from the table.

"Boys don't walk away from me." Her voice rose and became shrill. "You turn around right now, Gerald K. Williams, or we really are through!"

If everyone in the cafeteria weren't watching Jerry before, they were now, as Darla continued her rant at him. He maneuvered to an empty corner, grabbed a chair, and let his head drop. What a fabulous way to start the day. Jerry hoped he hadn't made a huge mistake. Darla was hot and smart, but he didn't want to ride that rollercoaster any longer.

"Mind if I join you?" a female voice broke through his thoughts.

Was Rachel chasing after him? One of the twins? Jerry raised his head. No, it was a smiling brunette with cute bangs and wearing a Pittsburgh Penguins sweatshirt. She looked familiar, but he couldn't place her.

"Uh sure, go ahead." Jerry gestured toward an open seat.

The brunette set her tray of oatmeal, toast, and orange juice on the table and sat. "Don't worry about that girl." She crooked her thumb in the direction of the still raving Darla. "I've got her in my English class, and she's a total psycho."

Jerry chuckled.

"I'm Angela, or Anj."

"Jerry."

"I know. I asked around. You disappeared so fast on Thursday after the EMTs showed up, I never got a chance to talk to you."

Jerry snapped his fingers. "You helped me with Kate's leg. I knew I recognized you."

"I was impressed with the way you took charge and wanted to ask you where you learned all that stuff. Haven't seen you in any of my nursing classes. Are you training to be a paramedic?"

Jerry shook his head. "I took a Wilderness First Aid course. It was my dad's idea. We do a lot of outdoorsy stuff: hiking, camping, canoeing. He thought it was a good idea to be prepared."

"Outdoorsy? I like that. Ever climb Mount Marcy?"

"The highest point in New York? Not yet, but it's on my list."

Anj grinned. "Mine too."

As the conversation turned to their mutual love of hiking and the outdoors, Darla slipped completely from Jerry's thoughts.

Thank you for reading! Did you enjoy? Please add your review because nothing helps an author more and encourages readers to take a chance on a book than a review.

And don't miss more from James Blakey's *The Secrets of Van Buren University* series, coming soon.

Until then, discover WITCHY WAY TO MURDER, by City Owl Author, Adrienne Blake. Turn the page for a sneak peek!

You can also sign up for the City Owl Press newsletter to receive notice of all book releases!

SNEAK PEEK OF WITCHY WAY TO MURDER

BY ADRIENNE BLAKE

We tumbled down the cold stone steps, a tangled mass of human and muscular animal limbs, locked together in a deadly embrace. The werewolf smelled of fire and stale pine, like an old magic tree that someone had torched. Adrenaline protected me from the worst of the pain, but it still hurt like hell. I heard the *clink, clink* as my wand trickled down the steps along with us, resting tantalizingly just out of reach in the wet night grass of the park.

My arms still held tight onto the werewolf's neck, desperate to keep those rancid, dripping wolf fangs from me. Not to mention the foul breath of the thing, as its snapping jaws tried to rip my throat out.

I wanted to scream, but the words stuck in my throat. If only I could reach that wand, but I dare not let go or I'd be dead in an instant. I closed my eyes; if my fingers couldn't get it perhaps if I concentrated....

The werewolf let go and howled. I thought I was free and turned my head to summon my wand properly—but too late, I realized my mistake. The beast still had me pinned to the ground. I was still trapped.

As the wand flew through the air to my fingers, the werewolf's red, fiery eyes narrowed. I lay terrified as his claws tore into my chest, seeking my heart which was beating as if it would explode. Wand or no wand, it was too late. Pain worse than anything I had ever experienced before enveloped me. The world became stained with my lifeblood, and then all went dark, as the moonlight faded, and I was dead.

I woke with a gasp, my hand instinctively flying to my chest, feeling for blood but finding only a scar. I wiped the sweat from my soaking forehead with my pajama sleeve, then reached for my phone. It was only five in the morning, dammit.

With a groan, I crashed back hard into my pillows. No decent witch should be awake at this ungodly hour. Especially since our days typically didn't start before midday. Goblins even later. I closed my eyes, desperate to sleep but afraid to fall back into that dream. How many nights had I had this same nightmare now? Was it a dozen? More?

After fluffing up my pillow more times than I cared to remember, I finally punched it and hauled my rear-end out of bed. Scratchpoop dropped down off the bed with a gentle *thud* and followed me out into the kitchen. Yawning, I flipped on the light, just as the cat jumped silently up onto the kitchen counter, his tail up high, showing me his butt and expecting food.

"Yeah, yeah. Gimme a minute." I said and reached for the kettle. In the mornings I typically liked coffee, but right now I didn't want a pick me up. I wanted something to put me back to sleep, and that meant tea. A nice, soothing, relaxing, sleep-inducing pot of herbal tea.

I definitely didn't feel like myself right now. Part-goblin, part witch, I had an acute sense of smell, razor-sharp hearing, greater than human strength, and was stirred when tribal skin drums played at funerals. I was the first to get swept up with hot-blooded goblin anger when surrounded by crowds of my own people—but not today. Today, all I could think of was my pillow, and how much I wanted to hug it.

After filling the kettle with fresh water and flipping the switch down, I dragged my feet to the fridge and opened the door. I reached inside and pulled out a half-eaten tin of Kitty-Kin food. I peeled off the lid and scraped the contents onto a saucer on the counter then dropped it to the floor. "There ya go, you bottomless pit of fur." Scratchpoop hunkered down and didn't seem to mind at all as I rubbed his black and white coat up and down. His fur was lovely, thick, and shiny. He was a good cat, really.

Still yawning, I slouched back to the kettle which should be whistling by now, but it wasn't. I cautiously rested the back of my hand against the shiny metal, only to find it stone cold. Was the darn thing plugged into the wall socket? I checked and it looked fine. I flipped the switch again. Nothing. It was dead. Great.

I sighed and poured some cold water into my mug and picked up my wand from the counter. I touched the surface of the water with the tip, and whispered, "*Calida Aqua!*" I watched as a goblin-green glow illuminated the cup, and the water began to boil. My grandmother would have tut-tutted at such gratuitous use of magic, but I needed my tea. I knew in my bones already that this was going to be a bad day. And it hadn't even started yet.

Harrison, my partner and co-founder of the unfortunately named Goblin Dicks Paranormal Detective Agency—*You lose 'em, we'll find 'em!* —was already sitting behind his desk when I arrived. He had just returned from a cruise to Bermuda, which he'd taken on doctor's orders, and his naturally green skin looked darker than ever. And he looked fit. The dark circles he'd had under his eyes were gone, suggesting restful nights, and his trim physique proved he'd been sensible with the onboard buffets.

"Good time, was it?" I asked.

He barely looked up from his computer. "You're early." Only Harrison could make that sound like a fault. Like me, he wasn't a morning person.

"Meet anyone nice onboard?"

Harrison grunted. I took that as a no. I suspected he hadn't been looking since his last boyfriend had turned out to be a demon who almost killed him. Had almost killed us both, in fact. Instinctively my hand went to my heart. Would I ever be able to forget?

"Well, you look good. I'm guessing those spa treatments really work." I always preferred my boss green. Some mixed-up sense of vanity had him change to a more human hue from time to time, but in my eyes, that made him look shifty. The green softened his features and made him look gentler. As far as a goblin could ever be described as gentle. I turned a little green myself once in a while.

"So, what's cooking? Anything hot?"

January had been dead as a dodo and this month wasn't looking much better. It was a typically flat time in the business, so I wasn't horribly worried. And the last demon gig had brought in enough money to keep us in the black for a bit. So, we were doing okay for now, but the pot would soon be running dry. We needed cases, pronto, and we both knew it.

Just as Harrison shook his head, the phone rang. I picked up the receiver since he clearly wasn't going to.

"Hello. Goblin Dicks Paranormal Detective Agency. How can I help —?" I listened as a leering voice made rude suggestions that would have made a hooker blush. "Yeah, that's real funny, pal. Get a life." I slammed the receiver down. Another of *those* calls.

"Look, Harrison, you sure we shouldn't change our name? I'm getting tired of these perverted calls."

"Nope. We're leaving it just as it is. I just had the name etched in our door and I'm not changing it again. Ignore them."

Damn. I looked back to the recently etched, frosted window in the upper panel of our door. *Goblin Dicks Paranormal Detective Agency* was neatly stenciled on the glass, in the tradition of other private dicks throughout history. Sam Spade would have been proud. Still, sometimes it sucked being only the junior partner in our business. Harrison's word was law, and frankly, Harrison wasn't always right. At least I didn't think so.

"Oh, by the way, I got this for you," Harrison said.

"Oh, what?" I turned around. "Something fun? Or chewy? Or choco-late? I could always eat more chocolate."

He slid a .38 in a leather holster across his desk.

"Oh, sweet!" Nothing says someone cares for you more than them buying you a new gun. "Aww, you shouldn't have!" I fluttered my eyelashes playfully. It was fun to tease him.

Harrison grunted. "That toy .22 of yours, wouldn't stop an angry dog. I was looking in the gun shop and saw that. I thought you could use it."

"Aww. People will say we're in love."

I pulled it out of the holster and checked it out, testing the weight and feel in my hand. I liked the balance, and it wasn't too heavy for me. Plus, it was fully loaded. Bless him; he'd thought of everything. "Thanks, Harri-son. You done good!"

I sat at my own desk and turned on my computer. I picked up the framed photo of my mom. It showed her on vacation in Miami and was the first time she'd been away on her own. She was the color of a lobster, but she looked like she was having fun. Next to that was a picture of me from my police days. With my dark hair and trim build, I looked pretty hot in my cop's uniform. I was kind of a Kelly Garrett from the original Charlie's Angels. Only greener. Except when I chose not to be.

While my computer booted up, I cleaned out the coffee maker and put in some fresh water and grounds. "Six sugars," Harrison said without looking up.

"Hey, I'm not your lackey." Harrison ignored me. I thought about spitting in his mug, but he'd only say it added flavor. Typical goblin.

I sat back down at my desk while the water boiled. There was nothing in my email except junk. And an email from my detective friend, Liam Wells with a funny about a dog trying to lick his own do-das but not reaching. I knew it was his warped way of reminding me he existed. He got one out of ten for trying and I grinned anyway. It was nice knowing someone cared.

After downing the last of my coffee, I shut down the monitor and got up, slipping into my new holster and popping my .22 into my purse. "Hold the fort for a bit, I'm heading out."

"You just got here!" he snarled.

"I know, but it's not like we're busy or anything. And my kettle conked out and you know what I'm like without a real cup of tea when I need one. I'm running down to Warlock Derek's to see what he's got. I won't be long."

Warlock Derek's Antique Shoppe was just down the end of our street, and he carried a wide range of modern and old-fashioned knick-knacks you could pick up for a song. Truth be told, it was little more than a second-hand magic store, but he carried some good stuff from time to time and I liked checking it out. Last year I'd picked up a pair of Elf-crafted leather boots, wearing them was like floating on air, until one of them developed a slow puncture and I began walking in circles without realizing it.

Harrison's eyes lit up, almost glowing, making him look like an entirely different goblin. He stood up and grabbed his coat. "Ah well then, now you mention it, I haven't been down there in a while. I'll come with you. My Fitbit says it's time I stretched my legs."

Yeah, right. I'd bought him the Fitbit for Christmas but since he hadn't used it for anything other than telling the time, I could only deduce he wanted to come with me to see Derek, the store's owner. The man was a hot commodity after all. If you were into long-haired warlocks with pony-tails, skull rings, and prison tattoos.

"But you haven't finished the coffee you asked for?"

"Oh well, I'll finish it later."

Yeah, right. "Whatever. Well, let's get going then."

I waited while he shut down his workstation and fluffed about with his hair in the reflection off the screen.

"You look super," I said.

Harrison grinned and straightened the collar on his shirt. "Yup, you're right," he said. "You lead, I'll follow."

A few minutes later we were back down on ground level, walking through Philly's Changeling Avenue heading toward the store.

It was freezing, and just about everyone was wrapped in thick scarfs and woolly coats, including myself. The sky was a dense yellow, and I would say the chance of snow was about eighty percent. The weatherman had said otherwise. Time would tell, but my money was on Mother Nature.

"So, what's with you and Derek?" I asked, just for something to say. Harrison wasn't much taller than I was, but at five-ten he was still tall for a goblin, and had a pretty good bod to boot, albeit stocky. He walked fast and I had a job keeping up with him. "You light up like a fairy fart every time I mention I go there. Got a thing for him?"

"None of your business," Harrison growled. He never looked more goblin than when he was annoyed. Which to me was kinda sexy, being part-goblin myself.

"Oooh, have I hit a raw nerve?" God, how I loved to tease him.

"Don't you have better things to interest yourself with other than my love life?"

"Nothing comes to mind. We're not exactly being rushed off our feet with cases. Or hadn't you noticed?"

Harrison growled again.

We passed a little girl sobbing on the street. She was crying over a balloon that had just popped though her mom wasn't paying much atten-tion. She was too busy talking to a hotdog vendor.

"*Sic faciet avolare!*" I whispered as we walked past her. Out of the corner of my eye I watched as the red balloon suddenly inflated and soared into the air. The little girl was so astonished she lost hold of the string, and the balloon was soon way out of her reach in the sky. *Dammit.*

The girl screamed even louder.

"That'll teach you," her mother scolded as she looked round to see what the fuss was about.

Oh well, win some, lose some. I hurried along as fast as I could.

Derek's magic shoppe had huge windows chock-full of everything you ever wanted, and a million other things you never knew you did. Its organized chaos of books, knick-knacks, and colorful effusions looked totally right on our paranormal avenue but walk around the corner to the normies cross street and it looked oddly out of place.

A little tinkling bell over the door announced our arrival. It was practically tropical on the inside compared to the sub-zero temperature outside, and there was a warm, real log fire to the side of the counter. It would magically vanish in the summer to make way for more stock, I knew. I headed straight for it, desperate to warm up my hands.

Derek was over in the corner, hanging a pixie box from a hook in the ceiling. He was a very manual warlock, preferring to do a lot of the physical things for himself rather than use magic, but I could see the swarming pixies that came with the box were busy giving him gyp. He balanced precariously on his ladder as he swatted the tiny terrors away, sending a few into a wooden sign on the wall behind him that read, *Don't Shoot, Love!* with a peace sign under it. I'd promised myself if I ever moved out of my apartment, I'd get a pixie box of my own. Pixies were awesome for tending your garden, even if they could be a pain in the butt. But right now, I only had a small balcony with a few potted plants overlooking the Schuylkill River, so there just wasn't a need. Plus, Scratchpoop would probably eat them.

The second Derek turned to face us I knew something was up. The handsome warlock looked surlier than usual, and he couldn't hide whatever was bothering him from his customers, which was odd. He kept looking over Harrison's head toward the door, clearly expecting someone else to come calling.

Harrison must have noticed it too because his usual awkwardness around men he fancied was gone and his gait had turned strictly business.

He glanced over his shoulder to see if anyone else was there, but we were alone.

"What can I get for you?" Derek asked, clearly trying hard to sound normal. Too hard. He stared at me, then my partner, no doubt wondering if we were here for business or pleasure, as he knew our particular line of work.

"I'm looking for a kettle," I said. "Mine died this morning and I can't live without my morning brew."

Without coming down off his ladder, Derek looked surprised, then pointed to the far corner of the shop where he kept most of the non-magical stuff. He then returned his attention to securing the pixie box. Another red flag. Though not overly chatty, I couldn't remember a single time when he hadn't at least spent a few minutes catching up on the local gossip with me. He'd always enjoyed a good natter and between us, we had a pretty good idea of what was going down in town. Maybe having Harrison with me was putting him off? Perhaps my partner wasn't his type after all. Oh well.

Convincing myself he was probably just having a bad day, I sauntered over to the corner he'd pointed out, and left Harrison where he was to ogle the warlock's butt, or strike up a conversation, whichever pleased him most.

On the way I passed a rather pretty little glass ornament. It had a round base and a long stem and was a purplish red color that looked rather unusual. The truth was, I wasn't given to knick-knacks, but I thought it would look pretty nice on a shelf in my bathroom. I turned it around and upside down in search of the sticker. $15.99 was a bit steep, but it wasn't that bad. I put it down and decided to think about it. Maybe if I found a cheap enough kettle, I could buy them both.

I spotted the kettles right in the back, surrounded by some seriously jaded electrical items that were clearly not magical at all. Some of them looked to be thirty years old and were as likely to burn down your house as make you a cup of tea. But then maybe their age spoke to their reliability. I toyed with a few, not liking anything in particular, they just wouldn't go with my kitchen decor. Don't get me wrong, I was no Betty Crocker, but even goblins liked things to look nice.

Out of the corner of my eye, on the top shelf in the farthest corner, in the darkest place, (which appealed to my sense of magical destiny), I spotted an old-fashioned silver kettle, the kind you put on a stove and didn't have to plug in at all. It was too high for me to reach, so I pulled out my wand and said, *"Veni ad me!"* Not that I needed to say anything at all. A simple summoning spell like that I could conjure in my sleep. Bigger things, yep, I needed to say the words.

The kettle was a big fat round one, quite old, with a hint of rust around the spout. It was nothing I couldn't fix with a little magic easily enough, and I kinda liked it didn't require a lead to boil water. Just a good old-fashioned stove.

Behind me I heard the doorbell tinkle again, but since I was focused on the kettle I didn't think to turn around. I soon wished I had.

Harrison shouted, "Get down!" But he was too late. His words came just as the whoosh of an evil spell zoomed around the shop floor, coating us all in a nasty black dust as the spell bomb danced around the counters and shelves, seeking its mark. And then *BOOM!* The small, ball-shaped bomb found Derek, and there was a terrible crash as the warlock went flying, and screeching pixies cried out, saved only by the circle of glittering energy Harrison managed to conjure in time to save them all from a nasty death.

Even so, the blast was powerful enough to send me sprawling, knocking the kettle out of my hand. It flew through the air, landing with a loud crash amid some glass and shiny whatnots in the middle of the store. Glass shattered everywhere, and I stayed down, face to the floor, while the splinters and shards came tinkling down, their pretty music a mockery of the mayhem around us.

Don't stop now. Keep reading with your copy of WITCHY WAY TO MURDER, by City Owl Author, Adrienne Blake.

ACKNOWLEDGMENTS

First, I want to extend my gratitude to City Owl Press for taking a chance on my manuscript, and a special thank you to my editor Danielle DeVor for refining and strengthening SUPERSTITION.

Second, a shout out to Vince, Ev, C.J., and the rest of the now disbanded Phoenixville Fiction Writers Group. They suffered through every chapter of my first draft and provided invaluable feedback.

Finally, I would like to acknowledge R.C. Goetter and Bob Joslin, my high school English Teachers. At Mullica Hill Friends School, they were known as Teacher R.C. and Teacher Bob. Decades later, their guidance and encouragement still prove to be instrumental in my development as a writer.

ABOUT THE AUTHOR

JAMES BLAKEY lives in Virginia's Shenandoah Valley where he writes full-time. He's a three-time finalist for the Short Mystery Fiction Society's Derringer Award, winning in 2019 for his story "The Bicycle Thief." He leads critique groups in Harrisonburg, Charlottesville, and Shenandoah County. When James isn't writing, he's on the hiking trail—he's climbed forty of the fifty US state high points—or bike-camping his way up and down the East Coast. SUPERSTITION is his debut novel.

Christa Gitchell, Photographer

www.JamesBlakeyWrites.com

instagram.com/JamesBlakeyAuthor
x.com/JamesWBlakey
facebook.com/JamesWBlakey